NO ORCHIDS FOR MISS BLANDISH

When Riley gets word that Miss Blandish is going out on the town with her new pearl necklace, he decides to stage a jewelry snatch. Things get a little out of hand, and the gang ends up snatching Miss Blandish, too. Now they've got a kidnapping on their hands. But that's when the Grisson Gang steps in and takes over. Ma Grisson wants the pearls, but her sadistic son Slim wants Miss Blandish. And whatever Slim wants, Slim gets—one way or the other. So the ransom is paid, but Mr. Blandish doesn't get his daughter back. That's when Fenner is hired, a detective as ruthless as the gang he's after. They've broken Miss Blandish, but will Fenner be able to break them?

TWELVE CHINAMEN AND A WOMAN

Hot off the Blandish case, Dave Fenner is contacted by a frightened young lady who is looking for her sister. Laying down six grand as a retainer, she tells him that all she knows is that her sister is mixed up with twelve Chinamen. Intrigued, Fenner agrees to take the case, only to find that someone has planted a dead Chinaman in his office. No sooner has he removed that problem, Fenner is than visited by two Cubans who search his office, pistol whip him— and lead him to an apartment where he finds his murdered client. Now it's personal and Fenner will stop at nothing to find the gang behind this strange operation. Which leads him to Pio Carlos, trafficker in human cargo…and Glorie Leadler, a beauty who is not at all who she seems.

"The king of all
thriller writers."

Cape Times

No Orchids for Miss Blandish

Twelve Chinamen and a Woman

by James Hadley Chase

Afterword by John Fraser

STARK
HOUSE

Stark House Press • Eureka California

NO ORCHIDS FOR MISS BLANDISH /
TWELVE CHINAMEN AND A WOMAN

Published by Stark House Press
1315 H Street
Eureka, CA 95503, USA
griffinskye3@sbcglobal.net
www.starkhousepress.com

NO ORCHIDS FOR MISS BLANDISH
Originally published in 1939 hardback and 1941 paperback by Jarrolds,
London; reprinted as such by Corgi, 1961. Revised edition published 1942 by
Jarrolds, and 1951 as Harlequin paperback. Original text version with some
of the 1942 changes published in hardback by Howell, Soskin (U.S.), 1942.
Another edited version published in paperback by Novel Library, 1948, as
The Villain and the Virgin; and under original title by Avon/Diversey, 1951.
Further heavily revised edition published by Panther Books, 1961; and
Penguin Books, 1980.

TWELVE CHINAMEN AND A WOMAN
Originally published 1941 by Jarrolds, London, as Twelve Chinks and a
Woman. Revised and reprinted as Twelve Chinamen and a Woman, Novel
Library, Chicago, 1950. Reprinted as The Doll's Bad News, 1970.

"Some Orchids for James Hadley Chase"
copyright © 2006, 2007 by John Fraser.

ISBN-10: 1-944520-06-6
ISBN-13: 978-1-944520-06-9

Book design by Mark Shepard, shepgraphics.com

First Stark House Press Edition: March 2016

No Orchids for Miss Blandish

by James Hadley Chase

I

It began on a summer morning in July. The sun came up early in the morning mist, and the pavements were already steaming a little from the heavy dew. The air in the streets was stale and lifeless. It had been an exhausting month of intense heat, rainless skies, and warm, dust-laden winds.

Bailey walked into Minny's hash-house, leaving Old Sam asleep in the Packard. Bailey was feeling lousy. He had been hitting the booze hard the previous night and the heat didn't help. His mouth felt like a bird-cage and his eyes were gritty.

Minny's was empty when he entered. It was still early and the woman had only just got through with wiping over the floor. He picked his way over the damp, wrinkling his nose a little at the stale smell of cooking and sweat that hung about the place.

The blonde, who was leaning over the counter, gave him a smile that made Bailey think of a piano. She had worked on herself until she looked as good as any movie star until you got close to her, then she wasn't so hot. She patted her tight, yellow curls and stretched, so that her large breasts poked at Bailey through her thin dress.

"I bet you couldn't sleep," she said. "Ain't this heat wicked? ..."

Bailey scowled at her and ordered a Scotch. She slapped a bottle on the counter and pushed the glass towards him.

"Ain't you a bright, cheery little boy?" she cracked at him. "You been hittin' things too hard last night, I can see."

Bailey took the bottle and glass and walked over to a table and sat down. He looked at the blonde, who was watching him with interest.

"Find somethin' to do," he said surlily, "and leave me alone."

"Aw, be yourself, Clark Gable," she said, once more spreading herself over the counter. "What's biting you?"

"Give your mouth a rest," he said, turning his back on her.

She shrugged and went back to her novelette. Bailey gave himself a long drink and felt better. He leant back in the chair and tipped his hat over his eyes. He was getting worried. Riley was gut-aching about dough. If the breaks didn't come very soon, they would have to stick up a bank again. Bailey was not so keen on busting banks now that the G-men were knocking around. The bastards were always gumshoeing about, patting your pockets for rods and so on. Still, things were certainly getting tough, and they all would be on the rocks if something didn't happen soon. From where he sat he could see Old Sam snoring in the Packard. Bailey sneered at the sleeping man. That guy was just useless, all he thought about was his next meal and his next sleep. It was up to Riley or himself to find something. He took another drink and gave himself a cigarette. The Scotch reminded him that he had a stomach, and he looked over his shoulder for the blonde.

"H'yah, Gorgeous," he called, "c'mon over here."

She walked over to him with her hands on her hips and stood close to his elbow, her breasts close to his face. He could smell her, and it stirred something in him.

"What about some eggs an' ham?" he said, poking at her breasts with his finger. She was too quick for him and jerked away.

"Be yer age, Romeo," she said, tossing her head. "You want building up before you start lying down."

Bailey thought that was a good crack and he grinned as he watched her flounce to the stove. She broke the eggs into the pan with a practised flip and slapped a thick slice of ham on the grill. While he was waiting, Heinie came in. Bailey waved to him, and Heinie's fat face split into a rubbery smile. He waddled over as fast as his short legs would take him, and sat down gingerly in the chair Bailey had pushed forward to him. He began blotting his face with a dirty handkerchief, putting his greasy hat under the chair.

"What's new?" Bailey asked.

"Gimme a drink," Heinie said, his little eyes fixed on the bottle. "Jeeze! Ain't it hot?"

Bailey poured him out a stiff one and watched him drink it with narrow eyes. Heinie was a right guy all right. He had his ear to the ground and passed it on. He was an outside man to a Society rag that ran blackmail on the side. A mighty useful guy to be friendly with.

"How you makin' out?" he asked Bailey with a friendly leer. "Things goin' good with you?"

"Lousy," Bailey said, tossing his butt on the floor. "Things are getting tight an' it don't look as if they're goin' to get better."

Heinie wagged his fat head. "Yeah," he said, "you're right. It's this goddam heat ... things don't happen when it's this hot."

Bailey shrugged impatiently. "What you doin'?" he asked.

The blonde came over with his order and stood waiting for Heinie to make up his mind what he was going to eat. She did not crack this time, because Heinie was raw with women and she knew it. Heinie said at last that he'd have a steak. Bailey waited with impatience while Heinie talked for some time about how he wanted the steak cooked and how many onions he wanted with it. When the blonde had left them again, he picked up the threads.

"What's doin' these days?" he asked. "Riley is sweatin' about dough. Can't you horn us in somewhere?"

Heinie shook his head. "Not a chance," he said. "I ain't been doin' a thing for weeks. Tonight is the only break I've had. I got to cover the Blandish story an' that ain't goin' to bring me in much."

"Blandish? Ain't he the meat king?"

"Yeah." Heinie was getting impatient for his food, he kept glancing over his shoulder at the blonde, and the smell of the onions frying was driving him crazy. "Ain't it a knock-out how I can eat in this weather?" he went on, showing an interest in himself. "Most guys jest fold up and drink, but it don't worry me."

Bailey finished his ham and eggs and sat back. "What's Blandish in the news for?" he asked.

"Ain't Blandish, it's his daughter. Ever seen her? Jeeze! What a honey! Is she the tops or is she? Listen, pal, I'd give a year's rent to lay that dame."

Bailey wasn't interested, but Heinie, once started, was difficult to stop. He wiggled his fat behind more firmly into the chair and spread his fat little hands on the table.

"This dame's gettin' the family rocks outa hock today!" he said. "There's to be a swell party tonight, and she's hanging fifty grand round her neck to celebrate."

"Fifty grand?" Bailey suddenly leant forward.

"Fifty G's goes round that little white neck tonight," Heinie said, smiling smugly. "An' this baby's goin' to write it up for ten lousy bucks."

The blonde came over with the steak and put it in front of Heinie. It looked good, and Heinie beamed. He patted her arm and nodded his head at her. She looked down at him with a stony eye and moved away quickly as he tried to make a pass at her. Bailey was sitting, thinking. He let Heinie get into a huddle with his food and stared out of the open door into the street. Fifty grand worth of rocks sounded like a big job. He creased his brows and wondered if Riley would have the nerve to go after them. He glanced quickly at Heinie who was eating noisily.

"Do you know if this dame's goin' straight home after the party?" he asked suddenly.

Heinie paused, his fork near his mouth. "What's eatin' you?" he asked suspiciously.

"Jest curious, that's all." Bailey looked at him with dead pan.

Heinie could never refuse to talk. "I got it from MacGowan's man—" he began.

Bailey interrupted him. "MacGowan? ...Where does he fit in?"

"MacGowan? Ain't you heard of Jerry MacGowan?" Heinie looked quite shocked. "You don't get about, do you? This MacGowan is one of our rich playboys ... he's got hot pants for this dame ... see? His man told me that he's takin' her to the Golden Slipper to hear Louis swing it after the celebrations."

"Jest the two of them, eh?" Bailey said thoughtfully.

Heinie looked worried. "I hope you ain't goin' to start anything," he said. "This is big stuff, Bailey, it don't suit your type of outfit."

Bailey grinned at him like a wolf. "I ain't startin' anythin'," he said.

Heinie looked at him with his little eyes, but Bailey met his stare without a flicker. He looked over his shoulder and signalled to the blonde. He settled his check and got up.

"I'll be seein' you," he said.

"You're in a sudden hurry ... ain't you?" Heinie asked, looking up at him.

"Got Old Sam outside in the wagon. He was poundin' his ear, but I guess he's about through by now. Christ! What a lousy night I had. Didjer ever know such heat?"

Heinie nodded his head up and down. He felt safer talking about the weather.

"Sure the heat was bad, an' it's gonna be bad today."

Bailey waved and walked over to the door. As he passed the blonde he aimed a slap at her, but she twisted like a lizard. "Aw, be your age." They both said it together, Bailey mimicking her voice. She squealed with laughter and Bailey grinned. He walked into the street. The heat hit him like a clenched fist. The haze on the road made him feel a little dizzy. He walked slowly over to the Packard. His brain was busy. So the Blandish rocks were coming to the surface again. Every little mobster in Kansas would be sitting up, licking his lips when the news got round. With Heinie, news got round mighty quick. He let everyone in on everything. Heinie had no favourites; he was a right guy all right.

Bailey found Old Sam still snoring. He looked at him with a grimace, and then turned into a nearby drug-store and shut himself in with a telephone. He dialled and began speaking with Riley. Hurriedly he explained what Heinie had told him. Riley seemed half-dead at the other end. Bailey had left him in bed with Anna, and he was surprised that he answered the telephone at all. He could tell that Riley was sore about something.

"Hold on for Christ's sake," Riley said suddenly. "This chippy is shouting an' I can't hear what you're sayin' ... just wait a minute."

Bailey could hear Anna's voice strident with fury and then he heard Riley's bellow and the sound of a sharp slap. Bailey grinned to himself. Riley and Anna fought all day—just for the fun of it. Bailey thought that it was the way they were made. Riley came back to the 'phone again.

"Listen, Riley," Bailey pleaded, "it's goddam hot in this box. Get your ears back so that I can get outa here quick." Riley began to beef about the heat at his end.

"Okay, okay," Bailey broke in, "it's hot your end, but it's murder here. Yeah!

Murder! No, I ain't done murder. I say it's murder in here … in this box. What box? … This goddam sonofabitch box I'm in here. What? … Aw! Skip it, will you? No! No, never mind the heat. Just listen to this a moment, before I die. The Blandish rocks are coming out of hock. Yeah, that's what I said … the Blandish rocks … THE MEAT KING! That's right, I keep tellin' you, don't I? Yeah, tonight. The dame's wearing them at the Golden Slipper after a big party. She is goin' there with Jerry MacGowan. What do you think?"

"Come right back," Riley seemed suddenly alive. "We got to talk this over … c'mon quick."

"Okay," Bailey grinned into the mouthpiece. Riley was not so yellow as he thought. "I'm on my way." He hung up and paused while he lit a cigarette, then he stepped into the street. The air was cool after the booth and he walked with quick strides to the Packard. He reached inside and jerked Old Sam roughly out of his sleep. "Wake up, Sleepin' Beauty," he said, sliding under the wheel. "Things are happenin'."

Bailey picked his way self-consciously through the crowded tables. The Golden Slipper was doing record business. Waiters were moving backwards and forwards like well-oiled machines, carrying trays held high. The noise of incessant chatter struggled with the blare of the band. The air was thick with smoke, and it was difficult to see across the room. Bailey felt awkward and irritable. It was like Riley to give him the inside job to work. He sat down at a small table and snarled at the waiter who looked at him doubtfully. He ordered a highball, and while the man went away to fetch it he looked round the room keenly. It was early and he knew that Miss Blandish had not arrived, but he did not know what she looked like, and he thought that he might spot the table which was reserved for her. He could see nothing in the haze, and he gave up with an irritable shrug. He was glad to have the highball to give his hands something to do. He sat there for some time, smoking and drinking and wondering how Riley liked waiting outside with Old Sam in the Packard. Then suddenly the drummer ran off a roll and the leader came to the mike.

"Just a word in your ear, folks," he said, his voice blaring round the room. "Miss Blandish is now arriving with our old friend, Mr. Jerry MacGowan. It's the little lady's birthday and she's here to have a good time. Give her a big hand when she comes in, folks, but don't crowd her. A little bird tells me that she will be wearing the famous pearls, so, ladies, here's your chance to see for yourself."

Bailey screwed his head round quickly and looked towards the entrance. Every head in the room was looking in the same direction. A bright white spotlight picked her out as she came in, followed by a tall young man, who grinned into the haze, waving a hand to unseen friends. Bailey watched her as she came down the narrow aisle between the tables. He had heard about her looks and had often wondered just how good she was, but now that he saw her for the first time, he drew in his breath sharply. The light caught her thick, red hair and reflected back on her white skin. Her eyes were large and bright, and Bailey sat gaping. He had seen plenty of good-lookers in his day, but Miss Blandish caught him by the throat.

What got him more than anything else was that she looked innocent. He didn't know the word for it, but she just wasn't like any of the girls he had run into. She had everything they had, but just the one thing that they lacked was there in her. He watched her wave her hand gaily to the crowd shouting and stamping round her, and, when the row had died down and she had seated herself with MacGowan, Bailey relaxed a little. He watched them closely, his eyes on the rope of pearls round her neck.

From where he sat he could tell that they were good, and at the same time he began to realize that this job was going to be big. They were not going to get away with it easily. He could imagine how tough Blandish would get with the cops. They would have all the State police in Kansas on their heels as soon as the news broke. Bailey found that he was sweating slightly. Perhaps they were nuts to try and pull a job like this. Blandish had millions and he'd raise hell. He gave himself a drink and tried to relax. What would Riley say if he went out and told him to throw in his hand. He shrugged to himself. He'd have to go through with it.

The band suddenly cut out with that slick precision of a well-trained troupe and let the clarinet and drums swing it. The clarinet fluttered the reed, dragging down the top register. The drummer, his eyes blank and bloodshot, jittered the gong. The floor was small and crowded, and the scrape of leather was as rhythmic as the wire brush on the trap-top. The ceiling lights were dimmed, and someone started raking the crowd with a spot. Round and round went the spot, picking out the white faces of the dancers. A girl in the middle of the floor was struggling to keep up her shoulder straps. The man dancing with her, his thumbs locked in the straps at the back, endeavoured to keep them on the move. The girl gave up struggling after a bit, and, giggling, let her peach brassiere show. Over in a corner a couple were facing each other, and every so often the woman would move her body towards the man without moving her feet.

Bailey saw that MacGowan was carrying a load. He was drinking steadily, and when he danced he lurched badly. Miss Blandish spoke to him and they went back to their table. This was interesting to Bailey and he watched Miss Blandish talking to MacGowan. Obviously she was trying to persuade him to ease up on the liquor, but he was already drunk enough to be obstinate. She suddenly shrugged a little and turned her shoulder away from him. This seemed to annoy him for he emptied his glass and immediately refilled it.

The crowd were getting rowdy, and Bailey could see some of the men trying to stitch their bodies into the women as they danced. Suddenly some raw horseplay broke out at one of the tables. A college boy began shouting at his black-haired companion who leant far over the table to smack his face. He grabbed her arms and, pulling her on to the table, sweeping the glasses and plates to the floor with a crash, he smacked her yellow-satin bottom. A crowd gathered round, laughing and cheering. The girl screamed till the roof quivered. Bailey thought uneasily that the vice squad would be along pretty soon. He looked across at Miss Blandish and saw that she was already standing. She was shaking MacGowan's arm impatiently. MacGowan got up unsteadily and followed her down the aisle.

No one but Bailey noticed them leave. Bailey hurried out. His broad shoulders jostled the crowd standing on the wooden terrace admiring the moon. A drunk, turning to protest, sobered suddenly when he caught Bailey's eye. Bailey walked down the drive quickly and on to the highway. The Packard moved out of the shadows and he climbed into the back. Old Sam was at the wheel, and Riley by his side.

"They will be out in a minute," Bailey said. "She will be driving. The fella is stewed to the gills."

"Drive as far as the farm we passed comin' and then park," Riley said to Old Sam. "We'll let them overtake us and then crowd 'em into a ditch."

Old Sam engaged the gear and the Packard slid away. Bailey lit a cigarette and pulled a gun from his shoulder-holster. He laid it on the seat beside him. There was plenty of power under the hood, and Old Sam knew just how to feed the gas. The farmhouse was on the next bend, so he stalled the engine and ran into a deep shadow.

Riley spoke over his shoulder: "Get into the road and watch for 'em."

Bailey took his gun; tossing his cigarette away, he stepped on to the road. His feet crunched on the loose gravel as he walked a little way back to clear the bend. He stood on the side of the road, watching. In the distance the lights of the road-house gleamed in the darkness. Faintly he could hear the band, swinging it hot. He waited there immovable for several minutes, then, turning suddenly, he ran back to the car.

"Okay," he said. "Here they come."

Old Sam started the engine. As the hum of the approaching car came nearer, he engaged the gear. The Packard slid into motion and, as Miss Blandish drove past, they fell in behind.

"Let her get a bit further on," Riley said, "then crowd her."

The road was lonely and broad with heavily wooded country ahead of them. They were waiting for that. The beam of their headlights clung to the back of Miss Blandish's car. They could see Jerry MacGowan's head through the rear window. He was slumped back and he rolled with the motion of the car.

"That punk ain't goin' to give trouble," Bailey said.

Riley grunted.

The next bend brought them to the woods. The road was pitch black.

"Crowd 'em," Riley said.

The speedometer showed sixty. The needle quivered and then crawled to sixty-five, and then on to sixty-seven.

The Packard held the road without any roll. The wind began to whistle and the trees looked smudged. The distance between the two cars remained the same.

"For Christ's sake," Riley said, looking at Old Sam.

Old Sam shoved the pedal to the boards. They crept up a few yards, then fell away again. Bailey leant forward, his hands gripping the back of the seat.

"Give her all you have, Sam," he shouted excitedly; "that dame's wise to us. In another mile she'll be in the clear!"

Old Sam clung to the wheel as the needle flickered to eighty. The gap was closing. The two cars began to sway a little on the rough surface of the road. Suddenly Old Sam saw his chance as they approached a fork in the road. He jammed on the foot-brake and flung the wheel over. The tyres screamed on the gravel and the Packard turned broadside on, skidding into the rough. Bailey was flung to the floor-boards. He felt the Packard lurch, the off-wheels rise and then slam back on to the road. The car quivered as Old Sam released the brake and trod hard on the gas, then it bumped and tore through the shrubs. Miss Blandish kept to the road; she had to come right round the crown while old Sam had cut through the rough and had come out ahead of her.

Bailey scrambled back to his seat, swearing hard. He savagely groped about for his gun and found it on the floor. Old Sam was forcing Miss Blandish to slow down. He zig-zagged about the road so that she could not pass, gradually reducing speed. Finally the two cars came to a standstill, the Packard broadside across the road. Bailey jumped out and walked over to the other car; he poked his gun at Miss Blandish.

"Come on out," he said. "This is a stick-up."

Riley didn't move from the Packard. He leant forward, his shoulder and arm out of the window, and watched. Old Sam chewed as he stared into the headlights of the car. He didn't even bother to look.

Miss Blandish couldn't see Bailey's face. He was standing in the shadow of the car, but the reflection of the headlights picked out the dull metal of his gun. She opened the door and stepped on to the road. There are ways in which a woman leaves a car. Some get out with a show of leg, others don't. Blandish didn't. She stood quite still, holding on to the car door, looking at Bailey with startled eyes. She was not scared, but badly startled. MacGowan called out from the car and raised his head with difficulty. He pulled himself out beside Miss Blandish, and Bailey's arm stiffened. The gun suddenly became menacing.

"Take it easy, bozo, this is a stick-up," he said.

MacGowan sobered up. He eased himself closer to Miss Blandish.

"You had better be careful," he said hoarsely. "You don't know who you are talking to."

"Pass over the pearls," Bailey said, ignoring him.

Miss Blandish's hands flew to her throat and she backed away.

"Cut out that stuff or you'll get hurt," Bailey said.

As she still backed away, he walked up to her with three quick strides. He had to pass MacGowan who lammed him on the side of the head. A sweet thing to do considering the circumstances, but he was still sufficiently drunk to be reckless. The road was uneven and Bailey's foot was off the ground, so he went over with a thud. Miss Blandish gave a little scream, not a loud one, but as if she had screamed to herself. Riley didn't move. He thought Bailey could handle it, but he did push Old Sam out of the car to watch Miss Blandish. The old man dug his .38 into her ribs, but she did not seem to see him, her eyes were fixed on Bailey sprawling on the road.

MacGowan stood still, instead of jumping in. The gun had shot out of Bailey's hands and vanished into the shadows. The blow jarred him and he crawled to his knees swearing softly and obscenely. He paused for a moment in that position, looking at MacGowan who, realizing his lost opportunity, came at him with a rush. Bailey was up to meet him and guided his feeble lead over his shoulder and smacked him across the jaw, bringing his wrist down as he did it. MacGowan reeled away, his arms flung wide to catch his balance. Bailey shuffled after him. He had a small life-preserver in his hand, which he carried tucked up his sleeve. He drove his left into MacGowan's body and, as the boy came forward, he socked him across the eyes and nose with the life-preserver. Miss Blandish heard the bone go, quite distinctly, like the sharp note of breaking wood. Jerry folded up. He lay on his back in the road, lit by the headlights, his long legs thrashing in agony, as he held his hands to his face. Bailey stood over him and kicked at his head. He still cursed softly. He kicked Jerry very carefully, aiming with his foot drawn back, then kicking very hard. Riley leant further out of the car.

Miss Blandish made a movement as if she wanted to go to him, but the gun in her side dug deeper. She could not scream. Her tongue curled in her mouth and she could not make a sound. She could not even shut her eyes. She just stood and looked. Suddenly Riley stiffened and opened the door. Bailey was still kicking. The sound of his boot was no longer sharp; it was dull, as if he were kicking dough. Riley came across very quickly, and violently shoved him away. They all looked at the tattered dummy that had once breathed and lived. Riley took a deep breath.

"You sonofabitch!" he said to Bailey.

Bailey began to wipe his boots in the long grass. Old Sam still stood near Miss Blandish, but his gun-arm hung at his side. He was scared. Miss Blandish had covered her eyes with her hands. She was shivering as if she were very cold. Riley went on one knee and looked closely at MacGowan, then he got up and shook his fist at Bailey. "You bastard!" he said, his face white and glistening with sweat. "You've started somethin' ... this is a goddam murder rap now ... you crazy rat!"

Bailey hooked his finger in his collar and jerked at it savagely. "He asked for it—" he jerked. "Didn't he ask for it?" He turned his head quickly to Old Sam who wouldn't look at him.

The three men stood and looked at MacGowan and then at each other. Murder was new to them, and they were scared to hell. Riley took himself in hand. He moved slowly over to Miss Blandish. She felt him coming and snatched her hands from her face.

"No row!" Riley snarled at her, almost crazy with fear that she would scream. "You'll get it if you make a row."

Miss Blandish was frightened. She thought he was going to kill her.

"Stay still and don't make a move," Riley told her.

Bailey came and pulled at his arm. "This dame's gotta go the same way," he said, keeping his voice low. "She's seen everything ... we gotta knock her off."

Riley pushed him away "Shut your mouth," he said. "You've done enough for tonight." He was looking all the time at Miss Blandish, letting his eyes soak in her beauty. He ran his eyes over her figure, and although he was jittery he found himself thinking that she was good all right. He walked towards her again and she took a step back so that the blazing car-lights were behind her. The beams went right through her clothes, showing her long legs in silhouette. Riley suddenly saw her like that and became implacable with lust. He wanted her so badly that he began to shiver.

She waved her hands at him as if imploring him to go away, but he came on. The touch of his cold, damp hands on her bare arms galvanized her into life. She jerked away from him and opened her mouth to scream. He shifted his feet and his fist, half-closed, hit her on the jaw. She sagged at the knees and he dragged her over to the Packard. He tossed her into the back seat and looked over his shoulder at the other two. "Shove the stiff into his car and drive it into the wood," he shouted. "Get goin'."

Old Sam helped Bailey get MacGowan into the car and then drove it through the rough until it was hidden from the road. They came back to the Packard in a hurry.

"What about the broad?" Bailey asked, leaning into the car.

"Get in and shut your trap," Riley said.

Bailey hesitated. "What's this?" he demanded again. "You ain't goin' to snatch this dame?"

Riley, leaning forward suddenly, grabbed the lapels of Bailey's coat and twisted them in his fist.

"Listen, you cheap mug," he said, biting off each word. "You've started a fast one ... okay, now I'm pullin' another. From now on you keep your trap shut and I'll do the talkin'. Get that?"

Bailey flinched away from his hard eyes. He stepped back as Riley released him, and straightened his coat; then he got in beside Old Sam. They sat there waiting for Riley to say something. Riley sat at the back, with Miss Blandish lying on his feet, biting his nails, "Hell," he thought. "If I ain't goin' to get fried, I've got to go mighty careful." He leant forward so that his arms rested on the back of the seat on which the other two sat.

"This is a murder rap, he said, groping for his words. "You suckers ain't got a thing to lose but your sweet lives. If they pinch us, we'll fry. They'll tie this to us as sure as hell, an' we ain't gettin' no smart mouthpiece to spring us on this rap. This dame knows all about it ... if we rub her out now, the heat will be on mighty quick, but if we hide her up and send in a ransom note, we stand to pick up some dough, an' we'll have a chance to look around, 'cos the cops won't put on too much pressure while she is with us. Her old man is in the dough an' he'll pay plenty. We go to Johnny's. We gotta good chance at his place. They won't find us there unless we have a bad break, but we gotta risk somethin'."

Bailey started to say something, but shrugged instead. Old Sam twisted in his seat and began to bellyache, but Riley shouted him down. "Can't you see we ain't got a thing to lose? Use your heads! It's an even break and, by Christ, it's the only thing to do!

"The heat's goin' on good," Bailey said. "That dame's goin' to get mighty hot."

Riley jeered. "Get goin—" he said.

The Packard moved off down the road, gathering speed until in lurched and jerked as Old Sam swung to the bends. The night was very dark, and they met few cars. As they went on, the roads got worse and they met no one.

Riley pulled Miss Blandish off the floor-boards and sat her up in a corner. He couldn't see her, but he could feel her. His hands went to her throat and he struggled with the clasp of the necklace. The car was lurching, and he could feel her soft cheek against his hands. Her hair got in his eyes and he liked it. It was only with patience that he unfixed the necklace, but he got it off at last, and put it in his breast pocket. He reached out his hands again and touched her lap. He could feel her soft, round thighs smooth under the silk dress. He suddenly felt himself sweating, but Bailey had been listening to his laboured breathing. A gleam of light struck him in the face as Bailey turned in his seat with a small flash in his hand.

"Want a light?" Bailey asked, keeping the flash steady.

Riley felt the light burning into him and he hurriedly jerked his hands away. Bailey let the light fall on Miss Blandish. "Nice dish," he said.

Miss Blandish was still unconscious. A small bruise showed on her white skin where Riley had struck her. She lay in her corner huddled up; the black silk wrap was open, showing her white dress. Bailey saw that the necklace had gone and his eyes narrowed.

"Put that light out," Riley said, his lips moving stiffly.

"Anythin' you say," Bailey said, sliding the switch. "If you can't see, jest holla."

He did not change his position after that, but stayed leaning over the back of the seat, watching Riley.

They had been driving solidly for two hours when Old Sam suddenly called for gas. Every mile or so they had passed a dark farmhouse, and they were well off the beaten track. The country was rough and hilly. Bailey turned his flash on Miss Blandish She was quite still and had drifted into a heavy sleep.

"She'll be dumb enough," Riley said. "Go ahead and get some."

They went on until they came to a lonely filling-station. A tall hick came tumbling out of the shack and shot the gas into the tank as fast as he could put it there. He was half silly with sleep and did not look once at the car. As he was screwing the cap home, an Airflow, without lights, slid up to the Packard. It startled the three men; not one of them had heard it approach Bailey dropped his hand on his gun. A tall, heavily built man with a black fedora pulled over his eyes climbed out of the Airflow and looked with interest at the Packard. He saw Bailey's movement and suddenly leant into the car.

"Kind of nervous, ain't you, pal?" he asked.

Riley handled it. "What you want, fella?" he said.

"Riley, ain't it?" the tall man peered more intently. "Well, well! If it ain't sonofabitch Riley."

The three men in the Packard suddenly stiffened. They looked over at the

Airflow. The thin tube of a tommy-gun had been pushed through the curtains and was covering them.

"That you, Eddie?" Riley said through parched lips.

"Yea, it's Eddie all right," the tall man said. "Flynn is nursing the cannon, so don't go puttin' on any big acts for me. Flynn is mighty nervous when he handles that tommy, and it might go off."

"Listen, Eddie, we don't want trouble." Riley was scared to hell. He thought that this was just one sweet time to run into a bastard like Eddie. Eddie took a cigarette and struck a match. Riley moved his body to hide Miss Blandish, but Eddie saw all right.

"Swell dame," he said, dragging the smoke down.

"Sure," Riley returned hurriedly. "We'll be seein' you some time ... we gotta get home ... shove her along, Sam."

Eddie kept his foot on the running-board.

"Swell dame, I said!"

"Sure she's a swell dame," Riley grated. "What of it?"

"You often have a four-handed pettin'-party?" Eddie asked with interest. "Sorta quiet, ain't she?"

"She's cock-eyed." Riley began to sweat.

"She's cock-eyed, is she? ... Ain't that too bad? Mind if I have a peep. You know my weakness ... don't you, pal?"

"Can't you lay off?" Riley said weakly.

"I wanta look at that broad," There was a sudden rasp In Eddie's voice. The tommy-gun moved a little. The two men looked at each other as their wills clashed, then Riley got out of the car slowly. He was a head shorter than Eddie and seemed to shrink a little when the other stood over him. Eddie took a powerful flash from his pocket and flung the beam on Miss Blandish.

"Swell dame," he said, "nice class." He leant forward a little. "Cock-eyed ... ain't she?"

"Sure, she's out." Riley fumbled for a cigarette. His hands were twitching with nerves. "Now skip the comedy and let us scram outa here."

"Okay, Riley, don't mind me buttin' in." Eddie stepped back. "You wouldn't take advantage of a nice dame like that when she's out ... would you? My Ma used to tell me to leave them alone when they had a load on. Jeeze, what a load she must've put on board. How she must've loved the booze. See where she bruised her puss with the neck of the bottle. You oughta tell a nice girl like that to use a glass ... she ain't likely to hurt herself so much that way."

Riley climbed back in the car, and Old Sam drove away from the filling-station as if hell were biting his heels. Eddie watched them go. He pushed his fedora over his eyes and scratched the back of his head. The tall hick was gaping at him, but Eddie ignored him. He walked over to the Airflow and stuck his head through the window.

"What you make of that, pal?" he asked Flynn, who was dismantling the tommy-gun. "That looked a phoney setup to me."

Flynn shrugged his shoulders. He was a man of few words.

"Now, what the hell are those cheap mugs doin' with a swell dame like that? Who is she?" Eddie spoke his thoughts out loud. Flynn looked into the darkness of the road and wasn't interested. They had been driving a long way and he wanted some sleep. "She's been socked in the puss all right. You don't tell me that a palooka like Riley is in the snatch game now. This is a funny business. I guess I'm goin' to have a word with Slim about this."

Flynn gave himself a cigarette. "Get a hustle on, will you?" he pleaded. "I want some shut-eye, if you don't."

Eddie turned to the tall hick who seemed to be falling asleep. "H'yah, doughface, take me to your 'phone."

The hick led him into the shack and stood over him while he dialled. He waited impatiently, listening to the crackling and the buzzing on the line, then Slim's dead voice floated to his ear.

"Listen, Slim, Riley and his mob have just pulled out of here with a swell dame, right out of their class. She's been socked and is still under the influence. Now this dame is a honey. Her clothes cost plenty, and she ain't the type that would go jazzin' around with Riley. It looks to me that Riley has snatched this dame and you oughta hear about it."

Slim was silent for a minute. "Hold on ... I'll have a word with Ma," he said at last.

He came back after a short delay. "Ma wants to know what the floozy was wearin'." He sounded incredulous.

"She was wearin' a white silk dress and a light, black wrap, shoes with paste buckles or somethin' that sparkled. Looks as if she'd been to some swell party. She had lots of red hair—an' say, Slim, was she a honey or was she? I've seen plenty of ritzy dames in my time, but this one had it all. One look at her an' a corpse would have wicked thoughts!"

Eddie heard Slim drawling to Ma and he waited impatiently.

"Listen, Eddie, Ma's gone crazy ... she says that this floozy is the Blandish girl. The meat king's daughter. Yeah! Can you see Riley takin' on a job as big as that?"

Eddie was going to speak, but he heard Slim talking to Ma again. Then Eddie heard Slim's voice; he seemed more awake.

"Maybe Ma ain't so crazy. She tells me that the Blandish girl got the famous rocks out today. She was due for a party at the Golden Slipper. Riley might have got a load of that an' risked his neck. If Riley has got those rocks an' the girl ... he's got plenty. I'm lookin' into this, Eddie. Where are you? ... Okay, now get a hustle on. I'll pick you up at the second cross-roads further on. There's only one place a little hoodlum like Riley can go to, and that's to Johnny's … get goin'."

Eddie slung the hick a dollar and hurried out to the Airflow.

"Come on, pal," he said, climbing into the car. "Slim wants to check up on this Riley angle. He thinks these mugs have put the finger on old man Blandish's daughter."

Flynn groaned. "Good-bye, sleep," he said. "Ain't this a sweet life?" The Airflow roared into the night.

Dawn was breaking over the hills and the Packard still whipped along the roads. Old Sam was huddled at the wheel, his face white and drawn with exhaustion. The other two were nervously looking through the rear window from time to time to see if they were being followed. They had to get under cover before it was light. Miss Blandish was awake now. She sat stiffly in the corner, as far as she could get, away from Riley. She was cold in the scurrying wind that beat round the car as it hurtled on. Riley watched her with cold eyes. She started to say something but he told her to keep quiet. "What a break," he kept muttering to himself. "Eddie, of all bastards. If he thinks of it he'll get on to Slim, an' then all hell'll start poppin'."

Bailey was thinking the same in front. He turned suddenly and said: "Shall we ditch the dame?"

"Will you shut your trap?" Riley snarled at him. He pulled his Luger and waved it in Bailey's face. "Another crack like that an' this heater's goin' off."

Bailey was not impressed. "Okay," he said, shrugging. "If Slim gets on our tail it ain't goin' to be so good."

"Slim ain't gettin' on our tail," Riley raved. "Why should he?"

"Eddie will tell him all right," Bailey said.

"All right … Eddie will tell him, so what?"

"Ma Grisson will know what to do," Bailey went on.

Riley said nothing. He knew Bailey was right. Ma Grisson would know all about it, she always did. Old Sam swung the Packard on to a small, narrow lane and he had to reduce speed. They were approaching Johnny's hide-out. The shack was a wooden, two-storey affair, screened by trees of a dense wood. Leading to it was a rough path that had been cleared of undergrowth. The Packard bumped up the path and came to a standstill outside the shack. Bailey got out and hammered on the door. There was a pause and then Johnny came out. Johnny was a rummy. He lived for drink and looked like it. He lived by hiding anyone on the run. His place was known to most of the hoodlums in the district, but the Federal Agents had not got on to him as yet.

He stood looking at Bailey with watery eyes. Drink had rotted him, and he was only one jump ahead of the nut factory.

Bailey started to haggle with him, but Johnny saw that he was jittery and started pushing his price to the ceiling. Riley listened to them wrangling for a little while and then got out of the car and joined them.

"Leave this to me," he said to Bailey; then, turning to Johnny, told him to shut up. "You'll get your dough okay," he said. "We ain't got it yet, but we're goin' to get plenty when we turn this dame in. Listen, Johnny, never mind who she is, but she's worth a hundred grand. You stand to pick up twenty of 'em. All you have to do is to feed us and keep your ear to the ground. We've taken the risks, you collect the dough ... how about it?"

Johnny said he'd do it for fifty grand. Riley lost his temper. He dug his Luger into Johnny.

"You'll take what I give you an' like it," he said. "Now get goin' an' get us somethin' to eat."

Johnny shrugged and turned to the shack, Bailey followed him. Riley went back to the Packard. "Come on out," he said to Miss Blandish. She hesitated a moment, then stepped on to the rough ground. She stood looking at him. Her head held high. She was getting over her scare and showed some spirit.

"You behave yourself, an' things will go easy for you," he said. "We want to exchange you for a parcel of dough an' that's all there is to it. You take things easy an' you'll be with your pa before you know it. If you make trouble you're goin' to have a bad time."

"You'll suffer for this," she said, keeping the tremor out of her voice with an effort. "Take me back at once."

"Cut that stuff out," Riley snarled at her. "That won't get you anywhere now ... you ain't Miss Moneybags no more ... get into that hut before I take a sock at you."

She stood looking at him. Her great eyes travelled over his shabby suit and his thick boots. He found himself squirming under her contempt. He raised his clenched fists at her, but she turned on her heel and walked with difficulty over the grass towards the hut. Bailey stood in the doorway, watching her. His eyes gleamed at her but she did not hesitate, so that he had to give ground, and she walked into the big living-room. It was dirty and rough. There was a rickety wooden stairway leading to a hanging balcony on the left. The furniture was fashioned by Johnny and looked solid but unfinished. An oil stove stood in the corner where he cooked.

"Where can this dame sleep?" Riley asked Johnny.

Johnny jerked his head upstairs. "Go ahead ..." he said. "There's no one there."

Riley looked at Miss Blandish and pointed to the stairs. She followed him

up the rickety steps, stumbling on the rotten boards. He kicked open a door
and she went into a small, dark room. He lit an oil lamp hanging from the ceiling and glanced round. There was a bed with a mattress that looked dirty, and
no bedding. A jug of water, with a thin film of dust floating on the top, stood
on the floor, and a tin basin stood on a wretched bamboo table. Thick sacking was nailed across the window, and there was a musty, stale smell in the
room.

"Ain't like home, is it?" he sneered, looking at her.

She did not flinch, but looked back at him with the same contemptuous
look. He leant forward towards her so that his stale breath hit her in her face.
"You can cut out those high-hat looks of yours," he snarled at her. "I got lots
of ways of putting little girls like you in their place.... So come off it!"

She turned her head away and he swung her towards him by her arm. "I
guess you can give me a kiss ... can't you?" but she had wrenched herself away
with surprising strength, and put the bed between them before he could grasp
what she was doing. He saw terror flash into her eyes for the first time and he
grinned. He hesitated, standing looking at her, wanting to grab her again. He
guessed she would scream and fight, and that would bring up Bailey. Bailey
was going to be tiresome about this dame ... not that he cared what happened
to her, but Riley guessed that Bailey wanted to do the jazzing himself. If Bailey spoke out of turn, he'd give him the heat. He turned to the door. "You
watch your step," he said to Miss Blandish, and walked out, shutting the door
behind him.

He went downstairs and found Old Sam putting food on the table. The food
was rough, but they were hungry. Riley told Old Sam to take Miss Blandish
some of it and a shot of Scotch. Old Sam seemed glad to do that, and he took
a plate of food up the stairs. He pushed the door open and shoved the food
at Miss Blandish. "Here, eat this," he said awkwardly.

Miss Blandish was standing in the middle of the room. She shook her head
at the food. "Come on," Old Sam said gruffly, "get this inside you." She
looked at him, seeing the lined, shifty old face, and then took the plate from
him. He looked at the dirty mattress and wrinkled his nose. "Not what you
been used to ... I bet," he said. "I'll get you a rug from car." He turned on his
heel and went down again. Riley grinned to himself when he saw him return
with the rug. Old Sam was beyond women, and he'd make a good nursemaid.
Bailey finished his meal and pushed back his plate. He lit a cigarette and
stretched himself. Old Sam came down and sat at the table, looking self-con-
scious.

"You tucked her in?" Riley sneered at him.

"No need to push her around, is there?" Old Sam mumbled with his mouth
full.

"If that little bitch don't lose some of her starch, she'll get pushed around all right," Riley snarled.

Bailey cocked an eye at him and yawned. "Hell, I'm beat!" he said. "All-night drivin' ain't my idea of a picnic. I'm goin' to snatch myself some sleep."

Old Sam had finished bolting his food and went over to a pile of sacks in the far corner and began snoring as soon as he lay down.

Riley looked at Johnny. "Not expectin' visitors?" he asked.

Johnny shook his head. He had taken a shot-gun and was going to bag something for the pot. Although his eyes were dim and his hand shook, he had an uncanny streak of luck with a gun. He had learnt just how much to give away with his unsteady hand, and if he drew a bead a foot too high and to the right he nailed most things. Johnny wasn't as soft as he looked.

Riley watched him go and then went over to the telephone. Bailey watched him with sleep-weary eyes. He had thrown himself down on the sacks near Old Sam and lay back, finishing his cigarette. He listened to Riley talking softly into the 'phone. He guessed he was 'phoning Anna, and a slight sneer went across his face. Riley hung up finally and looked over at him, nodded, and then went upstairs. Bailey watched him go into the room next to the one where Miss Blandish was, and then shut his eyes.

Riley lay on the rough bed and stared at the opposite wall. He tried to look right through the thin plaster and watch Miss Blandish as she huddled on the rug. He let his loose mind wander until the room became unbearable to him. He sat up and scratched his head viciously with both hands, letting his nails rasp on his scalp. He could feel the sweat running down the back of his neck. Swinging his legs over the side of the bed, he kicked off his shoes, letting them fall on to the floor with two distinct thuds. He sat there, looking at his trembling hands, breathing in short jerks. Then he rose to his feet and took off his coat. His gun worried him, so he unslung the holster and tossed it on to the bed. He wandered to the door and opened it softly. Stepping on to the balcony, he peered down into the living-room. Both Bailey and Old Sam were sleeping like dead men. He stood outside Miss Blandish's door, hesitating. Then, with one last look over his shoulder at the sleeping men, he turned the handle gently and went in. The sun was coming through the cracks round the nailed-up window. The lamp was out, but the room was not dark, just dim. He could see Miss Blandish lying on the bed, face down; her head pillowed on her arms, she seemed asleep. He shut the door gently and she moved a little, stretching out and turning on her side.

Riley leant over her, his sweating hands reached out and gripped her throat, nipping her scream as she woke. Her large eyes opened wide, the lids folding back like those of a doll that has been raised suddenly. He looked into the dark terror there and drew his lips off his teeth.

"Now you gotta be good," he whispered to her with his face close to hers.
"You can't get outa it an' you're not to scream. Get that ... no row! I'll sock
you if you do an' break your teeth for you. I'll hit you so goddam hard that
you'll never squawk again. No one ain't comin' if you do raise hell an' you'll
get it ... hard! I'm goin' to take my hands off your neck an' you can yell if you
wanta ... but mind what I've said."

He took his hands away slowly. Miss Blandish lay flat on her back, sound-
less. Her arms were flung wide, her hands, palm up, on the rug. She looked
into his blood-congested face, horrified at what she saw there. She shook her
head weakly and ground her knees together, arching her body stiffly. He came
at her suddenly, pinning her arms to the bed, his glistening face trying to find
her mouth. She turned her head quickly. The door opened and Bailey walked
in. The light came through the door and fell directly on to the bed. Bailey had
slipped into the room with the speed of a cat. Just for a split second he had been
outlined against the light, then he was in the room, a shadow in the gloom.
Riley did not move his body. He just withdrew his hands. He cursed himself
for not bringing his gun. He could see the gleam of Bailey's .38 and waited for
the lead to cut into him.

"Take it easy, Riley," Bailey whispered out of the shadows. "Don't move
outa turn."

Riley sat motionless, his head half-turned, looking at Bailey. Miss Blandish
rolled away from Riley and half sat up. She was now on the edge of the bed,
and she could feel her heart jumping wildly, half suffocating her.

"I'm wise to you, you yellow bastard," Bailey said. "You wanted to lay this
dame, an' you wanted so bad that you took the chance of us bein' picked up
to do it. Okay ... this dame ain't bein' laid ... do you get that? This dame is
goin' straight back to Pa, an' I'm collectin' an inscribed clock for takin' her
home."

"You're nuts!" Riley exclaimed, his face livid in the dim light. "It was you
that kicked hell outa that fella!"

"Yeah?" Bailey still kept his voice low, but he was trembling with excitement. "This dame is goin' to be mighty grateful to me for pullin' her outa a
jam with you. You get the heat, an' she tells Pa that it was you gave the bozo
the works."

Riley suddenly shivered. "You wouldn't do a thing like that?" he quavered.
"You ain't goin' to do that?"

Bailey stiffened. "I've been waitin' for this for a long time," he said. "This
is where—"

A soft knock came on the door, and Johnny put his head round. His weak
face looked startled. They could see his jaw trembling. "Slim an' his mob are
downstairs askin' for you," he said. "I told 'em you were still pounding your

ears."

Bailey's arm fell to his side, he turned hurriedly to Riley. They looked at each other, scared.

"For God's sake!" Bailey whispered. "I told you Slim'd be along."

"They mustn't find this dame here and they mustn't find the pearls." Riley slid off the bed. "Go down an' stall 'em along. Tell 'em that we ditched the girl before comin' here. See how many there are ... watch your chance an' rub 'em out if you can. I'll come down when I got my rod."

Bailey hesitated, then, getting a grip on his nerves, walked out of the room. Riley pulled Johnny towards him.

"Listen, Johnny, you stay here and don't let that dame squawk." He looked at Miss Blandish. "Listen, toots, down there is a man who would tread on your pretty neck an' not notice it. Slim ain't human ... if you wanta save your hide, you'll shut your mouth an' keep it shut."

Miss Blandish could just see the white circle of fear round his mouth as he left the room.

Riley stood on the balcony and looked down at the group of men, who, in turn, looked up at him. Eddie was there, both hands sunk in his raincoat, his black fedora pushed at the back of his head. Flynn was standing on the extreme left of the group, his hands also hidden, his eyes cold and watchful. Woppy and Doc Williams stood close to Slim. Their thumbs were hooked in their belts, both were smoking. Slim was the only one who did not look at him. It was Slim who kept Riley's eyes busy. Old Sam was sitting up on the sacks, his face bewildered and sodden with sleep. He looked as scared as hell. Bailey leant against the wall, his hands ostentatiously folded in front of him.

Slim Grisson studied the shiny caps of his pointed shoes. He was tall, reedy, and pasty-faced. A dopey look and a loose, open mouth, made him look a weak slob, without blood or gumption, but Slim was the coldest thing on two legs. A cold, inhuman spirit hid behind the idiot's mask and the sparse flesh of the thin body.

Slim Grisson was a killer. He had killed things when he was a child. Not for any reason, but because to kill was in his blood. He began early, wanting money. He had always been lazy at school, refusing to take the least interest in books. The old master who had taught him was nervous of him. He had enough insight to know that Slim was bad. It did not come as a surprise when he caught him cutting up a new-born kitten with a rusty pair of scissors. He was glad of the opportunity of running him out of the school. He was not rid of him as easily as that. One of the little girl pupils was found a week after Slim had left the school, wandering far away from her home. She had been interfered with, and named Slim. They never found him because Ma Grisson had got him out of the town.

He got a job in a pool-room cleaning glasses, and ran into a bootlegger crowd. He watched them handle wads of green-backed dollar notes. Although they treated him with contempt, he hung on until he became one of them. It was then that his ruthless disregard for human life built up a reputation for him. No job was too dangerous for him to handle, and the gang pushed all the dirty work on to him. He absorbed everything they gave him without making mistakes. Apart from his callousness, he had no brain to organize. It was not until Ma Grisson had taken him in hand that he became a gang leader. Ma Grisson had seen her opportunity for easy money for some time, but she was not ready to use it. She wanted Slim to knock around and get himself a reputation, and when he had done that she began to operate.

She built her son into a gangster, step by step. In the beginning he made mistakes when left on his own, and drifted in and out of prison on short sentences. She would wait patiently until he was free and then start again. Gradually he learnt not to make mistakes, and he learnt a lot from other convicts. He got in with a powerful mob, working bank holdups. He climbed slowly into the saddle by the simple method of killing anyone who opposed him, until the gang finally settled down and accepted him as their leader. Ma took over the reins then, and they found it paid them to work with her. Slim was useful for the dangerous jobs, Ma sat at home and pulled strings and the rest of the gang muscled in where the money was.

Riley hung his hands on his coat lapels. He could see Flynn was jittery and he wasn't giving him the chance to turn on the heat. He stood there trying to grin.

"H'yah, Riley," Eddie called. "Didn't expect to see us, did you?"

Riley began to pick his way down the rickety stairs. His eyes never left the group waiting for him. Down he came, each step measured and slow.

"'Lo, boys!" he said, trying to keep his voice casual. "This is a surprise!"

He stood near Bailey, but they didn't look at each other. Eddie did the talking. Slim didn't look up; he still admired his shoes.

"Where's the swell dame that you were carryin'?" Eddie asked.

"We ditched her," Riley said slowly. "She didn't stay cock-eyed that long."

Eddie tossed his cigarette butt on the floor and trod on it. "So you ditched her ... did you?" he said. "That's too bad ... I wanted another peep at that dame. Who was she, Riley?"

"Oh, just a broad," Riley said, keeping his eyes on Eddie's chin. "What's eatin' you boys ... ain't you seen a swell dame before?"

They were cold and immovable before his forced ease. Eddie said: "You didn't happen to pick her up at the Golden Slipper?"

Riley didn't give himself away. He acted amazement. "You're nuts! Golden Slipper? Say, that cheap little chiseller don't go places like that. We found her at Izzy's hash-house. She was stewed, an' we thought we would have some fun, so we took her along. When she came to the surface ... Boy! ... Was she sore? We couldn't do anythin' right with that female, so we let her walk home to cool off."

Eddie grinned, he was enjoying himself. "So she was a cheap little chiseller? An' you let her walk home because she wouldn't play ball? She looked swell class to me."

"All broads look swell these days ... it's the movies," Riley returned.

Slim dragged his eyes from his shoes. He looked at Riley who started to sweat. Slim had a mean look.

"Where's Johnny?" he asked. His voice was hoarse through smoking, and he seldom spoke above a whisper.

Riley shifted his position, leaning his shoulders against the wall. "He's upstairs," he said in a jerky gasp.

"Get him!" Slim said to Eddie.

The door opened above, and Johnny came out quickly. He leant over the rail. The men watched him. Johnny was nobody's enemy, but he wasn't taking sides. He had kept healthy and he was staying healthy. He looked at Riley and then at Slim. Riley frantically stared at him, but Johnny wasn't looking any more. He turned his head and looked at the door behind him. There was no movement from the men watching him. Then suddenly he leant forward. He said in his thin, cracked voice:

"The dame in there could use the can."

Nobody moved. Riley drew a sudden short breath and Bailey went green.

"Take her," Slim said.

Johnny turned and opened the door. He put his head round and said something, then he stood back. Miss Blandish walked on to the balcony. The men below watched her. When she looked down and saw them, she started back violently and shrank against the wall. Johnny spoke to her again and pointed to the stairs. She shook her head and tried to go back into the room. Johnny took her arm and shoved her. She hesitated, uncomfortable and frightened. The stillness in the room below could be felt. No one moved and every eye was on her.

Down she came, with Johnny on her heels. They passed through the room, into the daylight, across to the little lean-to outside. Flynn was the only one who did not take his eyes off Riley or Bailey. They all stood motionless, like a row of wax figures. They watched Miss Blandish come out and walk back, watched every step she took, watched her mount the stairs and disappear into the upstairs room again. Johnny went with her and shut the door. As the door shut, the tension snapped. Doc, Woppy, Eddie, and Flynn suddenly had guns in their hands.

"Get their rods," Slim said.

Doc eased himself over to Bailey and jerked his gun from the shoulder-holster. Bailey just stood there, licking his lips. Doc went on to Riley and did the same. He turned to Old Sam who suddenly went for his gun. He was surprisingly quick, and the heavy gun began to boom before Doc's brain could flash a warning. Flynn had seen the move and fired at the same time. Doc had flung himself clear, but Old Sam had the top of his head blown off. He fell on his face, the gun shooting out of his twitching hand. Riley and Bailey went green and stopped breathing. They waited. Slim looked at them and then at Old Sam. He had a starved, wolfish look on his face. Johnny came out and glanced down, then he went back to the room again.

"Get him outa here," Slim said. Doc and Woppy grabbed hold of Old Sam and dragged him into the clearing. They came back quickly. Eddie suddenly walked up to Riley.

"Listen, bozo," he said, "you're in a jam. Come on an' spill it. Who's the dame?"

"I tell you, I don't know," Riley jerked, his whole body shivering.

"Well, I'll tell you," Eddie said. "That's Blandish's daughter, an' you snatched her to get the pearls. You got those rocks on you right now ... ain't that the way it goes?" His huge hand was twisting the front of Riley's shirt as he talked and he shook Riley to and fro like a doll. "Sure, that's the way it goes." He dived a hand into Riley's inside pocket and fished out the pearls. He flipped them over to Slim, who caught them and held them to the light.

"Nice work," he said.

There was a tense silence as each man stared at the pearls hanging from Slim's bony fingers.

"Blandish is worth two million bucks," Slim whispered, staring with his dopey eyes at the pearls. "His daughter is worth a lotta dough to him. These rocks will hock for twenty grand or more ... very nice work." He said the last words slowly, letting them drip out of his loose mouth. He looked at Eddie and jerked his head towards the balcony. Eddie mounted the stairs and walked into the room where Miss Blandish and Johnny sat waiting. He nodded to Johnny, who walked outside, then he went over to Miss Blandish. She stood by the sack-covered window. Her breasts rose and fell quickly; one white hand covered her mouth.

"Listen, Toots," Eddie said, speaking quietly and rapidly. You're comin' for a ride. The boys down there won't hurt you if you behave. We're goin' to contact your pappy, an' then you'll go home. Now, don't go speakin' outa turn. Slim down there is a mean sorta guy and he can turn real rough if he gets put out. Jest you do what you're told and say nothin' and you'll make it ... get all that?"

Miss Blandish said: "Please let me go home now!"

Eddie took her arm, he thought she was swell and he gave her a friendly grin. "Come on," he said, "take it easy. You ain't got to get scared."

She hung back. "If you want money, my father will pay ... don't take me away with those men. That other man tried ... he had me alone—" she broke off, looking round the room wildly as if trying to find some place to hide.

Eddie patted her arm. "Come on," he said. "I could go for you myself in a big way, but it wouldn't be healthy. You keep your pants on an' I'll look out for you."

"Where are you taking me?" she asked. "Why don't you telephone my father now and he will give you the money? ... Why must I go away with you?"

Eddie went to the door and opened it. He jerked his head. "Get goin'," he said. "Remember what I said." There was a faint rasp in his voice, and suddenly alive to the hopelessness of the situation Miss Blandish followed him.

When Eddie had gone upstairs Slim turned to Flynn. "Take these guys outside," he said.

Doc and Flynn shoved Bailey and Riley out of the hideout. They were jostled into the thicket. Slim followed quickly. He carried in his hands two lengths of rope. His yellow eyes were gleaming. He had never killed a man slowly, and he began to tremble with excitement. His killings had all been fast, not from choice, but from safety. Now ... it was going to be different. He could hear Riley gabbling with hysteria. He could see his green, glistening face, and the way his mouth worked in his terror ... it pleased him.

Bailey walked without a word. His face was pale but dangerous lights smouldered in his eyes. They reached a small clearing in the thicket and, all realizing at the same time that this was the place of execution, stopped. Slim pointed to two convenient trees.

"Tie 'em there," he said.

While Flynn covered Bailey, Doc fastened Riley to the tree with the cord Slim tossed to him. Riley made no effort to save himself. He just stood shuddering and jerking, helpless in his terror. Doc stood back and turned on Bailey. Bailey walked deliberately to the tree and leant his back against it. As Williams came up to him, he kicked like a snake striking. His boot sank into Doc's belly and then Bailey was behind the tree, the slim trunk between him and Flynn's gun.

Slim suddenly got violently excited. "Don't pop him," he screamed out, "I want him alive."

Doc writhed on the grass, trying to get his breath, but no one worried about him. Flynn slowly began to walk towards the tree, while Slim stood motionless, a long two-edged knife in his hand. Bailey looked round for a way of escape. Behind him the shrub was thick; in front of him Flynn approached slowly; on his left, Slim stood with his knife. It was to his right that he must make his bid. He made a sudden dive, but Flynn was closer than he realized. He aimed a blow at Flynn, who was expecting it, and his fist went over Flynn's head. Bailey, unbalanced, floundered, and Flynn closed with him. For a minute they strained, then Bailey, who was the more powerful man, broke away. He smacked Flynn on the jaw with a crushing right-hand punch and Flynn went over with a crash. Bailey sprang away.

Slim had not moved. He stood there, his thin body drooping, his loose mouth half-open and the long knife hanging limply in his fingers. Doc was still out. Bailey suddenly altered his ideas. There was only Slim and then Riley, and he could surprise the others. He began to move towards Slim who waited with yellow, gleaming eyes. Bailey suddenly saw him grin. That grin told Bailey plenty. The idiot mask had dipped, and the killer was there. Bailey knew that he was dying fast, and he tried to stop his legs advancing, but he couldn't control them. He got nearer to Slim and he felt his nerve going. The sweat was running into his eyes. When he was a few yards from Slim he stopped walking. He had never felt so frightened; he knew that he was but one rapid heartbeat away from his end. Something flashed in the air, something shiny that caught the sun as it sped at him, and then he took Slim's knife in his throat.

Slim stood and watched him die and felt the same ecstasy run through his blood as a killing always gave him. He felt a little weak, standing in the hot sun, and he made no effort to move for several minutes. Doc had risen on his elbow, his face ashen, and began to curse softly. Flynn still lay on his back, a livid bruise on his jaw. Slim looked over at Riley who had shut his eyes. He walked to Bailey and withdrew the knife from the thin cut. He cleaned the knife carefully by driving it into the grass. Four times he did this before the blade gleamed again. He knelt on one knee as he worked. Doc watched him. Slim got to his feet and approached Riley who suddenly realized what was coming to him. He began to gabble again. Slim came quite close and grinned.

"Don't kill me, mister!" Riley shouted, his eyes protruding. "Gimme a break, for Christ's sake!"

Slim still grinned. This was good. He liked them to turn yellow. He felt big and tough when they ratted. He put out his hand and jerked Riley's shirt out of his trousers. With a powerful wrench he tore the shirt tail away. Riley stood there with his belly bare.

"I'm givin' it you there," Slim said, pricking the shuddering flesh with his

knife. "Right in the guts, Riley, an' you'll take a mighty long time to croak."
"Listen, mister, you wouldn't do that to me," Riley gasped. "You can't do
that to me ... I'm a right guy all right ... don't I keep tellin' you ... Slim, you
know me ... Riley? You ain't goin' to cut me like that ...? No! ... Slim! ... No!
... For Christ's sake ... don't ... don't do it! ... Don't do it ... Slim!"

Slim, still grinning, held the knife-point just below Riley's naval and put his
weight on the handle. The knife went in slowly as if it were going into butter. Riley drew his lips back. His mouth opened. There was a long hiss of ex-
pelled breath as he stood there. Slim stepped back, leaving the black hilt of the
knife growing out of Riley like a horrible malformation. Riley began to give
low, quavering cries. His knees were buckling, but the cord held him.

Slim sat on the grass a few feet away and gave himself a cigarette. He
pushed his hat over his eyes and squinted at Riley.

"Take your time, pal."

II

They pushed Miss Blandish into the hard light of the unshaded lamp. Her
hands were fastened behind her back with Flynn's muffler. Two pads of dirty
cotton wool were strapped across her eyes with adhesive tape. Eddie had to
hold her up right by putting his hand under her armpit. His hand felt warm
and hard, and she was glad of its comfort in her darkness. Slim lounged against
the wall, bored with the reaction of his killings. He was relaxed and eased like
a man sexually satiated.

Ma Grisson, from her chair, soaked Miss Blandish into her brain. Ma was
big, fat, and lumpy. The flesh hung in two loose sacks on each side of her
mouth. Her nose hooked sharply, and her little eyes were bright and un-
blinking. They were bad eyes, hard and shiny like bits of glass. Her big, floppy
chest sparkled with cheap jewellery. She was wearing a cream lace dress
which made her look like a stack of unwashed curtains. Her huge arms, mottled with veins, crawled through the network of the lace like dough bound in
wire netting. She sat in a heap, her hands grasping her knees.

Eddie loosed the muffler and whipped the tape off Miss Blandish's face. The
tape tore the fine hairs of her skin and hurt. It was a shock to find Ma Grisson sitting there like an old vulture. Miss Blandish started back and trod on
Eddie's toes. He pushed her forward a little and told her to take it easy.

"Meet Miss Blandish, Ma," he said. "Baby, this is Ma Grisson."

The old woman looked right into Miss Blandish. Those bits of glass tore
deep, and Miss Blandish would have folded up but for Eddie's hand.

Ma Grisson hated talking as much as she hated talkers. She said one word when most people said ten, but this time she spread herself.

"You're goin' to stay here until your old man comes across," she said. "If you're lucky you won't be here long. It all depends on your pa. If he tries to be smart, I'm goin' to take you apart in bits, and those bits will be sent to your pa every goddam day until he learns to play ball. Before I take you apart, I'll throw you to the boys an' what they'll do to you ain't nobody's business. You're going to behave, and you ain't causin' trouble. Do you get all that?"

She climbed out of the chair and stood over Miss Blandish. She was tall like Slim, but with shoulders like a gorilla. "Grab her an' hold her tight," she said to Eddie.

Eddie slipped behind Miss Blandish, gripping her arms hard. Ma Grisson slapped her across the face with heavy, sharp slaps that jerked her head from side to side. Eddie held her so that she could not move, only her head jerked like a pendulum. "Don't get ideas, an' do as I tell you," she said each word slowly and slapped at the same time. "Okay, now I guess you know what you're up against. Take her upstairs."

Eddie shifted his grip and hauled Miss Blandish out of the room. A red curtain hung over her brain and the nerves in her face revolted. She felt herself being pulled upstairs, and she offered no resistance. She was blind with shock. Her world had caved in, leaving her terrified and broken.

Eddie came down again and found them waiting for him. Doc and Flynn were leaning against the steel shutters that lined the windows. Slim had given himself an armchair and was picking his nose violently. Ma Grisson lumbered about the room. "You sure pushed her around," Eddie said, taking   a   chair.

Ma stopped and faced them. "Now, listen, I've said before, you boys have gotta leave girls alone. They bring trouble. You ain't gettin' ideas about this girl upstairs. Do you get that? … None of you. She may be this an' that, but you're to leave her alone. This job ain't goin' to be easy. Too much time has already been used up. I bet Blandish has contacted the Feds by now. Mac-Gowan has been found, too. We gotta work quickly … get the dough an' beat it."

Eddie poured out a shot of bourbon and folded up on the couch. He took a long pull and then balanced the glass on his chest, while he gave himself a cigarette.

"Give us the dope, Ma," he said.

"You get into town and 'phone the old man. Tell him to lay the Feds off or else. Tell him he'll get instructions tomorrow. That's the first thing. Tell him that we will get tough if he tries anything smart. When I say tough I mean tough. Tell him what will happen to the girl, an' make it raw."

Eddie groaned and drained his glass. "Okay, Ma," he said, getting up with an effort. "I'll give him the works all right." He hesitated before the bottle, but Ma told him to get going so he pulled his fedora over his eyes and left the room. They heard the car door slam and the tyres scream on the loose gravel.

Ma looked at Flynn. "Now use your head," she said. "Who knows we're in this?"

Flynn brooded. "There's Johnny," he said at last, "he saw everything ... but Johnny is a right guy. We left him plantin' those three stiffs an' takin' care of their car. Then there is the guy who served them with gas. He seemed half-dead, but he might remember Eddie. I guess that's all."

"We can't take chances," Ma Grisson said. "You go over and rub out that gas vendor. We'll be sure then. Up to now, the Feds will be lookin' for Riley's mob. They won't find them, but they may get on to their tracks. If they do, that gas feller will wise them up that we are in it. Get goin', Flynn, an' don't make mistakes."

Flynn took himself off.

"Now, Doc," Ma went on, "you get some paper an' write to Blandish. Tell him to get together five hundred grand in genuine used Federal Reserve currency in one-, five-, and twenty-dollar bills. Tell him to put this dough in a light-coloured bag and keep it handy. Tell him to run an ad in the Tribune for the sale of white lead paint in small kegs as soon as he has got the bills together, and that he'll hear from us again. Warn him how tough it will be for the girl if he tries a double-cross. Got all that?"

Doc, who had done this before, nodded and went into the next room to write. Ma Grisson lit a cigarette and looked at her son. "You ain't said much," she said.

Slim looked at her vacantly, his yellow eyes were glazed. "I'll trade the pearls for the girl," he said.

Ma sat very still. "I don't get that," she said.

"Just that." Slim dug into his pocket and dangled the pearls so Ma could see them. "I want that girl an' you can have these."

Ma closed her great hands into red fists. "Those pearls come to me, anyway," she said. "I ain't bargainin' with you ... you gone nuts or somethin'?"

Slim looked at her and swung the rope rapidly. "You been tight about women in this mob," he said, speaking in that low, hoarse whisper of his. "I ain't had any fun with women for a long time. You've kept women outa this mob an' the boys have had to like it. I'm lookin' for a break right now. This dame's got class an' I'm goin' to have her my way. You can handle these reluctant virgins an' you gotta fix it for me. Do that an' you get the pearls."

Ma relaxed. She knew Slim. She knew just how to handle him. "Give me the pearls an' stop talkin' wild."

Slim was shivering a little. His slack mouth hung open and his eyes gleamed hungrily. "Now, listen, Ma," he whispered, "I want this broad an' I mean to have her."

Ma tossed the cigarette into the empty grate. "Go ahead, I ain't stoppin' you."

Slim twisted in his chair. He got to his feet and walked to the door. The pearls hung in his hand, forgotten. Then he stopped and looked at Ma. She watched him indifferently. She knew he would not have the courage. She knew the only thing he could do was to kill. She knew his feelings were adolescent and he lacked the nerve to take what his body demanded. She knew, too, that all through his life women had scared him; that he wanted them, but he feared their ridicule of his clumsy inexperience. She understood how he was feeling now that he had something brittle, helpless, and beautiful in his grasp. She knew that he longed to revenge himself on the girl upstairs to ease the torture of the other women in his life. She knew, convincingly, that with the thing in his grasp his nerve would not carry him through.

Slim hung on to the door handle, his face crumpled with desire and fear. Ma watched him cracking and didn't move. Then suddenly he came stumbling over to her, falling on his knees, pawing at her great arms with his bony fingers.

"Come upstairs with me, Ma," he mumbled. "Come upstairs an' make her. Hold her for me, Ma, so she don't struggle. I can't do it on my own ... come an' help me."

Ma patted the thick oily hair. "Stop talkin' wild," she said in her deep, rich voice. "You shall have what you want, but not now. Go an' rest. You ain't had any sleep yet. When the dough comes you shall have her, an' she'll like it." She leant a little forward and gently took the pearls from his slack, unresisting fingers.

As soon as Eddie got into town he parked the Airflow and bought a newspaper. The headlines had it all. The kidnapping of Miss Blandish was news and it was plastered all over the front page. Photos of Miss Blandish and Mac-Gowan stared back at him as he read the violent type. It was all wind, anyway, because there was no lead and the police had made no statement. He walked over to a small cigar-store at the corner. He nodded to the fat man behind the counter and passed through a frosted panelled door into the pool-room. The room was heavy with smoke and full of men, smoking, drinking, and playing snooker. Eddie looked round quickly and spotted Woppy by himself at the far end of the room. He walked over and sat down. Woppy had been left in town to keep his ear to the ground.

Eddie helped himself to the rye Woppy pushed over him. "Anything moving?" he asked.

"Plenty," Woppy returned, screwing up his eye as the smoke of his cigarette curled upwards. "The heat is on all right, but the bulls are lookin' for Riley an' his mob. That little rat Heinie has blown the works. The police know that Bailey had cast eyes at the pearls and they can't find him, so the rest is easy. The Feds will be in town almost any time now an' they are goin' to have a clean-up ... mind they don't catch you with your rod."

Eddie grinned. "I'm contactin' Blandish an' then I'm blowing. You'd better come back with me. This spot is goin' to get mighty unhealthy soon an' we best get outa the way."

Woppy finished the rye regretfully. Sitting still and drinking appealed to him. "Okay," he said. "I'll wait for you here."

Eddie walked into the street and looked round for a 'phone booth. As he stood hesitating he saw a woman on the opposite pavement. He glanced at her casually because she was standing there, not moving. He looked her over and liked her a lot. She had a bold face without being vicious. She was his favourite height and her figure had it all. He wished he was not on business and turned regretfully on his heel.

He found a booth in a drug-store and searched through the directory until he found the number he wanted. Hanging his handkerchief over the mouthpiece to muffle his voice, he dialled. A deep voice came over the line almost at once, as if Blandish had been expecting him.

"That Blandish?" Eddie asked, making his voice rough. "Get an earful of this. We've got your daughter an' we're sending instructions. This is a straightforward snatch an' you play turkey with us an' it'll be okay. Call the bulls off ... that's your first job. Follow the instructions you'll get an' don't try to get smart. Don't forget that there are lots of things that can happen to a girl besides twistin' her neck. Your daughter is okay now, so keep her that way ... one smell of a double- cross an' she ain't goin' to be okay ... there are plenty of the boys wants to give that dame a tumble an' that's what she'll get if you start anythin' that ain't in the book." He slammed down the receiver before Blandish could say a word. He walked out of the box with a grin.

He noticed that the woman had crossed the road and was looking in a shop window quite close to him. He walked past her and their eyes met in the reflection of the window. He gave his hat a snappy tweak, but kept walking. At the cigar-store he paused, and she walked past him. A white card fell from her hand and fluttered near his feet. He grinned and watched her walk down the block. He liked the way her buttocks jerked under her tight green dress. He picked up the card. On it was scribbled *243 Palace Hotel, West*. He grinned again. She fooled him all right. She didn't look the kind to peddle it on the street. He shrugged and put the card in his vest pocket. She was certainly worth a visit when business got slack.

He picked up Woppy and they walked over to the Airflow. Suddenly Woppy nudged him and jerked his head. Eddie looked over and saw a long, powerful car coming to a standstill not far from them. There were two men sitting in the car, powerful, hard-looking men. The car was dusty, and had travelled far and fast.

"The Feds," Woppy said, speaking low.

Eddie climbed into the Airflow and Woppy got in under the wheel. They took tremendous care to seem casual. Their rods burnt in their holsters. The Federal Officers had seen them, but after a long look they showed no interest. The Airflow gathered speed and slid out of town.

Woppy heaved with relief. "That was too close," he said. "This burg is goin' to be lousy with dicks from now on."

"Take it easy," Eddie said, wiping the cold sweat from his face. "Blandish will call 'em off. I gave him the works all right an' he is in no state to get tough."

Ma Grisson's place was not conspicuously hidden away. It stood in a small plot of shrubs and trees, but there were some other houses around. Ma Grisson had taken her time in finding this place. The front door of the house was completely hidden from the road. No curious eyes could see who left or who got out of the cars that drifted to the house at all hours of the night.

Having selected a respectable neighbourhood, she had some Italian workmen in who knew how to keep their mouths shut, and they turned the house into a steel fort. When she was satisfied that it was bullet-proof and bombproof she moved in with the gang. Ma Grisson had lived long enough to know that she would have enemies, and she could feel reasonably safe entrenched behind her steel walls.

The Airflow ran up to the front door and Eddie climbed out while Woppy went round to the garage at the back. Flynn drove up a moment later in a Dodge.

Ma Grisson was waiting. "You first," she said to Flynn.

"Easy," Flynn said. "He was on his own. He came up to give me gas an' I let him have it smack in the face. The slug took the top of his head off. I stopped long enough to dig the slug outa the door, an' then beat it."

Ma Grisson rubbed her hands and told Flynn to go to bed. Eddie gave himself a drink and sat down near her.

"Blandish is scared to hell," he said. "I told him to turn off the heat ... but when he gets the girl back things will start all right. The Feds have pulled in.... I saw 'em arrive."

"He ain't gettin' her back," Ma Grisson said.

Eddie thought for a moment. "You rubbin' her out?"

"Slim wants her," Ma told him. "When he's through with her she gets knocked off. She's seen too much."

Eddie had Ma's confidence. He was the only one of the mob she would talk to. He looked at her sharply. "She's a swell dame ... seems a waste. Slim will use her meanly." He swung the knob and the radio began to hum.

"What do you care?" Ma Grisson asked, her eyes shrewd.

"I should sweat," Eddie said, setting the dial to ten.

The radio hummed into words. *"Calling all cars ... attention all cars.... Blandish kidnapping ... Persons wanted are: Frank Riley. Description: five-foot ten ... a hundred and forty pounds ... about thirty-seven ... black hair ... sallow complexion ... wearing dark brown suit and soft hat. John Bailey also wanted in connection with the Blandish kidnapping. Description: six foot ... a hundred and sixty pounds ... thirty-four ... sandy complexion ... Wearing dark blue suit and black hat. Also Sam Macton. Five foot seven ... sixty ... a hundred and fifty pounds ... grey hair and moustache.... These people are hiding near town.... Don't take any chances ... they are dangerous ... that's all. Maddistone."*

Eddie and Ma looked at each other. "That's the sweetest break we've had," Ma said. "While the Feds chase that lead we are sitting pretty."

Eddie got up and poured out another drink. He came to the couch and lay down. "Where's Slim?" he asked.

"In bed."

"Alone?"

Ma turned her head and stared hard at him.

"Sure he's alone," she said. "What you gettin' at?"

"Thought you turned him loose on the girl," Eddie said.

Ma laughed. "He can do what he likes when we've got the dough, but not before. He's got to keep his eye clear an' a woman can play hell with a man."

Eddie felt relieved. He thought Miss Blandish a class to herself. It made him feel low to think of Slim getting her. He stretched himself and yawned.

"Am I tired?" he said. "I'm goin' to snatch some sleep." He took out his silver-plated watch and glanced at it. The white card fluttered to the ground. Ma glanced at it. Eddie grinned and picked it up.

"This was slipped to me by one of those professional dames," he said to Ma. "Nice little dish. Tailed me for quite—" he broke off, staring at the card. "For the love of mike ..." he began. He turned the card over in his hand. The address was on one side and on the other was written: *What have you done with Riley?*

Just as a street clock was striking two the Airflow slid to a standstill near the Palace Hotel. Flynn eased himself wearily in his seat and looked at Eddie.

"Here we are," he said. "Now what?"

Eddie opened the door and got out. "I'm goin' in. You wait out here an' get ready to beat it if anything begins to pop. Slim will come in with me. This set-up stinks, but we've gotta know what it is all about."

Slim followed him and they walked quickly down the dim street to the hotel. It was not anything to rave about, but it had some class. There was a single light burning over the porter's desk. Eddie went in and looked round. The fat porter was dozing over the final night edition. He blinked sleepily at the two men when they leant over the counter.

"Listen, pal," Eddie said, keeping his voice low, "we are lookin' for information. Who's got room 243?"

The porter woke himself up and his stupid face frowned.

"Can't give you information like that, sir," he said sharply. "Will you kindly call round in the morning and ask at the office?"

"Wise guy, eh?" Slim sneered. He pushed his gun across the desk. "Open up! Who's in 243?"

The porter's face went like dirty dough at the sight of the gun. With fumbling hands he thumbed the register. Eddie snatched it from him. He ran his finger quickly down the list of numbers.

"Anna Borg," he said. "Who in hell is she?"

He noted that the rooms on each side of 243 were empty. Slim slid the gun in his hand until he held it by the barrel. He reached forward like a snake striking and hit the porter between the eyes. It was a hell of a belt and the porter spread himself behind the counter. Eddie craned his head to look at him.

"You shouldn't've hit him that hard," he said. "Maybe he's got a wife an' family."

Slim was looking mean. "Let's get upstairs and see this dame."

The lift was standing deserted and they took it up to the third floor. The corridor was dimly lit and they found the two hundreds on the floor above.

"Stay right here," Eddie said. "Don't start anythin' unless you hear trouble."

Slim backed into the shadows where he could see down the passage and the head of the stairs. Eddie started to gumshoe past the doors, looking for 243. He guessed that the room he wanted was at the far end, and he was right. He listened outside the door for several minutes but heard nothing. He eased the handle in his hand, and when he felt the catch slip he pushed gently. The room was in darkness and he stepped in and shut the door. He took a small flash from his pocket and swung the light slowly round. The room was empty all right. He snapped on the electric light.

With his gun ready he moved forward, slowly searching for likely places where anyone could hide. He found nothing and he relaxed. The room was untidy, as if the occupant had dressed hurriedly. A heap of clothes lay on the bed. A white silk thing was on the floor, as if someone had just stepped out of it and left it there. The dressing-table was crowded with cosmetic bottles, and a large powder-bowl had tipped a little of its contents on the carpet. Eddie opened some drawers and glanced inside, but found nothing to interest him. He turned to the open window and looked out. *The Airflow had disappeared.* He leant out, but the street was deserted.

Staring into the semi-gloom of the lights, he swore softly. What the hell was Flynn playing at? Where had he gone? He turned off the light and slipped out of the room. Slim joined him from the shadows and Eddie gripped his arm. "Flynn has scrammed," he said. "There's no one in the room. I guess she's out on a date."

Slim cocked his head. They both listened. Faintly they heard someone talking downstairs. Slim gumshoed to the head of the staircase and looked down the well into the hall. For a moment he stood there, leaning over the barrier, then he whirled round. "The Feds," he whispered. "They've found the porter ... that's why Flynn beat it. Come on ... we gotta get outa here."

"Take it easy," Eddie said, keeping his voice low. "There's somethin' phoney goin' on here."

"What the hell are you gabbin' about?" Slim demanded, his gun in his hand.

"Who's this Borg dame?" Eddie demanded. "What's Riley to her? How come when she dates me up the Feds move in?"

"For God's sake, let's get goin' an' do the thinkin' later," Slim returned.

"I'm staying an' watchin'," Eddie said. He walked back and Slim followed, grumbling.

"We'll park in the room next door, just in case the bulls are interested in 243."

They took up positions just inside the empty room, leaving the door ajar. They could see into the dim passage. They stood there waiting. Eddie could feel Slim's hot breath on his neck as he crowded behind him. Just as they were getting weary and were relaxing, a man walked softly down the passage. A big, powerful fellow, with wide shoulders and a hard bronze face. Eddie watched him walk out of his line of vision and heard him mount the stairs to the next floor. He did not move or make a sound. He knew that Slim and he were in a spot, and it wouldn't do to start popping guns. The man was an F.B.I. agent, Eddie was sure of that. He knew it was a bad thing to start swopping shots with a G-man, and he wasn't looking for trouble. They waited several minutes, and then the man came back. Slim's breathing became hurried. He was getting steamed-up.

The Federal Agent paused near their door and looked back over his shoulder. He seemed puzzled, as if trying to figure something out, then he walked downstairs again. They relaxed a little. Eddie was about to step into the passage when Slim pulled him back. *The door of the room opposite 243 was opening gently.* Eddie hurriedly pushed his door to, leaving enough space to watch. The opposite door opened and a woman put her head out. He recognized her at once. It was the woman who had dropped the card at his feet. He drew his lips back in a grin. She hesitated, looking up and down the passage, then, moving with the quickness of a lizard, she darted across the passage into 243.

Eddie looked over his shoulder. "What you make of that?"

"That's the broad who slipped you the card?"

Eddie nodded.

"What's she doin' over the way?" Slim asked.

"That's what I'm goin' to find out," Eddie said, stepping quietly into the passage.

"A sweet time to do that with a couple of dicks gumshoeing around."

"Listen, Slim," Eddie whispered, "I don't like it. This wants lookin' into."

Slim shrugged. He was getting jittery.

"I'm goin' into that room she just left, an' then, if I'm still in one piece, I'm goin' to have a word with her. Keep an eye on the bulls, will you?"

Slim nodded and Eddie stepped across the passage. He turned the knob slowly and entered the room. The lights were burning. He took the whole scene in with one glance. Then a little shock ran through him and he lowered his gun slowly. There was a dead man lying on the floor. There could be no mistake just how dead he was. The small blue hole in the centre of his forehead told Eddie that he was as dead as a lamb cutlet.

Ma Grisson had been staring at the wall for some time, and Doc Williams began to get uneasy. Whenever Ma got those brooding spells it meant that trouble was coming to someone. Doc was amusing himself with a tommygun. He fitted the round pan and inspected the bright-jacketed .45 automatic shells it contained; then, losing interest, he put the gun down on the floor and gave himself a cigarette. He kept his eyes off Ma because she did not like people taking an interest in her. She sat so still that he finally got to his feet and walked out of the room. He opened the front door and stood looking out at the garden, dimly lit by the moonlight. He felt more at ease, and leant his long, thin frame against the door-post.

Ma hadn't noticed him go, and she suddenly moved and got out of the chair. She looked as if she had made up her mind.

She lumbered over to the table and took from the drawer that fitted underneath, a length of rubber hose.

Doc heard her movements and turned his head. He could see her standing through the open doorway. He saw with interest the rubber hose in her hand, and watched her climb the stairs surprisingly quickly for her bulk. He pushed his hat over his face and scratched the back of his head. She had got him guessing.

Ma Grisson walked into Miss Blandish's room. She turned on the light. Miss Blandish hurriedly sat up in bed. Ma kept the rubber tubing in her hand and came over and sat down on the bed, quite close to Miss Blandish. She held the tubing up so that Miss Blandish could see it.

"Ever been socked with a thing like this?" she asked in a hard voice. Miss Blandish shook her head dumbly. She had just come out of a troubled sleep, and this seemed a continuation of her nightmare. "It hurts," the old woman said, and struck Miss Blandish across her knees with incredible force. Miss Blandish stiffened and went white as the sting went through her. The dull sleepy look in her eyes changed quickly to sudden anger. She struggled up in bed, pushing the bedclothes away and clenching her small fists. "You dare hit me like that again …" she began.

Ma Grisson grinned. Her big yellow teeth made her look wolfish and strangely like her son. "Gettin' high hat … are you?" she said, and one of her huge hands gripped Miss Blandish round her wrists, pinning them together, in her hot grasp. Miss Blandish wrenched and pulled, but she could not get her hands free. Ma Grisson began to beat her with the rubber hose viciously.

Downstairs Woppy came up through the garden and met Doc, still standing at the door. "Eddie back yet?" he asked.

Doc shook his head. He followed Woppy into the livingroom. Woppy picked up a bottle and held it to the light. "Ain't there anythin' to drink in this goddam hole?" he asked, putting the bottle back. Doc went to the cupboard and got out a full bottle. He pulled the cork and poured two drinks.

"Where's Ma?" Woppy asked, giving himself a long pull from the glass.

Doc jerked his head. He said: "She's upstairs. I guess she's givin' that dame the works."

Woppy filled his glass again. "What for?" he asked. "That dame's a honeypot all right.… What's Ma gettin' tough about?"

"Search me," Doc said uneasily. "The old wolf's been sittin' over there all the evenin', broodin', then she ups an' grabs some rubber hose and scrams upstairs."

Suddenly the two men looked at each other.

"What's that?" Woppy asked uncomfortably.

They stood there several minutes, then Doc turned on the radio. He blasted the swing music until it rolled round the room.

"She shouldn't make her scream like that," he said uneasily.

Upstairs Ma Grisson was sitting once more on the bed, breathing hard through her thick nose. She eyed Miss Blandish with her little black eyes. The rubber tubing lay on the floor where she had dropped it. Miss Blandish sat upright, twisting the sheet in her hands. Her face twitched and tears ran out of the sides of her eyes and down her face.

Ma Grisson said: "Now we can talk."

Miss Blandish said nothing, but she listened. Ma started speaking slowly, but she did not choose her words. Suddenly Miss Blandish said no; and then she kept on saying no. Ma Grisson still talked. Miss Blandish had recoiled to the head of the bed. She knelt up against the wall, her face hidden in her hands, saying no.

At last Ma lost patience. "You can't get outa it, you little fool," she snarled. "You'll never get back to your joint, not in a hundred years. You know too much ... do you get that? When your pa pays up that dough he ain't goin' to see his lovely any more ... don't get that idea in your nut. Slim's got to have some dame some time an' he's picked you. If you play ball you stay here, if you don't you get shoved in a sack with your throat cut, and it's the deep drink for you. I'm puttin' it to you plain. Are you goin' to give Slim the breaks? You know what I told you. What's the answer?"

Miss Blandish turned her face and looked at the old woman. "I won't," she said. "Nothin' you can do will ever make me...."

Ma Grisson got to her feet. "A real tough baby," she said. "Now I'll tell you somethin'. Slim's been a good boy to me an' he's goin' to have what he wants. I guess I could beat you into bein' dumb, but maybe I can't. That don't fin-ish things.... You're goin' to do what I say an' like it before I'm through with you ... get that? I gotta nice little pill downstairs that you're goin' to take, an' that's goin' to put you in a different frame of mind. You can think about that tonight ... it'll give you sweet dreams. We gotta way with girls like you. A lit-tle dope an' away goes the toughness ... you see."

She turned to the door and opened it. "You'll see me again," she said.

Eddie took a deep breath and pushed his hat to the back of his head. He told himself that he had to work quickly. With a break like this and the dicks down-stairs this was just one hell of a spot to be in. He stepped towards the dead man and knelt, keeping carefully away from the sodden carpet near the man's head. He recognized him all right. It was Heinie the news-hawk; the man who told the Feds about Bailey. Eddie asked himself if that was coincidence. Quickly he searched through the man's pockets, but found nothing of interest; just the usual oddments a man will carry. He opened the wallet and glanced inside, then he shoved everything back as quickly as he could.

He got to his feet and looked round the room. He could see at once that there had been no struggle. He reckoned that someone had knocked on the door, and when Heinie went he got the slug as he opened it. From the tiny hole, Eddie guessed that the gun was almost a toy. He thought maybe it was a woman who had done it. He lightly touched Heinie's hand. It was still warm. He must have been knocked off very recently. Certainly during the time Slim and he were on the floor. This was a sweet spot.

He looked into the passage. Slim was still watching by the head of the stairs. Eddie eased himself out of the room and shut the door. He carefully wiped the doorhandle with his handkerchief. It was a bit late in the day to take precautions, but habit dies hard. He walked across to 243 and tried the handle, but the door was locked. He tapped softly. Slim glanced over his shoulder at him, and then continued to stare down the wall. Eddie tapped again. He put his head against the panel and whispered: "Open up!" The woman did not answer. "Come on, sister, open up or I'll kick the door in." Still she did not answer.

Suddenly the wailing of police-sirens floated up from the street below. Eddie whirled round. Slim waved him to the stairs. The woman in 243 started to scream, piercing screams that tore Eddie's nerves in shreds.

"That bitch will sink us ... let's get outa here."

They raced for the stairs and tore up to the next floor. They heard doors opening and people shouting, then a pounding of feet as the coppers crowded up.

"The roof," Eddie gasped. "Jeeze, why in hell did we leave the tommy behind?"

The uproar going on downstairs came to them faintly. They blundered down the passage in front of them. A door at the far end was suddenly flung open and a scared man poked his head out. Slim hit him as they crowded past and he went over with a grunt. A woman started yelling from the room. At the end of the passage was the door leading to the roof; it was locked. Slim did not hesitate; he blew the lock off with two shots from his gun. The noise of the explosions in the confined space made both men rock. Gasping for breath, they flung themselves on to the flat roof. The cool dark night was a relief after the stifling closeness of the hotel.

Running to the edge of the roof they both took a stiff drop on to the next building, some twenty feet below. The shadows were thick, and they scrambled hurriedly under cover. Over the parapet they had just left, two heads suddenly appeared with flat caps. Slim paused and, aiming carefully, fired twice. One of the heads disappeared quickly, while the other appeared to slump forward as if hit.

"We gotta separate," Eddie said. "If you get outa this meet me at the Cosmos."

Slim drew his lips off his teeth. "I'll get outa this, okay," he said. "Takes more than a copper to stop me."

Eddie left Slim crouching behind a stack. Slim liked a tough spot, and Eddie told himself that he could get on with it. He looked down into the street. Crowds had collected and the street was blocked from end to end. Police-cars stood in a row in front of the hotel. The crowd was a sea of upturned faces. Keeping his gun steady, Eddie swung his legs over a close-by parapet and dropped on to another roof. He hid himself in the darkest shadows. He could just see some figures moving about cautiously on the hotel roof. He grinned to himself. Those bulls weren't taking chances. Suddenly he heard the roar of Slim's gun and saw one of the dicks fall. Slim was enjoying himself all right. The police fired steadily at the flash, and Eddie heard the slugs whine over his head. He hastily shifted his position.

There was no way of getting off the roof into the street. Everyone down there would be on the look-out. He would have to get into a building and wait until the heat cooled off, he told himself. Slim's gun crackled again; the sound was further off. Eddie was pleased that he was drawing the bulls off. He never had much use for Slim, anyway. He moved carefully, keeping in the shadows.

Suddenly he ran into a cop. He came round the stack quickly, and he was on Eddie before either realized it. The cop acted quickly, but Eddie was a fraction before him. He jumped in and lammed at the powerful head with his fist. The cop, instead of going back, came forward, and closed with Eddie. He was tough all right, and nearly had Eddie off his feet with the first rush. They reeled for a moment, then broke apart. Eddie didn't want to use his gun. He had kept out of sight up to now and didn't want to draw the bulls on to him.

Slim was still shooting some way off. The cop had a night-stick and a gun, but he was so excited that he didn't shoot. He charged in again, and this time Eddie was ready for him. He hit him as he came in with all he had, and the cop went over with a crash. Eddie was on him and struck him between the eyes with his gun butt. He got shakily to his feet and looked round cautiously.

All was quiet on his roof, although Slim was shooting on the hotel roof still. He seemed to have made up his mind to put up a battle. Eddie noticed a skylight near him, and running forward he hastily jerked it open. The bolt holding it in place was flimsy, and it snapped after his first heave. He flashed his light down into the empty room, and then quickly slid his legs into the void and dropped. He reached up and refixed the skylight.

Opening the door, he let himself out of the room into a dark passage. Quickly he ran to the stairs and with soft, hurried steps descended to the second floor. He looked over the banisters before going further and was glad that he did. Three flat caps were coming up with a rush. He hadn't a moment. The sweat was streaming down his face now. This was a jam all right.

He whipped round and noiselessly entered the first room near him. The light was burning, and for a moment he thought the room was empty; then he saw a woman leaning out of the window, intent on the excitement going on in the street below. He shut the door quietly and crossed the room with two strides. He jerked the woman round violently. She was so startled that she couldn't even scream. He rammed his gun into her chest and knocked the breath out of her body.

"Listen, sister," he said rapidly, "you've gotta play ball. One crack outa you an' you get it. The bulls are after me an' I ain't gotta minute."

He could see, now that he looked at her, that she was a young blonde with blue eyes. She wore neat black pyjamas that suited her.

"Get into bed quick," he said.

Terrified, she obeyed, and huddled the clothes round her. He leant over her. "You gotta cover me," he said, speaking low and quick. "If the bulls look in you gotta stall. One crack that's not on the level and I'll make a hole in you … get it?"

He reached out his hand and snapped off the light. Then he lay on the floor on the far side of the bed to the door. They lay in the darkness listening to the pounding feet and the short, sharp exclamations as the police went from room to room, routing out the occupants.

Eddie raised himself cautiously so that he could just see the girl lying there. "Keep your pants on," he said, "you ain't got any need to be scared. I ain't in bed with you, am I?"

She turned her head and looked at him in the dimness. He could just make out a white blob that was her face. She didn't say anything. He slid his hand inside the sheet and took her hand. "I'll just keep this until the bulls pass by," he said. "If you do get a fit of nerves, maybe you'll get a little strength from me." She lay as still as death, and he reckoned that she was scared to hell.

Suddenly heavy footsteps sounded outside the door. A head came round the door and a bright beam hit the girl between the eyes. She gave a little squawk and raised her head. Eddie kept below the side of the bed, but he pressed her hand hard.

"Who … is … it?" she said.

"Okay, miss," the cop said, taking a good look and liking it a lot. "You ain't been disturbed, have you?"

"What is it?" she demanded. Eddie handed it to her, she was running her act through like a professional.

"We're lookin' for a couple of birds," he explained. "But if you ain't heard anythin' you get off to sleep again … sorry to have woken you."

Eddie sneered. All this oil and bull from a cop.

"Will you please go away?" She sounded cross.

"Sure, sure." The cop withdrew his head. Eddie relaxed a little, but stiffened as the cop looked round the door again. "Sweet dreams," he said coyly, and withdrew again, chuckling.

"Take it easy," Eddie said to the girl, "you're doing fine."

She said nothing, but Eddie found that she was gripping his hand. Eddie lay on the floor, listening. The sound of the crowd swelled outside in the street. He wondered if Slim had been picked up. He felt safe lying there in the darkness, and gave himself a bouquet.

"That was a nice job of work," he said in a low voice, and she squeezed his hand. He sat up slowly and then got to his feet. The house was silent now. "Okay, sister," he said, grinning into the darkness. "Thanks for the buggy ride."

The blonde still kept his hand and she raised herself on her elbow. "You goin'?" she asked.

Eddie turned his head and looked at her. He could just make out her dim face close to him. He told himself that this dame was a honey all right.

"Yeah," he said regretfully, "I'm on my way."

"You ain't had the buggy ride yet," she said in a small voice.

Eddie was stupefied. "Well, for the love of Mike ..." he said, and burst out laughing.

He stayed all right.

Two days later an advertisement offering some kegs of paint appeared in the *Tribune*. Ma Grisson flung the paper over to Doc.

"He's got the dough ready," she said. "Now we've gotta collect it."

Doc glanced at the ad and grinned. Ma said: "It's goin' to be a cinch with the old man scared for his daughter. The Feds are standin' by, but they ain't goin' to start anythin' until he gets her back. Then the heat is goin' to be turned on good. Well, he ain't gettin' her back. We get the dough first an' fool 'em after. You write another note an' tell him how to pass the bag. Tell him to take a car out to the Maxwell fillin'-station. A mile from there he'll see a light. As soon as he sees that he is to sling the bag to the side of the road. He's to drive fast an' he ain't to stop an' he's to come alone. Tell him, too, that if he starts any wise stuff it will be just too bad for the doll. When girls get kidnapped there is plenty that can happen to 'em without gettin' rubbed out ... tell him that."

Ma looked over to Flynn who was lounging in an arm-chair, half asleep.

"You go on to the high road above Maxwell with a flash, an' when the old man comes along give him the signal. You ain't goin' to have trouble, but they may try an' trail you. The road is straight for miles, an' there's no way they can come after you without you spottin' 'em. If they do get on your tail, drop the bag right in the middle of the road and shake 'em. When they see that you have let the dough slide they'll draw off, 'cos they'll know what that will mean to the girl. It's a soft job, but don't mess it."

Flynn nodded his head. "Tomorrow night?" he asked.

"Yeah." Ma Grisson rubbed her huge hands. "An' it'll be a sweet night's work."

Flynn and Doc left her and went upstairs to Eddie's room. Eddie was lying in bed. He waved a hand when they blew in.

"The dough's ready," Flynn said, sitting on the bed. "I'm goin' after it tomorrow night."

Doc was walking about the small room restlessly. "Got a drink, Eddie?" he asked.

"Sure, you'll find one in the cupboard.... Pass it round."

Doc mixed three long drinks and passed them round. Flynn took a pull and then put his glass on the floor beside him. "Seen Slim?" he asked.

Doc grinned. "Slim's poundin' his ear. He ain't got over his little scare the other night."

Flynn looked at Eddie with a leer. "Jeeze, you're a lucky guy. Right in the middle of a battle you pick yourself a honey and fight it out in bed."

Eddie shrugged his shoulder. "Can't keep 'em away," he said with a grin. "Listen, you punks, these dames fall for me in a big way. Gee, did I have the laugh on Slim or did I?"

The three of them laughed in loud bellows.

"Mind you, Eddie," Doc said, wiping his eyes, "Slim gave those bulls the works all right. Three of the bastards knocked off an' four of them hurt bad. Slim didn't have a scratch, but they sure scared the pants right off him."

Flynn shook his head. "I bet he weren't scared," he said, picking up his glass again. "That guy is the coldest thing I know."

Doc winked. "Not so cold," he said. He jerked his head towards the ceiling. "He's getting hot pants for the dame upstairs all right."

Eddie looked up sharply. "What's been doin' with that dame?" he asked. "I've sorta forgotten about her in the rush of things."

Doc shrugged his shoulders. "Ma's put her under some dope she got off me," he said. "Ain't a bad idea really, keeps her outa mischief 'n' she takes what's coming to her."

Eddie tossed the bedclothes off impatiently and slid out of bed. He grabbed his trousers and began to dress hurriedly.

"I guess I'm goin' to look at that dame," he said' grimly. "I ain't seen her for several days, an' I wanta check up on what Ma's doin'."

Doc and Flynn exchanged glances.

"Take it easy," Doc said nervously. "You know Ma told us to lay off the dame."

"I don't care what Ma says," Eddie returned, fixing his tie, "I'm goin' to have a peep at that dame an' see what's poppin'."

"Okay." Doc shrugged. "I'll sit at the top of the stairs an' tip you off if Ma comes, an' Flynn can keep an eye on Slim."

Eddie grinned at them. "Nice work," he said. "I ain't goin' to be long."

He sidled out of the room, glanced downstairs, then mounted the stairs to the second floor with quick, noiseless strides. He reached Miss Blandish's room. The door was bolted on the outside. He slid the bolt back and put his head round. The bed was in line with him and he saw Miss Blandish sitting up in bed with the covers drawn up to her chin. Her knees were bunched up and she was sitting as far up against the end of the bed as she could get. She looked small, screwed up like that. Her face was flushed and her eyes had an unnatural brilliance. Eddie thought she was the swellest dame he had ever seen. They looked at each other and he grinned at her.

"Take it easy, toots," he said. "I thought I'd jest look in on you an' hear a few things."

"You had better go," she said.

He didn't move. He didn't step back or enter the room, he just didn't move. "Listen, baby, I'm all for you," he said, keeping his voice soft, "I want you to have the breaks. I ain't goin' to start anything ... honest. Just let me have a little talk with you."

She shrugged her shoulders indifferently and he came farther into the room, shutting the door quietly behind him.

"Here," he said impulsively, jerking out his flask, "have a drink."

She took the flask from him and he watched her tilt it. He watched her throat contract under the fiery bite of the liquor and saw some of it trickle down the side of her mouth. He leant forward and jerked the flask out of her hand. "Take it easy," he said in alarm, "that's tough stuff."

She passed her hand across her face as if she were wiping cobwebs away. He sat on the bed and looked at her with interest.

"What they doin' to you?" he asked.

She looked at him as if he were not there. He felt her big eyes looking through him at the wall beyond and it made him uneasy. "Open up, sister," he said gently, "I might do somethin' for you."

"There's a tall thin creature who comes in here," and she said slowly, talking to herself. He had to lean forward to hear her. "He just stands and watches me from the doorway and makes horrid little moaning noises. He came in last night. I was asleep. I woke and found him by the bed." She stopped and looked uneasily round the room.

Eddie said: "Did he do anythin'?" and she jerked her head around with a start, becoming aware that he was still with her.

"Do you ever dream?" she asked him. "Horrid dreams, and you wake up feeling frightened? You lie still wondering if you're still dreaming or if it is over? It was like that last night. I had been dreaming.... I can't remember what I dreamt ... funny how you forget, yet you know it was frightening. I once had a dog who used to dream in front of the fire; terrifying dreams. He used to twitch his legs and groan, I felt sorry for him, but he would wake up and go off to the kitchens ... he didn't seem to mind when he woke up."

Eddie dragged down smoke into his lungs. He was glad to light a cigarette. He guessed she wanted to talk and get this thing off her mind, but she wasn't sure of him. He sat quite still, just letting the smoke drift down his nostrils.

"Yeah," he said, "I've had bad dreams, but they don't amount to anythin'."

"This dream was bad. You see it was worse when I woke up. He was quite close to me. It was dark ... but I could hear him moaning quite close. Like the wind ... you know how the wind moans when there is rain about. It's fun listening when you are in front of a big fire ... it wasn't fun listening to him. At first I thought I was back home again ... but then, I knew that he had come in. I lay quite still in bed ... pretending to be asleep. I thought I would even pretend to be dead. It must be nice to be dead.... I was frightened of dying once.... I don't care now. The room was cold and the cold touched me when he pulled the covers off me. I pretended I was dead ... did I tell you that? I pretended I was quite dead and cold. I wasn't dressed ... the old woman had taken my clothes away ... I only had on my undies.... I wanted to be in a sack ... sewn tightly round my neck. Thick sacking would have been so comfortable...." She broke off and shifted her knees. Eddie tossed his butt into the empty grate and gave himself another cigarette.

"I hate being touched," she said suddenly. "I kept my knees together ... stiff ... just like a dead person would be. I wonder why people go stiff when they are dead. The dog I told you about, who had dreams, died. I found him in the morning. He felt horrid ... like a piece of wood. His legs stuck out and we couldn't do anything with him for a long time, then he went limp and we could bury him. I wasn't frightened of the dark. I was glad of it. You see, we couldn't see each other. I think he was glad of the dark, too, because he could have put on the light if he wanted to ... couldn't he?

"I tried to dig myself into the mattress. I pressed into the mattress as hard as I could, but it didn't do any good. His hand was cold, too ... light on me. There was a little hard something inside me that was growing and growing... I could feel it inside me ... like a spring uncoiling. I waited for it to uncoil so that I could scream ... but it grew and grew but never uncoiled. I wish I were a man ... men don't have to worry about those things ...do they? Girls have a bad time ... they get sick at times ... but you would know about that ... wouldn't you? I wish I could be sick even." She pounded her clenched fists in despair on the tops of her knees.

"I once read of a man who had an accident so that he wasn't like any other men any more. I wished all men could be like that ... but it didn't help. I felt his cold hand fiddling about. It was like a little snake in bed with me. I hate snakes... don't you?"

Eddie got to his feet. He couldn't stand any more. "Listen, baby," he said softly, "I'm goin' to watch you from now on."

"But he didn't do anything ... he went away. I know he is coming back ... the old woman told me." She began to cry weakly. "What am I goin' to do? He is such a coward ... he jut stands there and fiddles with his cold hands. If he would only do something instead of standing there. I wouldn't mind what he did if I could go home. I want to go home...."

"I'll fix this for you, baby," Eddie said. "Don't get upsettin' yourself." He opened the door and went out. He didn't look back. There are some things that don't stand looking at, and Miss Blandish was one of them. He joined Doc at the head of the stairs. They went down together in silence. Flynn, who was lolling against the wall near Slim's room, followed them into Eddie's room.

Eddie shrugged his shoulders helplessly. "That dirty sonofabitch will drive her nuts," he said angrily. "I guess she'd be happier dead."

"Now, for the love of Mike, Eddie," Flynn said, "let 'em alone ... will you? Women always bring trouble an' you know Ma won't stand you gettin' tough."

Eddie brooded. "I reckon that dame would be better off dead," he said at last.

RILEY MOB BELIEVED RESPONSIBLE FOR PALACE SLAYING

MURDERED MAN NOW IDENTIFIED

JOHN BLANDISH PAYS RANSOM MONEY TODAY

It has been learnt that the man who was brutally murdered in the Palace Hotel has been identified as Alvin Heinie, the freelance society gossip writer. It was Heinie who tipped the police that the Riley gang had questioned him concerning the movements of John Blandish's daughter, the kidnapped heiress.

It is understood that the ransom demand for 500 thousand dollars is being paid today. John Blandish, fearing for his daughter's safety, has refused to allow the State Authorities to interfere, although the Department of Justice is ready to participate in what will be the greatest man-hunt of the century, when it is known the kidnapped girl is safe.

The police have reason to believe that Alvin Heinie was murdered by the Riley gang. The two men, who escaped after a desperate gun battle on the roof of the hotel, have been identified by the porter at the hotel by police photographs...

Ma Grisson read the running story to the mob. They grinned round at each other when she put the paper down.

"That Riley louse did a sweet bit of work when he started this," Slim said. "Jeeze ... he's gettin' everythin' pushed on to him."

Eddie was looking thoughtful. "Yeah, maybe it's okay for the moment, but have you asked yourself just who did knock Heinie off? It wasn't Riley ... we know that, and it wasn't us. What worries me is where this Borg dame fits in. I bet my last nickle that she rubbed Heinie out ... but why? She knows somethin' that connects us with Riley, an' I don't like it."

Ma looked at him with her little black eyes. She nodded her head. "Eddie," she said, "you're right. There is something phoney that might trip us up. Before we collect that dough we gotta know somethin' about this Borg dame. Suppose you go into town an' see if you can get any dope on her."

"Okay, Ma ... anyone comin'?" He looked questioningly at Slim, who shook his head.

"Best go in alone," Ma said, watching Slim, "an' be mighty careful how you handle this. The dicks are goin' to be on the look-out for anyone they don't like the look of after the trouble you had the other night. It was a lucky break that the porter got you muddled."

Eddie saw that Slim was biting his nails savagely. He was getting the jitters all right. Eddie thought that Miss Blandish had it coming. He caught Ma's eye and jerked his head. She got up and followed him outside.

"Can't you tell Slim to lay off that dame upstairs?" he asked.

Ma looked at him carefully. "Listen, Eddie, this ain't your concern ... do you get that? You're a good boy an' you do as you're told ... but keep outa this."

"Aw, come on, Ma." Eddie tried a grin. "A swell dame like that honeypot don't want a hoodlum messin' her about. Why don't you give the girl a break?"

Ma's eyes snapped suddenly with rage. Her great lips curled off her teeth. She looked like an old she-wolf.

"You be careful," she snarled at him. "Slim can have that dame if he wants her. You know Slim's been a good boy about women, an' if he fancies this one ... well, he can have her."

Eddie sneered. He knew he was taking a risk, but he wanted to get to the bottom of this. "What you doin' to the girl ... preparin' the way for him?" he asked, speaking low and fast. "Is he so yellow that he can't take a girl without you doping the fight outa her?"

Ma struck him across the mouth with the back of her hand. It was a heavy blow and it bruised his lips. He reeled a little on his heels, but he managed to dig up a grin. "Okay, Ma," he said, moving off. "Forget it ... will you?"

He left her standing quite still, her fleshy face dark with rage. He guessed there wouldn't be any comeback on this, but he'd have to watch his step. He hesitated about taking the Airflow and decided to take the Dodge. The heat might be on the Airflow for all he knew, and he wasn't going to take chances.

The hands of the clock over the Cosmos Club were standing at twelve minutes past one as he drew up. He slid out of the car and walked into the club. The cleaners were still clearing up after the night before, and he had to pick his way through the buckets and step over the wet flags. The girls were rehearsing under the direction of a thin little man dressed in a white sweater and dirty flannel trousers. The pianist pounded away, a cigarette dangling from his lips. The girls smiled at Eddie; he was well known at the club and generally liked. He paused long enough to pinch a rouged cheek and pat a sleek behind before going on to the office.

Pete was sitting with his feet on his desk, brooding. He seemed surprised to see Eddie. Pete was fat and oily. His shifty eyes looked Eddie over before he offered a flabby hand.

"H'yah, Pete?" Eddie said, sitting on the corner of the desk. "How's it goin'?"

Pete began to bellyache. "Business is closed down," he said, giving himself a black cigar. Eddie helped himself from the box on the table. "This gunplay has got everyone jittery."

"Yeah!" Eddie grinned. "I read about it. This cluck Riley seems to be the big-shot around here these days."

Pete scowled. "There's somethin' phoney about this business," he said, chewing his cigar. "Riley ain't ever pulled a big job like this. He musta gone nuts or somethin'. Now, if it'd been Slim ..."

Eddie's eyes narrowed a little. "Slim's been outa town for a week," he said evenly. "I been with him an' the other boys."

"Sure, sure." Pete gazed vacantly up at the ceiling. "You been outa town all right. Ain't seen you around for some time. Still, if I'd pulled this Blandish snatch I'd go mighty careful. The bulls are just waitin' for the ransom to be picked up an' the dame to be returned before they start a war. They even got aeroplanes standin' by."

"Well, that's Riley's funeral," Eddie said carelessly.

"Yeah, as you say ... it's Riley's funeral."

"Ever run across a broad who calls herself Anna Borg?" Eddie was casual, he studied his cigar, but Pete flicked a sharp look at him.

"Sure, I know Anna," he said. "What of it?"

"We want to know somethin' about this dame," Eddie leant forward. "Who is she?"

"Say, Anna's a swell baby—"

Eddie cut in roughly. "Skip that," he said. "I know what she looks like. I want to know who she is an' what she does."

Pete regarded him through the thick cloud of smoke that was escaping from his moist mouth. "Properly interested?" he said.

"Come on, Pete, spill it," Eddie said curtly, "this is important."

"Anna's a gun-girl," Pete said slowly.

"Who's she carry the gun for?"

Pete smiled. He leant forward so that his fat face was close to Eddie's. "She carries a gun for Riley."

Eddie stiffened. "For Christ's sake ..." he said.

"Yeah, I thought that would give you a knock." Pete's black eyes were snapping. "An' believe me, Eddie, a lot of folks are havin' the same shock. They are askin' why Anna isn't with Riley. That's what's knockin' 'em around here. Funny, ain't it? Riley puts the finger on the Blandish dame an' leaves Anna flat."

"Maybe she is watchin' the way it goes for him," Eddie suggested.

"Maybe hell!" Pete returned. "It ain't my business, but I reckon Anna has had a sore deal. Furthermore, she ain't the dame to take it on the chin. She's goin' to cause plenty trouble before she's kicked through."

Eddie brooded. "Where's she stoppin'?" he asked at last. "Still at the Palace?"

Pete got out of his chair. He threw the cigar butt into the brass spittoon near the door. "What's all this?" he demanded sourly. "Why you interested in Anna?"

"Ma wants to know."

Pete shaped his lips to a noiseless whistle. "Ma's in on this?" He looked startled. Ma had a name in his circle and it wasn't a pretty one. "Well ... yeah, she's still at the Palace with two dicks sittin' outside her door. The Press don't know she's in the hotel when this Heinie gets himself knocked off, but the bulls do."

"Why don't they pinch her?" Eddie demanded.

"Say, these G-men are wise. They reckon that Riley came to see Anna at the hotel an' ran into Heinie an' just had to give him the heat for rattin'. Well, they figger it this way. If they keep on Anna's tail long enough they'll turn up Riley."

Eddie thought some more. "Listen, Pete, I gotta talk with this dame ... you gotta help me. I don't want the Feds gettin' ideas about me, so you gotta arrange a meetin'. You ring her an' tell her to come right over here. I'll wait an' talk with her in this office an' the cops won't know a thing."

Pete began to protest but Eddie cut him short. "Ma wants this done, so you'd better do it." He took a roll of greenbacks from his pocket and slid them across the table. "Better let me pay for the 'phone call," he added with a grin.

Pete hesitated a moment, then took the roll, glanced at it and pulled the telephone towards him. He dialled the Palace number. "I want Miss Borg," he said... Then: "That you, Anna? This is Pete of the Cosmos. Listen, baby, I want you to come right over ... yeah ... it's important. Can you come right away? Okay, I'll wait for you." He replaced the receiver on its cradle. "She'll be here in ten minutes."

"Swell." Eddie grinned. "They come easy for you ... don't they, Pete?"

"Treat her gently," Pete said. "I've gotta soft spot for that dame, an' if it weren't Ma doin' the askin' I wouldn't do it."

"Take it easy. I ain't gettin' tough ... not my way…. I just wanta have a brotherly talk with this judy, an' that's all there is to it," Eddie returned. "Now, you take a walk ... will you, an' leave me here? When you come back the office is yours again."

Pete hesitated for a moment, then picked up his hat and left the room. Eddie took his gun out and placed it on the desk. He wasn't taking any chances with a girl who carried a gun for Riley. Gun-girls had to have plenty of nerve, but it wasn't wise to startle them. He relaxed in his chair and waited. The minutes slipped by and he kept his eye on the electric clock on the desk. He heard the sharp click of wooden-heeled shoes and he put his hand on his gun. The door swept open and Anna Borg walked in. She was half-way across the room before she saw him. She had swung the door to as she entered. She stopped short, the colour leaving her face. He admired the steadiness of her crouch. She had a shock, but her brain wasn't frozen. He thought she was some looker. Riley knew how to pick 'em even if he had been a sucker. She had seen the gun and made no attempt to move.

"H'yah, baby?" Eddie said with a friendly grin. "Keep your pants on…. I ain't startin' anything just yet. Just put your bag on the desk… willya? That's where you honeypots carry your rods ... ain't it?"

She tossed the bag on to the desk and sat down. She was breathing quickly, but otherwise she was cool. Eddie took the bag, glanced inside and scooped it into a drawer. He shoved his gun back into its holster.

"You know who I am ... don't ya?" he asked.

She said nothing.

"You left me your visitin'-card the other day," he went on. "You asked where Riley was."

She relaxed a little, but her eyes remained watchful. He took out a packet of cigarettes and pushed them across the desk to her. She hesitated a moment, then took one. He got up, and moving round the desk he lit it for her. He sat himself on the corner of the desk quite close to her and grinned. "Now, listen, we gotta get together," he said. "You nearly had me in a spot the other night ... but I don't feel sore about it. What the hell ... I didn't knock off Heinie, but you did ... an' you know it."

She stared back at him without a flicker.

"What should I care? They've pinned it onta your boyfriend, an' he's nicely hidden ... so let's forget that part. Okay ... now you wanted to see me.... I came along an' it was certainly a warm welcome I had." He soft-pedalled her along the whole time. He could see that she was thawing out and getting over her scare.

"You an' I could get on well if you'd relax an' get a bit friendly."

"Where's Riley?" she asked abruptly. Her voice was husky, like those judys who moan over the air. Eddie sat back a little. He told himself that he was getting places.

"Now, why d'you think I know where Riley is?" he asked.

"You saw Riley the night he snatched that Blandish chippy," Anna told him, watching him with her hard eyes. Eddie told himself that she was a honey-pot all right. He liked the way her lashes curled. There was nothing of the cheap moll in this set-up. She was not just paint and powder. You could scratch this dame and still find her good underneath.

"How did you know that?" he asked.

"All right, wise guy," she said, "I'll let you know facts and then you can talk. Riley 'phoned me at Johnny's. He said that he'd run into you and he thought Slim might try and pull a fast one. I've been and talked to Johnny, but he says that Riley and the girl stayed the night, and then went on somewhere. He didn't know where."

Eddie handed Johnny a bouquet, but he didn't show how pleased he was. Things were going to pan out the right way after all.

"So what ...?" he asked.

"Riley's vanished. I'm left for a sucker ... that's what." Two bright spots of red marked her cheeks and her eyes flashed angrily. "I want to know where Riley is and I want to know why he hasn't sent for me."

Eddie scratched his head; he acted dumb. "I guess the dicks want to know where he is, too. He sure started plenty when he put the finger on that dame.

Jeeze! I didn't think he had it in him."

Anna suddenly got to her feet. "Quit stalling!" she snapped. "What do you know?"

"Okay, sister, keep your pants on!" Eddie got up also. "I don't know much, but what I do know is tough to tell. I know you useta run with Riley, and from what I've heard you've been a swell pal to him. Well, baby ... it certainly looks as if he's taken a runout powder on you."

Anna stepped up to him. She certainly looked good when she was mad. "I'm on to you," she said shrilly. "You're tryin' to put on a phoney act, and I don't take a word of it. Riley was a right guy. We used to fight a bit, but then who doesn't? He wouldn't have given me the run around, so that's out ... do you get that?"

Eddie shrugged. "You know best, sister," he said indifferently. "I saw him with this Blandish dame, an' he was goin' for her in a big way. I'm tellin' you when I saw him she was lying back in the car with a great bruise on her puss, an' Riley was goin' over her good. Do you get that? That punk's hands were all over her. He was givin' her the works. She had fought him to a standstill, an' he had got her just where he wanted her. Now, let me tell you that this dame's a looker. If I had been in that car with her instead of Riley I'd done the same as he was doin'. Okay, I figger it this way ... Riley gets hot pants for her. He has gone to ground with her. They wait for the ransom, and what the hell would he do with you? Would you sit around an' watch him jazz this dame ... that's a laugh. Riley knew that ... so you're out. What's more, you're out for good. He ain't likely to risk pickin' you up once the heat's on. I guess you're strung for a sucker...."

She slapped him across the mouth. It wasn't a hard blow and it made him grin. He liked them that way.

"Shut up," she shrilled. "Riley ain't like that!"

Eddie shrugged again. He walked over to the window and looked into the night. He saw that he had said enough. She believed him all right and she was certainly getting burnt up. She began to pace to and fro. Eddie let her work herself into a state. He stood there looking into the street at the traffic, grinning to himself. Suddenly she came over to him and stood at his side. She seemed to go slack and weary. Eddie could almost feel the fire going out of her.

"I haven't heard from him for so long," she said bitterly. "If I find he's crossed me up!" she began to beat on the wall with her clenched fist. "What am I going to do? I haven't a dime."

"Take it easy, sister," Eddie said, wondering if he could pat her somewhere, "dough ain't everythin'. Anyway, I could stake you for a bit until you get goin'."

She flashed round on him, spitting like a cat.

"I tell you this is a phoney," she stormed. "You're lying."

Eddie knew that he'd done a nice job of work. He was going to let it rest like that. He went over to the desk and took out her bag; turning his body so that she could not see, he shoved a roll of greenbacks under the .25. He went over to her and put the bag under her arm. He took her to the door. "Okay, baby," he said easily. "Forget it, maybe I'm lyin'. Wait for Riley, but don't wait too long. When you get tired of waitin', get Pete to send me a word. I could do things for a swell looker like you, an' I ain't a sucker enough to give you the run around." He pushed her out of the room and shut the door. For a full minute he leant against the panels giving himself a big hand. He'd see her again, he told himself.

Flynn checked his watch. He was sitting in the Airflow, a Thompson at his side, and a powerful flashlight on his knees. He was jittery and cursed softly to himself, He guessed it would be smooth going because Ma had said so, and he had great faith in Ma, but all the same he was uneasy. The Airflow was drawn up by the side of the road in the black shadow of a clump of trees. He had a clear sight of the road ahead of him for over a mile. He sat there waiting for John Blandish and the ransom. Doc had gone out and 'phoned Blandish a few hours back. He had again made it clear not to start anything. Blandish seemed resigned, but Flynn was not taking any chances. He wished Doc or Slim had taken on this job, although Ma had promised him an extra five hundred bucks. Five hundred bucks were nice if you weren't behind bars, but they were not much use if you were. He'd be glad to get this over. He looked at his watch again. It was getting on for the time. Overhead, dark clouds began to chase across the sky, blotting out the moon which rode high. It was a hot night, but Flynn was sweating ice.

Suddenly in the distance he caught the gleam of headlights. Instantly he was out of the car and standing in the road. The Tommy was tucked under his arm. He ran towards the lights and then got off the road. The car was moving at a high speed, he could hear the roar of the engine; the driver had cut out the exhaust. Flynn began to flash his lamp. The beam cut into the darkness. The approaching car slowed down a little, and as it went past something was thrown from the window—it fell almost at Flynn's feet. He turned his lamp on to it and saw that it was a strong leather bag. The car hadn't stopped but just went on into the night. Blandish was obeying orders.

Flynn looked hurriedly up and down the road, but there was no sign of another car; snatching up the bag, he ran back to the Airflow. He ducked under the wheel and hurriedly shoved in the gear. He found himself shaking, but managed to dig up a grin. Ma had been right. It had worked without a hitch.

Away shot the Airflow at a high speed. Flynn drove like a bat out of hell. The road ran straight for miles, and every so often he glanced into the driving-mirror, but there was nothing following him. He took his time and kept to the road until he was sure that he was not followed, then, relaxing, he spun the wheel and got off the main road into the rough. He jolted and bumped for over a quarter of a mile before he felt certain that he had beaten the rap; then he headed for home.

The whole gang were sitting round waiting for him. He came into the room and dumped the bag on the table. He felt good, coming in like that, the centre of the stage, with curious greedy eyes of the others watching him He grinned round at them.

"Not a squawk," he said.

Ma clambered to her feet and walked over to the table. She fumbled with the heavy straps. The others came over and stood watching. She jerked open the bag and began to pull out the neat stacks of money. She worked slowly and without excitement, but the others reacted each in his own way. She emptied the bag and pushed it off the table on to the floor. Slim hung over the pile of money; his mouth hanging open and his eyes like slits in his white face. He was getting more than the dough he told himself. Five hundred thousand dollars looked nice right there in a heap on the table. Ma counted the bundles and checked the notes. Finally she looked up. "It worked," she said. "An' now the heat's goin' on the wrong party. Ain't that a sweet break?"

She looked at the money thoughtfully and then bent down and picked up the bag and put the money in it again. When she had finished she sat down, her great arms resting on the table. "This dough is hot," she said, tapping the bag. "It is goin' to get so hot in a few days that it will be suicide to handle it. I want dough. I gotta plan that is goin' to land us all in the gravy for a long time. We got five hundred G's right here an' we can't use it. Okay, I'm sellin' this stuff for half price. I'm gettin' two hundred and fifty grand of real money. The stuff you can go out an' blow without a squad askin' questions. I'm tellin' you boys this, for you ain't figgered it this way. You guessed that we were sittin' pretty with a half a million bucks ... but we ain't. This dough is poison. Every dick in the country is waitin' for it to come to the surface. Right ... now we are in a sweet position. The Feds will look for Riley, an' they ain't findin' him because he's planted snug. There's no line on us at all. We get the dough an' we can go ahead."

Eddie was watching Ma with hard eyes. "Who's goin' to take a risk on the dough an' give us half for it?" he demanded.

Woppy broke in excitedly. He had been listening to Ma with growing restlessness. "You ain't goin' to part with all that dough?" he quavered. "Jeeze! Half ain't so hot."

Doc and Flynn nodded their heads, but Slim said nothing. Money was not worrying him at the moment. He was thinking of Miss Blandish upstairs, and his blood pounded in his ears. Ma had said that when the dough came he could have her. Ma kept her word and he hated this time-wasting blatter.

"Wait a minute." Ma looked round at the tense faces. Her little black eyes were glittering dangerously. "You don't want to part with two hundred and fifty grand ... is that it? I bet you don't, but you're goin' to, an' you'll like it. Listen, you cheap flops, you ain't thought about this. You can't see the jam you're headin' for. I can. We're usin' safe money ... get that? We're not gettin' gummed up for two hundred and fifty grand. I'm turning the dough over, and the gravy's round the corner. I've fixed the deal with Schunbaum. He's on his way now. Schunbaum has plenty of ways of handlin' hot dough ... we ain't."

The others looked at each other. Eddie relaxed. "Okay, Ma," he said, "anything you say."

The others fell in with his lead. "Now we got the dough what you goin' to do with it?" Flynn asked.

"I'm startin' a pay-out right now," Ma said, showing her yellow teeth in a grin. "We split a hundred grand between us in equal shares for the trouble we've had, an' the balance is goin' to be used on a proposition I've been givin' my mind to for some time. I'm goin' into business, an' you boys are goin' to handle it for me. As soon as things have settled down we're goin' to move outa this joint an' goin' to some other town. I wanta start a club, complete with girls, booze, an' clippin'. There's dough to be made in this game when the boys are wise an' wide. I'm sick of bein' a small-town hick with a mob of little gangsters around me ... from now on, boys, we move inta the big-shot class." She looked round at them to see how they liked the idea and she wasn't disappointed. "You've got to get wise to yourselves," she went on. "This idea of stickin' up banks and doin' small-time stuff is out now. I want you all to look on things from the big angle ... it's your chance. As soon as Schunbaum brings the right dough you shall have it ... an' it's up to you how you spend it."

Eddie eased himself in his chair and fixed his eye on the ceiling light. "How we sendin' the Blandish dame back?" he asked.

There was a heavy silence in the room. Ma looked at him, the dark blood flooding her face. Eddie glued his eye to the light. Slim sat suddenly very still. The others looked uneasy, and the atmosphere was charged with dynamite.

"I thought I told you to lay off that angle?" Ma said, speaking slowly.

"You got the dough; the girl had better be turned loose."

Ma leant forward. "Who says so?" she demanded.

Eddie hesitated, then he plunged on. "Say, what is this?" he turned his head and faced Ma. "You can't get away with this. Listen, Ma, can't you see you're spoilin' the business. If we don't turn this judy loose there is goin' to be a goddam row. Hell! What a row there'll be! No one will pay ransom any more. The business will just fold up."

Ma lumbered to her feet. Her face was twisted with rage. She looked as mean as hell. "That dame knows too much. Riley gets the blame now an' we're free to run into new business. Let that dame outa here an' she blows the works. The Feds will crack down on us. If you want your arse burnt ... I don't! So button your mouth, you gabby sonofabitch!"

Eddie shifted his eyes and said nothing. Slim got to his feet. His face was tense and his jaw muscles bulged.

"You lay off that broad," he said to Ma. His voice was loud and rough, but Ma only glanced at him.

"You shut up, too," she said, "that dame is gettin' the works ... so shut up, all of you!"

Slim groped inside his coat and jerked out his Luger. He kicked the table out of his way and it went over with a crash, the heavy bag going with it. There was a sudden stillness in the room. The blank stoniness of his face frightened them all. He walked up to Ma and shoved the gun in her face, "You lay off that broad," he repeated. "Do you get that? She's mine! You start any funny business with her from now on an' I'll give it to you. Do you get that, you old cow? I'll blow your guts out if you touch that broad."

Ma looked into the yellow eyes and saw that he meant it. She recoiled from him, scared. He followed her up and dug the gun hard into her floppy chest. She nodded her head at him quickly. "Sure," she gasped, "I got it."

He took the gun away from her and looked round at the others. They did not meet his eyes. "You all keep your noses clean on this ... or I'll start somethin'." He paused for a moment, then slouched out of the room. Ma watched him go. Her face had lost its colour and she was trembling with rage, but Slim had scared her badly. She knew that he'd kill her without hesitation, and suddenly, with all her pent-up, frustrated rage, she spat on the floor.

Slim began to walk upstairs. He still had his gun in his hand. The smooth, cold butt felt good. Each step he took brought him nearer to Miss Blandish, and he curled his toes inside his shoes, trying to grip the stair-carpet through the leather soles. On he went, noiselessly, taking care to put his feet down softly and spring up on his arches. He suddenly became aware of how he walked upstairs. He became conscious of the weight each foot had to carry as he lifted himself from stair to stair. He slowed down as he reached the head of the stairs, but he kept on, measuring each step.

He had thought about this moment for a long time. It had been with him for years. He had gone over and over the details in his mind, and he knew just what he wanted to do. He felt that he could do it now; nothing was going to stop him. It was his moment and he was almost blinded with the pounding of blood in his brain. He stopped on the landing when he had climbed the stairs, and shoved the gun back into the holster. His hands gripped the stair-rail, squeezing the varnished wood hard, until the heat from him made the wood sticky. His head was turned to Miss Blandish's door and he stared at it, trying to see through the panels. He stood there, shaking and jerking, his eyes boring into the wood. He felt his feet sidling on and he allowed his body to follow them. He moved forward slowly until he stood outside the door. He put his hand on the bolt, feeling the rough, painted metal cold to his touch.

He began to pull the bolt back, and he started to mutter and moan to himself. The bolt came out of the socket evenly and without a sound. Slim watched it come, then he eased it back again and pulled it out again. He did this several times, pulling the bolt back and pushing it gently into the socket. The action held him, then he let go of the bolt and opened the door.

Miss Blandish was wandering about the room in an old silk dressing-gown. It reached to her feet, and the sleeves were tucked back. She was wandering round aimlessly, her eyes blank and heavy, and she lurched when she manoeuvred the furniture. She looked up when the door opened and she saw Slim. They both stood perfectly still and looked at each other. They stood there for a long time. Slim just inside the room, leaning forward, the door-handle in his hand, Miss Blandish over by the bed. Slim gradually closed the door. He didn't make any violent move with the door, but shut it slowly, and by shutting it like that he didn't break the tension in the room. He leant against the panels.

Miss Blandish said in a little voice that she wanted a drink. "You won't come near me until I have a drink?" she said. "I couldn't bear it without a drink."

Slim said nothing, but he took a flask from his hip pocket and tossed it on the bed. She followed its flight all the way across the room. She flopped on the bed and took a drink from the flask. Slim watched her. He could hear himself moaning, but he couldn't stop himself doing it.

Miss Blandish got her eyes off him and kept her eyes off him. She gripped the flask in both her hands until her knuckles were white. She began whispering to Slim and rocking herself backwards and forwards as her drugged mind refused to waken itself.

"You coward," she said. "Coward ... coward ... coward. Why do you stand there like that ... doing nothing? Why don't you put out the light so that I can't see you? I don't want to see you.... I'm not looking at you, but I can see you ... you are coming over to me. I wish I were a man ... why wasn't I born a man?..." She dropped the flask on to the floor, and the whisky trickled on to the carpet. She lay on her side on the bed, hiding her head under her crossed arms, and began to cry weakly. "Can't you leave me alone? ... keep away just a little longer... don't touch me ... please don't...."

The naked lamp, swinging in the ceiling, suddenly went out. The darkness came down on her like a smothering blanket. She felt his cold hands turning her on her back so that she lay across the bed, her head hanging over the side. She stared up into the blackness, the tears welling up into her eyes and running down her face. The hot air of the room suddenly rushed over her body and a cruel and impossible weight pinned her to the crumpled sheets. Her resistance was gone, hidden by a heavy cloud that wrapped her brain. She whispered suddenly to him in a small, panic-ridden voice: "You're hurting me ... don't you know ... you ... hurt!"

III

Dave Fenner put his feet on his desk and tilted his chair back. His office was small and well enough furnished. The desk looked workmanlike with its chromium fittings and snowy blotter. The floor was covered by a fitted carpet and a bookcase of law books stood by the window. The law books looked new, and Dave admitted to his friends that they were just a front for those who expected to see them. He hadn't opened a law book in his life.

Fenner was big. His massive shoulders bulged over the chair back, and his hard muscles made the wood creak. He wore his hat in the office from habit. It lay over his eyes and he seemed to be asleep.

The outer office was larger. A strong wooden barrier divided the room, shutting out unwelcome visitors. Paula Dolan sat before an idle typewriter and thumbed through the pages of a lurid magazine. She sighed now and then and continually looked at the wall-clock. She had a superb figure, a mass of corn-coloured curls, and her blue eyes were enormous. Fenner had engaged her on the spot because her looks alone ought to bring in some business, even though her brains were not her strong point.

The buzzer suddenly jerked her out of a day-dream and she slid off her seat and walked into the inner office.

"Hullo, baby," Fenner said, "you makin' out all right?"

Paula went round the big desk and sat herself down on his lap, but he pushed her off gently and took his feet off the desk. "Behave yourself, baby," he said, "we ain't at home now."

She made a face at him and sat on the corner of the desk. "I'm getting so tired of this, Dave," she said. "Nothing ever happens. We just sit around waiting for something to turn up and it never does. Gee! I might just as well stay home."

Fenner stretched himself. "Aw, it ain't that bad," he yawned. "We started too quick ... that's what. We started with a bang all right ... didn't we? Well, this is the depression all over again. I guess there's no crime about these days."

"I wonder if you've done the right thing," Paula said, looking out of the window. "You were getting swell money on the *Tribune*, and this private sleuthing seems mighty uncertain."

"You thought it was okay when we started," Fenner said. "We made more dough in a week than it took me to pile up in a year with the old blatter. What's eatin' you? We got enough rent to last us another month ... so what the hell?"

"Okay, you're the boss," Paula dug up a smile. "But I'm getting mighty bored, sitting in front of that machine, twiddling my thumbs."

Fenner grinned. "Well, you can always come in here ... I'll amuse you, baby," he said. "Listen, honey, if we don't get the breaks pretty soon, I'm going right out an' start somethin' all on my own."

"Can't I go home now?" Paula asked, putting on a big act. "There are lots of things a girl has to do that a great big man like you wouldn't know anything about."

"I bet," Fenner looked her over and told himself that she was a grand looker. He reached out a long arm and pulled her close to his chair. She didn't need any encouragement and they remained in a huddle for several minutes, until Fenner remembered that it was still office hours. He slid his hand down her long back and then she suddenly gave a sharp scream and sprang away from him, rubbing herself rather tenderly. Hey!" she exclaimed angrily. "What do you think you are ... a lobster or something?"

"Okay, Paula," he grinned at her. "You're too unsettling to have around this office, get goin' an' leave me to look after this joint for a bit. What about puttin' the nosebag on with me tonight? I feel that a little spree wouldn't come hard."

"Yes," Paula said, "I'd like that. Will you pick me up?"

"Make it seven... that okay?"

She nodded and walked out of the room with a wave of her hand. Before she could shut the door Fenner shouted "Ain't you got nothin' to read in this goddam place?"

She came back with her magazine. "I think you're a bit young for this," she said, standing in the doorway. "It's full of ideas that might get you thinking."

Fenner began to heave himself out of his chair with pardonable annoyance.

"You see," she went on hurriedly, "a nice girl like me has to be careful about giving you ideas ... especially when I'm all alone...." She dropped the magazine and hastily skipped out of the room. Fenner picked up the paper and grinned to himself. She was a funny kid, he told himself. He settled himself at his desk again and began to look at the pictures.

Suddenly the door opened again and Paula slid in. Her face was bright with excitement. "Hold on to your hat," she whispered in a stage voice. "The drama begins to unfold."

"You gone screwy?" Fenner growled, but before he could get to his feet, she dropped a white card on the blotter in front of him. He picked it up and looked at it, then gave a low whistle. "For Pete's sake!" he said, gaping at her.

"He's out there waiting to see you."

Fenner got to his feet and dropped the magazine into the waste-paper basket. "Blandish?" he said. "John Blandish out there waitin' to see me? Gee! I've got a hunch right now, baby, that Fenner & Co. are movin' into action once more, an' my hunch tells me that there are a few sawbucks hangin' on to this, too. Look, Paula, send him in an' stick around ... I might need you."

Paula sighed. "Nosebags off ... I suppose?" she said. "I was getting a thrill out of eating with you."

Fenner grinned. "On your way, sweetheart, if this anythin' like my hunch, we shall be eatin' good, very soon."

He sat down at his desk and folded his arms. Paula came back, and stood holding the door.

"Mr. Blandish," she said.

John Blandish walked into the room with slow, measured steps. Paula closed the door behind him, leaving the two men facing each other. Fenner was surprised that Blandish was not a bigger man. He had had in his image of Blandish a tall, tough individual with a beefy face. Meat kings ought to be made like that, he thought. Blandish was quite the reverse. Just above middle height, a thin face, clean-shaven, and heavy jaw. His eyes gave his face its extraordinary power and character. Deep-set, in dark sockets, they were hard, shrewd, and vital. Fenner recognized the man who had made millions in those eyes. Blandish looked him over critically, from head to foot. He took his time, standing there, cold, impersonal, and unfriendly. Fenner told himself that this wasn't going to be an easy interview. He waved Blandish to a chair.

"Sit down, Mr. Blandish," he said quietly. "I'm glad to know you. I guess you want to have a talk with me."

Blandish sat down slowly like an old man. Apart from his hard eyes, he carried himself listlessly, as if he were utterly exhausted.

"So you're Fenner," he said abruptly.

Dave sat down again. "Yeah," he said.

"I've heard about you," Blandish went on. "You are supposed to be tough and you are supposed to be smart."

Fenner shrugged. This sort of talk told him nothing.

"I've come to put a proposition before you," Blandish said, "I just want a simple yes or no, because I'm in a hurry and I have got things to do."

"What's your proposition?" Fenner asked, fooling with a paper-knife.

Blandish selected a cigar from a pigskin case. He cut the end carefully with a little gold penknife and lit the cigar. He didn't offer his case to Fenner. He looked up sharply when the cigar was drawing well, but Fenner was still fooling with the paper-knife as if he wasn't interested.

"Three months ago," Blandish said, and it cost him an effort to keep his voice steady, "my daughter was kidnapped. This isn't news to you, you have read about the business."

Fenner nodded his head.

"She's not been found, nor have the kidnappers been caught," Blandish said evenly. "I am going to offer you the job of cracking this business wide open. If you have any doubts, don't touch it, but if you think you stand a chance of succeeding, say so. To make it easier for you to decide let me explain how you will stand. I shall be your boss. I an putting every dollar I have into this. Money is no object, but don't think that you are going to make a monkey out of me and feather your own nest, because I'm too old a bird to be caught like that." He paused and looked at Fenner, but Fenner said nothing, nor did he raise his eyes.

"The Federal Bureau of Investigation are still working on the case. They have a reputation second to none, and they will go on working until they crack it, but I cannot sit idle while they follow their routine investigation. I'm getting into this, myself, and maybe I'll beat them to it. I don't know, but I'm going to try. I have the facts of the case and I have their co-operation. I understand that you have knocked around a lot and have connections where they have not. You know a number of these hoodlums through your newspaper work. I have also heard that once you get going you are hard to stop. I believe that you are the man I'm looking for."

He paused again, but Fenner still said nothing.

"I will give you five thousand dollars as a retaining fee, and I will pay all expenses. If you don't succeed you won't be getting anything more. On the other hand, if you pull it off, I will pay you five hundred thousand dollars."

Fenner looked up slowly, his face was expressionless. It was not for nothing that he had learnt to play poker with some of the sharpest card-players in the press room.

"That's a mighty big sum of money," he said.

Blandish nodded. "I am aware of that," he said dryly. "But I think you will have some difficulty in earning it. For the money I pay you as a retaining fee I want action. I don't want you to sit about this office thinking up ideas. I want you to get out and keep out."

Fenner got to his feet and walked over to the window. He looked down at the fast-moving traffic far below. His hunch hadn't let him down. Five hundred grand was nice going.

"I'll take it on," he said, turning abruptly. "I'll drop everything and start right away. I'd like to go over the case with you first. I will get my stenographer, as I want our talk on the records."

Blandish raised his hand "Before you call her in," he said, "I want you to get this clear. From now on, I'm your boss. You are not to consider any other work. You are to report to me when you have got any information. If I think you are up the wrong street I shall tell you so, and you must start again. This is your one job and nothing is to interfere with it."

Fenner pushed his hat further over his nose. He might have guessed that all that dough had a sting in its tail. He walked over to Blandish. "Forget it," he said roughly "Be on your way and find a tame dick."

Blandish looked at him keenly. "You have just agreed to take on this job," he reminded him.

"Sure, I agreed," Fenner snapped, "but not on those terms. You don't want a guy like me, you want a private dick with fallen arches who's anxious to make a livin'. When I get on to a case I handle it my way or not at all. I want to be free to hop a boat to China at a moment's notice and not to run to some big-shot an' say, 'May I?' I gave the *Tribune* the bum's rush because the editor thought he could boss me around. No, sir I'm my own boss an' I ain't takin' orders from no one ... not even for five hundred grand. So forget it, an' thanks for the offer."

For the first time Blandish relaxed. "I heard you felt that way, but I wanted to see for myself. Very well, Fenner, let's get down to things. You handle this the way you want and I'll pay the bills."

Fenner grinned faintly, he couldn't help himself. He just hated seeing all that money trembling in the balance. He jabbed the buzzer and Paula entered with suspicious quickness. She sat near the desk, with a note-book and pencil. She caught Fenner's warning eye and hastily adjusted her skirt.

"Now, Mr. Blandish, let's go over the case," Fenner said, giving himself a cigarette and sitting down. "If I remember, your daughter was abducted about the 14th of June."

Blandish nodded. "Yes," he said, "that's right. She was attending a party with a number of friends and she went on to a dance at a road-house with a young fellow who had been friendly with her for some time. She was wearing the pearls. The police found MacGowan, that was the name of the man she was with, murdered in the early hours of the morning. My daughter had vanished and, as no trace of her has been found, the police still think that she is alive. Apparently a man called Heinie reported to the police that a gang of hoodlums had shown interest in the pearls on the morning of the crime.

"The police tell me that this gang used to operate in a small way as bank robbers in the smaller towns. They have been convicted several times for short sentences, but they have never touched any big jobs. The police are surprised that they should have taken on murder, kidnapping, and highway robbery."

"Heinie was killed," Fenner said, "in the same hotel as Riley's girl-friend was staying."

Blandish looked at him sharply. "You seem to know a lot about this case," he said.

Fenner glanced over to Paula. "Let me have the Blandish file," he said.

She got to her feet and found the file in the fire-proof cabinet. She put it on his desk in front of him. Fenner looked over at Blandish and tapped the file with his finger. "It is my business to watch things. I don't know when I might use this sort of stuff." He opened the file and glanced through the mass of typewritten notes. "When the excitement first started I followed it carefully, an' I have here suggestions which struck me as bein' useful. Now, Riley was identified by the night-porter of the Palace as the thug who killed Heinie. I guess Riley went along to have a word with this Anna Borg, ran into Heinie and killed him. Frankly, it stinks. I knew Riley, an' he had not the makin' of a real killer. Small stuff, yes, but killing ... no sir! I'm bettin' that when this case is cracked we're goin' to get a surprise. What I want to know is why did Riley suddenly become a big-shot gangster ... overnight, mind you?"

He turned some more sheets over and then looked up again. "On the morning after your daughter was snatched, a gas salesman was rubbed out. That gas salesman had a dump about a hundred and forty miles from the Golden Slipper. Did the Feds think anything of that?"

Blandish shook his head. "I didn't hear anything about it," he said.

"Riley and his gang had to buy petrol. Suppose they stopped at this place and your daughter screamed ... obviously they had to iron out the salesman. The murder was without motive. Nothing was stolen.... I may be wrong, but I guess there may also be somethin' in it."

He got up and took a large-scale map from a drawer. He spread it on the table. "This is where the garage was; now, did the Feds search the neighbourhood round here?"

Blandish leaned forward. "Yes," he said, "I know they did, they combed the whole place but found nothing. The extraordinary thing is that there has been no trace of the gang since then, or of the pearls. The three of them, with my daughter, have vanished into thin air."

Fenner leant forward, looking at Blandish.

"Tell me what you think?" he said.

"I think my daughter is dead," Blandish said quietly. "I hope she is, otherwise ..." he got to his feet abruptly and walked over to the window. Fenner and Paula exchanged glances. They could feel the tense atmosphere of tragedy that surrounded Blandish.

Will you consider things and get going?" Blandish said in a tired voice. "I want those men caught. I don't want them to get away with this. I should be more satisfied if they were killedthan arrested. These crooks have so many ways of evading the law. I'll leave everything to you." He turned and went over to Fenner, "I am glad I have come to you. I think you will do something. Will you let me know how you are progressing? I'll send you a cheque tonight."

Fenner got to his feet and walked over to him. He put his big hand on Blandish's arm and looked him in the face. "I'll get those thugs," he said softly, "if it's the last thing I do."

Paula put her head round the door cautiously. Blandish had been gone a good half-hour, and the street clocks were striking five. Fenner was pacing up and down the small office, smoking furiously. She slid into the room and sat herself on the corner of the desk.

"Sherlock's mighty brain continued to pound on the problem," she murmured softly.

Fenner looked up, his brows knit and a hard expression in his eyes. "I guess Blandish was right when he said I'd work for that dough," he said. "This is goin' to be a tough proposition all right. It looks as if I'm goin' to have a hard job to get started."

"What's the first move?" Paula asked, swinging her neat silk legs.

"The way I see it, Toots, is this. There is only one angle to follow, and that is the Borg dame. She sticks out of this case like a boil. The Feds are on to that, but they ain't uncovered anything. Borg is the only link we've got, so we've gotta make use of it. Okay, the first move is to contact Miss Borg." He scooped up the telephone and hastily dialled a number. "I wanta find out how helpful the local authorities are goin' to be," he said. "They know ... hello? Give me Mr. Lowes. Fenner talkin' ... that you Mr. Lowes? ... Fenner here. I've seen John Blandish about the kidnappin'. He told you he was comin' to see me ... did he? Right, then we know where we are. I want a line on this Borg dame. Brennan's coverin' that, is he? Thanks a lot ... sure, I know ... it looks like you're goin' to be a big help. Sure, we'll work together. Yeah, I'll be seein' you."

He slapped down the receiver and winked at Paula. "They are sunk on this case. Want me to turn in any information I can get. Gee! It certainly looks as if my reputation is good for somethin' after all."

"Don't get upstage," Paula said, "you've got a long way to go, and it beats me how you're going to get anything out of this Borg girl when the F.B.I. have already been over her."

Fenner moved to the door. "I got ways that the dicks can't try on," he said, "I'm goin' down now to see Brennan. Close up the office an' get home ... we ain't workin' for anyone now. I'll ring you at the apartment as soon as I'm through."

She slid off the desk and came over to him. "I suppose I'm going to sit at home and do nothing now," she complained. "You'll have all the fun and I shall have to sit still and listen to you brag about it."

"You go home, an' don't you talk so much."

"I guess I'll go to your home and camp out in your bed," she said.

"I get it. You think I'm goin' to bring that Borg home with me, don't you?"

"You've got me wrong there." She sidled quite close to him. "I know you. Aren't you the little boy who wouldn't touch a girl even if she asked you? I'd trust you, provided you were in a strait-jacket."

Fenner grinned. "One of these days I'm goin' to take you seriously an' just see how much of your talk is bluff."

"Well, don't be too long about it, you may get a surprise. And don't bring that Borg dame home ... three in a bed sounds like perversion to me."

Fenner gave her a pat on her fanny and left her, protesting. He found Charles Brennan waiting for him. Brennan, grimaced and fat, had already talked to Lowes and he was ready to give assistance.

"I'm glad you've come in on this, Dave," he said. "This job is costin' the State plenty. You, as an outside agent, can do a lot, and Blandish will foot the bill. We'll give you all the help you want."

Fenner nodded. "What about this Borg woman?" he asked. "Where is she now?"

"She pulled out of town about a month ago. She's got a new boy-friend now, no other than our old friend Eddie Schultz. Remember him ... the big guy who runs around with the Grisson gang? She gets tired of waiting for Riley and finds herself another meal-ticket. The Grisson mob have cleared out, too. They've moved to Springfield. The Old Wolf's come into money. Source unknown. I've had the boys go over her, but she talks of a backer and won't give names. We've nothing on her, so we can't get too nosy. Anyway, what the hell! She's gone into the entertainment business and runs a club."

Fenner raised his hat and scratched his head. "You've got a man taggin' Borg?" he asked.

Brennan shrugged. "Yeah, Doyley is watching her, but I guess it's a waste of time. She seems washed up with Riley, and this Schultz bird has sure knocked her plenty. Riley ain't goin' to show up on her any more. It's too obvious that we would watch Borg, and he ain't the type to risk his hide for a dame. I'll keep Doyley on for a little longer, then I'll have to set him to work on something else."

Fenner brooded. "Tell me, buddy, how do you really stand on this case?" he asked. "Forget I ever was a news-guy an' speak your mind."

Brennan shrugged hopelessly. "This is the god-damnedest case I've ever had," he admitted. "No trace of Riley's mob, no trace of the girl, no trace of the money, and no trace of the pearls. We can't get started. Jeeze! The money we've spent on this case. We've had aeroplanes out, house-to-house searches, and we've put out a drag-net and roped in anyone who smells a bit off, but we ain't found a thing. It's a bitch of a case."

Fenner got to his feet. He looked worried. "You sure are encouragin'," he said, "but I guess I'd better get busy an' do somethin'. I keep thinkin' of the dough I shall make if I crack this nut, an' it certainly has me steamed-up."

He shook hands with Brennan and turned to the door. Then a thought struck him and he shot out: "Where did this Borg dame work when she was around?"

"She did a bit of vaudeville work at the Cosmos Club, I believe," Brennan told him, "but she didn't have to work with Riley around."

"Cosmos Club? Sure, I know that joint. It's run by a Mex. I guess I'll look in an' have a little talk with him."

"He's a leery bird," Brennan said, "we've worked over him, but he didn't spill anything."

"He'll like me better than you professional dicks."

Outside in the street he paused to think. It was getting on for seven o'clock. Pete wouldn't be at the club yet. He thought that he would combine business with pleasure. He turned into a 'phone booth and rang up Paula. She answered at once.

"I'll stand you a feed after all," he said.

"Is that you, Micky?" she asked.

Fenner grinned into the 'phone. "You know who it is all right."

"Good gracious, I thought you'd got a date with the Borg woman."

"I would have, only she's pulled her freight, so I've got to be content to take you out."

"I don't know if I'm free, hold on while I look at my appointment book ..."

Fenner said, "I'll be around with the car right away," and hung up.

She was waiting for him on the door-step when he swung the car to the kerb. He thought she looked swell and told her so.

"What's the idea?" she asked him as they drove away. "Why the sudden change in your plans?"

"I've seen Brennan, an' he thinks Pete might know a little something. Good enough ... so we have dinner at the Cosmos an' then I'll have a little chat with this Mex, an' see just what he does know."

She relaxed into her seat. "I might have guessed it. I sit all alone eating all by myself while you do the heavy off-stage."

He patted her knee. "You're doin' fine," he said "Quit your beefing ... ain't I buyin' you a meal?"

The Cosmos was doing good business when they arrived, and there was some difficulty in getting a table. As soon as he had ordered the meal he asked the waiter if Pete was in.

The waiter nodded. "He's in the office."

Fenner looked at Paula with an apologetic grin. "I'm not wastin' time," he said. "You get on with the eats an' I'll join you in a little while."

She sighed. "Didn't I tell you that's the way it would go?"

He went across the room, passing the barrier behind which the professional dancers were sitting. One of the blondes dug up a come-hither smile and called softly: "Hello, handsome!"

"H'yuh?" he returned, matching her smile. He didn't pause, but went on straight into Pete's office. Pete was enjoying a cigar. He was sitting in his shirt-sleeves. Fenner looked him over and then shut the door. Pete's eyes shifted, and he seemed uneasy.

"H'yah, Pete?" Fenner said. "Remember me?"

"Sure, I remember you," Pete said uneasily. "What's the big idea, bustin' in like this?"

Fenner came over to the desk and leant over it. "I wanta talk to you," he said coldly. "I ain't wastin' time with a yellow belly like you, so here's what's comin' to you plenty if you don't spill what I want you to spill."

His fist, moving like a streak of light, thudded into Pete's face, sending the Mexican over backwards in his chair. He landed with a crash, his legs jammed under the desk. Fenner moved round quickly and, reaching down, closed his fist round Pete's shirt-front and hauled him to his feet. He stood the dazed man up against the wall and jolted his head back. The office door burst open, and two skinny wop waiters peered in nervously. Fenner looked at them. "Scram!" he said. "The boss an' me are busy." They hesitated a moment, then, seeing the hard eyes boring into them, they backed and shut the door again.

Pete was in a bad way. Blood was running down his chin and nose. Fenner slammed him into a chair.

"Okay, now we can start," he said viciously, "You're goin' to talk."

Pete cringed away and nodded wildly. "Sure, I'll talk."

"You know Anna Borg?"

"Yeah, I know her."

"What was she to Riley?"

"She carried his gun ... you know, when Riley went on a job she hung around with the gat. If the dicks pinched Riley they didn't find him rodded up. When he wanted to start trouble she was ready to slide the gun to him quick."

"Were they fond of each other?"

"Sure they were. They were like two love-birds. They fought all day an' made it up at night-time." Pete groped about for a handkerchief and began to pat his nose gingerly.

"Yet Riley ditched her when he put the finger on the Blandish dame?"

"Yeah, he did her dirt that time."

"How did she get in with Eddie Schultz?"

Pete hesitated and Fenner slapped him around the ears. "Get goin', you grease-ball, or I'll get tough!"

"She met Eddie here. Eddie made me get her down here. He said Mother Grisson wanted him to talk to her. I left them together," Pete mumbled.

Fenner wondered what the hell Ma Grisson wanted with this Borg woman. "Well? Go on, go on, let's have it."

"Honest, I don't know anythin' more," Pete groaned. "He used to come to the club an' see her a lot after that, an' when they opened up in Springfield she left me an' joined up with Schultz. I don't know a thing more ... honest I don't."

Fenner looked him over and decided that he was speaking the truth. He stood away from him and lit a cigarette. He felt faintly excited. He had already got just a little something new. Ma Grisson was interested in Anna Borg. Why? There was no use wasting time, he had got to see this dame.

"Okay, Pete, the heat's off you for a while. Take it easy, but don't go doin' things you oughtn't."

He turned to the door, and as he did so he caught a savage gleam in Pete's eye. A vindictive, satisfied smirk spread over the Mexican's face. Fenner paused and grinned to himself. He quietly picked up a chair and, opening the door suddenly, thrust the chair through the doorway. A small, wiry wop sprang forward and swung a leaded stick. He hit the chair hard before he could pull his stroke. Fenner drove the chair at him like a battering ram and struck him low down.

The wop curled up with a grunt of anguish and Fenner swooped down on him; seizing him by an arm and a leg, he tossed him violently into Pete's astonished face. He paused long enough to see the two men go over with a crash, then, grinning widely, he entered the dance room. The blonde behind the barrier was leaning forward with her neck craned, watching. She looked at him with open admiration. "A real tough guy," she said softly.

"Sure, baby," Fenner returned, not pausing in his walk, "but I could be mighty soft with a honey like you."

He found Paula enjoying herself. She had ordered an expensive wine and she had nearly completed her meal. Fenner put his hand under her arm and raised her from the chair.

"You are not goin' to dance?" she asked, pleased.

"You're right, I ain't," he returned. "Grab your wrap, we're leavin'." He looked over his shoulder at the office. "I guess we ain't goin' to be too popular in a minute, so this, is where we scram." He shoved some money at the startled waiter and walked quickly out of the club, still holding her arm.

"Isn't this sweet?" she said. "You're not taking me home to share your bed by chance!"

He grinned down at her. "You know all the answers, don't you?" he said. "You're goin' to pack. We're off to Springfield tonight."

The entrance to the Paradise Club was up a side alley off the main street on the East side. The alley was usually pitch dark except for the glow of the neon letters that spelt out the name of the club.

The door to the club was of three-inch steel with a small window of bulletproof glass let in, conveniently adjusted to investigate visitors. There was a bell-push on the side of the door and a code of long and short rings that pleased the members. The door was never opened to anyone who did not give the code ring. The membership was not very large, but the members brought friends, and a number of taxi-drivers brought suckers who were looking for girls, so the place did good business.

The club was on the first floor and the stairs were broad with a barrier and a little gate at the head. The barrier was of steel, and small loopholes were cleverly masked. Beyond the barrier was the cloak-room. The check-girl was hand-picked and generally caused a small riot in the reception hall. She wore a short red coat and white silk trousers, about a size and a half too small for her in the seat. The red coat had a zipper down the front and the boys could work it if they slipped her a dollar. As she had everything in the right places, the zipper put in some overtime and she picked up a nice living on the side.

The reception hall was white-and-gilt with a heavy pile carpet. Beyond that, through another steel door, was the restaurant and the dance floor. Beyond that, the office where Ma Grisson ran the club. Upstairs was nobody's business.

The Grisson mob had settled down. They had done themselves well and the club was making money. Springfield didn't take to them, but that did not keep them awake at night. They were a tough gang and they did not have to worry about things like that. It was serious for the small gangs that had flourished before their coming, and Rocco soon found that they played hell with his rackets.

Rocco was an unusual type of hoodlum. For one thing, he worked alone.

This in itself was original, but he had brains and he felt safer playing a lone hand and happier when he didn't have to split his takings. He had worked up several small, paying rackets, nothing very big and nothing very dangerous. He was unimportant enough not to excite the authorities and he only pulled small jobs that would prove profitable and safe.

He ran three taxi-cabs. On the face of it, harmless enough, but those cabs were linked closely with shady clip joints and he drew a satisfactory rake-off on a percentage basis. Now and then, when he thought he could get away with it, he used the cabs for a little white-slaving. Should some helpless-looking judy with sufficiently pleasing exterior hire one of these cabs, it might possibly be the last that was heard of her. This brought him in a nice slice, but he didn't often think the risk worth the dough. His real income was derived from the numbers racket. He got himself a job, as soon as he saw the possibilities of this system of illegal gambling, as a collector. His choice was wise because it was comparatively safe and certainly profitable. All he had to do was to find anyone who wished to try his luck and present them with a duplicate notebook in which they wrote the number they thought would turn up, the amount of their bet, and their initials.

He received a rake-off of ten per cent of the backer's win, plus a fat tip from the backer. Besides the numbers racket, he had made for himself a nice little corner in protection. This was only in operation amongst very small-time shopkeepers, but they willingly paid him ten dollars a week for his goodwill. So, taking it all round, Rocco was on to a nice thing ... until the Grisson mob moved in.

The first indication he had that they were going to cause trouble was when one of his taxi-drivers burst into his small office which he rented in a large block on a main street. The man was almost crying with rage. Rocco looked up sharply, his little black eyes looking startled.

"I'm quittin'," the man shouted at him. "I ain't standin' for it any longer."

"What the hell are you yellin' about?" Rocco asked, getting to his feet.

"There are six new cabs on the road an' they are made of steel. I've been crowded off the road by those bastards all day, an' I ain't takin' any more chances ... I'm through!"

Rocco was seriously alarmed. "I ain't seen any new cabs ..." he began.

"Maybe you ain't ... but that doesn't say they ain't on the road. I tell you it is a frame-up to get you off the road. How would you like to have some bum forcing you into the kerb all day at a high speed. I've saved my neck up to now ... but I ain't takin' any more chances."

"I'll fix that ..." Rocco said through his teeth.

Almost before the words were out of his mouth a dull crash, followed by shouts in the street, made them both run to the window. Far below, was one of his cabs lying on its side, the off-wheels revolving slowly. They were getting the driver out of the wreckage even as Rocco watched. A brightly painted cab was standing nearby, and the taxi-driver clutched Rocco's arm.

"There you are," he said. "That's one of them ... now do you see? It's a frame-up. By tomorrow you won't have a cab left. Give me my dough ... I'm quittin'."

Rocco took out his wallet and paid the man his salary. He did not say anything, but he was very thoughtful. His native caution warned him to go slow, and next morning he took a train to Kansas. Here he tried to find out just how tough this Grisson mob was. It did not take him long to realize that he was up against an outfit who could flatten him as easily as they could flatten a fly on the wall. Kansas seemed mighty relieved to see them go, and Slim's reputation as a killer was drummed into him during the few hours he spent in the town until he was genuinely scared.

With southern resignation he accepted the inevitable and withdrew his cabs. This meant a loss of income, so he raised his protection prices. This lasted only for a week, when the next set-back occurred. Going round for his weekly rake-off, he was met with the same answer.

"I'm sorry, mister, but I've been told to pay protection to the Grisson mob ... they say that if you start trouble they'll look after us."

By this time Rocco was getting in a frenzy. He decided to do something about it. He took himself round to the Paradise Club and introduced himself.

Ma Grisson had him in her office and Slim and Eddie stood about the room, watching him with contempt. Rocco stood in front of Ma's desk, and carefully put his bowler hat on the floor. He looked at Ma with a completely blank face, and she looked at him equally without interest.

"I have three cabs," he began in his soft voice. "I thought maybe I could do some business for you. My drivers take people to clubs and recommend the right places. Can't we arrange some business in that way?"

"We've got all the cabs we want ... if we want more we'll put them on the road. We ain't looking for competitors, but if we have 'em they'll get run off the road," Ma said.

Rocco raised his shoulders apologetically.

"My cabs are good—" he began.

Ma finished the interview. "You heard what I said. We've moved in, an' we're the big-shots around here. If you don't like it ... say so, an' we'll fix it for you."

Rocco bent down to pick up his hat. His face was expressionless. He could do nothing. "I thought we might do somethin' there, but we can't ... no?"

"No," Ma told him, and that was that.

Rocco went back to his numbers racket and had a thin time. He promised himself, however, that when the opportunity arrived, and he was sufficiently faithful in fate to believe that an opportunity would arrive, he would settle his differences to his own satisfaction.

A week after his first interview with Ma he got himself introduced to the club through a member. The actual business did not get going until after the theatres, and a small group of hoodlums were amusing themselves in a crap game. Rocco joined them and found himself next to a fat blonde with whom he had been extremely intimate in the past. Rocco was glad that he had found her again as her technique was extraordinary, even if she was as large as a house.

Eddie wasn't playing, but he wandered round the table, showing off his new tuxedo. He walked over to the cloak-room.

"Anna shown up yet?" he asked.

The check-girl was reading a lurid novelette. She looked up impatiently and shook her head. Just then Slim slouched up the stairs. His yellow eyes were half-closed with fatigue.

"H'yah, Slim?" Eddie said. "You seen Anna?"

Slim leant against the wall. "No, I ain't seen her," he said indifferently, "she'll be along."

"Some of the boys have blown in," Eddie told him; "they are inside, playin' crap."

Slim sneered. "Small-town stuff," he said.

"Rocco's in there an' he's found himself a judy."

Slim looked up quickly. "Rocco? What's he want round here?"

"Rocco's all right ...he won't start anythin'. He's scared of us."

Slim looked mean, "Rocco's a two-faced sonofabitch. I don't want him here."

Eddie shrugged. "He's spendin' dough here, so what the hell?"

Slim walked past him into the restaurant. He sidled past e group at the table. Rocco was enjoying himself. The big blonde sat close to him, giggling and chattering like a monkey. Slim sneered and the blonde, looking up, caught him at it.

"Hello, handsome, you gotta pain in your tail?"

Slim stood very still. "Tell your whore to lay off me," he said to Rocco. Rocco stopped smiling. His face stiffened. "What did you say?" he asked.

The others at the table quietly pushed their chairs back and looked at each other uneasily.

Slim said coldly, "I said, 'Tell your whore to lay off me'."

Rocco got slowly to his feet. He was half the size of Slim, but he was mad. Slim's yellow eyes didn't throw any scare into him. The office door at the end of the room suddenly opened and Ma Grisson bounced out; she was holding a riot-gun and she looked mean.

"Cut out that stuff," she bawled. "Rocco, take that blonde yapper outa here, and you, Slim, get to hell upstairs. This is a sweet thing, startin' a rough house in my joint. I won't have it, so get that straight."

The tension was broken, and even Rocco dug up a smile. "O.K., I'll scram," he said. He went off with his blonde, and the rest of the gang drifted away. The bell downstairs began to ring in jerky bursts. Ma laid down the gun and went off to the kitchens to start the wheels moving. Three jaded musicians climbed on to the low stage and began to swing it hot. Waiters materialized and took up their stations. The stage was set for another night's work.

Slim, still feeling mean, went upstairs. He entered a room at the end of the passage. Miss Blandish was filing her nails in front of a mirror. The room was richly furnished in bad taste and looked like a crazy movie set. Miss Blandish was in a silk dressing-gown, and her long legs were crossed. The dressing-gown fell open across her knees, but she made no movement to cover herself when she heard Slim walk in. She didn't even look up, but went on filing her nails as if he hadn't entered.

Slim looked at her and sat on the bed. He was feeling tired. He had been arranging for a load of liquor, and the day had been a heavy one. There was still money to be made supplying liquor, although repeal had come in. The authorities imposed a tax. The Grisson mob soon found a way to turn this into money. They contracted unbonded liquor from an illegal still and arranged for consignments to come regularly to the club. There was a risk in getting the stuff into the club, and Slim had to look after that angle. Once the liquor was in, the rest was easy. They had a supply of empty bottles complete with the genuine stamps and labels, and all they had to do was to fill the bottles and sell them at the usual rates, thereby putting the tax in their own pockets. They were making a nice line in this way.

Slim half-lay on the bed, content to watch her file her nails. He let his eye run over her thick red hair and travel slowly over her figure with the detached eye of a tired man.

"Ma been to see you today?" he asked.

Miss Blandish folded her hands in her lap and looked at him in the mirror. He was sitting behind her in the shadow. The small table-lamp lit up her reflection in the mirror, so that he could see her clearly. He noticed that her pupils were pinheads. He thought it pretty smart of Ma to give this judy dope. It took all the starch out of her and made her a languorous, consenting woman.

"Yes," she said listlessly.

"Come over here," Slim said.

She got to her feet at once and moved over to him, standing in front of him, her arms hanging limply at her sides. He pulled her down on the bed beside him. She gazed into his face blankly as if her brain refused to function. For a moment a small spark of resistance burnt up and her face curled a little in terror, but then she went blank again, the effort being too much for her.

Slim fondled her as if she were a doll. Because she offered no resistance to him and he could do what he liked with her, she meant much to him. At last he had a woman who would not jeer at him, who would not shrink at his touch, who did what he told her; and yet he knew that he was fooling himself, and sometimes he would turn on her brutally, trying to awake her resistance, but Ma had done her work too well.

"I gotta get downstairs," he said. "You got everything?"

She nodded, but said nothing. It was an effort for her to talk, she wanted to lie still and dream.

"Go to sleep. I'm tired. I shan't see you tonight." He clumsily pulled off her wrap and pulled the sheets over her. She lay still, looking at him with her great blank eyes, and he had to turn his head away sharply. Those eyes gave him the jitters. It was like playing with a corpse. He went downstairs again. The crowd was coming in fast and he hung about the reception hall, watching the people hand in their coats. Eddie came out of the restaurant. He looked worried.

"You seen Anna?" he asked Slim.

The check-girl, leaning over the partition, said shrilly: "She's comin' up now."

Anna Borg ran up the stairs quickly. She was sleek and trim and slightly breathless. Eddie went to meet her with a hard look.

"What's the big idea? I've been waiting for you over an hour."

Anna stopped short. "Well, what do you make of that?" she demanded in a loud voice to the hall in general. "Can't a girl take a little time puttin' on her rags without you startin' to beef? Think I'd run away or somethin'?"

Eddie looked round uneasily. "Pipe down, baby," he urged, "I tell you you're late."

Anna shrugged impatiently and whipped off her cloak which the check-girl took from her indifferently. "What if I am? No need for you to make a row like an elephant in childbirth, is there?"

"Okay, okay. What the hell …? Come on in an' have a drink."

"I got to get ready for my act. Go an' buy yourself one an' drown yourself in it." She flounced away from him, jerking her buttocks furiously as she went. Eddie grinned a little ruefully. She was a tough baby, he told himself.

Slim, who had been watching, said: "Why don't you take a swing at that chippy? She's gettin' too big for her pants."

Eddie eyed him and sneered. "Maybe, but she don't need dope to sleep with me."

Slim went livid. That crack hit him in his softest spot and he curled up under it. Eddie left him quickly and joined a party who were drinking in the restaurant. Slim felt someone looking at him curiously and turned his twisted face quickly. A short, powerfully built man had just come up the stairs. He gave his hat to the check-girl and stood talking. His hard face looked pleasant enough as he kidded the girl along. She showed him the zipper and the little medal hanging on it. "I work for a dollar", was engraved on its face. He shook his head with a grin. "No, Toots, I've outgrown that stuff," he said. Her pout slid into a smile when he tossed a sawbuck into the plate. He looked again at Slim and then walked into the restaurant.

"Who's that guy?" Slim came over quickly.

"Name of Flagherty," she said. "New member, registered a couple of days ago. Introduced by Mason."

"He looks like a dick. Ma in the office?"

She nodded. "I think he's a right guy."

"You'd think any palooka's a right guy if he fed you a buck now an' then," Slim snarled at her. He walked quickly into the office. Ma was smoking a cigar, adding up a ledger.

"Scram," she said, not looking up, "I'm busy."

"Who's this Flagherty bird?"

Ma looked up angrily. "Can't you see I'm busy? I gotta get—"

"Who's this Flagherty bird?" Slim repeated in a louder voice.

"How the hell should I know? One of Mason's pals."

"Listen, Ma, that guy looks like a bull to me."

Ma put her pen down. Her eyes narrowed and she nodded.

"Maybe you're right. There is somethin' phoney about that feller. You'd better keep an eye on him."

"You bet I'll keep an eye on him," Slim said viciously. He walked into the restaurant again and stood, looking round impatiently. He saw that Flagherty was sitting at a little table at the far end, near the band. He was talking to one of the professional "gimme girls". Slim gave Doc the high-sign, and Doc left his chair and joined him.

"That guy that's just come in. I think he's a bull."

Doc looked nervous. "How did he get in?"

"Mason got him in," Slim said, speaking rapidly. "Mason's all right, but I'd like to know something about this other guy." He went back to the cloakroom. "Mason showed up?" he asked.

"He won't be in tonight," the check-girl told him. "He's always on the dot."

Slim shrugged. "Okay, watch him, Doc, and pass the word round. That guy ain't to go upstairs, no matter what ... get that?"

Doc nodded. "I'll wise up the boys." He turned and went back to the restaurant. There was a slight lull. The band had stopped playing and a buzz of talk was hushed as the band leader minced his way to the mike. "Now, folks," he said, "here's the big act you're waitin' for. You all know what to expect by now. Tonight, Miss Anna Borg is givin' you just another of her wonderful passion dances. Oh, boy! Does she know her stuff or does she? Is she lovely or is she? You ask the drummer ... he knew her when the bubble burst. Now, folks, a big hand for the little lady. Miss ... Anna ... Borg!"

The drummer ran a roll as the lights dimmed. A spasmodic applause broke out round the tables. Anna appeared suddenly on the stage, and the electrician lit her with a spot. She wore a long white net dress, and underneath she was naked. The spotlight shining full on her made the dress look solid, but, when another spot got to work behind her, the guests saw plenty. The band broke into something hot, and she stood and sang. She certainly gave that song the works. Her voice was low and rich and she could tear the top notes down without effort. As she sang she moved about the room. No one made a pass at her because Eddie lounged about quite close, but there were a mighty lot of fidgety hands in that room, all the same. At the end of the song she got a big hand. Some of the men who had hit the liquor hard stood up and shouted at her.

The lights went lower still and faded right out. The whole room was just blackness and smoke-haze. There she stood, in a blue light, in the middle of the floor, with every eye fixed on her. She just stood, swaying to the music and then she began to undo the dress with tantalizing slowness. The spot focused to a small circle which just lit her face, the rest of her body was a shadowy white form. She dropped the dress at her feet and began to glide round the room with the spot chasing her. Sometimes it caught her and sometimes it didn't. She moved with incredible ease and speed. The room got properly steamed-up when the spot caught her in unexpected places. Then she was back by her dress and had slipped into it as the lights flashed up. The crowd howled their appreciation. She knew her job all right and she always went down big. She blew kisses as she ran up lightly to the platform and, turning, waved to the crowd, before ducking behind the curtain that covered her exit.

Slim had been watching her with a bored eye. She'd got a shape, all right, but no class, he told himself. She was just a small-town chippy. He glanced over at Flagherty's table and suddenly stiffened. Under cover of the darkness Flagherty had pulled his freight. The little table where he had been sitting was deserted.

Fenner got into Springfield in the early morning; Paula sat beside him in the car, heavy-eyed and weary from the all-night drive.

"Pinkerton never sleeps," she murmured drowsily.

"Ain't safe with you around," Fenner returned. "As this is our first job for a couple of months, what have you been doin' all this time?"

They drove down a couple of blocks in silence.

"I suppose you're going to snatch a little sleep some time?" she asked at last.

"I am, but it'll have to be a short one."

"Suppose we get married and pretend this is our honeymoon?"

Fenner grinned. "You're screwy," he said, "there are five hundred grand hangin' on to this job, an' you ain't worth all that dough."

She sighed "I thought you'd feel that way about it."

The street clocks indicated seven-thirty when he pulled up outside a quiet little hotel. He jogged her with his elbow. "This is the joint," he said. "Go in an' book two rooms, will you? Don't forget I said two rooms. I want some sleep for a couple of hours."

"I'd rather bed with a porcupine," she said, getting out of the car.

He paused midway between changing gears. "Yeah," he said thoughtfully, "that's an idea. Lookin' at it from every angle, it certainly might have its excitements." He drove the ear round to the garage, and when he got back he found her dozing over the reception desk, watched by an interested clerk. "Never mind her," Fenner said to him, "she's got sleepy sickness." He took her by her arm and led her gently to the lift. The boy took their grips and followed with a wide grin. Their rooms were next door, and he pushed her into one of them. "There you go," he said. "Take a good sleep, an' I'll ring you when I want you. When you've had enough sleep, 'phone down for some books, but don't leave your room until I ring."

"That's right," she complained, walking into the room wearily, "leave me out of it."

He grinned and softly shut the door on her. Going into his room, he took off his coat, jerked away his tie and, kicking off his shoes, threw himself on the bed. He slept heavily until ten o'clock, then sat up, feeling like hell. He rang the bell impatiently and put his head in a basin of cold water. By the time the boy brought him a long high-ball, he began to feel more himself. He swung down the stairs and made his way quickly to the garage.

It took him ten minutes to locate the address Brennan had given him. He found Doyley waiting for him. He took him upstairs to his room and seemed genuinely pleased to see him. "Just to keep the records straight," Doyley told him, "I'm known as Flagherty here, so watch that, will you?"

"Sure," Fenner said, resting himself on the horse-hair couch. "Brennan told me you're watchin' this Borg dame. I guess he's put you wise that I wanta little help."

Flagherty brought out a bottle of Scotch and mixed a couple of stiff ones. "You private dicks give me a pain," he said good humouredly. "You work for money an' I work for glory."

Fenner poured the drink down his throat and pushed the glass back again. Flagherty gave him another.

"I ain't so sure that I'm gettin' any dough," Fenner said with a wry face, "this case is tough. How you gettin' on? Had any breaks?"

Flagherty scratched his head. "There's something phoney goin' on at the Paradise," he said. "That's the Grisson's joint, you know. I was out there last night an' I nearly ran into trouble. This Borg dame does a strip-act there most nights, an' I persuaded a member to get me in. Well, while this dame was doin' her stuff, an' can she do it? I thought I'd do a bit of gumshoeing under cover of the dark. Okay. This is the way it went. I slid out into the hall as soon as the lights went off an' went into the can. I could watch the check-girl from there. Her position is just by the stairs, an' I told myself that I wanted to have a look up there. So I wait until she wraps herself round a dime novel, an' when she is busy I crawl outa the can and beat it upstairs. I do this quick, an' I get upstairs without her knowin' it ... which is nice work. Well, I gumshoe around an' stick my head round a few doors, but don't find anythin' to start me goin', except I guess there's plenty goin' on at that joint to justify a raid, because all the rooms have double beds, an' they all look ready for business. I get to the end of the passage and notice a door with a Yale lock on it. This looks phoney to me. I'm about to investigate when I hear the crowd downstairs shoutin' an' yellin', an' that tells me that the strip-act is over. I guess, too, that the lights have gone up, an' mother's little boy is among the missin'.

"I beetle back down the passage like a streak, but I'm not quick enough. The long, thin slob is comin' up with a high turn of speed. I just manage to duck into a bedroom as he arrives. He beats it down to the locked door and takes a key outa his pocket and in he goes. This gives me a break, an' I beat it downstairs. Now this check-girl an' I have got friendly in a friendly way, which is a good thing, because this crowd is a mean one, an' I think to myself that I might easily run into trouble. I give her a handful of bucks an' tell her that I had a faint feelin' an' had gone upstairs to cool off. She's wise enough to rumble what's happenin' and gives me my hat an' coat quick, an' I blow."

"The locked room sounds interestin'," Fenner said. "You gotta be careful from now on."

Flagherty nodded. "Sure, I'm goin' to be mighty careful. I'm off this job to-morrow. The chief tells me that I ain't earnin' my keep. I reckon he's right at that. I've been sittin' on that dame's tail for two months, an' not a crack from any of them."

Fenner got to his feet. "Okay. I'm havin' a look at her. Where do I find her?"

"She's got a nice little apartment down town," Flagherty told him. "Take it easy, won't you? Schultz hangs around there, an' he's a tough bird."

"I like 'em tough," Fenner said with a grin. "There's more to push round when they're big."

Flagherty scribbled the address down on a piece of paper, and Fenner went off with it. He glanced at his watch when he got into the street. It was just after eleven o'clock. The sun was hot and he was glad that he had a drink under his belt. He had no difficulty in locating Anna's apartment. It was a large block standing at the corner of a main street. He examined the row of mail-boxes and found she was on the fourth floor. He took the automatic lift up. The apartment was a large one and had the floor to itself. He walked to the front door and jabbed the bell-push. The door was opened by a coloured maid. She looked him over with open insolence.

"Miss Borg in?" he asked.

"Not at this hour, she ain't."

Fenner reached out a hand and jerked the woman into the passage. "Stay here an' wait," he said. He entered the apartment and shut the front door, leaving the woman speechlessly gaping. He stepped into the living-room. It was empty. He came back to the hall and stood listening. Down the passage he could hear voices. He pulled his Luger out and trod silently down the passage. He listened again outside a door and then jerked it open and went in.

Eddie was sitting on the bed talking to Anna. They both turned swiftly as Fenner walked in. They both saw the gun and froze.

" 'Mornin', folks," Fenner said, leaning against the doorway. "I feel right mean bustin' in this love-nest, but business before pleasure."

Eddie looked round the room hurriedly. His eyes fell on a heap of clothing by the window on a chair. It was a long jump. Fenner followed his eye and grinned. "I wouldn't," he said. "I ain't lookin' for trouble, but I can give it as well as take it."

"Who the hell are you?" Anna demanded from the bed. Fenner waved the gun at her. "I want a little talk with you," he said. "Let's all sit down an' have a get-together."

He walked over to the chair by the window. Fumbling amongst the pile of clothes, he found Eddie's gun. He slipped the magazine out and tossed the gun back. He put the magazine into his pocket. Then he sat down.

Eddie leant forward. "What do you want?" he asked. "What the hell ...?"

"Okay, okay." Fenner grinned. "I shall be seein' quite a lot of you mugs before I've finished, an' I thought I'd just look you over." He shoved the gun back into his holster. "Now, I suggest your boy-friend takes himself for a walk, an' you an' I have a little talk."

Eddie came at him like a cat. Fenner was waiting for him. He was out of the chair before Eddie reached him and blocked the right swing that Eddie tossed over. His own fist came up with a thud into Eddie's face. It was a peach of a punch with everything Fenner had behind it, and that was plenty. Eddie slumped forward on his hands and knees and then spread out flat. Fenner blew on his knuckles.

"These guys ain't so tough," he said.

Anna was sitting up in the bed, her eyes wide and dangerous. She had a .25 in her hand. "Reach!" she said in a hard voice. Fenner grinned at her, but he kept his hands still. At that range a .25 would not be so good.

"You sure keep plenty of cannons round this joint," he said amiably.

Anna cautiously pulled back the bedclothes and slipped on to the floor. Her eyes never left him, nor did the gun waver. Her scarlet pyjamas, with a black monogram on the pocket, showed off her figure. Fenner thought that most men would have raised a ringing cheer at the sight of it. He didn't feel like cheering at the moment, which was a pity.

"Don't you catch cold," he said.

"Now, Mr. Wise Guy, we'll fix you where we want you." She jerked the gun to an arm-chair. "Sit down."

Fenner didn't move. "Listen, Toots," he said quietly, "I want a little talk with you. I'm sorry I had to get tough with the boy-friend, but he started the fireworks."

"Sit down," she snapped. Fenner shrugged and collapsed into the chair; he crossed his legs.

She moved round the back of him and, slipping her hand over his shoulder into the inside of his coat, she jerked his Luger out and tossed it on to the bed. Her gun was pressing against the back of his neck the whole time, and he felt a faint tingling in his feet as the cold metal dug into him. He was glad when she took the gun away. He watched her move over to Eddie and turn his body over with her foot. He was still out.

"Nice smack, that," Fenner said; "he won't come round for some time yet."

Anna's eyes narrowed. He thought she had plenty of fire in her.

"Come on, spill it," she said. "Who are you?"

Fenner folded his arms. "I'm the guy who's interested your late meal-ticket," he said. "I'm lookin' for Riley."

"So you're a bull, are you?" she sneered.

"No, I ain't." Fenner scowled at her. "I'm a news-hawk. I wanta find this guy Riley bad, an' I figger that you might give me a line on him. Now listen, honey, why not help?"

Anna drew herself up. "There's one thing I hate more than a bull, an' that's a nosey press man. You get outa here, an' stay outa here."

Fenner put on a winning smile, but it made Anna wince. "Come on, baby, don't get tough."

"You get outa here right now. Comin' bustin' in like this, rough housin' all over my joint. Go on, get goin' and remember, the next time you start an act like this your relations will go into mourning."

Fenner got to his feet slowly, "Okay," he said regretfully, "I'm on my way." He pulled open the door, then hesitated. "It was a bad break when Riley took a run-out on you. Gee! He must've been a crazy guy to pass up a honeypot like you."

A deep red burnt up her throat and into her face, and her eyes flashed angrily.

"Get goin' and keep that big mouth of yours shut."

"Sure, I'm goin', but it sure makes me mad to think he's playin' around with some cheap little chiseller while you're sittin' on your fanny, waitin' for him to take you back."

Anna crossed the room with a rush. "Where do you get that stuff?" she shrilled at him. She was so furious that she waved the gun in his face. "Get out! Does it look as if I'm waiting for that punk?"

Fenner shoved his hat at the back of his head. "Okay, I'm only tellin' you what the town's sayin'."

"Well, it's a goddam lousy lie!" Anna stormed. "I wouldn't have that double-crossing son of a bitch back if he had his claws in the Federal Reserve."

Fenner suddenly took the gun out of her hand. She had been so mad that she just waved it about, and he took her by surprise. Instantly she made a dive for the bed where his Luger lay. Fenner shot after her and hit her in the small of her back with his knees. He slammed her face down on the bed and sat on her shoulders until he scooped up the gun, then he rolled her over; kneeling astride her, he pinned her arms down with his knees.

"Okay, baby, now we can have a nice little chat."

For a moment she was speechless with rage. Her large eyes were stormy and her lips drawn back off her teeth. Then she began to swear at him. He let her run for a minute or so, then he slapped her lightly across her mouth.

"I'm surprised at you," he said, looking pained. "I ain't keepin' you long like this. I guess it ain't so comfortable, but if you will get tough ... I ask you. Just one little question an' then I'll scram. Only one question, baby, and here it is. Where was Riley when you last heard from him? That's all. Tell me that, an' I'll beat it."

"You go to hell," Anna stormed, glaring at him, "I'm not telling you anything. You find out for yourself."

"I certainly will," he said. "I've plenty of ways to make little girls like you come across." He shifted his knees so that her arms were free, and as they came up at him he seized her wrists in his hands. "Now, I'm just goin' to fix you so that you won't be causin' trouble." He swung off her, and holding her wrists in one hand he untied the pyjama cord at her waist and pulled the cord through the loops. He shoved it into his pocket and stepped away from her. She hastily grabbed her trousers and held on to them tightly.

"No more fightin'," he grinned. "Maybe you do show your can off in a clip joint, but I guess you're too much of a lady to air it in here."

Anna sat there, livid with rage. "I'm going to get you for this, you dumb bastard."

Fenner laughed. "Be your age, baby," he said. "This is the funniest thing that's ever happened to you." He went over to the small portable electric stove, standing in the corner of the room, and switched on the current.

"Grand things, these stoves. I'm goin' to dump this on your boy-friend's pan when it's hot enough—if you don't spill things."

They both watched the filaments turn red. He picked up the stove. "What's it to be?" he asked. "I could get a hell of a kick clappin' this poultice on that rat's mug, but I'll hold off if you're goin' to play ball."

She had lost colour. "He was at Johnny's," she said in a small scared voice.

"Johnny the rummy?" he asked, swinging the stove in his hand.

She nodded, and he put the stove back and jerked the switch with his foot. Fenner knew Johnny all right. Most people who were in with the hoodlums knew Johnny. He told himself that he was doing fine.

"Okay, sister," he said, "sorry to crash in like this." He jerked open the door. Anna sat motionless. He turned back and tossed the cord into her lap. "Make your securities safe," he said with a little grin. "Sorry to have pushed you around."

Anna began to call him names again, but Fenner was hardened to abuse.

"You had better wash your mouth out," he said, "it ain't too clean." And he pulled the door behind him before the storm broke.

Downstairs he spotted a 'phone booth and called Paula.

Her voice came over the line after a delay that infuriated him. "Wake up, hophead," he shouted. "Things are poppin'."

"Well, well," she answered back. "Why didn't you call in and see me before you went off. I got myself up like Mae West and paid you an early visit, but you'd gone."

"Will you give your useless mouth a rest and get this. I'm scrammin' out to Johnny's hut. You know where that is? You do? Swell. Now, listen, baby, this is serious. Get hold of Brennan an' tell him to come over to Johnny's right away. I'll have the Grisson mob on my heels in a short while, if I don't get my bet wrong ... so snap into it. 'Bye, baby, I'll be seein' you soon," and he hung up.

Slim looked at Eddie and Anna, his yellow eyes blazing with cold fury. "You mean to tell me you let some lousy headline hunter come in here an' push you around?" he shouted at Eddie. "Christ! You goin' soft or somethin'?" Eddie felt his jaw uneasily. "Listen, Slim, this guy was tough. I ain't been hit so hard before. Ask Anna, she'll tell you how tough he was."

Slim turned his eyes on Anna. "What did this punk want?" he demanded. "What happened after he had put Eddie away?"

"Plenty," Anna snarled. She was sitting up in bed. Her eyes glittered viciously. "This heel wanted to know where Riley was when he 'phoned me for the last time."

Slim and Eddie suddenly stiffened. Eddie shot a warning glance at Slim. "So what?" Slim asked.

"Well, he was going to get funny with the stove, so I told him."

There was a heavy silence. The two men stood there thinking rapidly. Anna looked at them. She was puzzled why they were taking it like that. After all, she told herself, they weren't in this. If Riley did get pinched, what the hell? She tried to make herself plain. "Listen, this guy was going to put the stove on your face," she said patiently to Eddie. "He wasn't bluffing, and I wasn't standing for it. Don't you get it? He was the type to get a big kick out of frying someone's face with a red-hot stove. Riley don't mean a thing to me, so I spilt it."

Slim turned on her savagely. "You yapper!" he shouted.

Anna flew into another furious rage. "Did you hear what that sonofabitch called me?" she screamed at Eddie. "I'm not standing for it! Do you get that? I didn't give any of you guys away. What the hell does Riley matter to you?"

Eddie hastily climbed into his clothes. "Skip it, will you?" he pleaded. "Slim don't mean anythin'. Take it easy, for Pete's sake."

Anna struggled out of bed, clutching her trousers with one hand. "If this dumb bastard thinks he can get fresh with me, he's wearing the wrong pants," she shrilled "Listen, you long slob …"

Slim came at her with a sliding shuffle, but Eddie got between them. "For God's sake …" he said. He pushed Anna on to the bed. "Forget it, honey," he went on, "listen, I've got a job on. You don't think I'm stayin' around here an' let a tough get away with this, do you? Come on outa here, Slim, come on, let's get goin'."

Slim looked at Anna who pursed her lips and gave him a rude one. He hesitated for a moment, then lounged to the door. Eddie crowded him out. Going downstairs, Slim began to bellyache, but Eddie cut him short. "Forget it," he said impatiently, "I gotta do somethin' about this news-guy. If ever Anna got on to the truth, I reckon she'd turn mighty mean."

Slim shrugged. "What the hell? If she speaks outa turn, she'll get rubbed out."

Eddie stopped and jerked Slim round. "Get this!" he snapped. "You got your dame, I'm havin' mine! Anna's a swell kid an' I'm stayin' with her. She's not to know about this ... do you understand?"

"All right, all right." Slim moved on impatiently. "Ma's got to be in on this quick."

Ma Grisson sat and listened while Eddie went over the tale. She sat behind her desk, smoking a cigar, her heavy face expressionless. When Eddie had finished she brooded for a moment. Slim sat by the door, watching her. Doc and Flynn were looking nervous. She stared at them in turn; a cold, hard look that made them shift uneasily.

"Do you get all this?" she asked roughly. "This tough news-guy is goin' to beat it back to Johnny's as hard as he can lick. He's goin' to start askin' questions."

Eddie scratched his head. "Johnny's all right," he said uneasily. "Johnny won't squeal."

"This guy sounds tough," Ma went on. "Johnny's a rummy an' he'll crack fast enough if this guy starts pushin' him around. Can you see Johnny keepin' his mouth shut if he's gettin' fried with a stove? Not likely. Johnny's goin' to open his mouth so wide that you'll see all the booze floatin' inside him."

The others looked at each other. Slim reached inside his coat and pulled out his gun. He slipped out the magazine, glanced at it, and then put it back. Ma watched him. She nodded, "Sure, Johnny's got to go," she said. "Get goin'. This guy has started by now. Slim, you, Flynn, an' Doc, take the car an' get off at once. You'll do it by tomorrow morning. If this guy has got there first, get rid of him too. This ain't goin' to be a picnic, so don't ball it up. Don't forget, once the news leaks out we shall be on the run. The snatch business will come to the surface again. So watch your step."

The three men bundled out of the room, and rushed down the stairs into the alley. They climbed into the Airflow and, with a screeching of rubber, the car shot away from the kerb.

Rocco, leaning against the wall of the alley, watched them go with mild interest. He stood there in the sunshine, picking his teeth thoughtfully with a little wooden pick. His tight suit was pressed, and his trousers, too short in the leg, revealed brilliant white socks. A bowler hat perched on the top of his head. Rocco was funny to look at, but he was mean right through.

He wondered idly why three of the gang had left in such a hurry. He glanced at the club thoughtfully. He guessed someone was going to run into trouble. Just then Eddie came out of the club and nodded at him but didn't stop. He walked on down the street. Rocco looked after him, still chasing holes in his teeth. Eddie had a hell of a bruise on his chin, he noticed. This began to look interesting. He glanced at the clock across the way. It was just after one. Walking slowly down the street, he came to the "Tired Dog" restaurant. He pushed open the chromium-plated door and entered the cool, shadowy room. He glanced round quickly before handing his hat in. He saw the check-girl of the Paradise Club over at the far end. She was busy with a crab salad. He wandered over to her table and smiled in his thin way.

"This is a nice opportunity," he said.

She paused with a loaded fork suspended in air.

"I'll buy it," she said briefly.

"You know, Maisey, I been waitin' a chance to stand you a meal."

Her doll face smiled happily. "You go right ahead, big boy," she said brightly, "I won't stop you."

He pulled out a chair and sat down opposite her. She continued to eat with unexpected enthusiasm. He glanced down the menu and called for cold chicken and what went with it. He had a nice line of talk with dames, and he chatted away while he ate. Maisey said little but did herself well. She had not much time for wops, but when a wop paid for anything, she was brave about it. She'd do that for anyone, so long as they paid.

"You know, big eyes," Rocco said, leaving forward with his elbows on the table, "we ought to have got acquainted long ago. Where you been hiding that beauty so long?"

She giggled. "Be your age," she told him.

"Listen," he said in a low voice, "I ain't usually attracted to a dame, but when I run into a honey-pot like you, then I give up. Did anyone tell you you're lousy with the right stuff? When I saw you sitting here, I tipped my hat … this is the gravy, I tell myself, an' this is where Rocco digs inta his savings."

Maisy looked up coyly. This talk sounded like the berries all right, she told herself.

"Could you use a couple of hundred bucks?" he ask with that thin smile.

Her blue eyes flashed open. "A couple of hundred buck Gee! Could I use it?" She laughed. "I'd do a lot of this for that dough."

"Come over to my apartment an' earn it," he said.

For a moment she hesitated, greed battling with sham indignation. She thought she had better show a little front. "Here, where do you get that stuff from?" she demanded. "I'm not that sort of a girl."

Rocco waved his hands. "You got me wrong," he said hastily, "I wouldn't make a raw suggestion like that. I want you to come over an' have a talk with me. I'm offerin' to buy information."

"What's the big idea?" She looked puzzled.

"Save it, save it," he said patiently. "Will you come?"

She got to her feet. "No funny business," she warned him as they left the restaurant. They climbed into a taxi that was cruising by, and Rocco talked solidly about nothing until they reached his apartment. It was small and bare, but Rocco had been advised what to buy, and his stuff was good. The furniture was light wood and the floors polished. A few rugs lay like islands on the boards. The chairs were big and overstuffed. There was a big divan in the centre of the room, covered with brightly coloured shawls.

"Nice place you got here," she said, taking off her hat and fluffing up her brittle hair. She sank into the armchair, which gave nearly to the floor. She crossed her legs, and Rocco had an eyeful from where he was sitting. He reached over to a cabinet at his elbow and poured out a couple of drinks. He added ginger ale to the rye with the care of a chemist. He came over to her and put the glass in her hand.

"You're on the inside of the Grisson mob," he said carefully, choosing his words. "Since they've been here, business ain't so hot. I could use a little girl with brains if she could come across with some useful information. Now, listen, honey, if this idea don't appeal to you just say so, an' we'll forget it. I'll play some records to you instead. I've a swell radiogram here. If you wanta pick up some bucks now and then, well, it's here for the takin'."

Maisey finished her drink and Rocco gave her another shot. He saw that the liquor was already hitting her a bit. "What do you want to know," she asked.

Rocco smiled to himself. As easy as that, he said to himself. "What's going on at the club?" he asked.

Maisey puffed out her rouged cheeks. The liquor was making her dizzy. "Not a lot. They make dough, all right."

Rocco looked at her patiently. She was dumb, and he told himself that he'd have to take her along slowly.

"Anything phoney goin' on there?"

"Just the usual club business, with private bedrooms to let as a side-line," Maisey told him. She suddenly found it hot in the room.

"Where did the gang go to this afternoon?" he asked. "I saw Slim an' two of the boys scram outa the club as if all hell was poppin'."

Maisey shrugged. She was getting bored with this, "Search me," she said, finishing her drink. "I don't know."

Rocco lost patience. "You gotta do better than that for two hundred bucks," he said evenly.

She looked at him with bleared eyes. "Say, you're right. I ain't being a help, am I? Say, that poison's strong. I'm getting plastered."

Rocco laughed. "You're all right," he assured her, "just happy, that's all."

Maisey giggled. "I suppose you wouldn't be interested in Slim's girl-friend?"

Rocco shook his head. "Slim ain't got a girl-friend," he said; "I know that."

"Okay, smart guy." Maisey took another drink from him. "Slim ain't got a girl-friend, but let me tell you he's got some broad locked away upstairs that he spends a hell of a time with at nights."

Rocco's eyes narrowed a little. Was he getting somewhere with this dumb cluck at last? "Take a drink," he said.

She waved the glass at him, spilling some of the liquor on the polished floor. "What's the idea, getting a good girl stinko?"

"Come on," he said, giving her a cigarette and lighting it, "you can take it." She nodded her head drunkenly. "Sure, I can take it."

"What's all this about locking some dame up?" he asked.

"I dunno who she is, but I guess Slim's hot pants for her. She's on the second floor. She goes out late with Slim for a walk. She's all wrapped up. I've never seen what she looks like. She goes out about three o'clock in the morning for an hour. Most nights she takes this walk. I've spotted her when I'm clearing up. It is after the club shuts. She just walks along beside Slim and never turns her head. Gee! I don't mind telling you that that dame gives me the jitters sometimes. She looks like a walking corpse."

Rocco thought this was interesting. It might pay to investigate this business. He got to his feet and moved round the room, thinking. Maisey watched him from her chair. He came over to her and sat on the arm of the chair.

"If I could have a look at this dame," he said quietly, "I'd give you somethin'."

Maisey became generous. "S'all right,'" she said. "You keep away from your bye-bye till three o'clock and you'll see her most nights, taking her walk."

Rocco took out his wallet and thumbed out two hundred dollars in small notes. He got up and put them on the mantelpiece. Maisey watched him with interest. He looked at her and thought she was snappy on the eye, even if she was as dumb as a statue. He had nothing particular to do this afternoon. She'd do for the rough work, anyway, he told himself.

"There's some rent for you," he said, pointing.

Maisey got to her feet unsteadily, and he took her arm. Instead of taking her to the mantelpiece he led her to the divan. She collapsed on it with a little giggle.

"Now, positively no funny business ..." she warned him. He shoved her gently on to the shawls. They were smooth and cool and she stretched out lazily. Then she suddenly protested feebly, "Hey, didn't I tell you ..." she began, but stopped short and began to giggle again.

Fenner took some care in getting his car under cover. He manoeuvred it into the heavy undergrowth and, getting out, he walked back to see if it were visible from the road. He had to fix the bushes a little before it was completely hidden. All-night driving made his head muzzy and he felt like hell. He guessed that the Grisson mob would be coming up close behind him, and he had not much time to do things in. Almost he wished that he had picked up Flaherty before leaving Springfield. Two were better than one in a rough house, he told himself with a crooked smile, but time pressed. Flaherty was not at his hotel when Fenner called. He knew that Paula would get busy, and Brennan would be on his way.

Fenner was quite near Johnny's hide-out, but not too near. He began to walk up the twisting path to the shack. He carried his gun in his hand. Although he guessed that Johnny would not put on a rough act, he was not going to be caught on the hop.

As he approached the shack he moved with greater caution. He told himself that it was impossible for the Grisson mob to have arrived first, but he was on the look-out for trouble. The dawn was just breaking and the sun was coming up over the hills. It was going to be another hot day; there was a mist still hanging about the valley. This suited him because it cloaked his movements somewhat. He paused when he came to the clearing. Standing behind a broad tree trunk, he surveyed the scene before him. Although the shack door stood open, there was no sign of Johnny. Fenner guessed he was preparing to go out with his gun to find something for the pot. He slid across the clearing at high speed and entered the shack like a shadow.

Johnny was bending over the stove, shoving some rashers around in a frypan. His back was to the door and he didn't notice Fenner come in. Fenner saw a shot-gun, standing in a corner, but it was a good jump from Johnny, so it did not worry him. He pushed his gun forward and called softly. Johnny shuddered as the shock penetrated, and turned slowly. His face was ghastly and twitched with terror. He turned a mottled yellow when he saw Fenner. Dave felt sorry for him. "Take it easy," he said, "don't start anythin' an' you'll be okay."

Johnny just stood there, helpless with shock. "What you want?" he mumbled, a stream of saliva drooling from his mouth.

Fenner pointed to a chair. "Sit down," he said.

Johnny seemed glad to do so. His legs buckled, and he let himself go down heavily. His twitching hands jerked about on his knees.

"Listen, Johnny, I want some information from you," Fenner told him, his voice tense. "It's up to you to tell me straight. If I think you're lyin' I'm goin' to give you the works. Do you get that? I'm goin' to tear you apart. I ain't got much time, an' hell's goin' to pop mighty soon."

Johnny blinked at him stupidly. He glanced wildly at the door and then back to Fenner.

"Riley and his mob came here with the Blandish girl, didn't he?" Fenner shot at him.

Johnny nodded quickly—too quickly to please Fenner.

"That's right, mister," Johnny mumbled. "Sure, that's right."

"Then what?"

Johnny shifted his eyes. "I couldn't have them here, they were too hot, see, mister? I couldn't take a chance of gettin' in bad with the bulls, so I pass 'em up. Jest told them to keep goin', an' they did."

"How long did they stay here?" Fenner demanded.

"Jest long enough to eat, mister, straight. They beat it in a big closed car, soon as they had fed."

Fenner scratched his head. "The same story, an' it gets me nowhere," he told himself. He thought Johnny knew a bit more, but he was holding out on him. "Listen, you rummy, you know more than that. Come on, spill it! Where did they go?"

Johnny cringed. "Honest, mister, that's all I know."

Fenner hated doing it, but he had to crack this goddam case somehow. He hit Johnny right in the middle of his soft face. Johnny flopped over backwards, taking the chair with him. He crawled up on his hands and knees, whining. Fenner booted him hard as he struggled up, so that he went over again. Johnny began to squawk in a high-pitched voice. Fenner went over to him.

"What's the story?" he asked quietly. "Don't start sayin' you don't know, or else I'll get tough. Come on, open up!"

Johnny glared up at him viciously. The mess of blood across his face made him look like a street accident. "I tell you I don't know," he snarled. "Lay off me, will you?"

Fenner jerked up the fry-pan and stood over him. "You'll talk or I'll slop this fat in your mug," he said. The grease was hissing in the pan and Johnny cringed away. That scared him more than a punch, and he began to babble when Fenner swung the pan.

"Don't start on me, mister," he whined. "Ask Grisson, he knows … he was there…."

Fenner believed in hunches. All his life he obeyed an instinctive hunch when it came his way, no matter how foolish those hunches might be. As he was standing over Johnny he wanted suddenly to duck. He didn't look over his shoulder, he just slammed himself on the floor and rolled away from Johnny as hard as he could lick. There was a faint tinkle of glass as a pane in the window was shoved in and the black nose of a Thompson poked through. Fenner's brain raced. He was in a jam all right, and he had to get under substan-

tial cover or else he'd be decorating a slab in the local morgue. Grisson had
turned up and trouble was on the way. Close by him was an iron tank in which
Johnny used to mix his horse-feed. Fenner jerked himself behind this with one
swift movement, at the same time looking over at Johnny.

Johnny sat on the floor, gaping at the Thompson. He just stayed there paralysed. The sudden violent clamour of the gun burst through the room, and
Fenner could almost see the slugs as they cut into Johnny's chest. He ducked
back behind the tank as the Thompson swung round to him. Once more the
sharp clamour broke out. The slugs beat against the iron sides of the tank,
making a noise like a rivet-gun at work. Fenner sweated behind his cover. He
couldn't even pop out to have a shot back. That Thompson was pure hell. Behind him was the wall, and the tank covered him from the side. Unless they
came into the room they couldn't get at him. He lay flat and waited. There
was silence, accentuated far more after the violent noise. He could afford to
lie low, and he wasn't going to be a sucker and take a look round the side of
the tank. He cursed himself for leaving the shack door open. He was in a sweet
spot all right. Putting his ear to the boards, he listened, but he couldn't hear
anything. Any moment that Thompson might come round the corner to blast
hell out of him. He took a grip on his nerves and screwed himself further
against the wall. Suddenly he heard the murmur of voices outside. Then someone called: "Come on out. We know you're in there. Come on out with your
hands in the air."

He grinned crookedly. "An' have a handful of slugs tossed into my guts for
my trouble," he told himself. He just lay there and waited. He guessed Grisson and his mob hadn't the stomach to walk in and gun it to a finish. He began to feel better with that thought. After all, these heels were bright yellow,
and if he kept his nerve there was still a chance. He groped behind him and
his hand fell on an axe-shaft. He took off his hat; putting it on the end of the
shaft, he moved it cautiously round the corner of the tank. The hat jerked con-
vulsively as a stream of hot slugs tore it apart. Fenner grinned. "Glad my dome
wasn't in that," he said to himself.

"Hey, you punk, come on out, or you'll get it," someone shouted at him.

He lay there as dumb as a corpse. Suddenly he heard someone laugh outside. He stiffened. Something was going to start now, he thought. He took
hold of the edge of the tank and pulled it close to the wall, so that he was
wedged in tight. He heard something drop on the floor and he could just see
a small, round object hit the boards near Johnny. His eyes told him that it was
a pineapple, at the same time as the bomb went off. His head seemed to split
asunder with the noise, and the rush of air tossed him against the wall like a
doll. For a moment his brain cleared and he could see things clearly. He could
see the roof of the shack above him and the dirty walls of the room, then every-

thing began to disintegrate before his eyes. The roof began to crumble and the whole lot came crashing down on top of him.

It was a long way to struggle out of the pit. The goddam darkness wrapped itself round him like a rug. He'd like to take just one smack at that sonofabitch who was beating him on the head. Suddenly he opened his eyes and blinked in the sunlight. A shadowy figure was bending over him and he heard a distant voice telling him to take it easy. He shook his head and then wished he hadn't. Bright lights flashed before his eyes, and someone shoved a red-hot corkscrew through his brain. He heard himself groan. Relaxing limply, he tried to clear his brain. Things came back to him slowly and he sat up violently, "For God's sake ..." he muttered as his brain reeled under the effort.

"How you makin' out?" someone said to him. He screwed up his eyes. A tall hick in overalls was kneeling by him. In the background hovered an elderly farmhand, gaping like a fish. He gingerly began to move his arms and legs, and sighed faintly when he found they responded.

"Give me a hand up," he said urgently, and the old man shuffled over to him and they got him under the arms. He swayed a bit when they let him stand, but he was coming back quickly. "Seen anyone about?" he jerked out.

"An auto went by with three men in her a moment ago," the tall hick told him. "We heard the bang an' came running. We started to shout, an' these three beat it."

Fenner passed his hand over his sore head. "Listen, you two, I'm a police-officer. These men have just knocked a guy off. I want you to lend a hand."

The word police worked it. The two straightened up and became attentive. They gaped, but they were willing to help.

Fenner walked stiffly back to the ruin. He poked about for a moment, then shrugged. "What the hell ..." he said to himself. Johnny was dead. "Where's your place?" he said, looking at the two men. The old man pointed vaguely east.

"'Bout a couple of miles back."

"Where's the nearest 'phone?" Fenner asked.

The tall hick looked proud. "We gotta 'phone," he said.

"Okay. Come with me, I gotta car over there." Fenner moved off slowly. His brain banged about inside his head. The thin wail of a police-siren made him jerk his head. Coming up the narrow lane at a furious rate was a dust-covered car. It skidded to a standstill near him and Brennan scrambled out, followed by a number of uniformed officers. The last to get out of the car was John Blandish. Fenner waved to them grimly.

"Well, I guess you boys stepped on it," he said, "but you've missed the fireworks."

"Your girl 'phoned us," Brennan said, stretching his arms and legs gingerly. "She certainly got us worked up, an' we grabbed a car, and here we are."

Fenner turned to Blandish. "If what I think is right, then we shall have our hands on the kidnappers very shortly."

Blandish looked at him keenly "What's been happening?" he asked. "You look as if you've been in trouble."

Fenner grinned ruefully. "If you call a bomb-fight trouble, I guess you've hit it."

"What the hell's been goin' on round here?" Brennan demanded, looking at the shattered shack.

"Listen, Brennan, we can skip the story for a moment. There is urgent work to do. Can I use your men for a little while?"

The quick, sharp way he spoke told Brennan that something was breaking, and he nodded at once. "Sure, go ahead."

Fenner went over to him and said something in a low voice. Brennan looked at the two farmhands who were staring in the background. He went over to them and had a few words. They hesitated and then moved off. The group of men watched them until they had turned the corner, then Fenner said: "I want you boys to look round this place. You're lookin' for graves—do you get that? Look for any ground that's been disturbed, and let me know. Get going, I guess you won't take long on this job."

The State troopers moved off into the undergrowth and began a concentrated hunt. Brennan and Blandish walked over to Fenner who had sat himself on the running-board of the police-car.

"What is all this?" Brennan said.

"Wait," Fenner said briefly. "I may have made a hell of a bloomer, but I'm backin' my hunch. Without a little evidence I ain't talkin'."

Brennan shrugged his shoulders and moved off after his men. Fenner looked up and caught Blandish's eye.

"You've started something, anyway," Blandish said.

Fenner nodded. "Sure," he said. "You wanted action and, by God, I've given it to you."

"I'm anxious to hear what you have been doing," Blandish said quietly, "but I can understand that you don't feel inclined to tell me until your plans have materialized. You will remember that I am an anxious man." That was all he said, but Fenner knew it meant a hell of a lot to him.

He got to his feet. "Sure," he said again, "I know how you feel. I'll say this, if those cops find what I hope they'll find, then the lid is right off this case."

Blandish took out his cigar-case and offered it to Fenner. They both smoked in silence. The trampling and rustling in the undergrowth gradually faded as the beaters moved farther into the shrub. A small bird suddenly swooped down from the cloudless blue and hopped from twig to twig on a nearby bush. Fenner watched it with interest. He suddenly realized that he was sweating violently and his mouth was dry. A lot depended on what those bulls turned up. A sudden shout made both men turn sharply.

"I guess they've found something," Fenner said quickly.

They moved with urgent expectation to the undergrowth and began forcing their way through the thick bushes towards the shout. It did not take them long to catch up with the others. They found them in a small clearing. Brennan pointed to the ground significantly. The soil had obviously been disturbed, although it had been covered with leaves and dead branches which had been cleared.

"We gotta get a spade," Fenner said.

"I've sent one of my men for one already," Brennan returned. "Here he is, coming now."

One of the troopers peeled off his coat and took the spade. The others grouped round, watching. It was hot work, and they all had a turn before they found what they were looking for. One of the men abruptly put the spade down and knelt beside the shallow hole they had dug. Fenner came over and peered down. The man was scraping the soil away with his hand. A faint smell came from the hole, that made Fenner's stomach turn. He saw a mop of mud-matted hair coming to light. He stood back.

"It's a corpse, all right," he said. He turned to Blandish. "Let's get outa here, we ain't got time to mess around. Brennan will give orders to have those stiffs moved to the Springfield morgue. I gotta lot of things to talk about, an' this is urgent."

Brennan was still startled at the finding of the body, but he took things in hand. Fenner started off to the car and Blandish followed him. Brennan soon caught them up and they drove off rapidly. Fenner sat at the wheel, his face creased in thought. Brennan leant forward. He was sitting in the back. "What the hell is all this?" he demanded.

"Plenty," Fenner returned, "We're gettin' a 'plane back to Springfield and then we'll get together. I gotta think, so shut up an' let me do somethin' that's foreign to you."

Blandish smoked in silence. Fenner admired his nerve. He said to him in a low tone, "It's goin' to be all right," and Blandish looked at him hopelessly. Fenner told himself that the guy had given up.

Three hours later they were all seated round a table with drinks in front of them. Flagherty had joined them. Fenner looked round at each of them thoughtfully. He had given himself a bath and a fresh suit. This was his big moment.

"Now this is the way it goes," he said. He addressed Blandish the whole time. After all, he supplied the dough, so he had the best seat. "Your daughter was kidnapped by Riley and his mob who knocked off this MacGowan. They took her to Johnny's place, which was a good hide-out. This Johnny was used to hiding up hoodlums on the run, an' I guess he was gettin' well paid for the job. Now, somehow, an' I ain't sure how, but it don't matter, Grisson's mob got on to the kidnappin'. They made a surprise visit an' rubbed out Riley an' the other two. You have paid ransom to Grisson an' not to Riley, do you get that? Can't you see how it all fits? As soon as you paid out the dough, what happens? The Grisson mob come into money. They peddle this hot stuff for safe dough. That will explain why the ransom money hasn't turned up yet. Okay. These hoodlums move outa town an' start this night club. You supplied the sawbucks for that. Are they sittin' sweet or are they? All the dicks in the world are searchin' for Riley and they are spendin' the money. While Riley is givin' the worms their three whacks a day."

Brennan started up with an oath. He made a grab for the telephone. Fenner looked at him "What you startin'?" he asked.

"Why, you dumb bozo," Brennan spluttered, "you could have told me that in the car. We could have pinched that gang by now."

Fenner got out of his chair and took the phone away from him violently. "Will you sit down an' give me a chance to explain this thing. You dicks have got heads like stone."

Brennan scowled at him, but he sat down again.

"For one thing, we don't know if this is right, but I'm willin' to bet that it is. A smart lawyer would spring those birds as soon as we got the cuffs on them—so fast that it would make your head dizzy to see them go. What evidence have we got? Besides, I guess they have still got the girl."

Blandish started violently. For a moment there was a thick silence. Fenner turned and looked straight at him.

"Flagherty tells me that Grisson's got a room in his club that he keeps locked. He has seen him enterin' it. I may be wrong, but it looks as if your daughter is bein' held there."

Blandish got to his feet. "For Christ's sake," he shouted, completely out of control, "what the hell are you sittin' there for? Get men and raid that place!"

Fenner took it calmly. He looked round at the excited faces of the other three. "Flagherty will also tell you," he went on evenly, "that the Paradise Club is nothin' short of bein' a steel fort. You make a raid on that joint an' long before you get in, if you ever do, your daughter will be stiff. Listen, Blandish, I've been handlin' this my way, an', by God, I'll continue to handle it. I understand this business an' you don't, so shut up an' sit down."

Blandish hesitated a moment, looking round the table with feverish eyes, then he sat down again. Fenner looked at him hard and shrugged slightly. He turned to Brennan. "You can see that, can't you?" he demanded. Brennan looked at Flagherty.

Flagherty said: "He's right, boss, that place will want a lotta crackin'."

Brennan nodded at Fenner. "Go on," he said.

Fenner took a deep breath. "First I want that place surrounded. I want cops everywhere. In the opposite buildings, on the roofs, in the street, under cover, in fact I want the whole goddam place lousy with 'em. They may try an' get the girl out."

Brennan grabbed the 'phone and, after a moment's delay, got through to headquarters; he gave his instructions rapidly.

"I want Anna Borg picked up an' taken down to headquarters, an' if you can get hold of Schultz at the same time so much the better," Fenner went on. He waited until Brennan had finished, then he continued, "This Borg dame is at the bottom of the whole thing. She is our only witness that Grisson's mob knew that Riley had snatched Miss Blandish. She has told me that Riley 'phoned her from Johnny's, an' I'm wonderin' what else he told her. The question is: Did she know that Grisson wiped out Riley or did they kid her along? I'm bankin' that they kidded her, in which case she may rat on them when she hears the truth. She may be able to give us the low-down on Miss Blandish, too. Anyway, she is important. This thing's got to be handled carefully or else your daughter is goin' to be wiped out."

Blandish got to his feet slowly. He looked utterly tired and ill. He extended his hand to Fenner. "I'm sorry I made a fool of myself," he said quietly. "You've done a fine job of work. I did not understand…."

Fenner shuffled his feet. "Aw, nerts!" he said.

The telephone broke on their ears sharply. Fenner scooped it up and stood listening. "Okay," he said, and slammed the receiver on to its cradle. He turned to the others with glittering eyes. "They've dug up three bodies in that hole, an' the finger-prints match Riley's all right," he shouted excitedly. "We're on the right track now. Let's go!"

He sprang to the door, leaving the others to follow him.

IV

Rocco fixed his hair with a small white comb. He straightened his tight-fitting suit by pulling and patting the cloth. He stood in front of the mirror and looked at himself. His tie was straightened by a flip of his hand, and then he carefully perched his bowler hat on the top of his head. He looked round his room with satisfaction before leaving. He had made sure that Maisey had left nothing behind her. Maisey, he told himself, had been an amusing interlude. She had surprised him with her enthusiasm. He liked dames to get enthusiastic.

After Maisey had gone he had sat smoking in a relaxed position on the divan. He had smoked a number of cigarettes and he had come to certain conclusions. Slim was away. Of course he might come back that night, but then he had to take a chance. Rocco wanted to look at this mysterious jane that Slim was keeping under cover. Maisey must give him a hand there. He walked down the passage and waited for the lift. The bell-hop jerked his fingers respectfully to his pill-box as he slid back the grill. Rocco liked these little attentions. It wasn't so long back since he was a bum himself, and he could still remember what had been handed to him by those in the money.

In the street he flagged a taxi and was driven to the Paradise Club. He passed up the stairs with a number of other guests. The place was doing a brisk trade he thought, as he flipped his hat to Maisey. She looked at him with coy eyes. He admitted that she had her points. When she had time on her hands he came over and hung around the barrier, saying nice things to her. She took all he had and wanted more. Looking over his shoulder, he made sure that they were alone, then he said to her in a low voice: "Which room is this dame in?"

She took instant fright. "What's that to you?"

Rocco looked at her with narrowed eyes. "You mean, what's it to you, don't you, Toots?" he said softly. "The answer's another hundred bucks."

Maisey shook her head. "For Gawd's sake," she said, "this is dynamite, don't you be screwy."

Rocco nodded his sleek black head. "Okay, sister," he said, "I'm goin' upstairs to have a look around. You ain't seen a thing, an' you know nothin'."

Before she could protest, he left her and ran up the stairs quickly. He looked over the banisters at her when he reached the top, and she stared up at him with a white, scared face. He waved his hand at her and then walked down the corridor. He went to the last door and turned the handle. It was locked all right. A thin smile hit his mouth and he fumbled in his pocket. He inserted a thin piece of steel into the lock and twisted it sharply. The lock slid back with a click and he pushed open the door. With a quick glance over his shoulder into the deserted corridor, he entered the room and shut the door behind him softly.

Miss Blandish looked at him with complete indifference. She lay on the bed, smoking a cigarette. Her long green wrap reflected with a faint sheen the light of the table-lamp. Rocco stood and gaped at her. She was a big shock to him. He told himself that she was class all right. He stood by the door and said: "I guess I got into the wrong room."

Miss Blandish reached over and mashed the cigarette into the ash-tray. "Will you go away?" she asked, closing her eyes.

Something was persistently grinding itself at the back of Rocco's brain. He found himself asking where he had seen this dame before. The more he thought about it the more he realized that her face was as familiar as the face of his favourite film star.

"Who are you, lady?" he asked cautiously.

Miss Blandish opened her eyes with an effort and shrugged helplessly. "I can't remember," she said wearily; "I don't care very much, either." Rocco slid closer to the bed. He saw the pin-point pupils. They told him plenty. Suddenly he remembered. He could see the large splash pictures in the tabloids. For the love of Mike, he thought, it's the dame who was snatched. He had got on to something all right this time. He came nearer and looked at her intently. "Yeah," he said aloud, "I know who you are."

She opened her eyes with a start. "What are you doing here?" she asked. "You shouldn't be here; he wouldn't like it."

Rocco leant over the end of the bed. "Don't you worry your head about him," he said, "he's outa town."

"I think you had better go," she went on as if she hadn't heard him. "The old woman will hurt me if she finds you here."

Rocco came round to her and shook her shoulder gently. "Snap outa it, lady," he pleaded. "Listen to me for a moment. You're doped, do you get it? You're full of somethin' they've given you. You can't remember who you are or why you're here."

"Please don't touch me," she said. "I wish you would go away; I want to sleep."

"Your name is Blandish," Rocco said, keeping his voice low, and speaking close to her. "Your father is John Blandish. You were kidnapped nearly four months ago, an' the cops and your pappy have been huntin' for you. Now, ain't that right? Ain't your name Blandish?"

She looked at him with dazed, blank eyes. "Blandish?" she repeated. "That's not my name."

Rocco stood back and scratched his head. He was sure that this was the Blandish dame, but what could he do to get behind that blank wall? His brain raced. He could see a pile of jack in this for himself. If he could get this girl out and hand her over to Blandish, there would be a lot of dough coming his way. A nice backhand slap at Grisson, too. There were risks of course, but it had to be a gamble. He made up his mind quickly. He'd take the risks.

Sitting on the bed, he jerked Miss Blandish to a sitting position. She sat facing him, her face dazed and her eyes like great holes in a mask. "Your name's

Blandish," he repeated, speaking in a hard, low voice. "You've been kidnapped, ain't that the way it goes?"

She shut her eyes and tried to remember, but the heavy clouds that wrapped her brain were immovable.

He gave up with a grunt of disappointment. "Okay, sleep it off," he said, pushing her back on to the pillow. "I'll be back." He turned to the door and left the room.

Maisey was almost hysterical when he demanded his hat.

"My Gawd!" she said. "I've been steaming myself. What the hell do you think you're doin'?"

Rocco deliberately put his hat on his head and straightened his coat "I've been wastin' my time," he said with a thin smile, "an' been wastin' my dough too." He slid a small roll over to Maisey who grabbed at it with a nervous hand.

"Well," she said with a relieved smile, "you ain't mean."

Ma Grisson walked out of the restaurant and paused when she saw Rocco. Rocco lifted his hat high above his head. He liked to show that he knew his manners. "'Evenin', Ma," he said, "just been tellin' Maisey what a swell looker she is."

Ma stood looking at them. Her large face was blank.

"Don't go gettin' my girls into trouble," was all she said. They watched her plod up the stairs, and Rocco blotted his face with a silk handkerchief. He had judged his time close, he thought.

Maisey was watching the old woman with terrified eyes. Rocco gave her a sharp slap on her flank "Be yourself," he said, "there ain't nothin' to get scared about."

Maisey jerked her eyes away from the stairs. "Don't go pullin' any more fast ones, for Gawd's sake," she implored him. Rocco gave her his thin smile which said nothing. He walked out of the club and went over to the "Tired Dog". He sat down at a small table and took out his watch. It was nearly ten o'clock. He ordered a bottle of wine, and sent the boy for an evening paper. He placed his bowler on the seat beside him and carefully filled his glass with the sour red wine. He pressed his shoulders against the back of the chair and stretched. Maisey had tired him a little, he found. Women were hell, all right, but who would have thought that she could have got so enthusiastic. Yeah, if he got out of the business all right, he'd see some more of Maisey. He took the paper from the boy and gave him a nickel. "Save it, son," he said, looking at the headlines. "Money comes hard these days."

The boy looked at the nickel and sniffed. "You're dead right, mister," he said.

Ma Grisson stood squarely on her great feet and stared down at Miss Blandish as she lay on the bed. She had entered silently and had not disturbed the sleeper. She stood there, thinking of Slim. She tried to put herself in Slim's thin body, vainly trying to imagine how he must feel towards this girl so heavy in sleep. Ma Grisson knew the danger of keeping her, but she knew also what it meant to Slim. She wondered how long it would last. Not only how long Slim would want to fool around with her, but how long it would be before someone got wise to her being there.

She shrugged her massive shoulders. As soon as he tired of her she must be got rid of, she told herself. She hoped that it would be soon. Even her iron nerves were bending under the constant reminder that here was evidence that would get them all fried sooner or later. She glanced at the small wrist-watch, absurdly out of place on her great arm. It was nearly three o'clock. She turned to the door and plodded downstairs again. The Club was deserted now. Maisey was putting her hat and coat on, gaping with weariness.

Ma paused near her. "You gotta be careful of the wop," she said. "He ain't in love with us, an' he'd like to make trouble."

Maisey started nervously. "Sure," she muttered, "I don't encourage him."

Ma looked at her hard with her little glittering eyes. "Well, I've told you. He's poison to dames."

Maisey struggled into her coat and nodded good night. She was glad to get away from the old woman. She gave her the jitters. Ma watched her go and then went into the restaurant. The place was deserted except for Woppy who dozed in a chair. She shook him roughly.

"You gotta take the Blandish girl for her run," she said; "I'm gettin' her ready, so get goin'."

Woppy protested violently. "Aw, nerts!" he grumbled. "I'm beat. Can't she skip her walk for tonight? Slim'll be back tomorrow."

Ma jerked her head. "Get goin'. Slim wants her to go, if you don't like it you can argue it out with him."

Woppy got to his feet, cursing softly under his breath.

"Keep her off the main streets an' walk her fast. You're not to stop for anyone. Take your rod an' watch out for trouble," Ma told him. "This walkin' business ain't no picnic, so watch out."

"Eddie oughta do it," Woppy grumbled.

"Eddie's gone home with Anna," Ma said, "Get goin' an' shut your mouth." She went upstairs again and shook Miss Blandish roughly. "Come on," she said. "Come on, you're takin' a walk."

Miss Blandish started up hurriedly, her face twitching with nerves. She climbed out of the bed unsteadily and took off her wrap. She dressed herself mechanically while Ma stood and watched her. The drug was not holding her so much, and every time Ma made a move Miss Blandish felt her flesh cringe. She tried to brace her muscles, but it made no difference, she cringed just the same. Her body felt an independent being to her. She could do nothing about it. She took the dress Ma thrust at her and stood hesitating. She was frightened to put it over her head, because she would not be able to watch Ma for that short time. She hated to take her eyes off Ma for one moment.

"Get goin'," Ma said in a hard voice.

Miss Blandish made a small circle of the dress and raised her arms so that she could pull it quickly over her head. She scrambled into the dress with feverish haste. Ma said nothing. She gave her a black, light coat, and the hat that went with it had a thick, spotted veil.

"Woppy is takin' you," she said, throwing each word at Miss Blandish, slowly and deliberately. "You gotta behave. Don't you start anythin' or I'll come after you an' you'll get hurt."

Miss Blandish nodded her head. Her bones felt liquid inside her. She had no resistance left in her. They walked down the stairs, Ma keeping a large hand on her arm. Woppy was smoking in the hall. A black fedora was pulled over his face. He glanced at them as they came down, and scowled.

Ma took Miss Blandish up to him and shook her arm roughly. "Walk fast," she said, "and keep your eyes straight. If Woppy has any trouble with you I'll get tough."

Woppy took her elbow in a hard grasp. "Come on," he said. They walked into the street. Woppy glanced up and down, but the street was dimly lit and empty. They began to walk rapidly. Woppy hated this job. He was nervous and, besides, he could do with some sleep.

He kept one hand on his rod, tucked in his trousers' waistband. The other hand held Miss Blandish's elbow so that he could steer her straight. She walked along beside him, keeping her eyes straight. The night air was sweet to her, but not once did she think of breaking away. Her brain was still clogged with the drugs she had been given; and Ma scared her to hell.

Across the road, from a dark alley, Rocco watched them go past. He swung a short length of lead piping in his hand. He recognized Woppy and was glad to see that Slim hadn't come back yet. Woppy would be easy, he told himself. He let them get well up the road, then he slipped after them. Woppy walked round the block, keeping to the side-roads. He glanced over his shoulder from time to time, but the road seemed deserted. At the far end of the street he could see a cop standing under the standard lamp, and he turned abruptly down an alley, jerking Miss Blandish with him.

Rocco broke into a sprint. This alley would do. He came up quickly and silently. Woppy heard him when it was too late. He let go of Miss Blandish and swung round just as Rocco hit him. The blackjack bounced on his head. Woppy folded at the knees. He fell on his hands, his black hat wedged into his skull. Rocco hit him again. He hit hard, drawing his arm well back and slamming down as if he were breaking a rock with a hammer. Woppy made no sound. The lead pipe bounced again and stung Rocco's hand. There was no need to it again. The black hat began to fill with blood.

Miss Blandish stood against the dark wall, motionless. Her mouth was open, but she made no sound. Rocco tossed the pipe away. He stepped over Woppy carefully and took her arm.

"You remember me?" he whispered to her. She didn't know him. "I'm takin' you back to your father," he went on. Still she stood there, stiff and frozen. He took her arm and pulled her from the wall. "Walk!" he said sharply. "I gotta car at the end of the block."

She still hung back. "Come on, come on," he said, losing patience.

She began to struggle feebly, pulling her arm from his hand.

He tightened his grip. "Can't you understand that I'm gettin' you outa a jam?" he said.

"Let me alone," she said, "I must get back. The old woman will do things to me."

"Forget the old woman," Rocco said. "You're goin' a long way from her." He began to force her down the alley. She resisted for a moment, then gave up. He reached the main street. His car was parked in a shadow. He could see a cop examining the plates. He cursed quietly. He wanted the cops out of this. If he turned this jane over to them, they would take the credit and frame him on something. Maybe they'd even try and pin the snatch on to him. He ducked back into the alley again, pulling Miss Blandish with him. The cop didn't seem to be in a hurry. He put his foot on the running-board and took off his cap. Rocco just stood in the shadow, watching. Miss Blandish stood shivering, behind him. The cop looked up and down the street, then put his cap on. Rocco watched him move off. Still he waited, then, when the cop had turned the corner, he took Miss Blandish to the car. He pushed her into the front seat and got under the wheel.

She began to beat her hands together, but he took no notice. He drove fast and heaved a sigh when he ran into the underground garage. The place was deserted. A small light burnt the ceiling, but the attendant had gone home.

Miss Blandish began to cry. Rocco forced her out of the car. He found himself sweating slightly. This was not going to be a soft job, he told himself. He led her to the automatic lift and slid back the grill.

Only when he had shut the door of his apartment did he relax a little. He took her into his room and snapped on the lights. She just stood there help-lessly, her body jerking with nerves.

"Get your hat an' coat off," he said sharply.

She did nothing. He stepped up to her and jerked her hat off. Unbuttoning her coat, he took that off, too.

She let him lead her over to the divan. He went to the door and locked it then he turned to the kitchen. He made a quantity of black coffee, very strong. He made a lot of it. When he got back she was sitting on the divan, her hands, palms up, folded in her lap. She was crying weakly. He gave her a large cup of the coffee and forced her to drink it; he gave her another cup after that. He told himself that he had got to wake her brain up somehow.

She stopped crying after a bit, and he sat down beside her. "Get a grip on yourself, lady," he said urgently.

"What am I going to do?" she asked.

"Now, listen," he went on. "You gotta get your brain workin'. You've been doped—do you get that? You gotta try an' snap outa it."

She sat there, listening to him talk. He went on and on, drumming at her; waiting patiently for some sign of recognition to filter through. She tried to understand, feeling the clouds moving from her brain, seeing dim pictures of a nightmare gradually forming before her eyes. He went on and on, making a guess here and there, saying her name over and over again. He saw that he was making headway. She was beginning to get somewhere. He got up and dug about in a drawer. He gave her a number of old newspapers he had collected, carrying the story of her kidnapping in large black type. She stared at them with awakening interest.

He was limp with excitement when he finally asked her for her telephone number, and he grabbed at the telephone when she gave him the number in a faraway, terror-ridden voice.

The Airflow screeched to a standstill outside the Paradise Club. Its black body was covered with a film of white dust, and the wings were caked with mud.

Slim climbed out stiffly, followed by Flynn. Doc nodded to them and shoved the gear in. The two men paused for a moment, watching the Airflow shoot over to the garage, then they turned to the alley.

The time was just after eight o'clock, and the sun was bright and not too warm. Slim wiped his sleeve across his face. All-night driving could be tough, he thought, as he knocked on the door. The doorman looked swollen with sleep, standing there blinking in the sunlight. Slim pushed by him and walked up the stairs.

Ma was standing by the barrier. There was a frightened, brittle tension in her face that Slim hadn't seen before. He looked up at her and paused. One of his feet was on a higher stair than the other. His long, thin hand held the rail. He just stopped and looked. Ma stood there, her eyes shrinking as if she saw her death in him. His hand tightened on the rail so that his knuckles went white.

"The girl's skipped," Ma said.

Slim didn't advance his lower foot, but put his raised foot back and stood firmly on the one stair. He took his hand slowly off the rail and groped for his gun. Ma remained like a vast, misshapen statue.

"Go on," he jerked out.

"Woppy took her out an' they ain't come back."

Flynn watched them from the hall. Slim took a step forward, then stopped again. A white circle appeared round his mouth and spread to his nostrils.

"What have you done?" he asked softly. His hand had found the gun and he drew it slowly from his holster. His yellow eyes were gleaming.

"What can I do?" she answered, not moving any part of herself but her mouth. "The cops have got her by now."

"You old cow," Slim said, "you've framed this ... you killed her, ain't that right?"

"Woppy took her out an' they ain't come back," Ma repeated. "Use your head ... can't you think of something?" She knew that she had to turn his mind quickly or else he'd shoot her. His eyes wavered. Flynn broke the tension by calling nervously: "I'll get Doc."

Slim lowered the gun. "She's been gone about four hours?" he asked.

Ma nodded.

"The bulls would have been here by now if they'd got her," Slim went on. He walked up the stairs unsteadily and leant against the wall. The shock was beginning to hit him. "For Christ's sake get your brain workin'," he said; "there's more in this than the cops."

Ma said: "Last night Rocco was here. I saw him slip a roll of dough to Maisey."

Slim stiffened, "Rocco?" he said. "That heel would like to put one across us." He stood there looking down at his dust-covered shoes. His slack mouth hung open.

Doc and Flynn came in with a rush. Doc was shaking all over. "The dame gone?" he quavered. "Jeeze, this is where it blows."

Slim turned his eyes on him. "Rocco was here last night pushing dough to Maisey," he said. "I guess we'll have a little chat with that judy right now."

Ma relaxed a little. She had been expecting a lot of trouble from Slim. "You an' Flynn get hold of her," she said, taking command, "an' Doc can go out an' see if there's any news breakin' yet."

Slim ran downstairs with Flynn at his heels. Doc looked helplessly at Ma.

"Listen," he said urgently, "let's skip before somethin' starts that we can't handle."

Ma reached out a hand and shook him by his coat front. "Get going," she said, "we're all in this, an' we gotta keep our nerve. The bulls ain't here yet, an' it looks to me that Rocco is at the bottom of this."

Doc jerked himself away and went down into the street.

Slim let himself into Maisey's apartment with a pick. He trod softly. Flynn waited outside, shivering with nerves. He gripped his gun butt until his hand ached. He was ready to shoot at his shadow.

Maisey lay in her small bed, sleeping heavily. Her pouting mouth was open and she snored softly into the bedclothes. Slim shuffled into the room and stood looking at her. His yellow eyes gleamed in the dim room. He put his cold hand on her throat and squeezed; Maisey woke with a jerk. Her scream was throttled back.

"I want to talk to you," Slim said between his teeth. "Come on, wake up."

Maisey lay flat on her back, staring up into his twisted face. She was like a rabbit looking at a snake.

"Why did Rocco give you that dough last night?"

Maisey shook her head. He relaxed his grip slightly.

"Rocco didn't give me any dough," she whimpered.

Slim hit her across her face with his open hand. "Why did Rocco give you that dough?" he repeated.

She squirmed under his grip, her hands trying to pull her throat clear. He pinned her down and she could only thrash with her legs. He hit her twice. Her nose began to bleed and the blood ran on to his hand.

"All right, all right," she gasped, "he gave me the dough because he had me."

Slim showed his teeth, his face twisted in hate. "You can't pull that one," he snarled at her. "I know your sort. You want cash down for that sorta thing. Come on, spill it!"

"Honest, it's true," she whined.

He groped behind him and got hold of her stockings that were hanging over the bedrail. He dug one of them into her mouth and wound the other round her face to keep the gag in place. He moved with deliberate swiftness. Jerking off the bedclothes, he rolled her over, twisting her hands behind her. She struggled violently, but she was powerless in his hands.

He knotted his handkerchief round her wrists, then he stepped off the bed.

"You're comin' clean," he told her, "so get that straight."

Flynn, outside, paced up and down. He kept jerking out his large, silver watch and staring at the face with unseeing eyes. He felt the sweat oozing through his hat-band. Slim was a long time, he kept telling himself. He listened outside the door, his ear to the wooden panel, but he could hear nothing. He turned the handle, and looked into the room. What he saw made him jerk his head back, and he began to swear softly. Slim suddenly opened the door and came out. "Rocco's got her all right," he said. "I'm goin' right over to his place. Listen, Flynn, this bitch knows too much an' she talks too much. You gotta get rid of her right now. You're takin' her for a one-way ride. Take her out into the country. We don't want the bulls making inquiries round the club—get goin'."

Flynn watched him run down the stairs, then he walked into Maisey's room. She was lying on the bed, groaning through her gag. Her arms were scarred with little red circles where Slim had burnt her with a cigarette. Flynn jerked her to her feet. "Come on, sister," he said, "get a grip on yourself. You are in bad with Slim, but he's goin' to give you a break." He untied her wrists and eased the gag out of her mouth.

Maisey sat on the bed, holding her arms, and shuddering.

"Get goin', sister," Flynn said, "Get some clothes on. I've got to take you to see Ma."

"I ain't goin'," Maisey sobbed. "They'll do for me."

Flynn grinned. "Don't kid yourself," he said. "They want to get the girl back, that's all. If the bulls do get on to her trail all of us will be on the run. Ma ain't goin' to take a chance on you. We don't want you to be left behind. That's sense, ain't it?"

Maisey looked at him suspiciously. "Well, I ain't goin'," she said at last.

Flynn pulled his gun. "If you don't come along," he said quietly, "I guess I'll have to do somethin' about it."

Maisey got hurriedly to her feet. "Okay," she said nervously, "I'll come."

"Get goin'," Flynn said, sitting on the bed.

She dressed hurriedly under his cold gaze. Something told her that she wouldn't see her room again, and by the time she had pulled on her hat she was trembling and in a state of collapse. He had to support her down the stairs, and he hurried her across the pavement into the Airflow without attracting attention. She sat beside him, shivering and jerking. He looked casually down the street and then over his shoulder through the rear window. There was a group of men some way off, coming towards him, but otherwise the street was clear. He glanced at her quickly, then he pointed to the roof of the car. "What do you make of that?" he asked coldly. As she looked up he hit her on the point of her chin and eased her on to the floor-boards as she slumped forward. He started the engine as the group of men drew past him, and swung the Airflow towards the open country.

Rocco slammed the receiver back on to its cradle. He had wasted a whole goddam hour trying to locate John Blandish. He wouldn't admit it, but he was getting bothered. He looked over at Miss Blandish, sitting on the divan. What a sweet help she was! She was still turning over the newspapers, reading and re-reading the lurid story. Her hands were trembling so violently that she had to tuck them under her thighs and leave the tabloid spread out before her on the rug. Her head jerked constantly, and she gave Rocco the jitters.

"Listen, lady," he pleaded. "I wanta help you—can't you get that? What the hell am I to do? Your pappy is here somewhere. I've rung round every lousy number they have given me, but I can't find him. Can't you think of something?"

Miss Blandish didn't seem to hear him. She put the tabloid away from her as if it were suddenly unclean, and sat there looking at her feet. Rocco came over to her and patted her arm.

"For God's sake ..." he began.

She shied away from him. "Let me alone," she said fiercely.

"All right, all right, lady," he soothed. "Don't get jumpy. I wish to hell you'd help yourself. I gotta find your pappy, ain't I?"

She looked at him "No, no!" she said loudly, beating on her knees with her clenched fists.

Rocco was bewildered. "Don't you want to get outa this?" he demanded "Don't you want to see your pappy?"

Miss Blandish began to sob. She shook her head miserably. "Leave me alone," she said, swaying from side to side as if she were in pain "Leave me alone."

Rocco tore at his hair. "I gotta do somethin'," he shouted at her. "I'll have that mob round here if I don't do somethin'."

She sprang to her feet and ran to the door. She tugged and wrenched at the handle "Open it!" she cried shrilly. "Open it! I want to get away!"

Rocco dragged her away as she began to drum on the panels with her fists. "Take it easy," he said desperately. She twisted from him and sprang back to the door. He began to swear as he dragged her away again and forced her on to the divan. She opened her mouth to scream, but he slammed his hand across her mouth. He felt her teeth trying to nip the heel of his hand and he pinched her face, digging his fingers into her cheeks.

"Stop it!" he said. "Stop it, do you hear?"

She relaxed a little and lay slack. He shifted his grip so that he held her lightly.

"You're drivin' me screwy," he said. "I wanta help you an' this is the way you take it. What's biting you, for God's sake?"

She lay there trembling, her eyes roving round the room. "I'm goin' to get the bulls," Rocco said suddenly, "I've wasted enough time already."

"No!" She began to struggle again. "You're not to!"

"Aw, shut up!" Rocco snarled. He shoved her back hard and left her. He picked up the telephone again, watching her closely. She came at him with a rush, just as he began to dial the number. He shoved her away with a lunge of his body, and she lost her balance and went over hard on the floor. Her hand went to the cable.

"Leave it alone," he shouted, "take your hand off it. Christ! I'll sock you in a minute." She wrenched at the cable, throwing the whole of her weight backwards. The cable came away from the wall as the number connected. The line went dead. Rocco glared at her and threw the useless instrument on the floor.

"You bitch," he said.

She scrambled away from him. Her face was white and terrified.

"Hell," he shouted, "you must be nuts! I'm gettin' outs here ... you can go to blazes.... Grisson will come here, you little fool. He won't start a kissin'-party either ... you've sunk yourself."

"You must stay here until he comes," she said.

"Why, you—you ..." Words failed Rocco. He went spluttering over to the door. "Come on, come on, before it's too late." He paused by the door. "You don't want him to find you here an' take you back, do you?"

She nodded helplessly. "Yes," she moaned, "I can't do anything else. He must come ... you don't understand ... I can't see my father again ... not after what's happened. I can't see anyone ever again...." She began to weep, rocking herself to and fro.

Rocco came over to her. The sweat glistened on his olive skin. "Snap out of it," he said roughly. "You'll be all right. For God's sake, what's all the mystery about? Why can't you see your old man again? Don't talk nuts! Come on!" He jerked at her arm, but she twisted away fiercely. Rocco cursed her with exasperation. "Have it your own way," he said. "I'm through. You give me a pain. I'm gettin' outa here."

She ran over to the door and stood against it. Her eyes glittered madly at him. "You're to stay here," she told him "He's got to find you here."

"Like hell," Rocco came at her furiously. She slipped him when he made a grab at her and stood in the centre of the room. He fumbled for the key and shoved it into the lock.

Miss Blandish suddenly swept up a light chair and hit him on the back of the head. Rocco stumbled, dizzy under the blow. She swung at him again, but he got away from the door. He held his head in both his hands, trying to force the bright light out of his eyes. She had the key now. He could see her dimly and staggered over to her. She twisted lightly past him. He saw her toss the key through the open window; he suddenly felt frightened. Sitting down abruptly on the divan, he held his head in his hands. She got as far away from him as she could, leaning against the wall, moaning to herself.

"I'll kill you for that," he said evenly, "you goddam little fool!" The clock on the mantelpiece struck eight sharply. Rocco felt the sweat break out all over him. He was caught all right he told himself desperately. He pulled his gun and snapped open the magazine. He looked over at Miss Blandish and then shrugged helplessly. She was nuts he told himself. He got to his feet and looked out of the window. Far below he could see the traffic moving like toys and he turned away abruptly. Jeeze! He was in a spot all right.

If he got someone to bust in the door, this screwy dame might rat on him and even pin the snatch on to him. She was nutty for anything. If he didn't get out, Slim would be along. Anyway, Slim would have a job getting in, and, if he did, he'd get the first shot in. He walked to the door and carefully examined the lock. He knew it was hopeless, he had that lock fitted himself, and it was a tricky one. He turned back to the divan.

"Well, you certainly pulled a sweet one this time," he said. "I want to get this straight. If I shoot this lock off, we're goin' to have company. This block is full of nosey guys, an' they'll beetle around as soon as I start poppin'. Okay, what are you goin' to tell 'em when they do?"

"I don't want to see anyone," was all she said.

"For Pete's sake, can't you leave off playin' Garbo an' come down to earth?" he said impatiently. "I tell you I gotta get outa here. Suppose Slim don't arrive, you goin' to stay here all your life?"

"He'll come," she said.

Rocco got to his feet and walked over to her. She shrank away from him. "I want to find out just how nutty you are," he said, keeping his voice steady with an effort. "You know who you are, don't you?" She nodded her head. "You know Grisson kidnapped you?" Again she nodded. "You know you've been doped?"

She looked at him helplessly and her face crumpled a little. She began to cry. "All right," he said impatiently, "cut it out. It won't help you any. You been doped an' it has made you a bit nutty, only a bit, but you don't know what you want. Now, I've got you away from Grisson and want to take you back to your pappy. That is a good thing, ain't it? Your old man is goin' to get a mighty big kick outa gettin' you back, an' things are goin' to be jake for you again. When we get company, I want you to tell them how I helped you. Do you get all that?"

Over his shoulder she saw that the kitchen door was opening silently. Her eyes dilated. The door went on opening. Slim was caked with sweat, he had come up inch by inch in the box lift. His yellow eyes were half-closed.

"Do you get that?" Rocco repeated. He didn't give a damn now. He knew that Slim was behind him, but he couldn't turn. He knew that he was dying fast, but he just couldn't do anything about it. He looked at Miss Blandish, seeing her beauty, seeing her blank, terrified eyes. He wondered what would have been his end if he had not started this. Why the hell had he bothered with her? he asked himself. He had known the risks and had accepted them. He didn't want to die. Not the way Slim would kill him. He had seen Slim's knife before. The seed in his loins suddenly began to spring. He couldn't do anything about that either. It just came from him, unexpectedly and as a relief. He felt for the last time that urgent ecstasy that had been so necessary to him in his short life. He felt his muscles relaxing to it, and then the steel blade wiped out everything.

Eddie lay on top of the bed, his pyjama coat open down to his waist. A cigarette dangled from his mouth, and he lay listening to Anna as she stormed about the room. His complete indifference was rapidly coming to an end. Anna was a swell kid when she liked to be, but when she threw a temper she was not so hot.

In her red pyjamas, her hair wild, she stood at the foot of the bed and ranted at him. Eddie tightened his mouth and watched her with half-closed eyes.

"And, what is more," she told him shrilly, "it's time we got out of here. This burg will drive me screwy. Where the hell do you think it's getting me? Do you think I want to put on a cheap strip every night of my life ... not likely! I'm going to make a success in my life, do you hear? I'm not going to hang around with your small-time mob collecting rent that would make the poor-relief look like a banquet. You bet your socks I'm not. And you can take it from me that I'm not standing for any more cheap cracks from that long slob you go places with...."

Eddie sourly told her to pipe down, "For God's sake," he growled, "can't you give me a rest? Sure, you will be in lights one of these days. All you can-dancers think the same. The world is full of judys who show everything they've got ... what happens to 'em?"

Anna beat on the bedrail with her fist. "All right, smart guy, if that's the way you feel, I can get along very well playing solo. You can take your little mob and you can stick them on the wall one after the other. I'm through."

Eddie climbed off the bed lazily. "You're gettin' too big for your pants," he said evenly. "I guess you want somethin' to cool you off."

"You big sap," Anna shouted at him, "do you think I'm scared of you? Some chance! You're just a dime a dozen, and that goes for them all. Riley had more ideas than you ever thought of."

Eddie laughed. He thought that was funny. "Sure," he said, standing over her; "where's he now?"

"In the dough," Anna snarled at him. "Where you'll never be."

Eddie laughed again. It would tickle this dame it she knew just how deep Riley had been planted. "Come off it, baby," he said. "Forget it. Jeeze! We're always fightin' these days."

Anna turned away from him impatiently. "You don't start anything, do you?" she said bitterly. "You just sit around and do nothing. I tell you I'm quitting."

Eddie shrugged. "Go ahead if you want to," he said indifferently. "There's plenty of floozies who'd like your job. It's soft enough."

She turned like a wild cat "You calling me floozie?" she screamed at him.

"Naw!" he said with heavy sarcasm. "Who said you were a floozie?"

She swung back her hand and smacked him across the face, bruising his lips. Eddie's eyes gleamed. He liked a fight, and this judy had certainly asked for one. He walked over to his clothes lying in a heap on a chair. He carefully withdrew his belt from the loops, letting his trousers slide on to the floor.

"Okay, Toots," he said evenly, "this is where you get yours."

She rushed at him, scratching and kicking, but he swept her arms away and tossed her on to the bed. Before she could scramble up, he slashed at her with the belt, making her squeal. He aimed another blow at her, but she rolled off and crouched down by the side of the bed. His hand dropped to his side. He felt suddenly bored with her. What the hell, he thought, I used to get a kick out of fighting her; and now he felt it stale. He tossed the belt away and vaulted over the bed. He landed on top of her before she could get clear. His weight knocked her flat. Scooping her up, he ran with her into the bathroom. He slammed her into the empty bath hard. She saved her head by an unconscious forward movement, but she didn't save anything else. He jerked the shower-cord and stepped back, letting the ice-water hit her with force.

"That'll cool you," he said, breathing hard, and he left her floundering in the bath. After locking the door he dressed hurriedly, listening with indifference to her storming. She hammered on the panels and screamed names at him. When he was ready for the street he took the key from the lock and shoved it under the door to her. Then he left the apartment at a run.

When Anna bounced into the room she found that he had gone. She stood there, quivering with rage and making puddles on the floor. She tore off her pyjamas and went back to the bathroom for a towel. Her eyes glittered and she dressed herself violently. She told herself that she was through with him for good. She would pull her freight right away. She went from drawer to drawer, pulling her things out savagely, tossing her clothes into two suit-cases she had dragged from under the bed. She opened her handbag and glanced inside it. The roll of green-backs gave her some satisfaction.

She told herself that Pete would be glad to have her back. Pete had got ideas all right, he didn't let the grass grow. She slammed the lid of one of the suitcases down and knelt on it, snapping the locks to. The door-bell shrilled suddenly, and she got up impatiently. For a moment she hesitated about answering it, then she shrugged and walked out of the room. She jerked the front door open. Brennan and two other men were standing there. She stiffened. They had cops written all over them.

"Hello, Anna," Brennan said with his big smile, "we want a little talk with you."

She made as if to slam the door, but Brennan eased his way in, followed by his boys.

"What do you want?" she demanded angrily. "You've got nothing on me."

"Of course we haven't." Brennan seemed quite shocked. "Headquarters want to ask you a few questions, just routine ... ain't anything in it."

Anna put her hands on her hips. "Well, tell them to go take a pill. I'm busy!"

"Don't be awkward, Anna," Brennan pleaded, "we got a car outside, an' we shan't keep you long."

"I tell you I can't come," Anna snapped.

Brennan glanced at the other two and jerked his head to her bedroom. One of them drew a gun and walked into the room. He was expecting to find Eddie there. He came out again. "Pullin' out," he said briefly, "luggage an' all."

Brennan lifted his hat and settled it over his eyes. "Goin' away?" he asked mildly.

"Getting the weekly wash ready," Anna told him. Brennan folded his fat hand on her arm. "Come on," he said. "We want to be nice to you."

She hesitated a moment, then shrugged. "Okay, okay!" she said impatiently. "But make it snappy."

They went down in the lift in a body and the lift-boy kept looking at them. He didn't say anything, but stared the whole time. Anna asked him if he knew who his father was, and he was glad when she walked out of the lift. One of the bulls winked at him. "Nice, ain't she?" he said. The lift-boy said she was a bitch.

Anna sat in the car and sulked. Brennan talked the whole time. He just talked airily about the latest ball games, but she didn't answer him. Once she looked at him, and Brennan smiled; but the cold dislike did not melt from her face, and Brennan was quite glad when the ride was over.

They walked her into a large room. Fenner was sitting, smoking. He waved a hand to Anna. She stopped in the middle of the room, her eyes like granite.

"H'yah, baby?" Fenner said easily. "Told you I'd be seein' more of you."

She whipped round on Brennan. "What is all this?" she demanded. "Who's this guy?"

Brennan smiled some more. He was just one big host. "Take a chair," he said. "Make yourself at home."

She sat down, her hands gripping her bag.

"Nice of you to come," Fenner said. "I won't keep you long. I want to tell you a little story which will interest you."

"What the hell is this?" she wanted to know, but they just sat there looking pleased with themselves.

"I'm goin' to be frank with you," Fenner said. 'We're investigating the Blandish kidnappin'. Your boy-friend Riley started off by puttin' the snatch on this girl. You know about that part, so I'll skip over it. What you don't know is that Grisson heard about it an' thought it too good to miss. He thought that Riley was too small for a rake-off like that, so he muscled in and took the girl from under Riley's nose.

"Your new boy friend Eddie and the rest of the mob were in on this. What happened to Riley? You've been wondering about Riley ever since he faded out of the picture. You told yourself that he had taken a run-out powder on you. You thought he had gone nuts for this Blandish girl. You got so steamed up that you threw your cards in with Grisson's crowd; while all the time Grisson had the girl an' was makin' a monkey out of you. Wasn't that a laugh for Eddie?"

Anna sat quite still. Her brain was racing. "So what?" she managed to say. "Suppose this is the McCoy, what do you hope to get out of it?"

Fenner looked over to Brennan. He jerked his head at the small door on the right of the room. Brennan nodded.

"Take Miss Borg to see the exhibits," he said to the officer who was standing near the door.

"This way, miss," said the cop with a grin.

"Where do you get that stuff?" Anna demanded suspiciously. "I don't want to see anything. What is it, anyway?" She had gone suddenly pale as a thought went through her mind.

Fenner leant back in his chair. "Go along, sister," he said. "We've found somethin' that will interest you. Take a look an' then come on back ... we'll wait."

"What have you found?" She was getting jittery. Her breath came fast.

Fenner smiled at her. "Ain't nothin' for you to get scared about," he said. "Go an' have a look."

She went with the officer slowly, dragging her feet. Fenner glanced over at Brennan. "It'll work all right," he said. They sat there waiting. Suddenly they heard her scream. One short, disgusted scream. They didn't move. Fenner played with a pencil. This had got to be handled carefully.

She came stumbling back, her face contorted with horror. He came over to her fast. "Take it easy," he said, leading her to a chair. She sat there shuddering for a moment, then she looked up. "You bastard!" she said. Fenner kept his eyes on her "Sorry for that," he said, "They ain't pretty, are they?" She put her hands over her face. He thought she was going to be sick, but she held herself in hand.

"Yeah," he said, leaning forward, "Grisson knifed Riley to get that girl, and buried him out at Johnny's. He was gettin' the breaks all right. Five hundred grand and the snatch pinned to a dead man. A sweet set-up for Grisson, I must say. And you chuckin' yourself at Eddie. A sucker, if there was one. What a laugh for Eddie! Every time he tumbled you he was laughing at you. They had the girl, they had the ransom, and Eddie had you. You didn't even see any of that dough, did you? You bet your sweet life you didn't. You didn't know that Eddie had a hundred grand for his split. A hundred grand would have looked swell sittin' in your lap. All you got was a tumble every night and a snigger from Eddie.

"All right; here's your chance to get a smack at those rats. We wanta get into that steel fort of theirs without a battle, an' you can tell us how to do it. We want to know if that Blandish girl is in there, an' you can find that out for us. We want to get her out alive if she's in there. We gotta spring it on those birds so fast that they won't have time to pull a gun. You come across with that an' you even things up with them. You get out of this business with a clean sheet an' pick up a grand for bein' a good girl."

Anna sat there, her face dead-white and her eyes glittering wildly. She kept muttering to herself over and over again. Fenner let her work herself up.

"The lousy, double-crossin' bastards!" she said suddenly. "I'll fix 'em all right, but I ain't fixing them through you. I ain't squealed to a cop yet, an' I ain't starting now."

Fenner sat on the desk close to her. "You can't do a thing on your own without runnin' a risk of gettin' rubbed out. Why take that chance? You can get goin' with a thousand bucks an' you can have a big laugh when we fry those guys. Think, they've got that girl in there, an' I guess you would hate to be in her place with Grisson and Eddie ridin' her."

She looked at them sullenly but said nothing.

Fenner tried again. "Come on, Toots," he said. "Use your head. This will be a nice break for you. Now, listen, this is what we want to know. How can we get into that joint without a battle? Is there any way round it? You can tell us that and then you'll be in the clear."

"You cheap bulls can go to hell," was all she said. Fenner glanced over at Brennan. Time was pressing and this was getting them nowhere. He went over to Brennan and, taking his arm, led him away from Anna.

"I can crack this dame," he said in a low voice. "Haul your boys off an' give me a few moments with her alone."

Brennan looked puzzled. "What's the idea?" he asked.

Fenner tapped him on the chest. "Get the boys outa her and skip. This is urgent. Let me handle this."

Brennan said okay, and went over to the door. He jerked his head to the others and they followed him out of the room. Fenner stood looking at Anna. She sat in the chair indifferently. Her face was obstinate and hard, but Fenner knew he had her where he wanted her, and he could afford a grin.

"Riley has been dead over four months," he said, speaking rapidly and low. "Just get the dates right. A month ago there was a murder committed at the Palace Hotel. You remember Heinie was shot there and Riley had the shooting pushed on to him. Riley couldn't have done the shooting. The bullet came from a small-calibre gun, the type of rod a woman would use. You were on the same floor as Heinie and you loved him a lot. Didn't Heinie squeal on your boy-friend? Okay, add that up an' tell me the answer."

Anna was watchful now. Her eyes shifted to the floor. "You're nuts," she said.

"Maybe," Fenner went on, "the cops haven't given this angle any thought yet, but I have. Either you play ball with me or else I'm goin' to remind Brennan about Heinie's shootin.' I want you to get this clear. It's sweet fanny to me who happened to Heinie. That little rat's nothin' to do with me. I want the Blandish girl. Give me what I want an' I shan't say anythin' about the shootin'. Brennan may get on to it himself in which case you're goin' to have a thin time beatin' the rap, but Brennan is mighty busy at the moment, an' I don't think he'll come round to that angle for a time. Anyway, it'll give you a chance of skipping with the grand that Blandish will pay you. Now, what's it to be?"

She thought for a moment. "What do you want me to do?" she asked.

Fenner breathed a faint sigh. Things were going the right way, after all. "I want you to go straight down to the club an' find out if the girl is there or not. I'm comin' with you and I wait outside. We must know if she's there. We can't go bombing that joint regardless unless we know where she is. Now, will you do that?"

"How the hell can I?" she demanded. "They've got her under cover now, an' it's not likely that they'll let me stick my nose around."

Fenner got to his feet. "You'll find a way," he said grimly. "That's your part of the bargain. This is urgent, so let's step on it."

They left the room together. Brennan was hanging about in the outer office. Fenner didn't stop, but he gave him a wink as he passed him. Brennan watched them leave the office and then scratched his head. "What the hell is that bozo up to now?" he asked himself.

Fenner let Anna go on alone when they reached the street. Before she left him, he said: "Now, understand, you gotta be quick. Go in an' find out, then meet me at the corner in double-quick time. Rush it, sister!"

She had to knock several times before the door-man slid back the small trap. He hesitated before opening the door, then he grudgingly did so. Anna went straight up the stairs. She ran into Ma who was coming out of the deserted restaurant. Ma stopped short when she saw her, and her face hardened. "What the hell do you want?" she demanded impatiently.

Anna was startled. She hadn't seen Ma look so mean before. "Eddie an' I had a fight," she said, speaking casually, "I thought I'd better see if he'd come in here. Has he?"

Ma shook her head. "Scram outa it," she said. "He ain't here. I'm busy. She turned back to the office. Just then Doc came blundering up the stairs. His face was white and glistening with sweat. Anna stared at him, but he didn't even see her. He went straight into the office on Ma's heels and shut the door. Anna stood still. What was going on around here? she asked herself.

The atmosphere was tense and charged with dynamite. She hesitated, wondering what to do next. She had the place to herself for a moment. Turning quickly, she ran up the stairs. When she reached the top landing, her breath was coming fast, and she paused and looked over the rail into the reception hall. Ma and Doc were still in the office. She continued down the corridor until she reached the last room. The locked door had never interested her. She had accepted Eddie's explanation that it was a store-room without any thought. The door stood half-open and she looked into the room. She stood looking round and her face hardened.

So it was on the level, she thought. This was obviously where they had kept the girl. Somehow they had taken her out of the club. Her eyes narrowed. Fenner should know this. She'd take his offer and skip. The lousy, double-crossing bastards. She turned on her heel and sped down the corridor again. At the head of the staircase, she stopped short. Ma was standing in the hall, looking up. Anna felt herself flinch. Ma's face was stolid, but her little eyes had a murderous gleam.

"I thought I told you to get outa here?" Ma said.

"I was looking for Eddie," Anna stammered. She tried to get a grip on herself. She began walking down the stairs, without taking her eyes off Ma. She got half-way down and then her nerve went back on her. She stopped. "I tell you was looking for Eddie," she quavered.

Doc came out of the office and joined Ma. They both watched her. "Where are you goin' now?" Ma asked,

Doc suddenly touched Ma's arm. "She knows," he said in a low voice. Anna heard him, and she lost her head. "I don't know anything." she stammered. "What are you talking about?"

Ma said: "You're goin' to stay right here."

Anna nodded. "Sure," she said, "I'll stay."

Outside, Fenner waited impatiently. As the minutes went by he got more and more worked up. Something had gone wrong he told himself. Anna had either crossed him or else she had over-played her hand. He knew the Grissons weren't to be trifled with. He stood there waiting and then decided to start something himself. He slid back into his car and rapidly drove off to Anna's apartment.

Miss Blandish watched Rocco fold slowly to the floor. She put both her knuckles into her mouth, forcing her mouth wide open. She leant against the wall biting her knuckles because she couldn't scream and because she wanted to. Rocco had fallen on his knees, his hands spread on the polished floor. He remained like that for a moment, then he slid further down, his hands opening slowly as if he were swimming. He stretched out on the boards, rubbing the skin off his nose.

Slim stood over him, watching indifferently. He held the stained knife at his side; dangling loosely from his fingers. He stared for quite a long while, then he looked at Miss Blandish. She cringed away trying to work her body into the wall.

"You're comin back with me," he said.

She turned her head away, so that she could not see Rocco lying there. He didn't bleed at all. She couldn't understand why. She wanted to tell him to get up. He looked absurd lying there. She wanted him to get up, but she knew that it wouldn't make any difference if she had told him to get up. Slim wiped the knife on Rocco's coat. Rocco's coat was light grey. The bloodstain spoilt the suit. Slim went over to the window and looked down into the street.

The traffic was getting heavy, and people were moving in the street. Time was getting on, and the streets would be dangerous. He thought for a moment, then looked at Rocco. Rocco was a little guy. Neat and narrow. Slim went over to the wardrobe, he pulled out a dark suit and tossed it on the bed. He rummaged in some drawers and found a shirt.

"Get into those," he said to Miss Blandish.

Miss Blandish shook her head. "Please ..." she began. Slim walked over to her. "Do it!" he said, his eyes hating her.

She undid her blouse and then, hesitating, fumbled at the waist of her skirt. She stepped out of the skirt. He began to breathe quickly. She saw the look on his face and she backed away from him. He just stood there watching. "Go on," he said. She picked up the shirt. He walked slowly over to her and took the shirt out of her paralysed hands. His mouth pursed, pushing his wet lips forward. His eyes were blind. He began leading her to the divan, moaning to himself.

A large bluebottle settled on the bloodstain on Rocco's coat. It stretched its legs and buzzed excitedly. It remained there some time, enjoying itself.

The room was disturbed suddenly by Miss Blandish, clawing with her nails frantically on the shawl that covered the divan.

Eddie bought himself a big breakfast. All the time he was eating he thought about Anna. He kept telling himself that she could go to hell, but at the back of his mind he wanted her to stay. He had got used to her, and she was swell when she felt that way. He pushed his plate away impatiently and gave himself a cigarette. He told himself that he had better look the boys up. He wished that Slim would get rid of Miss Blandish. With that dame popping around anything might happen.

He picked his teeth thoughtfully. Perhaps it would be safer to slide while the going was good. Perhaps Anna's beef was justified. Eddie believed in a woman's instinct. Maybe Anna had a hunch. He got slowly to his feet, pushing the chair away with the back of his legs. He jerked his finger to the waitress, who gave him his check; she wrote laboriously, putting her tongue out a little. He paid at the desk and walked out into the street. He stood hesitating in the sunshine. He couldn't make up his mind whether to go back to Anna or to go on to the club. He had a hunch to see Anna, and he flagged a taxi. His hunch was urgent.

He stood waiting for the lift to come from the top floor. The boy slid back the grating and looked surprised to see him again.

"Ain't no use goin' up," he said to Eddie, "they've pinched her."

Eddie asked him what the hell he was talking about. The boy waved his hands excitedly. "Sure," he said, "ten minutes after you had gone the bulls arrived. They took her off in a car." ·

Eddie stood motionless. His mouth twitched nervously. His hunch had been right. "Get this," he said quickly, "I ain't been back, do you understand?" The lift-boy grinned as Eddie stripped off some notes from his roll. "Sure," he said, "you ain't been back."

Eddie turned hurriedly to the door again. He looked into the street. He saw nothing to arouse his suspicions. He thought for a moment, his brain racing. Grisson ought to know about this. Anna, in the mood he had left her, was unreliable. He stepped across to the 'phone booth. He dialled hurriedly.

"Hang up," Fenner said behind him, "and keep your hands still."

Eddie dropped the receiver back on to its cradle. He looked over his shoulder. Fenner was quite close and had a gun in his hand. He looked tough all right.

"I want you," Fenner said, speaking low.

The lift-boy leant out of the lift, watching with big eyes. This was a big day for him. Eddie stepped out of the booth with his hands raised above his hips.

"You ain't got nothin' on me, copper," he said.

Fenner said: "I'm clairvoyant; if we ain't got anything on you now, we soon will."

Two uniformed policemen stepped out from behind the booth where they had been waiting. They hustled Eddie into the waiting car. Eddie sat trembling. What the hell had happened? he asked himself. He dug into his pocket and found a cigarette. He put it in his lips, but one of the coppers smacked it with his open hand. Eddie snarled at him: "Tough, eh?" he said. The copper grinned at him. "You bet," he said.

They hurried him into Brennan's office when they reached headquarters. Brennan was pacing up and down, smoking a cigar. He was looking savage, and Eddie's mouth went dry. The bastards had got him all right. He stood in the middle of the room, looking at each man in turn out of the corner of his eyes. He twiddled with his hat held in his hands.

Brennan went over to sit behind the desk.

"We're on to you, Schultz," he said abruptly. "Come on, get it off your chest."

Eddie shrugged, but his knees began to knock. "You ain't got a thing on me," he said. "What's the charge?"

Brennan said: "We're holding you for kidnapping John Blandish's daughter, and for the murder of Riley, Bailey, and MacKay."

Eddie held himself in. Jeeze! The lid had blown right off this time. "You're nuts," he said. "You can't make that stick."

Fenner walked slowly over to him. "Ain't it right that you rubbed out Riley to get the girl?"

Eddie looked round wildly. "I tell you you're screwy," he shouted. Fenner threw out a hand and hit Eddie across the nose. It hurt, but Eddie had taken a smack or two. He reeled back on his heels.

"You ain't goin' to do this to me," he shouted. "I want my mouthpiece. I gotta right to have him, an' I gonna use that right."

"You ain't goin' to get outa it as soft as that," Brennan told him, behind a cloud of smoke. "You are goin' to spill all you know before you get any outside help. We're used to handling rats like you, an' we ain't taking chances with one of your crooked lawyers."

Eddie whirled on Fenner. "Who're you?" he snarled.

Fenner grinned. "We're doin' the questioning now," he said. "Just open your trap when we tell you."

Brennan put his thumb on the bell-push and kept it there. Three uniformed policemen eased their way into the room. They were big, tough-looking birds with large, red faces, and thick necks. They crowded round Eddie.

"This guy thinks he's tough," Brennan said, his elbows on the desk. "Take him away and talk to him."

'The men grinned at each other. "Come on, bozo," they said to Eddie.

For a moment Eddie showed fight. He clenched and unclenched his fists. He saw that they were hoping that he'd start something. One of them had a night-stick in his hand, the thong tight round his wrist.

"Pass it up," Eddie said. "I don't know a thing."

"Get going," Brennan said impatiently.

They pushed Eddie to the door. He went with them, and Fenner brought up the rear. Fenner was getting worried. Time was moving too fast, and there was still a lot to do.

They took Eddie into a small soundproof room. There was a massive chair in the centre which was fixed to the floor with iron bolts. To Eddie it looked like the hot-squat. Leather straps hung from the arms and the legs.

"Sit down," Fenner said, leaning against the wall.

Eddie drew away. "You go to hell," he said. "You can't push me around, I tell you."

One of the cops hit him across the knees with his nightstick, and Eddie fell forward. Another of them booted him from behind. They grabbed him while the pain gripped him and slammed him into the chair. They worked fast, fixing his arms and legs with the straps. Then they hauled off. Eddie snarled at them. His knees gave him plenty. Fenner stood over him.

"Who killed Riley?" he asked.

Eddie spat at him. "I tell you ..." he began.

They jerked his head back by his hair, and one of them hit him across his bared throat with a club. He hit him very hard and straight. Eddie suddenly stiffened, straining at the straps. The chair creaked with his movements. He jerked and pulled while he fought to get the air into his lungs. His face was blue with his effort, and for a moment Fenner thought he wouldn't make it. They stood back and watched him have his convulsions. Gradually the air got back into his lungs again and he ceased to thrash.

"Who killed Riley?" Fenner shouted at him. "Come on, you rat, spill it, or you're goin' to get it again."

They wound thick fingers in his hair, forcing his head back once more, dragging at the roots so that his head felt on fire. Back went his head, inch by inch, and he fought them with his neck muscles until his eyes stood out in his face like lamp globes. When his chin pointed to the ceiling they hit him again. He thought they had killed him this time. His throat closed up and his lungs screamed at him. He snapped one of the straps as he strained to get free, but they hit him on the wrist with the club, so that his arm went dead. He didn't know that they had hit him, he just felt his arm fall to his side, and the frantic commands from his brain for his arm to go to his throat didn't amount to anything. Again they hauled off, waiting for him to come back.

"Who killed Riley?" Fenner droned.

"I don't know ..." Eddie moaned. "You got me wrong, mister. For Christ's sake gimme a break, can't you?"

They hit him across the knee-caps twice with the club. Each time hauling off and swinging down hard. Eddie bit his bottom lip through, but he didn't say anything. Fenner turned sour. "Quit playin' with him, can't you?" he said to the cops. "This guy's tough, ain't he? Well, get tough, too."

One of the cops peeled his uniform. Eddie watched him with terror in his eyes. He knew he was going to crack. He couldn't stand any more of this. These bastards would go on until he did split. He clenched his sound hand and strained on the strap. The pain from his knees and his throat nearly drove him crazy. "You can't do this to me...." he wailed. "I ain't goin' to be framed."

He saw the cop coming at him with a raised club, and he tried to duck his head away, but a blinding light burst before his eyes.

Fenner watched them work on him for a long time, then Eddie slumped in the chair. One of the cops caught up a pail of water and tossed it into Eddie's face. The shock of the water brought him back again, and Fenner signed them to stand back.

"Who killed Riley?" he demanded, leaning over the shuddering man.

"Slim did it ..." Eddie moaned faintly. "Slim wiped 'em all out...."

"Where's the girl?"

"Slim's got her ... he had her all the time at the club ... don't touch me any more ... leave me alone..."

Fenner whirled round. "Shove him away," he said. "We've got to get goin'."

He burst into Brennan's office. Brennan was getting fidgety. He looked up hopefully as Fenner came in.

"Slim's got the girl at the club," Fenner said swiftly. "We know where we are ... we ain't gotta minute to waste now. Get your boys and let's get goin'."

Brennan slid open his drawer and took out a gun. He glanced at it and then shoved it into his hip pocket. He left the office at a run. Fenner could hear him shouting orders in the squad-room, and he went after him fast.

Slim lowered Miss Blandish to the street level in the box-lift. It was tricky work, but he was desperate. He slid down after her and jerked her out of the cramped space roughly. Rocco's suit was on the big side and it hid her figure. Her thick hair was tucked up under a black fedora which Slim had pulled over her eyes. She walked a little drunkenly. Slim had given her a long shot of raw liquor. She looked odd enough, and Slim was jumpy. He kept his hand on his gun butt. He thought she would do, huddled in the car, but she was not so hot walking for anyone to see. They would tumble that she was a dame unless they were pretty dumb. The Airflow stood at the end of the alley, and he took her arm.

"I'm goin' to open the door for you," he said.

She didn't say anything.

"As soon as I've opened the door you come quickly. Get into the car an' don't stop on your way."

He left her and crossed the pavement. He got in the car and started the engine. Leaning forward, he swung the off-door open. Miss Blandish ran across, holding her head down. He had shoved the gear in before she had reached him, and as she tumbled in the car shot away. He looked into his driving-mirror, but the street was quiet. There was an old woman who was looking after them, but she didn't count. He told Miss Blandish to sit low.

The Airflow shot on towards the club. Suddenly he slammed on the brakes and slowed down. The air was violently split with police-sirens. He saw five cars overtaking him, loaded with police. He drew to the side of the kerb, slowing the car down to twenty. His gun was out and he began to curse softly. The police-cars swept past him. They were heading for the Paradise Club.

He followed behind cautiously, telling himself that they weren't after him. As he got nearer he suddenly realized with alarm that they were pulling up outside the club. He swung the Airflow to a side-turning. He heard a sudden shout and saw a speed-cop on a motor-cycle coming after him. The street was busy, so, still swearing softly, he drew in to the side of the road and stopped. He leant against the side of the car, hiding his gun with his body. The cop came up with a rush. He stuck his red Irish face into the car.

"What's your hurry?" he demanded.

Slim kept Miss Blandish hidden by his body.

"I ain't in no hurry," he said. "I thought I'd get out of the way of your speed boys ... makin' a raid or what?"

The cop said: "Come outa that."

Slim's eyes turned yellow. He shoved in his clutch. The cop jerked open the door. "Come on out."

Slim let him have it low down. The gun roared with a savage explosion. The cop buckled, holding his belly with his two gauntleted hands. The gloves turned red. Slim sent the Airflow leaping forward. The people in the street began shouting, but none of them moved. They had seen street shootings before, and they knew it was safer to sit tight.

Fenner was just bundling out of his car when the cop got shot. The noise made him jerk his head. He saw the Airflow tearing down the street, scattering the other traffic. He hesitated, but he knew his job was to get the girl out of this place alive. He ran over to the trooper, but he was dead. Brennan joined him. "Who the hell was that?" he asked.

Three motor-cycle police had ridden after the Airflow. They could hear their noisy exhausts dying in the distance. Fenner shrugged. "It was one of the rats," he said uneasily. "I hope to Christ they don't let him get away."

Brennan was looking worried.

"My men can't get into the club," he said.

Fenner cursed. "We've got a sweet job on our hands now," he said. "I guess the girl ain't got much chance."

Brennan said: "She'll have to take what's comin'. We gotta get into that place, an' we gotta get tough doing it."

More police began to arrive, and a fire-engine came clanging up. The street became congested with staring crowds. The police were pushing them back and clearing a large space in front of the club.

At the first sign of the raid, heavy steel shutters were hastily swung across the windows of the club. An enterprising trooper tossed a gas-bomb, but the shutter had already swung to, and the bomb burst in the street, adding to the confusion.

Fenner came running over to Brennan. "Give me some boys," he said, "I guess we might hack our way through the roof."

Brennan nodded. "Yeah," he said, "that's a good idea. You can get on the roof from the next-door building. You make a start there and I'll get some other men to kick up a row in the front."

He gave orders in a fog-horn voice, and a number of the police ran up the alley and began battering on the steel panels with their clubs. They made a big uproar, but it didn't get them anywhere. Fenner watched them for a moment, then he darted off with four policemen close on his heels. As they ran across the empty space before the club, someone opened up with a Tommy-gun. The slugs scattered at their feet. One of the cops gave a howl and his legs doubled up under him. Fenner raced forward until he was out of range. The gun fired again, smacking more slugs into the cop as he lay there. From behind the police-vans the cops began firing. The sharp clatter of the Thompsons and the heavy impact of the slugs as they flattened against the steel were an added uproar to the shouts of the excited crowd and the wail of sirens as more police arrived.

Next door to the Paradise Club was the Hotel Lexham. A tall, narrow building, overtopping the club by a couple of floors. Fenner raced up the stairs of the hotel. Police were standing about the hall with drawn guns, grimly watching. He pelted breathlessly until he reached the attics. The others came panting behind him. He shot the skylight back and scrambled on to the roof. Below them was the roof of the Paradise Club. Fenner swung his legs over the parapet and took a grip on the stack pipe. He went down with a rush, skinning his hands and tearing his trousers at the knee. The others followed more slowly. They could hear the hammering on the front door, and the spasmodic firing of the machine-guns.

The police attacked the roof with crowbars, wrenching off the tiles and revealing the rafters. It didn't take them long to hack a hole in the plaster, and one after the other they dropped into a small, dark room.

Fenner pulled his gun. "This ain't goin' to be a picnic," he said. He turned to one of the cops. "Get back the way you came an' tell the boys that we're in. Send some more up here, pronto."

He waited long enough to see the man swing himself out through the hole in the roof, then he gently turned the handle of the door and stepped into the passage. He stood there listening. On the next floor he could hear someone swearing obscenely. He hesitated for a moment, holding his gun steady. Two of the officers behind him had submachine-guns clutched tightly to their chests, and the other one had a gas-gun.

Fenner gumshoed down the passage to the head of the stairs. He began going down, feeling the sweat start under his arms. Suddenly Flynn came blundering round the corner. He saw Fenner just as Fenner shot at him. Flynn threw his arms above his head with a dramatic gesture, just like an Italian singer reaching for a high note. He went over backwards, with a choking shout. Fenner shot him again. He took the rest of the stairs with a jump. He was off balance when Doc appeared from a door down the passage, but he managed to throw himself on his face as Doc fired. The two police on the stairs let Doc have it with two bursts from their guns. Doc just managed to scramble back under cover, and the slugs ripped the woodwork of the door.

"Take it easy," Fenner gasped from the floor. "These rats will fight to the finish now."

Doc had slammed the door to and now he began to pump lead through the panels so that they could not get near. The police replied with a terrific burst of fire, riddling the door from top to bottom. They heard Doc give a sudden scream and Fenner thrust the door open with his foot. They found Doc slumped in a corner, the blood running in a thick stream from his mouth. He looked at them with glazed eyes and tried to raise his gun, but the effort was too much for him. The gun slipped out of his hand and fell with a little thud on the floor beside him. His eyes suddenly rolled up.

Fenner said: "Number two."

They backed out of the room and stood hesitating in the passage. "Go through the rooms," Fenner said, "We gotta find that girl."

They walked slowly down the passage, pausing at each door. It was nervy work, and Fenner was glad when it was over. The last door in the row he knew must have been Miss Blandish's room, but it was empty. "This is where they kept her," he said; "but she's skipped!"

They headed for the stairs once more. "This is where we meet the rest of the birds," one of the cops said uneasily. "I ain't lookin' forward to shakin' hands with the old woman."

Fenner grinned. "It's up to you to get your slugs in first," he said, moving cautiously down the stairs.

Ma Grisson watched them come from behind the cloakroom barrier. She held a Thompson in her huge hands, and her little eyes glittered like glass. Her heavy face was twisted in a snarl. She was going to give as much as she got.

Fenner saw a slight movement from the barrier when he reached the half-way line on the stairs. It was only because his eyes were sharp that he saw it. The thin tube of the Thompson came slowly over the counter-top. He gave a yell and threw himself down the stairs, falling with a crash on his hands and knees. He heard the Thompson clatter, and the police, for a moment paralysed by his shout, were caught in the open.

Fenner, rolling against the barrier, saw the three officers crumpling up under the stream of slugs. One of them tried to scramble back up the stairs, but he was caught by a fresh burst. Fenner put his hand against the wall and felt cold steel. He drew his lips off his teeth. That was sweet, he told himself. The old woman on one side of the barrier and he on the other. He guessed he'd have to lie there until someone came and gave him a hand.

"Listen, honey," he called, "I've gotta gun an' I know how to use it, so take it easy. You can't get me before I get you, an' I guess that goes for me, too. Why don't you be a good girl an' toss the gun over an' take it quietly?"

Ma cursed him. Fenner lay still on his back watching the top of the barrier. He held his gun ready.

"Come on," he coaxed. "Turn it in, an' take what's comin' to you."

Ma gently shifted the gun from the barrier. She moved her bulk inch by inch until she was standing. Fenner was lying so close to the barrier that she could not see him. She eased herself against the wall. Fenner caught a glimpse of her in the opposite mirror. She saw him at the same time. They stared at one another in the mirror. Both of them were unable to shoot and they just watched each other's reflections for the next move.

"Like the movies, ain't it?" Fenner said from the floor.

Ma's face twisted again. "I'll get you, you bastard," she said.

"Well, don't stand there all night, get goin' if you want to," Fenner said.

Brennan, from the top of the stairs, watched them. Ma was right in the open now, she had eyes only for Fenner. Brennan raised his gun, but the slight movement caught Ma's attention. She whipped up the Tommy-gun and fired burst after burst. Brennan only just got himself under cover as the slugs churned up the wood of the chairs.

Fenner took a chance and slid quickly along the floor, watching Ma who had forgotten him for the moment. He made the restaurant on his belly and when he turned the corner he scrambled to his feet. The room was in darkness and he wondered if Slim was hiding there. He had to risk that, but he felt his nerves crawling up his spine. He heard Brennan swopping shots with Ma, and he left them at it.

He groped for the light-switch and suddenly the restaurant sprang into view. The place was deserted. He walked with great care into Ma's office. Standing in the doorway he thought for a moment that his quest was over. A girl lay on the floor, her head hidden by the desk. Then he realized that it was Anna. She had been dead some time. Someone had shot her at close quarters. He glanced round the office and swore to himself. Slim and Miss Blandish had skipped somehow.

Suddenly there was a terrific burst of firing in the hall, then silence. He heard Brennan give a shout. He stepped cautiously back to the entrance and looked round the corner. Brennan was running downstairs.

"She's done for," he shouted. "I caught her when her slugs gave out."

Fenner lifted his hands helplessly. "The girl ain't in the building," he said wearily. "There ain't a sign of Slim either."

Brennan was shouting orders to his men to search the place, but Fenner knew that it was a waste of time. "I tell you she ain't here," he said impatiently. "I went through all the rooms upstairs, an' I've looked down here. There's nowhere else they could have hidden her."

"Well, they're in the open now," Brennan said. "I'll get back to headquarters and put out a general call. We'll pick 'em up quick enough. Once these rats are out of their holes it's easy to run 'em down."

Fenner went with him into the street. The crowds were still gaping with excitement. Brennan was surrounded by a mob of urgent press men as soon as he stepped into the street.

"Okay, boys," he said impatiently. "Don't hold me up now, come on down to headquarters and you'll get the story all right. The girl ain't there and Grisson ain't, either." He didn't stop while he spoke, but elbowed his way to his car, followed closely by Fenner.

At headquarters they found the desk-sergeant steamed-up. "The boys

have located Slim," he said excitedly. "He is heading for Kansas as fast as he
can lick. All the roads are being watched, but they ain't picked him up yet."
A speed-cop, his face cut and his uniform ragged, sat nursing an aching
wrist. He got to his feet when Brennan glanced at him,
"It was Slim who killed Murphy just before the raid," he said. "We followed
him for several miles but that car of his can move. It had us nowhere. I had a
blow-out an' took a toss, but got on to headquarters and warned them where
he was heading."
Brennan nodded shortly. He took Fenner's arm and led him into his office.
Fenner said to the speed-cop, "Was he alone?"
The cop shook his head. "He had another little guy with him."
"It wasn't the girl?"
"Not unless she'd got dressed in men's clothes. I never got near enough to
see."
Brennan stood impatiently in his office doorway. "It looks as if it were go-
ing to be played out on the home ground."
"Well, come on, come on," Fenner said savagely. "What the hell are we go-
ing to do now?"

During the first mad rush out of town Miss Blandish crouched down in her
seat, staring ahead, but seeing nothing.
Slim gripped the wheel with both hands, pushing the Airflow forward, ruthlessly driving other traffic to the kerb. His loose mouth hung vacantly and his
skin glistened with sweat. He could hear the wailing sirens behind him, but
he did not once look into his driving-mirror. The open country was ahead of
him, and if he could once make that he guessed his speed would put him in
the clear. The Airflow had plenty under its hood. He spun the wheel suddenly,
ripping round a corner. He felt the off-wheels rise, then thud back. He did not
ease down the speed.
Another car suddenly appeared from a side-turning, but he kept on, roar-
ing past the startled driver and missing him by inches. He was leaving town
rapidly. At the end of the street the traffic lights were in operation. The red
light had just flicked on. Slim put his hand hard on the horn button. The horn
screeched its warning, and he cut out the exhaust at the same time. The Airflow roared, thundering down on the red light.
The crossing traffic heard him coming and crowded on their brakes. One
driver lost his head and kept on. Slim hit him a glancing blow, but he kept the
Airflow steady. Then he was in the clear. The busy streets dropped behind
him, and the broad road leading to the open was under his wheels. The
sirens behind became menacing and he heard the crack of a revolver. The Air-

flow had been built in Chicago, and the builders had seen that it could laugh at slugs.

Slim glanced in his mirror. There were two speed-cops behind him, both leaning over the bars of their motor-cycles, one of them shooting. He kept his pedal on the boards. They couldn't overtake him at that speed. He guessed that they were flat out as it was. Suddenly he heard a sharp noise, and he grinned. One of the cops had a blow-out. He glanced into the mirror again. He saw, in the rapidly receding distance, one of the cyclists wobbling to a standstill. The other cop grimly kept on behind him. Slim eased his foot slightly, so that the Airflow lost speed. Up came the motor-cycle with a rush. The cop fired twice at Slim. The bullets made a cobweb of lines on the bullet-proof glass, but that was all. Slim drew his lips off his teeth and swerved suddenly, pulling his wheel to the right and then to the left.

The side of the car hit the motor-cycle and Slim almost went into a skid. He dragged on the wheel, cursing hard, then, as the Airflow righted, he shoved the pedal down again. The motor-cycle had swerved into a ditch and had disappeared. The road was silent now, but Slim kept his speed.

Without immediate pursuit to harass him, he could think. He glanced at Miss Blandish, but she was sitting like a statue. He was on the run now, he told himself, they had got him in the open and it was going to be tough going. He knew well what it meant. The dame was going to be poison from now on. Yet he didn't for a moment consider ditching her. He'd play it out to a finish.

After a few miles, he slowed down and shoved on the brake. He got out of the car stiffly and checked his gas. He still had plenty. The first thing to do, he thought, was to switch cars. The Airflow was hot now. The bulls would be looking for it. He came round to the off-side of the car and put his head into the open window.

"We ain't goin' to be together much longer," he said to Miss Blandish, "but it's goin' to be mighty lively for you until we do get picked up."

She sat there, crushed. Words were nothing to her. She had her own nightmare that obsessed her. He didn't expect her to answer; he was used to her silences. He went round the car and got in again. He drove on at a steady sixty.

He had to drive some time before he saw what he wanted. In the distance there was a car drawn up on the side of the road. Two women were sitting on the running-board, eating from paper bags. As he came up, he saw that one of them was young and the other looked like her mother. He shoved on his foot-brake and disengaged his clutch. The Airflow slid to a standstill. He looked the other car over with a keen eye. It was a small tourer that ran on the streets in its thousands. He climbed out of the Airflow and the two women looked at him curiously. The long road was empty and lonely. Slim didn't waste any time. He walked round the Airflow and raised the hood. He opened the toolbox on the running-board and took out an oily rag and a spanner. He loosened a plug with difficulty and wrapped it in the rag, which he put in his pocket. The women still stared at him. He put the hood down carefully and then groped for his gun. They both started up when he swung round on them.

"Get into the car," he said, opening the back door of the Airflow. "Make it snappy. This is a stick-up."

The women scrambled into the Airflow, terrified. He told Miss Blandish to get into the tourer. He had to jerk her out before she obeyed him. Again he saw how odd she looked in Rocco's suit. He looked at the younger woman.

"Take off that dress and give it to me," he said. "Come on, I ain't got all day, get goin'."

In the car she wriggled out of the dress, white with fear. He took the dress from her and tossed it to Miss Blandish. He leant into the Airflow. "Keep your mouths shut," he said. "The boys will get you, sure, if you report this."

He got into the tourer and drove off again. Miss Blandish held the dress on her lap. Slim said: "Further on we'll stop an' you put that dress on." She said nothing.

A mile down the road he stopped again. "Get into it," he said. She took Rocco's clothes off in the car and pulled the dress over her head. It fitted her all right. Slim rolled the discarded suit up and shoved it under the back seat. He told himself that he had to switch cars again pretty soon. Those women would raise a squeal when someone passed, which might be any time. He drove into a small town and pulled up by the post-office. He said to Miss Blandish: "You stay here. I'm goin' to 'phone. You're to stay here, understand? You ain't goin' to start any funny business. It's too late for that now."

He went into the booth. No one in the place looked at him. They were small-time stuff; just village hicks. He rang Pete. Pete was jumpy. "I can't do a thing for you," he said excitedly. "The heat's on good. The cops are all looking for you. I've had 'em in here. You're too hot for me, Slim; you know I'd give you a hand if I could, but keep out of Kansas. They are expecting you here."

Slim hung up on him, and stood before the 'phone, cursing. He didn't know where to go. He felt suddenly trapped and he began to sweat again.

He came out into the street and then stopped suddenly. An elderly man was leaning into the tourer. He was speaking to Miss Blandish. Slim paused for a moment, then he slid his hand inside his coat. He loosened his gun. The elderly man felt him staring, and he straightened. He turned so that Slim could see him. Slim saw that he wore a sheriff's badge on his coat. The man looked dumb enough, but Slim was nervous.

"What's the matter?" Slim asked, standing there with his hand inside his coat. The sheriff glanced at him curiously. "I'm tellin' the lady that she can't park here," he said.

Slim said he didn't know that. "I'll be movin'," he said, walking to the tourer with stiff legs.

The sheriff seemed burnt up with curiosity. "What's the matter with her?" he whispered to Slim. "She nuts or somethin'?"

"Yeah," Slim said, pausing for a moment. "Don't take no notice of her … lost her ma, an' it's taken her that way."

Miss Blandish had hidden her face in her hands. The sheriff blew out his fat cheeks. "Got me guessin'," he said. Slim wished him to hell. "Where you headin', stranger?"

Slim told him Kansas and got in the car. The sheriff continued to stare after them. Slim drove down the street, keeping the car steady. When he got out of the town he increased his speed. All the time he was thinking that the news had got round that he had switched cars. The bulls would be looking for this small black tourer as they had been looking for the Airflow. Once you were on the run the heat was on good, and it stayed on. It was just a matter of time before you got pinched. Slim had no illusions about that. Before you got pinched you had a chance to shoot the other guy. He would rather swap slugs than run like this. If he knew where he was going he wouldn't mind so much, but he didn't know where the hell to go. He just felt that he had to keep going so that he was one jump ahead of the bulls. They had him on the run now, and his brain could think up nothing.

The road began to mount. He was leaving the woods and getting into the hills. The mountain road twisted with sudden, sharp, hairpin bends. His foot did not relax from the pedal, and he tore up the road in second, dragging at the wheel. Half-way up, an idea struck him, and he slowed down and then stopped.

"Get out," he said to Miss Blandish. 'We're goin' to walk a bit."

He leant over her and opened the off-door, then, putting his hand under her armpit, he shoved her into the road. She stood there in the sunshine, looking across at the panorama. He climbed out of the car, leaving it in the middle of the road.

Further back, the road twisted out of sight in a sharp bend. He said: "Stay here," and walked back to the bend, so that he could see round the corner. The road was deserted. Standing on the edge of the steep hill, he could look far down into the valley, and he could see the white ribbon of the road twisting snakelike as it climbed. He walked back to the tourer and, leaning into the window, he released the hand-brake. Instantly the car began to run backwards fast. He had to throw himself clear, and sprawled in the white dust. He knelt in the road, watching the car as it gathered speed. Miss Blandish watched too.

The car reached the bend, then its wheels ran off the road. It hovered against the white wooden posts that skirted the bend. The posts began to sag, and finally bent over like candles in the sun. The car hovered, dusty in the sunlight, then it was gone. Slim remained kneeling in the road, listening to the distant crash. He got to his feet and walked over to Miss Blandish with stiff legs.

"Come on, walk," he said.

Together they began to walk up the dusty road in the hot sun. They walked slowly and in silence. Slim kept close to her, making her walk on the inside. When they breasted the top they both paused and looked back. The valley lay below like a green carpet patterned with unusual designs.

Slim sat himself on the bank, jerking Miss Blandish down beside him, "I want you to get this straight," he said; tipping his hat. "We're goin' to jump a truck, an' you gotta keep dumb. You just gotta say nothin' and do nothin'. If you start anythin' I'll start shootin', so it's up to you. I'm gettin' out of this somehow, an' I'm takin' you with me."

Miss Blandish turned and faced him. "Why don't you kill me?" she demanded fiercely. He was startled to see the wild look in her eyes. "You can't keep this up, and you know it. Why don't you get rid of me? Do you think I want to live? I don't, I tell you."

Slim told her to pipe down, uneasily. "I'll start on you in a minute," he said. He put his hands on her throat and squeezed. She let him; her hands on the grass beside her. He let her go and got to his feet. He pulled a short rubber stick from his hip pocket and threatened her with it. Instantly the wild light went out of her eyes and she cringed back. "No, no! Don't touch me with that," she said, terrified.

"Another crack from you," he said savagely, "an' you'll get it." She pulled away from him, her face twisted. She acted like an animal that is threatened with a whip. Her eyes were fixed on the stick, and she cringed back.

"Come on," he said, jerking her to her feet. "Watch out or I'll get tough. "

They walked on. The road began to wind down and the going was easy. They let their legs do the walking, the weight of their bodies carried them down the steep hill almost at a run.

A light truck overtook them after they had reached the bottom of the hill. They heard the swish of the wheels as the truck coasted, and Slim stood in the middle of the road waving his hand. The truck stopped, and the driver grinned at him. The driver was a wizened little man with a cocky, sparrowlike face, burnt brick-red with the sun and wind.

Slim wanted to know where he was going.

"Jefferson City," the driver told him. "You two want a lift?"

Slim nodded "I'll give you a couple of bucks," he said briefly "The dame's tired."

The driver opened the door 'Sure," he said "Hop up. Where do you want to go?"

Slim said Jefferson would do as well as the next. He climbed up first and sat next to the driver. Miss Blandish sat by Slim. Slim saw that his body blocked the driver's' view of Miss Blandish.

"Jim O'Keik, that's me," said the driver, releasing the brake. "Just back from haulin' a load. Business is mighty bad. This is the second time I've been back empty."

The truck was light and it bounced a little on the road. Slim stared ahead and let Keik talk. Keik kept up a flow, but he noticed that Slim said nothing. "That your wife?" he asked Slim.

"What the hell's that to you?" Slim snarled at him, his face twisting. He was getting tired of this hick's voice.

Keik looked startled and shut his mouth. They rode on in silence. Keik couldn't stay that way long. He leant forward and switched on the radio. "I put that in meself," he said proudly. "Comes in mighty handy on a long haul. I would have fallen asleep many a time without that to listen to."

The radio crackled and a thin sound came through. Someone was playing an accordion. The music sounded sad. "Ain't that swell," Keik said. Slim said nothing. He took out his nickel watch and glanced at it. "What time shall we hit Jefferson?" he asked.

"It'll take about eight hours," Keik told him. Slim grunted and relapsed into silence.

The radio suddenly crackled once more into life. "Attention, everybody. This is important. The police are looking for Slim Grisson, believed heading for Kansas City. With him is another man, small, maybe a boy. Grisson is wanted for the kidnapping of John Blandish's daughter, and also for the triple murder of another rival gang. Was last seen driving a Ford tourer, licence number XXX42. Description of wanted man is as follows …" The voice went on to give a full description of Slim. "The police think that it may be possible that Grisson's companion is the missing girl, disguised as a man. You are warned that this man is dangerous. Do not attempt to apprehend him in any way, but report immediately to the police if you think you have seen him. Please look out for anyone answering this description…."

Slim reached forward and turned the radio off. Keik said nothing, but he suddenly lost his red colour. Slim looked at him from under his hat. "Keep going," he said.

"Sure," said Keik.

They drove on.

At one-thirty in the morning, Brennan still sat in his office. A large-scale map was spread before him on the table. His hat was tilted at the back of his head, and a damp cigar, long since forgotten, gripped between his small, yellow teeth. Fenner sat near him with the telephone clamped to his ear.

Brennan said: "This guy is losing his head."

A police-officer poked his head round the door. "Mr. Blandish would like a word."

Brennan looked up with an impatient scowl, but Fenner nodded to him. "Okay, shoot him in," Brennan said.

John Blandish walked in. His face was lined with exhaustion. "Have either of you gentlemen anything to report?" he asked briefly.

Fenner hung up. "We'll have 'em by tomorrow," he said.

Brennan put a stubby finger on the map. "This guy's leaving some trail behind him," he said. Blandish leant over his shoulder, peering with short-sighted eyes at the map. "He pulled out from here with two of my boys on his heels. One of them had a blow-out. He managed to ditch the other. Mad, murderous driving. My boy was hurt bad. He went on from there to this little hick town. There he 'phoned, and the sheriff spoke to him. You know what these small-town sheriffs are; he suspected who he was, but wasn't taking any chances of a shooting-match. Before that, he held up two women, took their car and, what is more important, grabbed one of these dames' dresses. The sheriff reports there was a woman with him. We guess that must be your daughter.

"He went further on, up this mountain road here; he spills the stolen car over the side and foots it. A truck-driver reports driving him into Jefferson City. He left them on the other side of the town. I guess that driver is lucky to be alive. Grisson seems to be losing his taste for murder. Every road is being watched out of Jefferson. There is a drag-net so thick that a fly couldn't get through it. He's bound to be picked up soon."

Blandish sat down. He passed his hand wearily across his eyes. "You have done well," he said.

Brennan shrugged his massive shoulders. "Get those rats into the open and it's easy," he said. "We're going out to Jefferson City right away."

"I'll go with you," Blandish said, getting to his feet.

Fenner went over to him. "It would be better for you to stay here," he said. "There's goin' to be a battle. Grisson ain't goin' to let himself be taken alive. These hoodlums always fight when they are cornered. Jefferson City is going to take a mighty big interest in this case, an' I guess you will want a little quiet when you get your daughter back. I suggest that you fix up rooms at some hotel here, an' wait for me to bring her back. Otherwise you're going to have the Press an' God knows who causin' a riot all around you."

Blandish hesitated "I want my daughter," he said finally.

Fenner nodded understandingly. "Sure you do," he agreed, "but if you just think for a moment, you'll see what I suggest ain't a bad idea. Your daughter has had a bad time, an' we are in a better position to get her away quietly than you are. Besides, she may want an hour or so to herself before she meets her family." Fenner said this looking on the floor.

Blandish looked at him sharply. "I don't know what you mean by that," he said.

Fenner shrugged. "I don't know myself," he said shortly. "I just gotta hunch, that's all."

Blandish brooded for a moment. "Very well," he said. "You will bring her to me as quickly as possible."

Fenner nodded. "You bet I will," he said.

Blandish hesitated, as if he wanted to say something else, but then he turned to the door. "I am confident that you will do the best you can," he said.

Brennan nodded impatiently. "It's in the bag." He turned an inquiring eye on Fenner when Blandish had gone. "What's on your mind?" he asked.

Fenner sat on the edge of the desk and swung his leg. "This girl has been in the hands of these thugs for four months now," he said slowly. "You've seen pictures of her, ain't you? Well, you don't want me to tell you that she is something outa the ordinary as a looker. She's got everything that makes up a swell dame. You knocked around enough to know what those hoodlums have done to her in that time. That girl ain't goin' to be happy when we find her; most like she'll be a bit screwy.

"Ever bothered to read Grisson's record? Sure you have, well, what do you expect from a rat like that? Ain't he been inside for two charges of child assault? Did you know that he used to cut up live cats and birds with scissors when he was at school? What's he hangin' on to her for all this time? Why ain't he slit her throat an' dumped her in the drink? Ever asked yourself that? Grisson ain't ever had a record for goin' after women, but he's had a bad name for little girls. That ought to tell you something. I guess that Blandish girl has had a mean time."

Brennan swore under his breath.

"So you see I ain't goin' to be so wrong when I said that she'd like a few hours to herself before meetin' her old man."

Brennan got to his feet, "Let's go over to Jefferson City an' wait there," he said. "Heck, what a case this is!"

The door jerked open and the police-officer came in. He looked excited. "'Phone message just come through," he reported. "Grisson and the girl have been located at a farmhouse just outside Jefferson City. The farmer spotted Grisson entering one of his barns just now. He 'phoned through immediately.

There ain't a doubt that it's Grisson."

Brennan began to give orders and Fenner grabbed the telephone. He called Paula.

"Listen, Paula, they've located the girl outside Jefferson City. Yeah! This looks like the end of the case. I want you to get over there as fast as you can, I want you to go to the Bonham Hotel and arrange for a room on the top floor. Tell them that I want service and no publicity. Get food and drink up there an' a lot of flowers. I'm bringing the girl there. Get goin', sister. Take an air-taxi... step on it."

He hung up and gathered up the map. He looked round the little office, seeing nothing, his mind busy with his thoughts. "I guess that girl would be a lot better off if she were dead," he said in his mind.

Brennan had already left the office, and Fenner followed him out at a run.

Slim woke from sleep with a start. His brain instantly cleared. His gun jerked away from its holster under his coat. He lay in the darkness, listening with straining ears.

The smell of the barn was unfamiliar to him, and in the darkness he had to think for a moment where he was. He heard a rustling in the straw, and he shifted his gun round in that direction cautiously. He lay on his side, motionless, staring into the thick darkness. A faint squeaking reassured him, and he relaxed once more on the granary floor. He became aware of a faint gnawing inside him, a strong desire for food. He turned on his small pocket-flash and swung the bright beam round the loft. Miss Blandish was curled up in the straw away from him, deep in heavy sleep. Her dress was rucked up. He could see her long, slim legs and the splash of white underwear as she lay there. Her face was tear-stained and pale.

His bones ached from the hard floor. He was lying immediately on the trap-door that led down into the barn. There was no window in the loft; as long as he lay there no one could get in, nor could she escape him without waking him. He got stiffly to his feet and pulled a truss of straw from the pile in the far corner and spread it over the trap. He lay down again, making himself comfortable. It was hot and stuffy up there, and it made him drowsy. He looked once more at Miss Blandish, then he lay back.

Dimly he began to realize that the net was settling round him, drawing him into its folds. Up to now he had been content to keep moving just ahead of pursuit; but now he was getting scared. He knew that he could not keep this up for long. The constant need of food and the urgent necessity of a good hiding-place was becoming more and more difficult. He guessed Keik had reported to the police. That meant that they knew he was in the neighbourhood.

He had walked with Miss Blandish, keeping to the side-streets until he had put Jefferson City at the back of him. Exhausted, they had taken shelter for the night in the barn. The large farm had appealed to him in the darkness of the night. He told himself that he would get a car and food from the farmhouse in the morning. He vaguely wondered if they were on the telephone, and how long it would be before they reported him.

He shut his eyes impatiently from the darkness. He found that his brain was suddenly clear and full of uneasy alarm. He tried to sleep, but although his long, thin body ached for rest, his brain would not relax. He sat up again, this time savagely swearing to himself. He turned on his flash-lamp and again looked at Miss Blandish. He got to his feet and walked over to her. Turning out the light, he knelt down where she was lying. He groped for her, and slid his arm under her head. She woke with a start, trying to struggle away from him. He spoke to her, telling her to keep quiet. His hoarse voice numbed her, and she lay still, sobbing with hopeless exhaustion, while he took her with brutal urgency.

Later, sleep came to both of them again. His muffled, choking snores disturbing the rats so that they darted with alarm in the straw.

The bright sunlight coming through the warped walls of the barn woke him in the morning. He sat up quickly, listening. His mouth was dry and he was seriously hungry. Miss Blandish woke at his movement. She dragged down her dress and backed away from him miserably.

"I'm going down to talk to the farmer," he said. "You stay here an' wait. We gotta get grub somehow." He lifted the trap and looked down into the barn. It was full of farm rubbish. He climbed down the rickety wooden ladder and walked stiffly to the double doors. He opened one of them cautiously and looked out. He could see no one.

Some distance away the farmhouse stood deserted. The front door was closed. Slim looked for a long time, getting more and more uneasy. He dragged out his watch and glanced at it. He saw that it was a little after nine o'clock. He looked again at the closed door. He had always heard that farmers got up early. This looked phoney to him. He felt suddenly weak and frightened. He stood hesitating at the door of the barn, trying to make up his mind.

Suddenly he stiffened. Two cars were coming up the road, filled with men. He could see the flat blue caps and the sparkle of the sun on guns. He dodged back into the barn swiftly and pushed the door to. His gun leapt into his hand, and he began to shiver unconsciously. Through a chink in the wood he watched the men pile out of the cars. They began to run over in his direction. He fired without hesitation. The foremost cop fell to his knees. The others, with cool assurance of ultimate success, took cover behind various shelters offered by the farm rubbish that lay about the untidy yard.

Brennan and Fenner directed the second car-load to go round the back of the barn.

"This rat ain't got many shells," Brennan said. "On no account must you boys fire unless you get a chance at him on his own. We ain't takin' risks of ploughing the girl at this part of the case."

Fenner worked his way past the barn on his stomach. Feeling acutely aware of Slim and his gun, he was glad when he got out of range. He stood up and wiped his face with his sleeve. He knew now that this was the end of the case. It was just a matter of time. Grisson, caught in a net, must find his finish in death. The barn was completely surrounded. The police were lying secure behind their shelters, their guns pushed forward, and eager fingers on the triggers. Fenner was anxious not to throw away any lives, but at the same time he realized that, if Grisson could wait until nightfall, there might be an entirely different ending to what he had hoped. Under cover of the dark, Grisson might still slip through the net. Anyway, there was time yet. It was early and things ought to start soon. He grinned a little as he watched Brennan drag his heavy bulk over the rough ground. Crawling was not in his line, and he was swearing when he reached Fenner. He got stiffly to his feet.

"I'll give him a chance," he said. "Then if he wants trouble he shall have it." He cupped his fat hands over his mouth and gave Grisson a shout.

"Come on out of it with your hands in the air, Grisson," be bawled. "You're fixed, sure, so take it quietly."

His voice echoed back in the still fresh air of the morning. Grisson didn't answer.

Fenner said, "He'll try an' get the girl before he goes."

"If he ain't already rubbed her out," Brennan said uneasily. "I have a hunch this case ain't goin' to break as cleanly as it might. We've had a nice run up to now."

Inside the barn Slim stood watching through the chink in the door. He held his gun tightly and his loose mouth was closed in a bunched-up mass of wet lips. It was quite true that he was short of shells. Brennan had guessed right. He had a full magazine, but that was all. He yearned as he stood there for a Thompson gun. He cursed himself for being trapped like this, but he could think of nothing else he could have done, anyway. He heard Brennan call and he snarled silently. He wouldn't make it easy for the bastards, he told himself savagely. He wasn't going to let himself be fried. It would be a quick bullet and he'd take some of them with him.

Upstairs in the barn Miss Blandish crouched, shivering. She realized that this was the end of the nightmare and the beginning of another one. The four months that had passed were now drawing to a close. Her dazed mind refused to look back on those months. Her body, wracked and yearning for the peace of drugs, did not belong to her any more. Although she had not eaten for many hours, hunger did not torment her. She just felt weak, as if she had been very ill for a long time. With an effort she crawled over to the open trap-door and looked into the barn.

She could see Slim standing with his back to her, peeping through the trap-door. His long thin back was tense, and she saw the dull metal of his gun as he pushed it forward. She watched him raise the gun and shoot suddenly. The violence of the noise made her start back involuntarily. When she looked again he was standing still, and she could hear him muttering to himself. There was silence outside the barn. Her concentrated attention on his back was conveyed to him.

He turned slowly and they looked at each other. He, standing by the door, looking up, and she, lying stretched out, her head and shoulders framed by the trap-door, looking down at him. They stared at each other for a long time. His face was glistening with the sweat of fear. He looked almost phosphorescent in the dim barn. His lips came off his teeth and he swore at her, calling her obscene names, picking his words and hurling them at her in his hatred. She lay there, not listening, but hoping that he would shoot her. She willed him with all the strength of her mind to raise his arm and release the bullet into her. He did nothing but glare at her with his feverish yellow eyes. It did not cross his mind to kill her, otherwise he would have done so. His mind was gradually becoming paralysed. The obsession of sudden death was striking at his morale. This standing, looking out at the deserted litter of the farmyard, knowing that everywhere was a hidden death waiting for him, was gradually wearing down his nerve.

He jerked away his gaze from her, and looked once more into the yard. He thought he saw something move and he fired instantly. The noise of the shot echoed in the silence, and he saw the puff of dust and the white splinters of wood fly from the side of the cart behind which he had seen a movement

Once more he heard them shouting for him to come on out. His legs began to go back on him. He felt them suddenly weak and he realized how desperately he needed food, and what he would give for just one shot of liquor. His thin, wolfish, idiot's face began to crumple like a child's before it weeps. He fell on his knees, letting his hands slide down the rough wood of the door. He let his gun drop on the floor. Miss Blandish still lay and watched him. For a sickening moment she thought that he had been hit when he slumped down, but when he began to moan in that horrible way he had she hastily drew herself away from the trap.

Brennan, anxious to get it over, was giving orders in a low voice. Several uniformed men began to trundle a heavy cart towards the barn. They kept well behind the shelter of its heavy wooden sides, feeling that their legs were unpleasantly exposed as they moved. They kept on steadily, sweating under the labour.

Slim saw the cart coming and got to his feet. He looked hurriedly over his shoulder, but the trap-door was deserted. Then he lost his head completely. He jerked the barn door open and ran out. He held his gun forward stiffly, and his ghastly face was wild with despair. He had not taken three paces in the open before the clamour of submachine-guns broke out from all sides. He stopped running suddenly, as if he had come against an invisible wall. Blood suddenly appeared on his coat, and his gun slid out of his hand. The guns stopped as abruptly as they had started.

Fenner watched Grisson, standing bewildered in the bright sunshine, and saw him pitch forward. He knew before he reached him that he was dead. He cautiously turned him over with his foot. The yellow eyes looked up at him blankly; the thin white face, upturned, looked pathetically defenceless; the loose, fleshy mouth hung open, and Fenner turned away with a little grunt of disgust.

Brennan joined him.

"It's finished," he said.

Fenner drew a deep breath, then he walked slowly towards the barn.

It struck Fenner as he sat at the wheel with Miss Blandish at his side, that she had had all the bad breaks. He overlooked that she had lived a life of richness and had enjoyed the things that money could buy ever since she was old enough to appreciate them. Against the good things of life she had had four months with Grisson. Most people would have preferred a life of drabness to that. He believed that each person had their pre-arranged destiny to live; that, though the small things came under control, the big things were plotted like the green holes on a golf course. He felt sorry for the girl and awkward at not being able to say the right thing that might bring her comfort.

Leaving the police and Brennan at the farm, he had taken Miss Blandish away. She had not opened her mouth, nor had she looked at him after the first uncomfortable meeting. He had found her crouching in the loft. She hid her face from him as his head and shoulders appeared through the trap. He had spoken to her softly, telling her that it was finished, and that he was going to take her home. He was utterly impersonal to her, and he could see that she was glad of that. She went with him down the ladder, in her borrowed dress, looking dirty and untidy, with great, blank eyes in a white mask.

Brennan had moved his men away from the barn so that no one was there to stare at her. Brennan had shown surprising human feeling. He had taken himself off, too. The car had been run up close to the barn and left empty, with the engine running. Fenner wondered uneasily if they were all making too much of a tragedy out of this. Whether it would not have been better to have greeted her more normally, but a quick glance at her face told him that he had done right. He did not touch her when she got into the car. He stood well back and let her sink into the seat unaided. Then he ran round and slipped under the wheel, driving off at a high speed.

When they had left the farm several miles behind, he said quite casually, "I'm takin' you to a quiet hotel. Your father is in Kansas waitin' for you, but I guess you would like a rest an' some new clothes before you meet him."

She didn't say anything, but he saw her relax from her tense position. He drove on in silence. He could watch her reflection in the windscreen, and he saw that she was crying to herself. He guessed that she would be better in a little while.

The hotel was certainly quiet. Paula had done a good job of work. He got her upstairs without meeting anyone. The room that was prepared for her was loaded with flowers; their heavy scent hung in the still air, and the cleanness of the room looked invitingly secure.

She walked slowly over to the window and stood looking out at the white clouds that piled up in the blue sky. One of her hands caressed the flowers, although she did not look at them.

Fenner stood quietly by the door.

"There's food over there," he said, "an' a bathroom on your right. I've got you some clothes; you'll find 'em in the cupboard. Is there anythin' else you want?"

"Get me a drink," she said in a low voice.

"Sure, what do you want?"

She said nothing. He noticed that she was pulling the flower to pieces with feverish fingers. The petals were falling on the carpet at her feet.

He walked over to the dumb waiter that stood against the wall. He selected a bottle of Scotch and poured out a small drink. He put the bottle and the glass on the table and stood back.

"Will you go away?" she said, still standing with her back turned. He could see that her shoulders were quivering.

He stepped out of the room and softly shut the door. Then he leant against the wall and gave himself a cigarette. He tilted his hat over his eyes and waited. He was patient, and waited for some time. He just stood there, listening and smoking. He was uneasy about her, and wondered what the hell he should do next. Finally he levered himself away from the wall and looked into the room again. She was still standing looking out of the window, the glass, full of raw spirit, in her hand. He drew a sharp breath when he saw that the bottle was nearly empty.

"Why don't you eat?" he said, closing the door behind him and leaning against it.

"I don't want any food." Her voice was suddenly loud.

"Shall I ring your father? I guess he's anxious to know you're safe," he said, after a long pause.

"No!"

"I guessed you wouldn't want that," he said.

She stood hesitating, then, over her shoulder, she said: "Why do you say that?"

"I can guess what you've been through," he said, choosing his words carefully. "You want to get adjusted to things, don't you?"

She turned slowly on her heel and stood looking at him. Her face was slightly flushed, and her eyes made him uneasy. "I don't know who you are," she said, "but you have been very kind. I want to be alone now. I've got to think. Will you come and see me tomorrow? I shall be quite ready to see father tomorrow. I can't see anyone now." Her voice broke, and she quickly put her hands to her eyes.

"Sure, I'll leave you," he said gently. "But, before I go, try to relax. You've got nothin' to be scared about now. Grisson is dead ... all that's over."

She snatched her hands from her face. "No, you're wrong," she said, her voice high-pitched and hysterical. "He's not dead. He's with me now, I know he is—at first I thought I was wrong, but I know I've got him with me. I've got him inside me, he wouldn't leave me alone, ever—and he never will."

Fenner stood undecided. He blew out his cheeks and swore in his mind. He knew Blandish must handle this, and his first thought was to get him. He turned to the door and ran to the lift. Then he hesitated and turned back to the room. The door had closed behind him and, as he put his hand on the handle, he heard the lock snap to. He rapped with sudden panic, but she did not answer, He drew himself back against the wall and drove his shoulder against the door, but although it trembled it did not give. As he made another heave he heard a thin wailing scream ... it sounded a long way away. He stopped and raised his hands helplessly, then, jerking out his gun, he shot the lock away. He pushed open the door and stood looking round the empty room.

In the street there was a sudden rush of people. A shrill whistle blasted in the still air. Cars came to a hasty standstill, and people began to push forward.

A richly dressed woman, fondling a long-eared little dog, raised her head and looked inquiringly out of her car.

"Why have you stopped?" she asked her chauffeur angrily. "You know I'm late already."

"I'm sorry, madam, but there seems to have been an accident."

She lowered the window and looked out. A tall, boneless man was watching the crowd from the kerb with a bored eye. She beckoned to him and he lounged over to her.

"What has happened?" she asked, her face showing her annoyance.

He looked at her with disapproval. "Some dame gone nuts an' tossed herself outa a window," he said.

The woman leant back into her cushions and tapped impatiently on her patent-leather bag.

"How tiresome," she said irritably. Her eyes suddenly looked hungry, and she felt an envious pang. "How disgusting of her," she said to herself. "I suppose she made a fool of herself over some man."

She was sorry when the car took her away from the curious, gaping crowd that the police held back with difficulty.

THE END

Twelve Chinamen and a Woman

by James Hadley Chase

I

Fenner opened one eye as Paula Dolan put some elegant curves and her fluffy head round his office door. He regarded her vaguely, and then settled himself more comfortably. His large feet rested on the snowy blotting-pad, and the swivelled desk-chair inclined perilously at an angle of 45°. He said sleepily, "Run away, Dizzy, I'll play with you later. Right now I'm thinking."

Some more curves filtered through the half-open door, and Paula came to the desk. "Wake up, Morpheus," she said; "you've got a client."

Fenner groaned. "Tell him to go away. Tell him we've gone outta business. I gotta catch up some sleep sometimes, haven't I?"

"What's your bed for?" Paula said impatiently.

"Don't ask questions like that," Fenner mumbled, settling himself further down in the chair.

"Snap out of it, Dave," Paula pleaded; "there's a passion flower waiting outside, and she looks as if she's got a load of grief to share with you."

Fenner opened an eye again. "What's she like?" he asked. "Maybe she's collecting for some charity."

Paula sat on the edge of the desk. "Sometimes I wonder why you keep that plate on your door. Don't you want to do business?"

Fenner shook his head. "Not if I can help it," he said. "We're in the dough, ain't we? Let's take it easy."

"You're passing up something pretty good. Still, if that's the way you feel..." Paula slid off the desk.

"Hey, wait a minute." Fenner sat up and pushed his hat off his eyes. "Is she really a passion flower?"

Paula nodded. "I guess she's in trouble, Dave."

"Okay, okay, send her in, send her in."

Paula opened the door. She said, "Will you come in?"

A voice said, "Thank you," and a young woman came in. She walked slowly past Paula, looking at Fenner with large, smoky-blue eyes.

She was a shade taller than average, and pliantly slender. Her legs were long, her hands and feet narrow, and her body was very erect. Her hair, curling under her prim little hat, was raven black. She wore a severe two-piece costume, and she looked very young and very scared.

Paula gave her an encouraging smile and went out, shutting the door quietly behind her.

Fenner took his feet off the desk and stood up. "Sit down," he said, "and tell me what I can do for you." He indicated the arm-chair by his desk.

She shook her head. "I'd rather stand," she said breathlessly. "I may not be here very long."

Fenner sat down again. "You can do just what you like here," he said soothingly. "This place is anyone's home."

They remained looking at each other for a long minute. Then Fenner said, "You know you'd better sit down. You've got a lot to tell me, an' you look tired."

He could see she wasn't scared of him, she was scared of something that he didn't know anything about. Her eyes were uneasy, and she held her high-breasted body as though she was ready to jump for the door.

Again she shook her head. "I want you to find my sister," she said breathlessly. "I'm so worried about my sister. What will it cost? I mean, what are your fees?"

Fenner squinted at the inkwell by his hand. "Suppose you don't worry your head about the cost. Just relax an' tell me all about it," he said. "Tell me who you are for a start."

The telephone jangled at his elbow. The effect on the girl was startling. She took two quick graceful steps away from the 'phone, and her eyes went cloudy and big.

Fenner grinned at her. "I guess I get the same way," he said quietly, pulling the receiver towards him. "When I fall asleep an' the bell goes off, I guess it scares the shirt right off my back."

She stood very tense by the door, watching him.

Fenner said, "Excuse me a moment," as he took off the receiver. "Yeah?" he said.

There was a lot of crackling on the line. Then a man said with a very liquid accent: "Fenner?"

"Yeah."

"Any moment now, Fenner, a girl is going to call in and see you. I want you to hold her until I get round to your office. I'm on my way now. Do you understand?"

Fenner let his eyes fall on the girl, and he smiled at her reassuringly. "I don't get it," he said to the telephone.

"Well, listen, only get this right. A girl will come and see you about a story of her missing sister. Well, hold her for me. She's suffering from delusions. She got away from an asylum yesterday, and I know she's heading for your office. Just hold her for me."

Fenner pushed his hat on to the bridge of his nose. "Who in hell are you?" he said.

There was more crackling on the wire. "I'll explain when I get around. I'm coming right away. Your fee will be paid on a generous scale if you do this."

Fenner said, "Okay, you come on up."

The girl said, "Did he say I was crazy?" The hand that wasn't holding her bag fluttered up and down the seam of her skirt.

Fenner put the receiver on its prong. He nodded shortly.

She shut her eyes for a second, then her lids rolled back like a doll's that has been sat up suddenly. She said desperately, "It's so difficult not to believe him." Then she put her bag on the desk, stripped off her gloves and hastily pulled off her coat. Fenner sat quite still, his hand on the telephone, watching her. She gave a little sob and then, with trembling fingers, she began to undo her shirt blouse.

Fenner shifted. "You don't have to do this," he said uneasily. "I'm interested in your case without any act."

Once again she caught her breath in a sob and turned her back on him. She pulled the blouse off. Fenner's hand strayed to the bell. Maybe this dame was nutty, and was going to hold him up for assault. Then he stiffened and took his hand away. Her back showed distinct, livid bruises, startlingly vivid against her white skin. Some of them were in the shape of finger-prints. She put on the blouse again, fastened the buttons, and then put on her coat. Then she turned round and looked at Fenner with her eyes bigger than ever.

"Now do you believe I'm in trouble?" she said.

Fenner shook his head. "You didn't have to do that," he said. "You came to me for help. Okay, why look further? You don't have to be scared."

She stood there, torturing her lower lip with her glistening teeth. Then she opened her bag and took out a roll of notes. She put them on the desk. "Will that do as a retainer?"

Fenner touched the roll with a thick finger. Without actually counting the money he couldn't be sure, but he was willing to bet that there was at least six grand in that roll. He got up swiftly, picked up the roll, and stepped to the door. "Stay here," he said, and went outside into the outer office.

Paula was sitting at the typewriter, her hands in her lap and her eyes expectant.

Fenner said, "Grab your hat quick, an' take this baby to the Baltimore Hotel. Get her a room there and tell her to lock herself in. Take this roll and when you've fixed her, sock it in the bank. Find out all you can about her. Tell her I'll look after her. Give her the you're-in-good-hands dope. Feed her a good line of syrup. She's got the jitters; she's in trouble and she's still young enough to need a mother."

He went back to the office. "What's your name?" he said.

The girl beat her hands together. "Do get me away from here," she said.

Fenner put his hand on her arm. "I'm sending you out with my secretary. She'll look after you. There's a guy on his way up who's interested in you. I'll take care of him. What's your name?"

"Marian Daley," she said. Then she swallowed and went on hurriedly: "Where shall I go?"

Paula came in, pulling on her gloves. Fenner nodded. "Go with Miss Dolan," he said. "Go down the back way. You'll be okay now. Don't get scared any more."

Marian Daley gave him a timid little smile. "I'm glad I came to you," she said. "You see, I'm in a lot of trouble. It's my sister as well. What can she want with twelve Chinamen?"

Fenner blew out his cheeks. "Search me," he said, leading her to the door. "Maybe she likes Chinamen. Some people do, you know. Just take it easy until I see you to-night."

He stepped into the passage and watched them walk to the elevator. When the cage shot out of sight he wandered back into the office. He shut the door softly behind him and went over to his desk. He opened the top drawer and took out a .38 police special. He was playing hunches. He put the gun inside his coat and sat down behind the desk. He put his feet up again and shut his eyes.

He sat like that for ten minutes or so, his mind busy with theories. Three things intrigued him: The six thousand dollars, the bruises on the girl's back and the twelve China men. Why all that dough as a retainer? Why didn't she just tell him that someone had bruised her instead of stripping? Why tell him *twelve* Chinamen? Why not just say, 'What did she want with Chinamen'? Why twelve? He shifted in his seat. Then there was the guy on the 'phone. Was she fresh from a nut farm after all? He doubted it. She had been badly scared, but she was normal enough. He opened his eyes and glanced at the small chromium clock on his desk. She had been gone twelve minutes. How long would this guy take to come up?

As he was thinking, he became aware that he was not concentrating as he should. Half his mind was listening to someone whistling outside in the corridor. He moved irritably and brought his mind back to the immediate problem. Who was Marian Daley? Obviously she was a rich girl of the upper crust. Her clothes must have cost a nice pile of dough. He wished the guy outside would stop whistling. What was the tune, anyway? He listened. Then very softly he began to hum the mournful strains of *Chloe* with the whistler.

The haunting tune held him, and he stopped humming and listened to the fluting sound, beating out the time with his index finger on the back of his hand. Then he suddenly felt a little chilled. Whoever was whistling was not moving. The low penetrating sound kept at the same degree of loudness, as if the whistler was standing outside his door, whistling to him.

Fenner took his feet off his desk very softly and eased the chair away gently. The mournful tune continued. He put his hand inside his coat and felt the butt of the .38. Although there was only one entrance to his office, and that was through the outer office, he had an exit in his own office, which he kept locked. This door led to the back entrance of the block. It was from outside this exit that the whistling was coming.

He walked to the door and softly turned the key in the lock, carefully keeping his shadow from falling on the frosted panel. As he eased the door handle and gently began to open the door, the whistling stopped abruptly. He stepped out into the corridor and looked up and down. There was no one about. Moving fast, he went to the head of the staircase and looked down into the well. The place was deserted. Turning, he walked the length of the corridor and looked down the well of the other flight of stairs. Still nothing to see.

Pushing his hat on to the bridge of his nose, he stood listening. Faintly, he could hear the roar of the traffic floating up from the street, the whine of the elevators as they raced between floors, and the persistent ticking of the big clock above his head. He walked slowly back to his office and stood in the open doorway, his nerves a little tense. As he went in and shut the door the whistling started again.

His eyes went very bleak and he walked into the outer office, the .38 in his hand. He stopped just in the doorway and grunted. A small man in a black shabby suit sat hunched up in one of the padded chairs reserved for visitors. His hat was pulled so far down that Fenner could not see his face. Fenner knew by just looking at him that he was dead. He put the gun into his hip pocket and moved nearer. He looked at the small yellow bony hands that rested limply in the man's lap. Then he leant forward and pulled the hat off the man's head.

He was not a pleasant sight. He was a Chinaman all right. Someone had cut his throat, starting just under his right ear and going in a neat half-circle to his left ear. The wound had been stitched up neatly, but just the same, the Chinaman was quite a nightmare to see.

Fenner blotted his face with his handkerchief. "Quite a day," he said softly.

As he stood, wondering what the hell to do next, the telephone began to ring. He went over to the extension, shoved the plug in and picked up the receiver.

Paula sounded excited. "She's gone, Dave," she said. "We got as far as the Baltimore and then she vanished."

Fenner blew out his cheeks. "You mean someone snatched her?"

"No. She just took a runout on me. I was fixing up her room at the desk, turned my head, saw her beating it for the exit, and by the time I got into the street she'd gone."

"What about the dough?" Fenner said. "That gone too?"

"That's safe enough. Right now that's in the bank. But what am I going to do? Shall I come on back?"

Fenner looked at the Chinaman. "Hang around the Baltimore and buy yourself a lunch. I'll come on out when I'm through. Right now I've got a client."

"But, Dave, what about the girl? Hadn't you better come now?"

Fenner was inclined to be impatient. "I'm runnin' this office," he said shortly. "Every minute I keep this guy waitin' he gets colder and colder, an' believe me, it ain't with rage." He dropped the receiver into its cradle and straightened up. He looked at the Chinaman unemotionally. "Well, come on, Percy," he said. "You an' I gotta take a walk."

Paula sat in the Baltimore lounge until after three o'clock. She had worked herself up to a severe tension when, at quarter-past three, Fenner came across the lounge fast, his eyebrows meeting in a heavy frown of concentration and his eyes hard and frosty. He said, pausing just long enough to pick up her coat lying on a vacant chair beside her, "Come on, baby, I wantta talk to you."

Paula followed him into the cocktail lounge, which was almost empty. Fenner led her to a table at the far end of the room, opposite the entrance. He took some care to pull the table away from the wall, so that he could sit facing the swing-doors.

"Are you usin' booze as perfume these days," he said, sitting down, "or do you think we can get some hard liquor in this joint?"

"That's a nice crack," Paula said; "what else can a girl do in a place like this? I've only had three martini's. What's the idea? I've been sitting on my tail for three hours now."

Fenner beckoned to a waiter. "Don't say tail. It's vulgar." He ordered two double Scotches and some ginger-ale. He sat with his back turned to Paula and watched the waiter order the drinks and bring them all the way back. When the waiter had set them down he reached out and poured one of the doubles into the other glass, filled the empty glass half full of ginger-ale and pushed it over to Paula. "You gotta watch your complexion, Dizzy," he said, and poured half the neat Scotch down his throat.

Paula sighed. "Well, come on," she said impatiently, "let me in on the ground floor. I've been out of circulation for three hours."

Fenner lit a cigarette and leant back in his chair. "You're quite sure Miss Daley walked out on you without any persuasion?"

Paula nodded. "It was like I told you. I went up to the desk and started making arrangements for a room. She was standing behind me. I took off my glove to sign the book and I felt sort of lonely. I looked round and there she was drifting into the street. She was on her own and moving fast. By the time I'd got through the revolving door she'd gone. I tell you, Dave, I got a nasty shock.

What was worrying me more than anything was I'd got all that money on me.
I guess you were nuts to have given it to me."

Fenner grinned unpleasantly. "You don't know just how smart I was,
baby," he said. "I guess I did myself a nice turn sending you out with that
dough. Anyway, go on."

"I went back to the hotel, asked for an envelope, put the money in and gave
it to the cashier to hold. Then I shot out into the street and had a look round;
didn't get anywhere, so I 'phoned you."

Fenner nodded. "Okay. If you're sure she ran out without some guy pushin'
her to it, we'll let it ride for a moment."

Paula said, "I'm positive!"

"Now let me tell you somethin'. There's somethin' mighty phoney about
this business. Someone planted a dead Chink in the outer office after you'd
gone, and tipped the cops."

Paula sat up. "A dead Chink?"

Fenner smiled mirthlessly. "Yeah. This Chink had a slit in his throat and had
been dead some time. He would want some explainin' away. Soon as I saw
him, I asked myself why. Either that guy was left as a warnin' or else a plant.
I wasn't takin' any chances, so I moved him out quick and tossed him in an
empty office at the end of the corridor. Well, I was right. It was a plant. I had-
n't got back more than a few minutes before three tough bulls bust in. They
were lookin' for that Chink, and, believe me, it took all I had not to laugh in
their faces."

"But why?" Paula asked, her eyes very wide.

"Suppose they found him there? I should have been taken down to the sta-
tion and held. That's what was wanted. To get me out of the way long enough
to catch up with this Daley dame. These bulls softened up a lot when they
found nothin' to holler about, but they searched the two offices. I had my fingers crossed. If they had found that six grand it might have taken a little explainin' away."

Paula said, "But what's all this mean?"

"Search me. It just amuses me; but it don't mean anythin' yet. What did you
get out of Miss Daley?"

Paula shook her head. "She just wasn't talkin'. I asked her the usual line for
our records, but she said she would only talk to you."

Fenner finished his Scotch and stubbed out his cigarette. "Investigation
seems about to peter out," he said. "We're six grand to the good an' no work
to do for it."

"But you won't sit around doin' nothing?"

"Why not? She paid me the dough, didn't she? Then when I fix it so she can
talk in comfort she blows. Why should I worry? When she wants more ad-

vice she'll contact me."

An elderly man with a lean face, all nose and chin, came into the lounge and sat down a few tables from them. Paula looked at him curiously. She thought by the look of his eyes he'd been weeping. She wondered why. Fenner broke into her thoughts.

"What did you think of this Daley dame?" he said abruptly.

Paula knew what he wanted. "She was educated. Her clothes were class and cost plenty. She was scared about something. I could guess at her age, but I'd most likely make a mistake. I'd say twenty-four. I might be six years out either way. If she was anything but a good girl, she was a good actress. Her makeup was mild and she'd been living in the sun a lot. She was modest—"

Fenner nodded his head. "I was waiting for that. Sure, she was the modest type. Then why should she take off her clothes to show me her bruises?"

Paula put her glass down and stared at him. "This is a new one," she said.

"Oh, I'll get round to everythin' in time." Fenner waved his glass at the waiter. "You don't know about the guy who 'phoned me while I was talkin' to her an' told me she was nuts. That's when she went into the strip-tease. That's what's gettin' me. It don't line up with her type. She just took off her coat and blouse and stood around the office in her brassière. It don't add up."

"Someone had bruised her?"

"I'll say someone had bruised her. The marks on her back looked like they were painted on, they were so vivid."

Paula thought for a moment. "Maybe she was scared that you'd think she was crazy and, by showing you that, you'd see she was in a jam."

Fenner nodded. "It might go like that, but I don't like it."

While the waiter was fixing him another drink, Paula glanced at the elderly man again. She said to Fenner, "Don't look now, but there's a man over there taking a great interest in you."

"What of it?" Fenner said impatiently. "Maybe he likes my face."

"It couldn't be that. I guess he thinks you're made up for the films."

The elderly man got up abruptly and came over. He stood uncertain, and he looked so sad that Paula gave him an encouraging smile. He addressed himself to Fenner.

"You'll excuse me," he said, "but are you Mr. Fenner?"

"That's right," Fenner said without any enthusiasm.

"My name's Lindsay. Andrew Lindsay. I wanted your help."

Fenner shifted restlessly. "I'm glad to know you, Mr. Lindsay," he said, "but I couldn't be any help to you."

Lindsay looked disconcerted. His eyes wandered to Paula and then back to Fenner.

"Won't you sit down, Mr. Lindsay?" Paula said.

Fenner shot her a hard look, but Paula wouldn't see it.

Lindsay hesitated and then sat down.

Paula went on with a show of manners that almost embarrassed Fenner. "Mr. Fenner's a very busy man, but I've never known him to turn down anyone who was in trouble."

Fenner thought, "This little smartie's goin' to get smacked when we're alone." He nodded his head at Lindsay because he had to. "Sure," he said. "What's bitin' you?"

"Mr. Fenner, I've read about how you found the Blandish girl when she was kidnapped. I'm in the same trouble. My little girl disappeared yesterday." Two tears ran down his thin face. Fenner shifted his eyes. "Mr. Fenner, I'm asking you to help find her. She was all I had, and God knows what has become of her."

Fenner finished his whisky and put the glass down on the table with a click. "You've told the police?" he said abruptly.

Lindsay nodded.

"Kidnappin' is a Federal offence. I can't do better'n the F.B.I. You must be patient. They'll turn her up."

"But, Mr. Fenner—"

Fenner shook his head. He got to his feet. "I'm sorry but I can't get round to it."

Lindsay's face puckered like a disappointed child's. He put out his hand and held on to Fenner's sleeve.

"Mr. Fenner, do this for me. You won't regret it. You can charge what you like. You can find my little girl sooner than anyone. I know you can. Mr. Fenner, I beg you to do this."

Fenner's eyes were chips of ice. He took Lindsay's hand off his arm gently but firmly. "Listen," he said. "I'm my own boss; I don't work for anyone. If I want to take an assignment, I take it. If I don't, I turn it down. Right now, I've got something that's giving me an itch. I'm sorry your kid's got herself into trouble, but I can't do anythin' about it. The F.B.I. is big enough to take care of your daughter and hundreds of other guys' daughters. I'm sorry, but I'm not doing it."

He jerked his head at Paula and walked out of the lounge. Lindsay dropped his hands helplessly, and began to cry very quietly. Paula patted his arm. Then she got up and went out of the lounge. Fenner was standing waiting for her. He said savagely, as she walked up,

"You must start crimpin'. What the hell do you think we're runnin'—a dog's home?"

Paula gave him a mean look. "That old guy's lost his daughter; doesn't that mean anything to you?"

"It means a pain in the neck to me, that's all," Fenner snapped. "Come on back to the office—we've got work to do."

"There are times when I think you're cute," Paula said bitterly, moving towards the reception hall. "But right now I'd swop you for a lead nickel and a bad smell."

A tall young man uncurled himself from one of the big lounges and stepped up to Fenner. "I'm Grosset of the D.A.'s office. I want to talk to you."

Fenner grunted. "I'm busy right now, pal," he said. "Call round at my office to-morrow some time, when I'm out."

Grosset apologetically indicated two big cops in plain clothes who stood right in Fenner's exit. "We can talk here, or at my office," he said primly.

Fenner grinned. "A hold-up? Okay, let's talk here, and quick."

Paula said, "I've forgotten something. I'll be right back." She left them and went back into the cocktail lounge. Lindsay was still sitting there. She sat down beside him. "You mustn't feel that Mr. Fenner means to be unkind," she said softly. "He's got a case that's worrying him. He gets like that. He doesn't mean anything."

Lindsay raised his head and looked at her. "I guess I shouldn't have asked him," he said helplessly; "but my little girl means a lot to me."

Paula opened her bag and took out a flat note-book. "Give me the facts," she said. "I can't promise anything, but I might be able to persuade him."

The heavy eyes lit up a little hopefully. "I can do that," he said huskily. "What facts do you want?"

In the lounge outside, Fenner followed Grosset to a quiet corner and sat down with him. He was very watchful and distrusting.

Grosset was smooth, just a shade too smooth. He flicked open a thin gold cigarette-case and offered it to Fenner. He then lit the two cigarettes with a gold lighter.

Fenner said dryly, "You guys live well."

Grosset said, "I don't think we've run into you before." He crossed his legs, showing black-and-white check socks. "I've checked your licence. You were the guy who made so much money out of the Blandish kidnapping case. That was when you were a down-at-heel investigator new on the job. You got a lucky break and you pulled out of Kansas and put up a plate here. That's right, isn't it?"

Fenner forced a long stream of smoke down his nostrils. "You're tellin' the story," he said; "you've got it right up to now."

Grosset looked wise. "You've been in New York six months. You don't seem to have done much in that time."

Fenner yawned. "I pick an' choose," he said indifferently.

"We got a pretty hot tip about you this morning." Fenner sneered pleasantly.

"Yeah? So hot you sent some bulls out to haul me in and they went away with fleas in their ears."

Grosset smiled. "Since then, we've looked over the block," he said. "We've found a murdered Chinaman in an empty office near yours."

Fenner raised his eyebrows. "What you squawking about? Want me to find who killed him for you?"

"The tip we got this morning was about a dead Chinaman who was to be found in your office."

"Ain't that sad? What happened? Did they plant him in the wrong room?"

Grosset dropped his cigarette butt into the ash-tray.

"Listen, Fenner, you and I don't have to fight. I'll put my cards on the table. That Chink had been dead thirty-six hours. The tip was clumsy and we guessed it was a plant, but we had to look into it. Well, we're interested in this Chinaman. We want to get a line on him. Suppose you give us your angle of this?"

Fenner scratched his nose.

"Brother," he said, "I feel like I want to beat a drum in the Salvation Army after that speech. If I knew a thing about it, I'd tell you. If that Chink meant anything to me I'd give it to you fast, but he doesn't. I've never had a Chink in my office. I've never set eyes on your dead Chink, and I hope to God I never will."

Grosset looked at him thoughtfully. "I've heard you were like that," he said gloomily. "You like to run on your own and then turn the whole thing over to us after you've got it sewn up. All right, if that's the way you want to play it, go ahead. If we can help you, we will, but if you get into trouble we'll crack down on you so hard you'll think the Empire State building is on your neck."

Fenner grinned and got to his feet. "All set?" he said. "If you're through, I got some work to do."

Grosset nodded. "Hang around, Fenner; I'll be seeing you again before long." He jerked his head at his two watch dogs, and the three of them walked out of the lobby.

Paula came out of the cocktail lounge and caught up with Fenner as he moved to the exit. He said, "Where have you been?"

"Listen, Dave," she said, "I've been talking to Mr. Lindsay. I've got a record of what's been happening to his daughter. Why don't you have a look at it?"

Fenner regarded her with a cold eye. "You wearin' your armour-platin'?"

"What's it to you what I'm wearing?"

"Only when I get you back to the office I'm goin' to apply somethin' pretty hard to it, an', baby, you'll keep perpen dicular for a fortnight after I'm through with you. And listen, not another word about Lindsay and his daughter. I ain't interested, I've never been interested, and I never will be in-terested. I've got enough on my mind to last me a lifetime."

"Considering the size of your mind, it doesn't surprise me," Paula said coldly, and followed him out into the street.

Back in his office, Fenner went straight to his desk and sat down. He lit a cigarette and shouted to Paula. "Come on in, Dizzy."

Paula slid through the door and sat down at his elbow, her pencil poised over her note-book. Fenner shook his head. "I ain't dictating," he said. "I want you to keep me com pany."

Paula folded her hands in her lap. "Okay," she said. "I'll be your stooge."

Fenner brooded. "Maybe I could get an angle if I turned that money over to the cops to track up. I should be lettin' 'em in if I did. Grosset is worried about the Chink. He'll keep his eye on me. Anythin' I do is goin' to be shared with that bright boy."

"Why not? He might find the girl for you if you let him have a chance."

Fenner shook his head. "I'm still playin' hunches," he said. "Somethin' tells me that the cops are best outta this."

Paula glanced at the clock. It was getting on to five. "I've got some work to do," she said. "You won't get any where right now."

Fenner said impatiently, "Stick around, stick around. Ain't you on my pay-roll no more?"

Paula settled herself more comfortably. When he was like this she knew it was better to let him have his way.

"Unless this dame contacts me, the case will peter out. I've got no lead to go on. I don't know who she is. She might come from anywhere. All I know is she's got a sister who's interested in twelve Chinamen. If the dead Chink was one of them, there are only eleven for her to be interested in now. Why did she give me all that dough, and then take it on the lam?"

"Suppose she saw someone she knew, got scared, and lost her head?" Paula put in softly.

Fenner thought this one over. "Did you see anyone who might have given her a scare?"

Paula shook her head. "You know what the Baltimore lobby's like that time of day."

"It's an idea." Fenner got up and began walking up and down the gaily pat-terned carpet. "If that's how it went, then we've gotta stick around this tele-phone for her to ring back. Maybe she won't ring, but if she does, I want to know about it quick."

Paula groaned.

"Yeah, I guess you'd better run home, pack a bag an' move in. You can sleep on the lounge."

Paula got to her feet. "You go home and sleep in your nice warm bed, I take it?"

"Never mind what I do. I'll let you know where you can get me."

Paula put on her hat and coat. "If the office downstairs knows that I'm sleepin' here, they'll begin to think things."

"That's all right. They know I'm particular. It won't blow into a scandal."

Paula swept out, shutting the door with a firm click behind her. Fenner grinned and grabbed the telephone. He dialled a number.

"D.A. office? Give me Grosset. Tell him Fenner wants him."

Grosset came through after a barrage of crackles. "Hello, Fenner. You changed your mind and want to talk?"

Fenner grinned into the receiver.

"Not just yet, pal," he said. "I want you to talk instead. This Chink you found lyin' around. Did you find anythin' on him that might help?"

Grosset laughed. "By God, Fenner! You've got a nerve. You don't expect information from me, do you?"

Fenner said seriously: "Listen, Grosset, this case hasn't started to break yet. I got a hunch that when it does, some one's goin' to yell murder. I want to stop it before it starts."

"I warn you, Fenner, if you're holding back anything it's going to be just too bad for you. If something happens that I could've stopped, and I find you knew about it, I'm going to ride you."

Fenner shifted in his chair.

"Skip it, Jughead," he said impatiently. "You know I'm in my rights to keep my client covered. If you like to play ball an' give me the information, I'll turn it back to you with interest if I think trouble's startin'. How's that?"

"You're a smooth bird," Grosset said doubtfully. "Still, what I know won't be much good. We found nothing."

"How did they get him in?"

"That wasn't so difficult. They brought him in a big laundry basket, up the trade entrance, and unpacked him in an empty office before shooting him into your room."

"Don't try to pull that one," Fenner said. "They didn't bring him to me. They left him in the empty office."

Grosset made a noise like tearing calico.

"Did anyone see the guys who brought him?"

"No."

"Well, thanks, pal. I'll do the same for you one day. Nothin' else? Nothin' that seemed odd to you?"

"Well, no, I don't think so. Someone had cut his throat and sewn it up for him—that's odd, I suppose."

"Yeah, but I could see that. Nothing else, huh?"

"I guess not."

Fenner hung the receiver on its prong. He sat staring at the telephone for several minutes, his face blank, and a puzzled look clouding his eyes.

Paula, coming back a couple of hours later, found him sitting slouched in his chair, his feet on the desk, tobacco ash all over his coat, and the same puzzled look in his eyes.

She put a small suit-case on the lounge and took off her hat and coat. "Anything break?"

Fenner shook his head. "If it wasn't for that dead Chink, I'd write it off as easy money. Those guys wouldn't have risked carting the stiff all the way up to my office unless they were mighty anxious to get me out of the way."

Paula opened her case and took out a book. "I've had my dinner," she said, sitting in the padded chair near the desk. "I'm all set. If you want to be excused, you can go."

Fenner nodded. He got up and brushed himself down. "Okay," he said. "I'll be back in a little while. If she rings, tell her I want to see her bad. Get her address and still feed her syrup. I want to get close to that dame."

"I was afraid of that," Paula murmured, but Fenner went to the door without hearing her.

Just outside, two men, dressed in black suits, stood shoulder to shoulder. They looked like Mexicans, but they weren't. Fenner thought they were Spicks, but then he wasn't sure. Each of them had his right hand in the coat pocket of his tight-fitting suit. They were dressed alike: all in black, black fedoras, white shirts and dazzling ties. They looked like some turn that comes first on a vaudeville bill, only when you got a look at their eyes you began to think of snakes and things that haven't any legs.

Fenner said, "Want to see me?" He knew without being told that two guns were pointed at his belly. The bulge in the coat pockets couldn't lie.

The shorter of the two said, "Yeah, we thought we'd drop in."

Fenner moved back into the office. Paula slid open the desk drawer and put her hand on Fenner's .38. The short guy said, "Hold it." He talked through his teeth, and he made his message convincing.

Paula sat back and folded her hands in her lap.

The short man walked into the outer office and looked round. There was a puzzled expression on his face. He went over to the big cupboard where Paula kept the sta tionery and looked inside. Then he grunted.

Fenner said, "If you'll care to wait, we can give you a hot meal and a bed. We like you guys to feel at home."

The short man picked up the heavy ash-tray that was by his hand and looked at it thoughtfully, then he smacked Fenner across his face with it very hard. Fenner dropped his head on his chest, but he didn't move quickly enough. The embossed edges of the tray caught him high up on the side of his face.

The other man pulled out a blunt-nosed automatic from his pocket and jammed it into Paula's side. He jammed it so hard that she cried out.

The short man said, "Start something and we'll spread the twist's guts on the mat."

Fenner pulled out his handkerchief from his breast pocket and held it to his face. The blood ran down his hand as he did so, and stained his shirt cuff. "Maybe we'll meet again," he said through his teeth.

"Back up against the wall. I want to look this place over," the short man said. "Get goin' before I hang another one on you."

Fenner suddenly recognized them as Cubans. They were the kind you ran into on the waterfront of any coast town if you went far enough south. He stood with his back to the wall, his hands raised to his shoulders. He was so furious that he'd've taken his chance and started something if Paula hadn't been there. He somehow felt that these two were just a shade too tough to take chances.

The short Cuban ran his hands over Fenner. "Take your coat off and give it to me," he said.

Fenner tossed it at him. The Cuban sat on the edge of the desk and felt through the lining very carefully. He took out Fenner's note-case and examined that. Then he dropped the coat to the floor. Again he went up to Fenner and patted him all over. Fenner could smell the spiced food he had been eating recently. His fingers itched to grab him round the neck.

The Cuban stepped back and grunted. He then turned his head. "You—come here."

Paula's mouth set in a line, but she stood up and took a step forward. "Don't put your filthy hands on me," she said quietly.

The Cuban said something to the other man in Spanish. The other man jerked his head at Fenner. "You come here."

Fenner moved across the room, and, as he went past, the short Cuban hit him on the back of his head with his gun butt. Fenner went down on his knees, dizzily, and fell forward on his hands. The Cuban kicked at him with his square-toed shoe, catching him where his collar ended, below his ear in the soft part of his neck. It was a very hard kick and Fenner rolled over on his side.

Paula opened her mouth to scream, but the other Cuban poked her with his gun barrel low down. Instead of scream ing, she caught her breath in agony and folded up at the knees.

The Cuban caught her under the armpits and held her straight. The short man searched her. He didn't find what he was looking for, and with a vicious spurt of rage he slapped her with his open hand. The other Cuban tossed her on the lounge and then sat on the corner of the table.

The short Cuban searched the office quickly. He didn't make any mess, and he acted as if he'd done that sort of job many times before. Then he went into the outer office and searched that, too.

Fenner heard him moving about, but he couldn't get his muscles working. He tried to get up, but nothing moved at his frantic efforts. A red mist of rage and pain hung like a curtain before his eyes.

It was only when they had gone, slamming the office door behind them, that he managed to drag himself up from the floor. He put his hand on the desk to support himself, and looked round the office wildly.

Paula was sitting in a huddle on the lounge. She was crying with rage. "Don't look at me, damn you!" she said. "Don't look at me!"

Fenner lurched into the outer office and into the small washroom on the left. He ran the cold water into the hand basin and bathed his face carefully. The water was very red when he had finished. He walked a little more steadily to the wall cupboard and found a half-bottle of Scotch and two glasses. He took a long drink. His head ached like hell. The Scotch burnt him, but it knitted him together. He poured another two ounces into the other glass and wandered back into the office.

Paula had got herself straightened out. She was still crying quietly.

Fenner put the Scotch on the edge of the desk, near her. "Put it down, baby," he said. "It's what you want."

She looked at him and then at the Scotch. Then she reached forward and snatched up the glass. Her eyes blazed in her white face. She threw the whisky in his face.

Fenner stood very still, then he took out his bloodstained handkerchief and wiped his face. Paula put her face in her hands and began to cry properly. Fenner sat down behind his desk. He unpeeled his whisky-soaked collar and dropped it into the trash basket, then he wiped his neck carefully with the handkerchief.

They sat there for several minutes, the silence only broken by the harsh sound of Paula's sobs. Fenner felt like hell. The back of his head threatened to split open. The side of his face ached with a deadly throb, and the grazed, livid bruise on his neck smarted from the whisky. He selected a cigarette from his case with fingers that trembled a little.

Paula stopped crying. "So you think you're tough," she said, without taking her head from her hands. "You think you're good, do you? You let two cheap gunmen walk in here and do this to us? My God, Dave! You're slipping.

You've got soft and you've got yellow. I teamed up with you because I thought you could look after yourself and you could look after me, but I was wrong. You sat around and got soft ... do you hear? You're yellow and you're soft! Then what do you do? You let them walk out of here and you crawl round to the bottle. Okay, Dave Fenner, I'm through."

She beat the cushions with her clenched fists and began sobbing again. Then she said:

"Oh, Dave ... Dave ... how could you let them do that to me?"

While she had been talking Fenner just sat there, his face wooden. His eyes were half shut, and they looked like chips of ice. He said, when she had finished, "You're right, honey. I've been sittin' around too long." He got to his feet. "Don't run out on me now. Just take things easy for a day or so. Shut up the office. I'm goin' to be busy." He jerked open his desk drawer, snatched up the .38, shoved it down the front of his trouser band and adjusted the points of his vest to cover the butt. Then he walked quickly out of the office, shutting the door behind him.

An hour later, changed and neat again, Fenner thumbed a cab and gave a down-town address. As he was rushed through the heavy evening traffic he sat staring woodenly before him. Only his tightly clenched fists, that lay on each knee, indicated his suppressed feelings.

The cab swerved off Seventh Avenue and plunged into a noisy back street. A moment later it stopped, and Fenner climbed out. He tossed a dollar to the driver and picked his way across the pavement, avoiding the group of fighting kids milling around his feet.

He ran up a long flight of worn steps and rang the bell. The door opened after a while, and an old, disreputable woman squinted at him.

"Ike in?" he said shortly.

"Who wants him?"

"Tell him Fenner."

The old woman slid the chain on the door and pulled it open. "Careful how you go up, mister," she said. "Ike's restless to-night."

Fenner pushed past her and mounted the dark stairs.

The stench of stale cooking and dirt made him wrinkle his nose. On the first landing he rapped at a door. He heard a murmur of voices, and then a sudden hush. The door opened slowly and a slim, muscular lad with a pointed chin like a hog's looked him over.

"Yeah?" he said.

"Tell Ike I want him. Fenner's the name."

The lad shut the door. Fenner heard him say something, then he pulled the door back and jerked his head. "Come on in," he said.

Ike Bush was sitting at a table with four men; they were playing poker. Fenner wandered in and stood just behind Bush. The other men looked at him suspiciously, but went on playing. Bush studied his cards thoughtfully. He was a big, fat man with a red rubbery face and ingrowing eyebrows. His thick fingers made the playing cards look like a set of dominoes.

Fenner watched him play for a few minutes. Then he leaned over and whispered in Bush's ear: "You're goin' to take an awful hidin'."

Bush studied the cards again, cleared his throat, and spat on the floor. He threw down the cards in disgust. Pushing back his chair, he climbed to his feet and led Fenner to the other end of the room. "What you want?" he growled.

"Two Cubans," Fenner said quietly. "Both dressed in black. Black slouch hats, white shirts and flashy ties. Black square shoes. Both little punks. Both wear rods."

Ike shook his head. "Don't know 'em," he said; "they don't belong here."

Fenner regarded him coldly. "Then find out quick who they are. I want to get after those two fast."

Ike shrugged. "What've they done to you?" he said. "I wantta get back to my game—"

Fenner turned his head slightly and showed the gash on his cheek-bone. "Those two punks came into my joint, gave me this ... and got away."

Ike's eyes bulged. "Wait," he said. He went over to the telephone that stood on a small table across the room. After a long whispered conversation he hung up and jerked his head at Fenner.

Fenner want over to him. "Find them?"

"Yeah." Ike rubbed his sweaty face with the back of his hand. "They've been in town five days. No one knows who the hell they are. They've got a joint out Brooklyn way. I got the address here. Seems they've taken a furnished house. Got dough, an' no one knows what their racket is.

Fenner reached out and took the paper on which Ike had written the address. He got to his feet.

Ike looked at him. "You goin' into action?" he asked curiously. "Want one or two of the boys?"

Fenner showed his teeth in a mirthless smile. "I can manage," he said shortly.

Ike reached out and picked up a dark bottle without any label. He looked inquiringly at Fenner. "One before you go?" he said.

Fenner shook his head. He patted Ike on his shoulder and walked out. The cab was still waiting. The driver leaned out as Fenner ran down the steps. "Didn't think that was your home," he said with a grin, "so I hung around. Where to?"

Fenner pulled open the door. "You might get far," he said. "You been learnin' your job by mail?"

The driver said seriously: "Things are pretty bum these days. You gotta use your nut. Where to, mister?"

"The other side of Brooklyn Bridge. I'll walk the rest."

The cab shot away from the kerb and headed for the lights of Seventh Avenue.

"Someone been knockin' you around?" the cab-driver asked curiously.

"Naw!" Fenner grunted. "My Aunt Fanny likes to keep an edge on her teeth."

"A tough old lady, huh?" the driver said, but after that he piped down.

It was almost dark by the time they crossed Brooklyn Bridge. Fenner paid the cab off and went into the nearest bar. He ordered a club sandwich and three fingers of rye. While he bolted the sandwich he got the girl who waited on him to find out where the address was. She took a lot of trouble, finding it on a map for him. He paid his bill, had another short rye, and went out again.

Ten minutes quick walking got him there. He found his way without asking and without making a mistake. He walked down the street, looking closely at every shadow. The house he wanted was on the corner. It was a small two-storey affair, with a square box hedge so arranged that it masked the front door completely. There were no lights showing in any of the windows. Fenner pushed open the gate and walked up the slightly inclining path. His eyes searched the black windows for any sign of movement. He didn't stop at the front door, but went on round the back of the house. There were no lights there. He found a window that was open a few inches at the top, and he shone his small torch into the room. It was empty of everything. He could see the dust on the floor-boards. It took him a few seconds to raise the window and step into the room. He was careful not to make any noise, and he trod on the boards tenderly.

Quietly he tried the door, pulled it open and stepped into a small hall. The light of his torch picked out a carpet and a large hall cupboard. The stairs faced him. He stood listening, but no sound came to him except the faint hum of distant street traffic.

He went up the stairs, the .38 in his hand. His mouth was drawn down a little at the corners, and the muscles of his face were tense. On the landing he paused again, listening. He was conscious of a strange unpleasant smell that was vaguely familiar to him. He wrinkled his nose, wondering what it could be.

There were three doors facing him. He chose the centre one. He turned the handle softly and edged the door open. The smell came to him stronger now. It reminded him of the smell from a butcher's shop. When he got the door half

open, he paused and listened, then he stepped in and pushed the door to behind him. His torch lit up the light switch and he snapped it on.

He looked round the well-furnished bedroom, his finger itching on his gun
trigger. There was no one there. He turned and twisted the key in the lock.
He wasn't taking chances. Then he wandered round the room thoughtfully.
A woman's room. The dressing-table had the usual stuff. The bed was
small, and a big nightdress case in the shape of a flaxen-haired doll lay on the
pillow.

Fenner went over to the wardrobe and looked inside. There was one costume
hanging on the peg. Nothing more. There didn't have to be anything more;
it was the costume that Marian Daley had worn when she called on him.

Fenner touched it thoughtfully while he tried to visualize Marian Daley. He
took the costume out of the cupboard and tossed it on the bed. There was more
spring in his step as he went over to the chest of drawers. In the top drawer
was the prim little hat. He tossed that on the bed too. In another drawer he
found a bundle of underclothes, a suspender girdle, stockings and shoes. He
threw all these on to the bed. Then he went over to the dressing-table and
jerked open the small drawer under the mirror. Stuffed inside was her hand
bag. He pulled it out with difficulty, and walked with it across the room. He
sat on the bed, slapping the bag on his open palm and staring hard at the carpet. He didn't like this at all.

He opened the bag and spilled the contents on to the bed. The usual junk
a woman carries around clattered into a small, rather pathetic pile. He stirred
the pile with his finger and then looked in the bag again. There was nothing
there that he could see, and he put two fingers inside and ripped out the lining. Crumpled at the bottom of the bag, either hidden there, or else slipped
through the lining, was a piece of paper. He spread it out and peered at it. It
was a letter on a single sheet of notepaper in a large careless hand. It read:

Key West.

Dear Marian,
Don't worry. Noolen has promised to help me. Pío doesn't know anything yet.
I think things will come out all right now.

The letter was unsigned.

Fenner folded the paper carefully and put it in his cigarette-case. He sat on
the bed, thinking. Key West and the two Cubans. Something was beginning
to add up. He got to his feet and made a systematic search of the whole room,
but he found nothing else. Then he unlocked the door, snapped off the light
and stepped quietly into the passage.

He eased his way into the room on the left. His torch showed him that it was a fair-sized bathroom. Making sure that the curtain was drawn over the window he reached out for the light switch. The smell in the room was making him feel a little sick. He knew now what it was and he was steeling himself to turn on the light. It flashed on as he turned the switch down with exaggerated care.

In the hard light the room looked like an abattoir after a full day's work. The bath stood against the wall and was covered with a blood-spotted sheet. The wall was marked red and the floor by the bath was red. A table stood near the bath and that, too, had a blood-soaked towel on it. Fenner could see that it covered something.

He stood very still, looking round the room, his face white and set. He took a slow step forward and, hooking his gun-barrel under the towel, he flicked it off the table. A slender white arm, ruthlessly hacked off at the shoulder, wobbled on the table and then rolled off and fell on the floor at his feet.

Fenner felt the cold sweat of sickness break out all over him. He hastily swallowed the sudden rush of saliva that filled his mouth. He looked at the arm carefully, but he couldn't bring himself to touch it. The hand was narrow and long, with carefully manicured finger-nails. There was no doubt about it. The arm and hand belonged to a woman.

With a hand that shook a little, he lit a cigarette, drawing the smoke down into his lungs and forcing it through his nostrils, trying to get rid of the nauseating smell of death. Then he walked over to the bath and turned back the sheet.

Fenner was tough. He'd been in the newspaper racket for years, and sudden death didn't mean much to him. Violence was just another headline, but this business shook him. It shook him more because he'd known her. She was his client, and only a few hours before she had been a living pulsing woman.

The thing in the bath told him he couldn't be wrong. The tell-tale vivid bruises still decorated her body.

Fenner dropped the sheet and stepped out of the room. He pulled the door gently to and leaned against it. He'd have given a lot for a drink. He stood there, his mind blank, until the first shock drifted away from him. Then he wiped his face with his handkerchief and moved to the head of the stairs.

Grosset had to hear about this. He'd got to get those two Cubans fast. He stood thinking. The legs and one arm were missing. The head was missing, too. A heavy enough burden for two men to carry without exciting comment. That was it. They were planting her somewhere, and they'd be back to get rid of the rest of the body.

Fenner's eyes narrowed. All he had to do now was to wait for them to come back, and then give it to them. Before he could make up his mind whether to hunt for a 'phone and get in touch with Grosset or to just wait and handle it on his own, he heard a car draw up outside and a car door slam

He stepped quietly back into the bedroom, letting the .38 slide into his hand. He stood inside the room, holding the door open a few inches.

He heard the front door open and shut. Then a light snapped on in the hall. He moved out a little and peered over the banisters. The two Cubans were standing in the hall. They were very tense, listening. Fenner remained where he was, motionless. The Cubans each held a large suit-case in their hands. He saw them exchange glances. Then the short one murmured something to the other, who put his case down and came up the stairs fast. He came up so fast Fenner hadn't time to duck back.

The Cuban saw him as he rounded the bend in the stair way and his hand flew to the inside of his coat. Fenner drew his lips off his teeth and shot him three times in the belly. The noise of the gun crashed through the still house. The Cuban caught his breath in a sob and bent forward, holding himself low down.

Fenner jumped forward, heaved him out of the way, and dived down the stairway as if he were taking a header into the water.

The short Cuban had no chance to get out of the way. The sudden crash of gunfire had paralysed him, and although his hand went unconsciously to his hip, he could not move his feet.

Fenner's fourteen stone of bone and muscle hit him like a shell. They both crashed down on to the floor, the Cuban underneath. The Cuban had given one high-pitched squeal of terror as he saw something coming at him, then Fenner was on him.

The crash made Fenner's head spin and for a second or two he was so dazed that he could only lie, crushing the Cuban flat. His gun had shot out of his hand as he went down, and as he struggled to his knees he was dimly conscious of a jabbing pain in his arms.

The Cuban didn't move. Fenner cautiously got to his feet and stirred him with his foot. The odd angle of the Cuban's head told him all he wanted to know. He'd broken his neck.

He went on his knee and searched the Cuban's pockets, but he didn't find anything. He looked inside one of the suit-cases, but it was empty. The smear of blood on the lining confirmed his idea that they were taking the body away in bits.

He found his gun and cautiously went upstairs to have a look at the other Cuban. He, too, was as dead as a pork chop. He lay twisted in a corner, his mouth drawn up, show ing his teeth. Fenner thought he looked like a mad dog. A quick search revealed nothing, and Fenner went down stairs again. He wanted to get out of this fast. He turned off the light in the hall, opened the front door and stepped out into the night.

Outside, the car still waited. There was no one in it, but Fenner let it stay. He walked down the street, keeping in the shadow, and it was only when he got into the Fulton Street crowds that he relaxed at all.

A taxi took him back to his office. During the short ride he had decided on a plan of action. He took the elevator up to the fourth floor and hurried down the passage to his office.

A light was still burning, and for a moment he hesitated before entering. Then, keeping his hand on his gun, he turned the handle and walked in.

Paula was sitting in an arm-chair before the telephone. She jerked up her head quickly as if she'd been asleep.

"Why haven't you gone home?" Fenner said shortly.

Paula indicated the telephone. "She might have rung," she said quietly.

Fenner sat down beside her wearily.

Paula said, "Dave, I'm sorry about—"

"Skip it," Dave said, patting her hand. "You were right to blow off. Right now things are happenin'. Those two Cubans got hold of that girl, killed her and carved her up. I caught them cartin' her away. They're dead. I killed 'em both. Don't interrupt. Let me tell you fast. The cops must be kept out of this. This is between me and whoever started it. Those cheap punks are only the dressin'. They ain't the whole salad. Take a look at that." He gave Paula the letter he'd found in Marian's bag.

Paula read it through. Her face had gone a little pale, but otherwise she was calm. "Key West?" she said.

Fenner's smile was mirthless. "That make you think?"

Paula puzzled.

"That dame wanted to find her sister. She said she didn't know where she was. Why didn't she tell me Key West? You know, baby, it looks like a plant. There's something very funny about this business."

"Who's Pío?" Paula said, reading the letter gain. "And who's Noolen?"

Fenner shook his head. There was a hard look in his eyes. "I don't know, baby, but I'm goin' to find out. I've got six thousand dollars of that girl's money, an' if I have to spend every dollar of it, I'm goin' to find out."

He went over to the telephone and dialled a number.

While the line was connecting, he said, "Ike's goin' to earn some of that dough I've been slippin' him."

The line connected with a little plop. Fenner said, "Ike?" He waited, then he said, "Tell him Fenner. Tell him if he don't come to this 'phone at once, I'll come down and kick his teeth in." He waited again, his right shoe kicking the desk leg continuously. Then Ike's growl came over the wire.

"All right, all right," Fenner said. "To hell with your game. This is urgent. I want to find someone I can contact in Key West. Do you know anyone down there? He's gotta have an in with the guys that count."

"Key West?" Ike grumbled. "I don't know anyone in Key West."

Fenner showed his teeth. "Then hustle up someone who does. Ring me back right away. I'll wait." He slammed the receiver down on its cradle.

Paula said, "You going down there?"

Fenner nodded. "It's a long way, but I think that's where it'll finish. Maybe I'm wrong, but I'm going to see."

Paula got to her feet. "Do I go with you?"

"You stick around here, baby. If I think something's goin' to start, I'll have you down. Right now you'll be more of a help here. Grosset's got to be looked after. Tell him I'm out of town for a few days, but you don't know where."

"I'll go over to your place and pack a bag for you."

Fenner nodded. "Yeah," he said, "do that."

When she had gone, he went over to his reference shelf and checked the Pan-American air time-table. There was a 'plane for Florida at 12:30. He glanced at his watch. It was five past eleven. If Ike 'phoned back quickly, he could just make it.

He sat behind his desk and lit a cigarette. He had to wait twenty minutes before the 'phone jangled. He snatched the receiver.

"The guy you want is Buck Nightingale," Ike said. "He's got his finger in most pies down there. Treat him easy, he's gotta brittle temper."

"So have I," Fenner said unpleasantly. "Fix it for me, Ike. Tell him that Dave Ross'll be down on the next 'plane an' wants introductions. Give me a good build up. I'll tell Paula to put a cheque in the mail for five hundred bucks for your trouble."

"Sure, sure." Ike's voice was quite oily. "I'll fix it for you," and he hung up.

Fenner dialled another number. "Paula?" he said. "Hurry with that packing. I'm catching the 12:30 'plane, Meet me at the airport as fast as you can make it."

He pulled open a drawer, took out a cheque-book and signed five blank cheques quickly. He put his hat and coat on and looked round the office thoughtfully. Then he snapped off the electric light and went out, slamming the door behind him.

II

Fenner arrived at Key West about nine. He checked in at a nearby hotel, had a cold bath and went to bed. He was lulled to sleep by the drone of an electric fan that buzzed just above his head.

He had two hours' catnap, then the telephone woke him. The telephone said "Good morning." He ordered orange juice and toast and told the voice at the other end to send him up a bottle of Scotch. While he was waiting, he went into the bathroom and had a cold shower.

It was half-past eleven when he left the hotel. He walked south down Roosevelt Boulevard. All the time he walked he kept thinking about the heat. He thought if he was going to stay long in this burg he'd certainly have to do something about the heat.

He stopped a policeman and asked for Buck Nightingale's place.

The cop gaped at him. "You're new here, huh?"

Fenner said, "No, I'm the oldest inhabitant. That's why I come up an' ask you. I wantta see if you know the answer," and he went on, telling himself that he'd have to be careful. Already the heat was doing things to his temper.

He found Nightingale's place by asking a taxi-driver. He got the information and he got civility. He thanked the driver, then spoiled it by not hiring the cab. The driver told him he'd take him all over the town for twenty-five cents. Fenner said that he'd rather walk. He went on, closing his ears to what the driver said. It was too hot to fight, anyway.

By the time he reached Flagler Avenue his feet began to hurt. It was like walking on a red-hot stove. At the corner of Flagler and Thompson he gave up and flagged a cab. When he settled himself in the cab he took off his shoes and gave his feet some air. He'd no sooner got his shoes off than the cab forced itself against the oncoming traffic and pulled up outside a small shop.

The driver twisted his head. "This is it, boss," he said.

Fenner squeezed his feet into his shoes and had difficulty in getting his hot hand into his trouser pocket. He gave the driver twenty-five cents and got out of the cab. The shop was very clean and the windows shone. In the right-hand window stood a small white coffin. The back of the window was draped with heavy black curtains. Fenner, fascinated, thought the coffin looked lonely all by itself. He read the card that stood on a small easel by the coffin.

MAY WE LOOK AFTER YOUR LITTLE ONE
IF THE LORD DOES NOT SPARE HIM?

Fenner thought it was all in very good taste. He went over to the other window and inspected that, too. Again, it was draped in black curtains, and on a white pedestal stood a silver urn. A card bearing the simple inscription 'Dust to Dust' impressed him.

He stepped back and read the facia over the shop:

B. NIGHTINGALE'S FUNERAL PARLOUR.

"Well, well," he said, "quite a joint."

He walked into the shop. As he opened the door the electric buzzer started, and stopped as soon as the door shut. Inside, the shop was even more impressive. There was a short counter dividing the room exactly in half. This was draped with a white-and-purple velvet cover. Several black leather armchairs dotted the purple pile carpet. On the left of the room was a large glass cabinet containing miniature coffins made of every conceivable material, from gold to pine wood.

On the right was a six-foot crucifix cleverly illuminated by concealed lights. The figure was so realistic that it quite startled Fenner. He felt that he'd wandered into a church.

Long white, black and purple drapes hung behind the counter. There was no one in the shop. Fenner wandered over to the cabinet and examined the coffins. He thought that as a permanent home the gold one was a swell job.

A woman came quietly from behind the curtain. She wore a tight-fitting black silk dress, white collar and cuffs. She was a blonde, and her big gash-like mouth was very red with paint. She looked at Fenner and her mouth shaped into a smile. Fenner thought she was quite something.

She said in a low, solemn voice, "Can I help you, please?"

Fenner scratched his chin. "Do you sell these boxes?" he said, jerking his thumb in the direction of the glass case.

She blinked. "Why, sure," she said. "They're just models, you know; but was that what you wanted?"

Fenner shook his head. "No," he said; "I was just curious."

She looked at him doubtfully.

Fenner went on: "Nightingale in?"

"Did you want to see him particularly?"

"That's why I asked, baby. Tell him Ross."

She said, "I'll see. He's very busy right now."

Fenner watched her go away behind the curtain. He thought her shape from behind was pretty good.

She came back after a while and said, "Will you come up?"

He followed her behind the curtain and up the short flight of stairs. He liked the scent she used, and halfway up the stairs he told her so. She looked over her shoulder at him and smiled. She had big white teeth. "What do I do now?" she said. "Should my face go red?"

He shook his head seriously. "I just like to tell a dame when she's good," he said.

She pointed to a door. "He's in there," she said. Then, after a little pause, she said, "I like you. You've got nice eyes," and she went downstairs, patting her blonde curls with long white fingers.

Fenner fingered his tie. "Some frill," he thought, and turned the door handle and walked in.

The room was obviously a workshop. Four coffins stood in a line on trestles. Nightingale was screwing a brass plate on one of them.

Nightingale was a little dark man with thick-lensed steel-rimmed glasses. His skin was very white, and two large colourless eyes blinked weakly at Fenner from behind the cheaters.

Fenner said, "I'm Ross."

Nightingale went on screwing down the plate. "Yes?" he said. "Did you want to see me?"

"Dave Ross," Fenner repeated, standing by the door. "I think you were expectin' me."

Nightingale put down the screwdriver and looked at him. "So I was," he said, as if remembering. "So I was. We'll go upstairs and talk."

Fenner followed him out of the workshop and up another short flight of stairs. Nightingale showed him into a room which was large and cool. Two big windows opened out to a small balcony. From the window Fenner could see the Mexican Gulf.

Nightingale said, "Sit down. Take off your coat if you want to."

Fenner took off his coat and rolled up his sleeves. He sat by the window.

Nightingale said, "Perhaps a drink?"

"Sure."

When the drinks were fixed, and Nightingale had settled himself, Fenner sparred for an opening. He knew he'd have to go carefully with this little guy. He didn't know how far he could trust him. It was no use getting him suspicious.

He said at last, "How far you carryin' me?"

Nightingale fingered his glass with his thick weak fingers. He looked a little bewildered. "All the way," he said. "That's what you want, isn't it?"

Fenner stretched out. "I want to get in with the boys. New York's got too hot for me."

"I can do that," Nightingale said simply. "Crotti said you were an all-right guy and I was to help you. Crotti's been good to me; I'm glad to even things up with him."

Fenner guessed Crotti was the guy Ike got on to.

"Maybe five C's would be more concrete than lovin' Crotti," he said drily.

Nightingale looked a little hurt. "I don't want your dough," he said simply. "Crotti said 'help this man,' and that's enough for me."

Fenner twisted in his chair. It quite shocked him to see that the little man was sincere.

"Swell," he said hastily. "Don't get me wrong. Where I come from there's a different set of morals."

"I can give you introductions. But what is it exactly that you want?"

Fenner wished he knew. He stalled. "I guess I gotta get into the money again," he said. "Maybe one of your crowd could use me."

"Crotti says you've got quite a reputation. He says you've got notches on your gun."

Fenner tried to look modest and cursed Ike's imagination.

"I get along," he said casually.

"Maybe Carlos could use you."

Fenner tried a venture. "I thought Noolen might be good to throw in with."

Nightingale's watery eyes suddenly flashed. "Noolen? Noolen's the south end of a horse."

"So?"

"Carlos has Noolen with his pants down. You won't get any place with a piker like Noolen."

Fenner gathered that Noolen was a wash-out. He tried again. "You surprise me. I was told Noolen was quite a big shot around here."

Nightingale stretched his neck and deliberately spat on the floor. "Nuts," he said.

"Who's Carlos?"

Nightingale got back his good humour. "He's the boy. Now, Pío'll get you somewhere."

Fenner slopped a little of his Scotch. "That his name—Pío Carlos?"

Nightingale nodded. "He's got this burg like that." He held out his small squat hand and closed his thick fingers into a small fist. "Like that—see?"

Fenner nodded. "Okay," he said, "I'll be guided by you."

Nightingale got up and put his glass on the table. "I've got a little job to do, and then we'll go down and meet the boys. You rest here. It's too hot to go runnin' around."

When he had gone, Fenner shut his eyes and thought. The lid was coming off this quicker than he'd imagined. He'd have to watch his step.

He felt a little draught and he opened his eyes. The blonde had come in and was gently shutting the door. Fenner heard her turn the key in the lock.

"Jumpin' snakes," he thought, "she's goin' to grab me!"

He swung his legs off the chair Nightingale had sat in, and struggled to his feet.

"Stay put," she said, coming over. "I want to talk to you."

Fenner sat down again. "What's your name, honey?" he said, stalling for time.

"Robbins," she said. "They call me Curly round here."

"Nice name, Curly," Fenner said. "What's on your mind?"

She sat down in Nightingale's chair. "Take my tip," she said, keeping her voice low, "an' go home. Imported tough guys don't stand up long in this town."

Fenner raised his eyebrows. "Who told you I was a tough guy?" he said.

"I don't have to be told. You've come down here to set fire to the place, haven't you? Well, it won't work. These hoods here don't like foreign competition. You'll be cat's meat in a few days if you stick around."

Fenner was quite touched. "You're bein' a very nice little girl," he said; "but I'm afraid it's no soap. I'm down here for a livin', and I'm stickin'."

She sighed. "I thought you'd take it like that," she said, getting up. "If you knew what's good for you, you'd take a powder quick. Anyway, watch out. I don't trust any of them. Don't trust Nightingale. He looks a punk, but he isn't. He's a killer, so watch him."

Fenner climbed out of his chair. "Okay, baby," he said. "I'll watch him. Now you'd better blow, before he finds you here." He led her to the door.

She said, "I'm tellin' you this because you're cute. I hate seein' a big guy like you headin' for trouble."

Fenner grinned, and, swinging his hand, he gave her a gentle smack. "Don't you worry your brains about me," he said.

She leaned towards him, raising her face; so, because he thought she was pretty good, he kissed her. She wound her arms round his neck and held him. They stood like that for several minutes, then Fenner pushed her away gently.

She stood looking at him, breathing hard. "I guess I'm crazy," she said, colour suddenly flooding her face.

Fenner ran his finger round the inside of his collar. "I'm a bit of a bug myself," he said. "Scram, baby, before we really get to work. Beat it, an' I'll see you in church."

She went out quickly and shut the door. Fenner took out his handkerchief and wiped his hands thoughtfully. "I think I'm goin' to like this job," he said aloud. "Yeah, it might develop into somethin'," and he went back and sat down by the open window again.

Nightingale led him through the crowded lobby of the Flagler Hotel. Fenner said, "This guy does himself well."

Nightingale stopped before the elevator doors and thumbed the automatic button. "Sure," he said; "what did I tell you? Pío's the boy to be in with."

Fenner studied the elaborate wrought ironwork of the gates. "You're tellin' me," he said.

The cage came to rest and they stepped in. Nightingale pressed the button for the fifth, and the cage shot them up.

"Now I'll do the talkin'," Nightingale said, as the lift stopped. "Maybe you won't get anythin', but I'll try."

Fenner grunted and followed the little man down the corridor. He stopped outside No. 47 and rapped three times fast and twice slowly, on the door.

"Secret signs as well," Fenner said admiringly.

The door opened and a short Cuban, dressed in a black suit, looked them over. Fenner shaped his lips for a whistle, but he didn't make any sound.

Nightingale said in his soft voice: "It's all right."

The Cuban let them in. As he shut the door after them, Fenner saw a bulge in his hip-pocket. The hall they found themselves in was big, and three doors faced them.

"The boys in yet?" Nightingale asked.

The Cuban nodded. He sat down in an arm-chair by the front door and picked up a newspaper again. As far as he was concerned they weren't there.

Nightingale went into the centre room. There were four men lounging about the room. They were all in shirt-sleeves and they all were smoking. Two of them were reading news papers, one of them was listening to the radio, and the fourth was cleaning a rod. They all glanced at Nightingale, and then fixed wooden looks on Fenner.

The man with the rod got up slowly. "Who is it?" he said. He'd got a way of speaking with his teeth shut. He wore a white suit and a black shirt with a white tie. His wiry black hair was cropped close, and his yellow-green eyes were cold and suspicious.

Nightingale said, "This is Ross. From New York. Crotti knows him. He's all right." Then he turned to Fenner. "Meet Reiger."

Fenner gave Reiger a wintry smile. He didn't like the look of him.

Reiger nodded. "How do," he said. "Stayin' long?"

Fenner waved his hand. "These other guys friends of yours, or are they just decoration?"

Reiger's eyes snapped. "I said, stayin' long?" he said.

Fenner eyed him. "I heard you. It ain't no goddam business of yours, is it?"

Nightingale put his hand on Fenner's cuff. He didn't say anything, but it was a little warning gesture. Reiger tried a staring match with Fenner, lost it and shrugged. He said, "Pug Kane by the radio. Borg on the right. Miller on the left."

The three other men nodded at Fenner. None of them seemed friendly.

Fenner was quite at ease. "Glad to know you," he said. "I won't ask you guys for a drink. Maybe you don't use the stuff."

Reiger turned on Nightingale. "What's this?" he snarled. "Who's this loud-mouthed punk?"

Miller, a fat, greasy-looking man with a prematurely bald head said, "Somethin' he's dug outa an ash-can."

Fenner walked over to him very quickly and slapped him twice across his mouth. A gun jumped into Nightingale's hand and he said, "Don't start anythin'—don't start anythin', please."

Fenner was surprised they took any notice of Nightingale, but they did. They all froze solid. Even Reiger looked a little sick.

Nightingale said to Fenner, "Come away from him." His voice had enough menace in it to chill Fenner a trifle. Curly was right. This guy was a killer.

Fenner stepped away from Miller and put his hands in his pockets.

Nightingale said, "I won't have it. When I bring a friend of mine up here, you treat him right. I'd like to measure some of you heels for a box."

Fenner laughed. "Ain't that against etiquette?" he said. "Or do you take it both ways? Bump 'em an' bury 'em?"

Nightingale put his rod away, and the others relaxed. Reiger said with a little forced smile, "This heat plays hell." He went over to a cupboard and set up drinks.

Fenner sat down close to Reiger. He thought this one was the meanest of the bunch and he was the one to work on. He said quietly, "This heat even makes me hate myself."

Reiger looked at him still suspiciously. "Forget it," he said. "Now you're here, make yourself at home."

Fenner rested his nose on the rim of his glass. "Carlos in?" he said.

Reiger's eyes opened. "Carlos ain't got time for visitors," he said. "I'll tell him you've been in."

Fenner drained his glass and stood up. Nightingale made a move, but Fenner stopped him with a gesture. He stood looking round at each man in turn. He said, "Well, I'm glad I looked in. I thought this was a live outfit, an' I find I'm wrong. You guys are no use to me. You think you've got this town by the shorts, but you're fat an' lazy. You think you're the big-shots, but that's where you're wrong. I think I'll go an' see Noolen. That guy's supposed to be the south end of a horse. All right, then I'll make him the north end. It'll be more amusing than playin' around with guys like you."

Reiger slid his hand inside his coat, but Nightingale already had his rod out. "Hold it," he said.

The four men sat still; their angry faces made Fenner want to laugh.

Nightingale said, "I asked him to come along. If he don't like us, then let him go. A friend of Crotti's 's a friend of mine."

Fenner said, "I'll drop round some time an' see you again."

He walked out of the room, past the Cuban, who ignored him, and took the elevator down to the street level.

The commissionaire at the door looked as if he had some brains. Fenner asked him if he knew where he could find Noolen. The commissionaire said he'd got an office off Duval Street, and beckoned a cab. Fenner gave him a fin.

The commissionaire helped him into the cab as though he were made of china.

Noolen's office was over a shop. Fenner had to go up a long flight of stairs before he located the frosted glass-panelled door. When he got inside, a flat-chested woman whose thirties were crowding up on her, regarded him suspiciously from behind a typewriter.

"Noolen in?" he asked, smiling at her, because he felt she could do with a few male smiles.

"He's busy right now," she said. "Who is it?"

"Me? Tell him Ross. Dave Ross. Tell him I ain't sellin' anythin', and I want to see him fast."

She got up and walked over to a door behind her. Fenner gave her a start, then he took two strides and walked into the room with her.

Noolen was a dark, middle-aged man, growing a paunch. He'd a double chin and a hooked nose. His eyes were hooded and mean. He looked at Fenner and then at the woman. "Who's this?" he snapped.

The woman jerked round, her eyes popping. "Wait out side," she said.

Fenner pushed past her and wandered over to the big desk. He noticed a lot of spots on Noolen's vest. He noticed the dirty nails and the grubby hands. Nightingale was right. Noolen was the south end of a horse.

Fenner said, "Ross is the name. How do?"

Noolen jerked his head at the woman, who went out, shutting the door with a sharp click. "What do you want?" he asked, scowling.

Fenner put his hands on the desk and leant forward. "I want a hook-up in this burg. I've seen Carlos. He won't play. You're next on my list, so here I am."

Noolen said, "Where you from?"

"Crotti."

Noolen studied his dirty finger-nails. "So Carlos couldn't use you. What's the matter with him?" There was a sneer in his voice.

"Carlos didn't see me. I saw his flock of hoods an' that was enough for me. They made me puke, so I scrammed."

"Why come to me?"

Fenner grinned. "They told me you were the south end of a horse. I thought maybe we could do something about it."

A faint red crept into Noolen's face. "So they said that, did they?"

"Sure. With me, you might have a lotta fun with that gang."

"Meanin'?"

Fenner hooked a chair towards him with his foot and sat down. He leant forward and helped himself to a thin greenish cigar from a cigar-box on the desk. He took his time lighting it. Noolen sat watching him. His eyes intent and bright.

"Look at it this way," Fenner said, stretching in the chair; "my way. I've come from Crotti. I want a chance like the rest of you for some easy dough an' not much excitement. Crotti said either Carlos or Noolen. Carlos's mob is too busy big-shotting to worry about me. I can't even get in to see Carlos. You—I walk in an' find you sittin' around with a flat-chested bird outside as your muscle guard. Why did Crotti tip you? Maybe you've been someone an' Crotti's getting behind in the news. Maybe you are someone, an' this is a front. Take it all round, I think you an' me might get places."

Noolen gave a little shrug. He shook his head. "Not just now," he said. "I don't know Crotti. I've never heard of him, an' I don't believe you've come from him. I think you're a punk gunman bluffing himself a job. I don't want you an' I hope I'll never want you."

Fenner got up and yawned. "That's swell," he said. "I can now grab myself a little rest. When you've looked into things, you'll find me at the Haworth Hotel. If you know Nightingale, have a word with him—he thinks I'm quite a boy."

He nodded to Noolen and walked out of the office. He went down the stairs, called a cab, and drove to his hotel. He went into the restaurant and ordered a turtle steak. While he was eating, Nightingale came in and sat down opposite him.

Fenner said, with his mouth full, "Ain't you got any boxes to make, or is business bad?"

Nightingale looked worried. "That was a hell of a thing to do—walking out like that."

"Yeah? I always walk out when I get a Bronx cheer. Why not?"

"Listen, Reiger ain't soft. That ain't the way to handle Reiger."

"No? You tell me."

Nightingale ordered some brown bread, cheese and a glass of milk. He kept his eyes on the white tablecloth until the waitress brought the order, and when she had gone away he said, "This makes it difficult for me."

Fenner put his knife and fork down. He smiled at the little man. "I like you," he said. "You're the one guy who's given me a hand up to now. Suppose you stick around, I might do you some good."

Nightingale peered at Fenner from under his hat. The sun, coming in through the slatted blinds, reflected on his glasses. "You might do me some harm, too," he said dryly.

Fenner resumed his eating. "Hell!" he said. "This is a hell of a burg, ain't it?"

When they had finished their meal, Fenner pushed his chair away and stood up. "Okay, pal," he said. "I'll be seeing you."

Nightingale said, "We might talk some time." He said it hopefully.

Fenner took off his hat and ran his fingers through his hair. "I don't know," he said vaguely, "I don't know."

He nodded to the little man and went out to the office. The hotel manager was busy at the desk. He looked up as Fenner passed and gave an oily smile.

Fenner said, "I'm goin' to sleep. This place's killin' me."

Before the manager could say anything, he went on up the stairs to his bedroom. He shut the door and turned the key. Then he took off his coat and hat and lay on the bed. He went to sleep almost immediately, a pleased smile on his mouth.

The 'phone woke him. He sat up with a jerk, glanced at the clock, saw he had slept for two hours, and reached out for the 'phone.

A voice said, "Come over to the Flagler Hotel right away. The boss wants you."

Fenner screwed up his eyes. "Tell the boss I came this mornin'. I don't visit the same place twice," and hung up.

He lay back on the bed and shut his eyes. He only lay there a minute or so before the 'phone went again.

The same voice said, "You'd better come. Carlos don't like bein' kept waitin'."

Fenner said, "Tell Carlos to come out here, or tell him to go roll a hoop." He put the receiver on the prong with exaggerated care.

He didn't bother to answer the 'phone when it rang again. He went into the little bathroom, bathed his face, gave him self a short shot from the Scotch, put on his hat and coat, and went downstairs.

The heat of the afternoon sun was blistering. The hotel lobby was deserted. He went over and sat down near the entrance. He put his hat on the floor beside him and stared out into the street. He knew that he wasn't going to get very far with this business unless he turned up Marian Daley's sister. He wondered whether the cops had found the two Cubans and the remains of Marian. He wondered what Paula was doing. From where he sat he could look into the hot, deserted street. A big touring car suddenly swept into the street, roared down to the hotel, and skidded to a standstill.

Fenner relaxed into the long cane chair and, reaching down, picked up his hat and put it on.

There were four men in the car. Three of them got out, leaving the driver sitting behind the wheel.

Fenner recognized Reiger and Miller, but the other guy he didn't know. They came up the few steps quickly and blinked round in the semi-gloom. Reiger saw Fenner almost at once. He came over.

Fenner looked up at him and nodded. "Want to see anyone?" he said casually. "The clerk's gone bye-bye."

Reiger said, "Carlos wants you. Come on."

Fenner shook his head. "It's too hot. Tell him some other time."

The other two came and stood round. They looked mean. Reiger said softly, "Comin' on your dogs, or do we carry you?"

Fenner got up slowly. "If it's like that," he said, and went with them to the car. He knew Reiger was itching to slug him and he knew it wouldn't do any good to make too much fuss. He wanted to see Carlos, but he wanted them to think he wasn't too interested.

They drove to the Flagler Hotel in silence. Fenner sat between Reiger and Miller, and the other man, whom they called Bugsey, sat with the driver.

They all went up in the small elevator and along to No. 47. As they entered, Fenner said, "You could have saved yourself a trip by playin' ball this mornin'."

Reiger didn't say anything. He crossed the room and rapped on another door and went in. Bugsey followed behind Fenner.

Carlos lay on a couch before a big open window. He was dressed in a cream silk dressing-gown, patterned with large red flowers. A white silk handkerchief was folded carefully in a stock at his throat, and his bare feet were encased in red Turkish slippers.

He was smoking a marihuana cigarette, and round his brown, hairy wrist hung a gold-linked bracelet.

Carlos was young. Maybe he was twenty or maybe he was twenty-four. His face was the colour of old parchment and he had very red lips. Thin lips, paper-thin lips, and red, just like someone had slit his throat with a razor and moved the wound above his chin. His nose was small, with very wide nostrils, and his ears lay tightly against his head. His eyes were large and fringed with dark curly eyelashes. He had no expression in them. They were like dull pieces of black glass. His hair grew away from his forehead on either side of his temples. It was black, glistening, and inclined to wave. Take a quick look at Carlos, and you'd think he was a pretty handsome guy, but when you looked again you got an eyeful of his mouth and his lobeless ears, and you weren't sure. When you got to his eyes you were dead certain that he was bad.

Reiger said, "This is Ross," then he went out with Bugsey.

Fenner nodded to Carlos and sat down. He sat a little way from the sickening smoke of the marihuana cigarette.

Carlos looked at him with his blank eyes. "What is it?" he said. His voice was hoarse and unmusical.

"This mornin' I came round to see you, but your hoods told me you were busy or somethin'. I ain't used to bein' handled that way, so I went back to my dump. I ain't sure I wantta talk to you now."

Carlos let his leg slide off the couch on to the floor. "I'm a cautious man," he said; "I have to be. When I heard you'd been in, I got on long-distance to Crotti. I wanted to know more about you first—that's reasonable, I think?"

Fenner's eyelids narrowed. "Sure," he said.

"Crotti says you're all right."

Fenner shrugged. "So what?"

"I can use you. But you gotta show me you're my type of guy."

"Let me hang around for a bit. Maybe you ain't my type of guy either."

Carlos smiled. There was no mirth in it. "You've got a lot of confidence. That's all right in its way."

Fenner stood up. "I get along," he said abruptly. "Where do we go from here?"

Carlos got off the couch. "Go an' talk to the boys," he said. "Then we'll go down to the waterfront. I've got a little job to do. It'll interest you."

Fenner said, "Do I come on your pay-roll?"

"Suppose we say a hundred bucks until we get used to each other?"

"We've got to get used to each other pretty quick," Fenner said without humour. "That's chicken-feed to me."

He went out and shut the door behind him.

Fenner, Carlos, Reiger and Bugsey entered a coffee-shop an hour later. The place was full, and curious eyes watched them walk to the back through a curtained door and out of sight.

Fenner found that Bugsey was ready to be friendly. He was a short, thickset man, very much inclined to fat, with a round mottled face, gooseberry laughing eyes, and lips like sausages.

Reiger hated Fenner, and they both knew it. He walked with Carlos, and Fenner and Bugsey tagged along behind. They went down a short passage and down a flight of stairs. It was dark and rank in the passage, and very silent.

At the bottom of the stairs was a door. Carlos unlocked it and went in.

The room was very large, and Fenner noticed, when Bugsey pushed the door to, he had to use a lot of beef. The door was solid and shut to with a thud.

The room was dark but for two clots of brilliant light at the far end. Carlos and Reiger went towards the light and Fenner stood still. He looked inquiringly at Bugsey. Bugsey pursed up his mouth. "This is his office," he said in a low voice.

"What do we do—just stand around?"

Bugsey nodded.

Carlos sat down at a big table under one of the pools of light. He said to Reiger, "Bring him in."

Reiger went into the darkness, and Fenner heard him unlock a door. A minute or so later he came back dragging a man with him. He led him by the front of his coat just like he was a sack of coal, not looking at him, not seemingly aware that he was bringing him in. He went over to a chair close to Carlos and dumped the man into it.

Fenner wandered a little nearer. The man was a Chinaman. He wore a shabby black suit and he sat huddled in the chair, his hands under his armpits and his body bent double.

Fenner looked at Bugsey, who again pursed his lips, but this time he didn't say anything.

Reiger dragged the Chinaman's head back.

Fenner made a slight movement forward, then stopped. The Chinaman's face glistened in the bright light. His skin was so tightly stretched that his face was skull-like. His lips had shrunk off his teeth, and only black shadows showed where his eyes were.

Carlos said, "You goin' to write that letter now?"

The Chinaman just sat there, silent. Reiger jerked on his pigtail, wrenching his head back and then jerking it forward.

Carlos smiled. "An obstinate punk, ain't he, Reiger?" He pulled open a drawer and took something out, which he put on the table. "Put his hand on the table."

Reiger put his hand on the Chinaman's skinny wrist and pulled. The Chinaman kept his hands hidden under his arm pits and Fenner could see the tremendous effort he made to keep them there. There was a long silence while Reiger struggled. Fenner could see the hand coming inch by inch from its sanctuary. Beads of perspiration started out on the Chinaman's face and a low moaning sound came through his teeth.

Fenner said to Bugsey, "What the hell's this?"

Bugsey waved at him, but said nothing. He just stared at the group at the table as if fascinated beyond speech.

The thin claw-like hand gradually came into view and Reiger, his mouth set in a hard grin, forced the hand on to the table. From where he stood, Fenner could see red-stained rags tied round each finger.

Carlos pushed a cheap pad of notepaper, a small bottle of ink and a brush towards the Chinaman. "Write," he said.

The Chinaman said nothing. He did nothing.

Carlos looked in Fenner's direction. "Come here," he said; "I want you to see this."

"I can see where I am," Fenner said evenly.

Carlos shrugged. He picked up the object that he had taken from the drawer and carelessly fitted it on to one of the Chinaman's fingers.

Fenner turned his back slowly on the group and took Bugsey's arm. "If you don't tell me what this means, I'm going to stop it," he said hoarsely.

Bugsey's face was like green cheese. He said, "The old guy's got three sons in his home town. Carlos wants him to send for them, to hook them up in his racket. Those three guys are worth four grand a head to Carlos."

A sudden exclamation came from the other end of the room. Fenner turned his head. The Chinaman was writing. Carlos got to his feet, his dull eyes watching every stroke of the pen. When the letter was finished, the China-man fell back in the chair.

Carlos put his hand inside his coat and pulled a .25. He took a quick step towards the Chinaman, put the muzzle of the gun at the back of his head and squeezed the trigger.

The crash of the gun sounded incredibly loud in the silent room.

Carlos put his gun away and walked over to the table.

He picked up the letter, folded it carefully and put it in his wallet.

"Tell Nightingale to get rid of him," he said to Reiger, then walked directly over to Fenner. He stood and looked at Fenner narrowly. "Now do you like my racket?" he said.

Fenner itched to get his hands on him. He said very gently, "Maybe you've got a reason, but right now I think it's a little too tough."

Carlos laughed. "Come upstairs. I'll tell you about it."

The coffee-shop had an air of reality, not like the room downstairs that gave Fenner the jitters. He sat down at a small table in a corner and took three quick deep breaths of hot air. Carlos sat down opposite him. Bugsey and Reiger went out and disappeared down the street.

Carlos pulled out a pouch and began to roll a cigarette. The tobacco was stringy and yellow-brown. A mulatto girl with enormous eyes brought two small cups of very strong black coffee. When she had gone, Carlos said:

"You're in this game now. If you don't like it, say so, and you can get out. If you want to go ahead, I'll tell you how it works. Once you know how it works, you'll have to stay in. Get the idea?" He smiled bleakly.

Fenner nodded. "I'm stickin'," he said.

Carlos said, "Don't rush it. A guy who knows too much about my affairs is likely to run into a lot of grief if he wants to get out sudden."

"What have you gotta worry about? If I don't like it, that's my funeral."

Carlos sipped his coffee and stared across the café with blank eyes. Then he said abruptly: "There's a big demand on the West Coast for cheap Chinese labour. When I say cheap, I mean cheap. The authorities look on Chinks as undesirables, so they won't let them in. Now, that's a cock eyed way of doin' things. The demand's there, but the guys who want them can't get them. Well, that's my racket. I get 'em in."

Fenner nodded. "You mean you smuggle them in?"

"It's easy. On this coast there are hundreds of places I can get them in. The coastguards don't give me no trouble. Sometimes I'm unlucky, but I get along."

Fenner scratched his head. "There ain't any dough in this line, is there?"

Carlos showed his teeth.

"You ain't quite got the angle," he said. "Look at it this way. First, the Chinks are crazy to get in here. I've got a guy in Havana who contacts them. They pay him to smuggle them across the Gulf. These Chinks are so hot to get in that they'll pay as much as five hundred to a thousand dollars. We take a load of twelve Chinks at a time. Once those guys have got on one of my boats and have coughed up the dough, they become my property. I see them to the West Coast, and a good Chink will fetch again as much as five hundred bucks."

Fenner frowned.

"You mean the Chinks pay to get in, then you sell them once they're in?"

Carlos nodded.

"That's it," he said. "A two-way pay-off. It's quite a game. I've shipped fifty Chinks over this week. Taking everything into consideration, I'll pick up around thirty grand for that bit of work."

This quite startled Fenner. He said: "But why in hell don't these Chinks squawk? What happens to them?"

"How can they squawk? They got no right to be here. They can't go to the cops. It'd mean jail and bein' deported again. We send them up the coast and they get their food and that's all. You can find 'em workin' everywhere. In wash places, restaurants, laundries, everywhere."

"Why did you want the old guy to write that letter?"

Carlos looked at him. "I'm tellin' you quite a lot, ain't I?"

Fenner met his glance. "Be your age. You don't have to worry what you tell me."

"That old guy's got three sons in China. We ain't gettin' enough Chinks over. I got him to write to his sons askin' 'em over. You know the stuff, sellin' them the idea of what a grand time he's havin' and what a lot of dough he's makin'. They'll come all right. Those Chinks are suckers for that stuff."

Fenner pushed back his chair. "Where do I come in?" he said.

"Maybe you'd like a trip over the Strait and collect some cargo for me. I'm sendin' over in a day or so."

Fenner nodded. "Sure, I'll do that," he said. "I'll look in each day. Your joint's a little too elaborate for me. It makes me feel coy. I guess I'll stick to the Haworth for a while."

Carlos shrugged. "Suit yourself," he said; "Bugsey'll keep in touch with you."

Fenner nodded and pushed back his chair. "Sure," he said.

He went out into the street, leaving Carlos still sitting at the table.

Bugsey suddenly appeared from nowhere and tagged along behind Fenner. Fenner turned his head, saw him and stopped. Bugsey drew up with him, and they went on together.

Fenner said, "Quite a racket, ain't it?"

Bugsey nodded. "It's all right if you're some big-shot," he said, without enthusiasm. "I ain't gettin' places."

Fenner looked at him sideways, thoughtfully. "Ain't you gettin' anything out of this?"

"Sure, sure," Bugsey said hastily. "I'm not grumblin'."

They wandered along the waterfront. Fenner thought this guy looked simple. He began to get ideas. He said, What's your rake-off?"

Bugsey said, "A hundred bucks."

"That's chicken-feed."

"Sure, but it's tough these days."

Fenner agreed that it was.

They moved along the waterfront, idly watching the shipping. Fenner paused suddenly. He regarded a large luxury motor-launch that was lying off the short jetty. He said, "Swell boat."

Bugsey screwed up his eyes. "Yeah," he said wistfully. "I'd like a tub like that."

Fenner looked at him curiously. "What in hell would you do with it, anyway?" he asked.

Bugsey heaved a sigh. "Me? I'd get a flock of dames an' I'd take 'em out in that tub. That's what I'd do."

Fenner wasn't listening to him, he was staring at a girl who had come up from the big cabin. She was a red-gold blonde with a neat figure, long legs, and long, narrow feet. She wore white trousers, red sandals and a red high-necked jersey. Fenner felt a little prickle of excitement. He knew who she was. He could see the points of likeness. This was Marian Daley's sister.

Bugsey noticed her, too. He whistled softly. "What a frill!" he said.

Fenner said, "Know who she is?"

"Me? Don't make me laugh. Think I'd be standin' here if I did?" Bugsey looked at her wistfully.

Fenner didn't hear him. He saw the name on the boat, *Nancy W*, and he wandered on. "Havin' you around cramps my style," he said. "Alone, I'd 've made that dame."

Bugsey sneered. "You wouldn't 've got to first base. A frill like that's class. She's got no time for hoods."

Fenner led him to a bar. "All the same, pal, I'm goin' to have a try," he said.

When the barman came to take the order, Fenner said, "That's a swell boat out there."

The bartender stared vacantly out through the open door and nodded. "What'll you have?" he said.

Fenner ordered two gin slings. When the bartender brought them back, he tried again. "Who owns her?"

The bartender scratched his head. "What boat is it?"

"*Nancy W*."

"Sure, that's a swell boat. Thayler's the guy. He's gotta heap of jack."

Bugsey sighed. "You'd wantta heap of jack to make a dame like that."

"Thayler? What's his line?" Fenner went on.

The bartender shrugged. "Just spends dough. One of these rich playboys, I guess."

"Does he live around here?"

"A guy don't want to live around here when he's got a boat like that, does he?"

Fenner lowered half the gin sling. "Who's the dame?"

The barman grinned. "I can't keep up with them," he said. "I guess that guy's got a contract with the authorities to test them."

Bugsey said, "That's a swell job. Maybe he could do with a little help."

Fenner said, "Where can you meet a guy like that?"

"Meet him? He gets about. He's out a lot at Noolen's Casino."

"So Noolen's got a casino, eh?" Fenner said, looking at Bugsey.

Bugsey sneered. "Noolen's the south end of a horse."

Fenner put his glass down on the counter. "I'm beginning to believe that," he said, and, putting his hand under Bugsey's arm, he led him into the sunlight.

Noolen's casino was close to Ernest Hemingway's house at the corner of Olivia and Whitehead.

Fenner stopped his cab to get a look at the Hemingway house. Then he went on to the casino.

It was a hot evening, full of noise and river smells. The casino stood back in a landscape garden, with a half-circular drive leading to the big double front doors. Double porches and arched windows, fitted with yellow-slatted shutters, gave the big house a touch of distinction.

A lot of cars crawled up the drive, unloaded, and crawled on back to the street.

Fenner paid off his cab and wandered up the long flight of broad stone steps. The front doors were open, and he could see a brilliantly lighted lobby as he mounted.

There were two men standing by the door who looked at him hard. He put them down as Noolen's muscle men. He went on through the lobby into a big room where two tables were in action. He wandered around, keeping his eyes open and hoping to find the girl from the boat.

He hadn't been in the room five minutes before a short Cuban in evening dress came up to him. "Mr. Ross?" he said politely.

"What of it?" Fenner said.

"Will you come into the office a moment?"

Fenner smiled. "I'm here to enjoy myself," he said. "What do I want in your office?"

The two men who had been standing at the door suddenly moved through the crowd and stood each side of him. They smiled at him, but the smile didn't reach their eyes.

The Cuban said softly, "You'd better come, I think."

Fenner shrugged and moved with him. They crossed the room, went out into the lobby and into a small room on the left.

Noolen was walking up and down, his head on his chest, and a big cigar clamped between his teeth. He glanced up at Fenner as he came in.

The Cuban shut the door, leaving the other two men outside.

Fenner thought Noolen looked in better shape. He seemed cleaner and his tuxedo suited him.

Noolen said, "What are you doin' here?"

"This is public, ain't it? What's bitin' you?"

"We don't have any of Carlos's mob in here."

Fenner laughed. He went over and sat in a big leather arm-chair. "Don't be a mug," he said.

Noolen stood very still. "You better get out an' stay out...."

Fenner raised his hand. "Send the monkey away—I want to talk to you."

Noolen hesitated, then he gave a sign to the Cuban, who went out.

"You're not going to get anywhere being tough with Carlos," Fenner said, stretching his long legs. "Why don't you get wise to yourself?"

"What's your game?" Noolen said. "There's something about you I don't like."

Fenner said seriously, "I don't know. But string along. If my bet comes right, I may have to bust this town wide open. To do it, I might want you. I don't like Carlos and I don't like his racket. I think I'll wash him up."

Noolen laughed. "You're crazy. Carlos's big enough to smear you."

Fenner nodded. "That's how it looks, but that isn't the way it'll pan out. You'd like to see that guy go, wouldn't you?"

Noolen hesitated, then nodded. "Yeah," he said; "but he ain't goin' in my lifetime."

Fenner studied the toes of his shoes. "You got a mob if I wanted one?"

Noolen came and sat down. "I've gotta mob," he said cautiously, "but they're not in the same class. They'd be scared to start anything."

Fenner grinned. "Not when Carlos starts to slip. That's when your mob's got to go to work."

Noolen clasped his hands. There was a long silence while he brooded. Then he said, "You're playin' a tricky game. Suppose I have a little talk with Carlos."

Fenner shrugged. "Why should you? You've got every thing to gain by just sittin' tight waitin' for me to clean up the town."

"Okay. Then go ahead. I'll come in when I see you gettin' somewhere. Don't think you're going to clean my territory, because you ain't. One move from you I don't like, an' I'll clamp down on you."

Fenner got to his feet. "We won't worry about that for a little while," he said. "There'll be plenty of time to take care of that angle later."

Noolen looked up at him suspiciously. "I don't trust you, Ross, you're too cagey."

"Who's Thayler?" Fenner asked abruptly.

"Thayler? What's he to you?" Noolen's eyes were sud denly hot and intent.

"Saw his boat this afternoon. Swell job. Heard he came out here. Thought I'd like to look him over."

Noolen got up and walked to the door. "He's out there now."

Fenner followed him into the main hall. "Show him to me," he said. "I want to meet him."

Noolen wandered through the crowd, looked right and left, then said, "He's playin' on the third. The guy sittin' next to the blonde twist."

Fenner saw the girl. She looked fine sitting there. The soft light reflected on her red-gold hair, making deep shadows of her eyes and making her red lips glisten. She was wearing a black dress that fitted her too well.

Fenner said, "Who's the frill?" He said it very casually.

"Glorie Leadler. She's good, isn't she?" The blood had mounted in Noolen's face, and his blue eyes were watery. Fenner looked at him curiously. Noolen went on, "You'll have to wait if you want to meet Thayler. He won't want to be interrupted."

"That's all right. This Leadler girl, what is she?"

Noolen turned his head and looked at Fenner. "Why the excitement?"

"Why not? She's a riot, ain't she?"

Noolen sneered. "I'll leave you for a little while. I've got things to do," he said, and walked away.

Fenner looked after him, wondered what it was all about, and walked over to the small bar at the other end of the room. He ordered a rye and ginger and leaned against the bar. From where he stood he could just see Glorie's head and shoulders. He looked at Thayler and studied him, a big man, with a very sunburnt complexion and black crinkly hair. His china-blue eyes and his long thin nose made him look handsome.

When Fenner glanced at Glorie again he found she was looking at him. Fenner regarded her thoughtfully, wondering at the uncanny likeness. If this dame wasn't Marian Daley's sister, then he was a three-legged horse.

Thayler leaned over a little and spoke to her, and she started. Fenner couldn't be sure, but he thought she had smiled at him. He thought maybe it had been a trick of the light, but it certainly had seemed that she'd given him a come-hither. He watched her closely, but she didn't look in his direction again. He stayed there for several minutes, then he saw her speak to Thayler and stand up. Thayler looked angry and put his hand on her wrist, but she shook her head, laughed at him and walked away from the table. Thayler screwed his head round to watch her, then turned back to the table again.

She came over to the bar. There were two other men standing close by, and the small Cuban manager. Fenner said, "Drinking alone is a vice. Will you have one with me?"

She didn't look at him, but opened her small bag and took out a ten-dollar bill. "I like vice," she said softly, and ordered a gin sling. She stood with her back three-quarters to him. He could just see the lobe of her ear and the strong line of her chin.

Fenner finished his rye and ginger quickly and signalled the bartender for another. He studied her back thoughtfully, wondering. When the bartender put his order down on the polished wood, and had gone away, he said, "Miss Leadler, I want to talk to you."

She turned her head. "Me?"

"Yeah. That's your name, ain't it?"

"Yes." Her gaze began to embarrass him. He had a sudden uncomfortable feeling that she was seeing through him. No one had ever given him that feeling before. It confused him.

"My name's Ross. I'm staying at the Haworth. I want—" He broke off. Thayler was coming over fast. A heavy scowl darkened his face, and he came up to the bar with long quick strides. He said to Glorie, "For God's sake, can't you just drink?"

Glorie laughed at him. She said in a clear voice, "I think he's marvellous. I think he's absolutely, incredibly mar vellous."

Thayler looked uneasily at Fenner. "Cut it out, Glorie," he said under his breath.

She went on. "He's the most beautiful thing I've seen. Look at his arms. Look at the size of them. Look at the set of his neck—the way he holds his head."

Fenner took out his handkerchief and wiped his hands. He finished his drink. The Cuban manager was watching him, a cold look of contempt on his face.

Thayler said savagely, "You don't have to rave about his arms or his neck."

"Ask him to have a drink. He's cute. Do you know what he said to me? He said, 'Drinking alone's a vice.'" Glorie turned her head and smiled at Fenner.

Thayler said to Fenner, "Get out of here, you dope."

Glorie giggled. "Be friendly. You're making him embarrassed. That's no way to talk to a lovely man like that."

Fenner said, "Watch yourself, playboy! You're a little too soft to talk big."

Thayler made a move, but the Cuban manager slid between them. He said something to Thayler in a low voice. Thayler looked at Fenner over the top of the Cuban's head, his face was flushed with suppressed rage; then he turned, took Glorie by the wrist and walked out of the room.

Fenner said to the Cuban, "Nice girl."

The Cuban said, "Maybe you'd better go, too," and turned away.

Fenner stood thinking, then he snapped his fingers and left. He ran through the lobby, out into the black night. A cab shot up to the entrance and the driver swung the door open. Fenner said, "Waterfront, fast," and climbed into the cab.

Although the cab went fast, Thayler was already on board the *Nancy W.* when Fenner arrived. Fenner saw the light in the cabin flash as he paid off the cab driver. He looked hastily up and down the deserted waterfront, then ran along the jetty and climbed on board. Moving quietly, he reached the cabin. By lying full length, he could look down through the glass panel, which was half open.

Glorie was standing in the middle of the cabin, rubbing her wrist and looking at Thayler, who was leaning against the door. "It's time we had a showdown," he said. His voice came quite clearly to Fenner. "I've been a sucker long enough."

Glorie turned her back on him. "Once I get out of here," she said unevenly, "I never want to see you again."

Thayler went over to the sideboard and poured himself a drink. His hands shook so that the liquor slopped on the polished surface. "I've done a hell of a lot for you," he said. "It's always the same. I know you're crazy, but can't you try? That's what gets me, you don't even try."

Glorie moved round the room. She reminded Fenner of a caged animal.

"I'm sorry for you," Thayler said.

She spun round. "You're crazy. Do you think your sorrow means anything to me?"

"No one's sorrow has ever meant anything to you. You haven't any feeling, anyway."

"Yes, I have."

"Not that sort of feeling."

Thayler held the glass in his hand very tightly. Fenner could see his knuckles were white. "After this, I'm through with you. I'm not going to have another evening like this one."

Glorie laughed suddenly. "I'm sending you away, not you sending me. Shall I tell you why?"

"I'm sick of hearing it. I know it backwards."

Glorie said spitefully, "No, you don't. It's because you're no good. You were never any good. You're a flop. You don't know anything. You only think you do."

Thayler put his glass carefully on the table. He walked over to her, and put his hands on her shoulders. His face was white. "You know that's a damn lie, don't you?" he said.

She flung his hands off. "I've got through telling lies to you, Harry," she said. "It isn't fun any more. One time I'd 've let you keep your silly little pride. I can't be bothered now."

Thayler smacked her face.

Fenner pushed his hat to the back of his head and moved a little further forward.

Thayler said in a trembling voice, "I'll kill you for that."

Glorie felt her cheek. "You haven't the nerve to kill a rumour," she snapped back. "Don't you get tired using your head as a hat stand? Why don't you get wise? I'm through with you. I'm giving you the air."

Thayler went very white. "It's this other guy, huh?" he said. His hand touched the glass and he picked it up.

"Go easy with your blood pressure," Glorie sneered, "or you'll bust something."

As she opened the door, Thayler flung the glass at her. It splintered against the wall, a yard from her head.

Fenner drew away from the cabin skylight and stood up. "Let 'em fight," he thought, and, turning, he went away from the boat, heading towards his hotel.

III

Fenner was in Nightingale's workroom, watching the little man staining a box when Reiger came in.

Reiger said, "We got a job for you. I'll pick you up here at eight o'clock."

Fenner lit a cigarette. "What's the job?"

"You'll see."

"Listen, Reiger. You ain't gettin' that way with me. Either you work with me or to hell with it. What's the job?"

Reiger scratched the side of his mouth with his thumbnail. "We've got a consignment of Chinks. We're bringin' them over to-night."

Fenner said, "Okay, I'll be here."

Reiger went out.

"Friendly guy that," Fenner said to Nightingale. "Some how, I don't think he an' I hit it off."

Nightingale looked worried. "You're handlin' that guy wrong," he said, shaking his head. "He's mean. You'd better watch him."

Fenner drummed on the top of a coffin-lid with his fingers. "I'll watch him all right," he said. He nodded to Nightingale and went downstairs. Curly was sitting at the desk writing in a ledger. She looked up hopefully as he went past.

Fenner paused. "Hyah, baby, he said. "That's a nice face and figure you're wearin' this mornin'."

Curly opened her big eyes. "Gee!" she said. "I don't get much of that syrup."

"Never mind. It comes as a nice surprise when you do."

Curly nibbled the top of her pen. She looked at him with thoughtful eyes. "You're in this now?" she said.

Fenner nodded.

"Seen Pío?"

"I've seen him."

Curly sighed. "Ain't he a beautiful guy?"

"I wouldn't call him that. You don't think a lot of him, do you?"

Curly said bitterly, "What does it matter what I think?"

Fenner had a sudden idea. He sat on the edge of her desk. "Wait a minute, baby, don't get that way. Carlos mean anythin' to you?"

Curly said, "No guy means anything to me. You keep your nose out of my business, will you?" Her eyes told him quite a lot.

He stood up and grinned. "Sure, sure," he said. "Don't get me wrong. I thought maybe you'd like to put your curly little head on my shoulder an' tell me all your troubles."

"Well, you're wrong," she snapped. "I've got no troubles."

Fenner grinned again and went into the street. So that's the way it is, he thought. Curly had gone soft on Carlos and was getting nowhere. It was tough to fall for a little rat like Carlos.

He walked for some time through the narrow streets, retracing his steps, going into a bar for a short drink, and all the time checking to find out if anyone was tailing him. When he was satisfied no one was, he headed down-town again.

When he reached the Federal Building he loitered outside, keeping a close watch on the street; then he ducked into the building and took the elevator to the Federal Field Office.

The Federal Agent was named Hosskiss. He stood up behind his desk and offered a moist hand.

Fenner shook hands and sat down heavily in the chair opposite Hosskiss. He took some papers out of his inside pocket and handed them over. "The name's Fenner. Here's my licence that permits me to operate as a private investigator. I'm on business for a client down here, and I want you to know some facts."

Hosskiss examined the papers, frowned, and then said, "Fenner? You the guy who broke the Blandish kidnapping case?"

Fenner nodded.

"Well, that's fine," Hosskiss grinned. "I used to know Brennan. He told me all about it. Why, sure, if I can help you I'll be glad."

"I can't give you all the facts, but I'm looking for a girl. Somehow or other Carlos is tied up to the business. I've got an introduction to Carlos which was a fake and I've got a hook-up with his gang. I want you to know about this because I don't want to run foul of your boys. To-night I'm going with Reiger to collect a cargo of Chinks. We are due to leave around eight o'clock. I thought maybe you'd like to hear about that."

Hosskiss blew out his cheeks.

"Hell," he said, "you don't seem to know what sort of an outfit you're bucking. Listen, if Carlos hears about this you'll be cat's meat. That guy is the most dangerous rat on the coast."

Fenner shrugged.

"I know that," he said. "I was careful. I don't think anyone spotted me coming here. Why haven't you clamped down on that gang?"

"No evidence. We know what his game is, but we've never caught him at it. We've got aeroplanes and boats watching the coast, but he seems to slip through easily enough. Once we did catch up with him, but he hadn't anythin' on board. They're a tough gang. I'm betting they dumped the aliens overboard as soon as they saw our boat heading towards them."

Fenner scratched his head. "If you catch up on us to-night you've got to let me out somehow. It's Reiger I'd like to see in a cage, but I've got to be in the clear so I can carry on with my investigation."

Hosskiss said, "I'll fix that for you. You wouldn't like to tell me what it's all about?"

Fenner shook his head. "Not right now," he said cautiously. "I guess maybe I'll need your help for the final clean-up, but all I want now is for you to keep me in the clear if trouble comes my way." He stood up.

Hosskiss shook hands. "You don't know your course for to-night?"

Fenner shook his head. "No," he said; "you'll have to find us."

"We'll find you all right. I'll have the Strait lousy with boats."

Out in the street again, Fenner went on to the waterfront and picked up Bugsey. They went on to the Flagler Hotel.

Carlos was by himself when they entered No. 47. He nodded to them. He said to Bugsey, "Go outside and rest yourself."

Bugsey looked surprised, but he went out. Carlos looked at Fenner. Then he said, "Why did you go to Noolen's joint the other night?"

Fenner said, "I'm workin' for your mob, but I don't have to play with them, do I?"

Carlos said, "You didn't play. You went into Noolen's office—why?"

Fenner thought quickly. Carlos was standing very still, his hand hovering near the front of his coat. "I did go in to play, but Noolen sent for me an' told me to clear out. He didn't want any of your mob in his joint," Fenner said.

Carlos said, "You tried to talk with the Leadler woman—why?"

"Why not?" Fenner thought this was getting on dangerous ground. "Any guy would try for a frill like that. She was on her own, so I thought we might get friendly. What do you know about her?"

Carlos's eyes snapped. "Never mind about that. I don't like the way you're acting, Ross. Both those stories come too easy. I think I'll watch you."

Fenner shrugged. "You're losing your nerve," he said contemptuously. "You ain't scared of Noolen?"

Carlos jerked his head. "You can go," he said, and walked to the window.

Fenner went out thoughtfully. This guy wasn't such a dope as he'd thought. He would have to play his cards carefully. He said to Bugsey, "I'll be with you in a second. I wantta 'phone my hotel an' tell 'em I won't be in to-night." He shut himself in a booth and called Noolen. Bugsey hung about outside. Fenner said, keeping his voice low, "Noolen? Ross speakin'. Listen, Carlos has got a plant at your gambling house. He knew you an' me had a talk, and he knew other things. That Cuban manager of yours—had him long?" "Two months." Noolen's voice sounded worried. "I'll check up on him." "Yeah," said Fenner grimly, "I'd get rid of that guy quick," and he hung up. He walked out of the booth and took Bugsey's arm. "We'll go an' take things easy," he said. "Looks like I'll have a little hard work to-night." Bugsey went with him. He said in a low, confidential voice, "I gotta date myself." He closed his eyes and smiled.

Fenner showed at Nightingale's two minutes before eight. Reiger and Miller were already there. Miller was greasing a sub-machine-gun. They both looked up as Fenner followed Nightingale into the workroom.

Fenner said, "I smell rain."

Reiger grunted, but Miller said in a false, friendly way, "That's what we want, rain."

Nightingale said to Fenner in a low voice, "You got a rod?"

Fenner shook his head.

Nightingale went over to a drawer and took out a big automatic. Reiger jerked up his head. "He don't want a rod."

Nightingale took no notice. He handed the gun to Fenner. Reiger seemed to get quite excited. "I tell you he don't want a rod," he said, standing up.

Fenner looked at him. "Give it a haircut," he said. "I feel safer with a rod." They stared at each other, then Reiger shrugged and sat down again.

Nightingale gave a peculiar smile. "You given up packing a rod?" he said to Fenner. "They tell me you're dynamite with a trigger."

Fenner balanced the automatic thoughtfully in his hand. "I get by," was all he said.

Miller looked at the small watch that seemed out of place on his thick wrist. "Let's go," he said. He wrapped the machine-gun in his dust-coat and picked up his hat.

Reiger moved to the door. Nightingale said softly to Fenner: "Watch those two birds."

There was a big sedan parked outside the Funeral Parlour. Reiger got under the driving-wheel, and Fenner and Miller got in behind. Fenner waved his hand to Nightingale as the car slid away. He caught a glimpse of Curly watching behind Nightingale. He could just make out the blurred outline of her face.

He said to Miller: "Carlos never comes on these runs, does he?"

"Why should he?" Miller said shortly.

Reiger swung the car south. "You're always askin' questions, ain't you?" he said.

They rode the rest of the way in silence. When they got down to the waterfront they left the car parked and walked rapidly down to the line of small shipping. A tall Negro and Bugsey were waiting alongside a forty-foot boat. As soon as the Negro saw them coming he climbed aboard and disappeared into the engine-room. Bugsey stood ready to cast off.

Reiger said, while Miller climbed aboard, "You don't do anythin until they come alongside. Then you gotta watch them as they come aboard. Not one of these Chinks must have guns. The safest way to deal with them is to make them strip as they come on board. It takes time, but it's safe. If you think one of them's got a rod, take it off him. If he looks like startin' anything, give it to him. Miller will take them from you and put them in the forward cabin."

Fenner said, "Sure," and followed Reiger on board. Bugsey cast off and tossed the bowline to Reiger. He waved his hand to Fenner. "Nice trip," he said.

The Negro started the engines and the boat began to shudder a little. Miller was already down in the cockpit, his hand on the wheel.

Reiger said, "All right—let her go," and the boat began to show her heels.

Reiger went over to the small but powerful searchlight on the foredeck. He squatted down behind it and lit a cigar ette. His back was intent and unfriendly, and Fenner didn't bother to follow him. He climbed down into the cockpit with Miller and made himself comfortable.

"What time will you pick these guys up?" he asked Miller.

"Around about ten, I guess."

As the boat headed for the open sea, it grew suddenly chilly and a drizzling rain began to fall. There was no moon and the visibility was bad.

Fenner shivered a little and lit a cigarette. Miller said, "You get used to these trips. If you feel cold go into the engine-room. It'll be warmer there."

Fenner stayed with Miller a little longer, then he went off to the engine-room. He noticed Reiger still sitting behind the searchlight, immovable.

The boat bounced a good bit in the rough, and Fenner suddenly lost interest in smoking. The Negro didn't say a word. Now and then he rolled his eyes at Fenner, but he didn't say anything.

After some time Miller yelled and Fenner joined him. Miller pointed. An intermittent flash of light came from a long way off. Miller had altered the course and the boat was running directly toward the light. "I guess that must be our man," he said.

Reiger suddenly switched on his searchlight, and almost immediately he snapped it off again.

Very faintly Fenner heard the drone of an aeroplane. He smiled in the darkness. Miller heard it, too. He bawled to Reiger, "There's a plane coming." Reiger stood up and looked up into the blackness over head. Then he hurriedly put out the running lights. The boat went on through the curtain of blackness.

Miller said savagely, "Those coastguards give me a pain."

The aeroplane droned on, then, after a few minutes, faded away. Reiger flashed on the searchlight again, let the beam cut the darkness, and then turned it off. The other light kept on flickering. It was drawing nearer and nearer.

Miller handed Fenner a torch. "Go forward," he said; "we're nearly there."

Fenner took the torch and climbed out of the cockpit. He felt the boat roll as Miller cut speed.

Reiger, who was standing well forward, shouted, "Kill it," and with, a flurry the engines stopped. Reiger came over to Fenner, walking carefully as the boat rolled and heaved. "Get your rod out," he snapped, "and watch these guys." He was holding the sub-machine-gun. "I'll pass them to you. Make sure they ain't got guns, then pass them to Miller."

They both stared into the inky blackness. Reiger flashed on a small torch suddenly. He had heard the creak of oar locks.

A small rowboat came bobbing towards them. Fenner could see four men huddled in it and two men at the oars, then Reiger put his lamp out.

"Keep your ears back for that aeroplane," Reiger muttered to Fenner. Then, as the rowboat bumped gently alongside, he put his lamp on again.

A thin scraggy Chinaman came aboard. "I got four here," he said to Reiger. "I'll bring the others in four lots."

"What about the special?"

"Sure, sure, I'll bring the special last."

Reiger said to Fenner. "Okay, let's start."

Fenner stepped back and waited. The Chinamen came on board one by one. Reiger counted them, letting only one come at a time, waiting for Fenner to pass them to Miller, who directed them to the forward cabin. Each Chinaman wore the same clothes, tight shirts and knee-length trousers. They stood sheep-like before Fenner, who patted them down and shoved them over to Miller.

Two more boatloads came out and it all took some time. The scraggy Chinaman, who had stood on the right-hand side of Reiger while this was going on, said, "Okay, that's the lot. I'll go back for the special now."

Reiger said to Miller, "You locked those Chinks in?" His voice sounded uneasy to Fenner.

"Bolts on," Miller assured him.

Fenner wondered what the 'special' was. He sensed a sudden tension between Miller and Reiger. They all waited in the darkness, their ears straining for the long-boat to return. At last they heard the faint splash of oars. Reiger snapped on his torch and, reaching out with a boat-hook held the long-boat steady.

The scraggy Chinaman climbed on board. He reached down and the oarsman handed a small figure over to him. A quick pull, and the special was aboard.

"Don't you worry about this," Reiger said to Fenner.

Fenner flashed his torch on the special. He gave a soft grunt. It was a girl. He'd guessed as much. She was about thirteen or fourteen years old, Chinese, and pretty. She looked very scared and cold. She wore the same tight shirt and knee-length trousers.

With an oath Reiger struck the torch from his hand. "Keep out of this," he said between his teeth. "Miller, get her under cover."

Reiger turned to the Chinaman, who gave him a package wrapped in oilskin, and then climbed into the long-boat which disappeared into the night.

Fenner said between his teeth: "There's a nice rap hanging to this sort of racket."

Reiger said, "Yeah? You gettin' milky?"

"I guess I was entitled to know you were runnin' women. That ain't a thing that gets passed over easily."

"What do you think? A twist is worth ten Chinks, if you can get them. So shut up, will you?"

Fenner didn't say anything, he let Reiger go to the cock pit. He stood there brooding. Was this the answer to the riddle? They'd picked up twelve Chinks and a woman. Was that what this sister of Marian's was trying to hint at? Or was it just a coincidence? He didn't know.

Miller shouted. "Take her back, Reiger, I've had enough of it."

Reiger said, "Sure, tell the Nigger to start her up."

The boat quivered as the engines sprang into life. Fenner sat down with his back to the cockpit roof and searched the darkness. His ears strained, hoping to pick up the sound of a patrol boat. He neither heard nor saw anything.

Reiger shouted suddenly. "Ross—where the hell are you? Hi, Ross!"

Fenner dropped into the cockpit. "What's the matter?" he said. "Scared of the dark?"

"Listen, bright boy, suppose you lay off the funny angle? I want you to go into the Chinks' cabin and chain them together. There are the chains over there."

Fenner looked at the heap of handcuffs linked together with rusty chains that lay in the corner. "What for?" he said.

"What you think? We gotta be careful, ain't we? If a patrol boat gets on our tail, we shove the rats over. Chained like that they go down quick."

Fenner said, "The things you think of!" He took the wheel out of Reiger's hand. "Do it yourself. That ain't up my street."

Reiger looked at him in the dim light of the navigation lamp. "Somehow I don't think you're goin' to be a lotta use with our mob," he said, and picking up the chains, he climbed out of the cockpit and disappeared.

Fenner made a little face. He couldn't see how much longer he was going to keep this up. He was nearly satisfied that he'd got as much information as he wanted. It depended on what this Glorie Leadler would have to say. If he got what he hoped from her, then he could strike and wash the whole business up.

A muffled sound of a gun going off jerked his attention to the boat again. He listened, peering ahead but seeing nothing. There was silence, and after a little while Reiger came back into the cockpit again.

Fenner glanced at him as Reiger took the wheel from him. Reiger's face was hard and cold. "Trouble?" Fenner said.

Reiger grinned. "They don't like the chains. I had to shoot one of the punks in the leg before they'd quiet down."

Fenner ran his hand through his hair. It had stopped raining, but he felt cold and damp.

"Go along an' tell Miller to watch that broad," Reiger said suddenly. "She looked quiet, but if she starts a squeal, there'll be hell on this ship."

Fenner went aft to the small cabin behind the galley. He walked into the cabin and stopped. Miller was struggling with the Chinese girl. She fought him silently, blood running from her nose and from her lips.

Fenner took a step forward and grabbed Miller by his collar. He heaved, dragging Miller away from the girl. When he got him clear, he booted him hard, sending him sprawling to the other side of the small cabin.

Miller sat up slowly. His great white face glistened in the lamplight. He focused on Fenner by screwing up his eyes.

"Get out of here, an' leave me alone," he said thickly.

Fenner didn't say anything. He just stood, his hands hanging loose at his side. Miller looked round the cabin, saw the girl, and scrambled over to her.

Fenner, white-faced and thin-lipped, slid his gun so that he held it by the short barrel. He sucked in his breath and hit Miller on the top of his head. Miller stiffened, went limp. He twitched once, as if trying to command his muscles, then his forehead hit the floor with a little thud.

Fenner shoved his gun away and took him by his arm and dragged him out of the cabin.

Reiger shoved his head over the top of the cockpit. "What the hell's goin' on?" he shouted.

Fenner took no notice. He dumped Miller in the scuppers.

Miller sat up, holding his head. He mumbled a hoarse stream of obscenities. Fenner didn't look at him; he went over to the cockpit and climbed down.

Reiger said, "What's goin' on?"

Fenner had difficulty in keeping his voice steady. "That heel Miller was after the girl. I bounced him."

Reiger shrugged. "You should worry about her."

Fenner didn't answer. He was looking at a tiny moving light on their port side. He hastily looked away before Reiger noticed. He wondered if it were a patrol boat.

Miller, who had staggered to his feet, saw it and yelled a warning. Reiger looked and spun the wheel.

"Coastguards," he said; "maybe they won't spot us."

The boat was still running without lights, but the moon had climbed above the belt of clouds, and the big white wash showed up pretty well.

Fenner watched the light, saw it swing round a little and head towards them. He said gently, "They've seen us all right."

Reiger yelled for Miller. He gave the boat all the gas she'd take. Miller came staggering down into the cockpit. He glared at Fenner murderously, but Reiger snarled, "Take the wheel. I'm gettin' the gun out. Maybe this guy's faster'n us."

Miller took the wheel and Reiger disappeared aft. Fenner climbed out of the cockpit and followed Reiger. The light was coming up now, and as the moonlight began to flood the sea, Fenner could make out the boat. It was fast all right. He could see the way the bows were lifted right out of the water.

He said to Reiger, "This boat's goin' to catch us."

Reiger shouted down into the engine-room, and the Negro handed up a Thompson gun. Reiger gave it to Fenner, and took another from the Negro.

"You get on the port side," Reiger said, lying down flat. "Keep firing at them."

Fenner lay down. He fired two bursts, taking care that the bullets would go well over the top of the boat. Almost immediately, Reiger fired with his gun. Even from where he lay, Fenner could see a shower of white splinters spurt from the bows of the oncoming boat.

Fenner ducked his head as the coastguards replied. He saw the long yellow flashes and heard the thud of bullets as they bit into the sides of the boat. The coastguards kept up such a heavy fire that it was impossible for either Reiger or Fenner to show themselves to fire back.

Miller, watching from the cover of the cockpit, screamed out, "Do somethin'. They'll be up in a few seconds."

Reiger peered from behind his cover, saw the boat was within six feet or so and ducked back as the wood began to splinter again.

Fenner turned his head. He could see Reiger lying flat. Reiger shouted to him, "Stand by for a headache," and leaning over on his side he tossed a small ball-like object right into the other boat.

There was a blinding flash and a violent explosion and the coastguard boat immediately began to fall astern.

"Keep her going," Reiger shouted to Miller, and sat up to watch the coastguard boat burst into flames. He scrambled over to Fenner. "That's the first time we've tried that stunt. Carlos's some guy with his ideas. If we hadn't had that pine apple on board the Chinks would be feedin' the fishes by now, an' we'd have had a lost journey."

Fenner grunted. He couldn't take his eyes off the burning boat, which was rapidly becoming a little red glow in the darkness. He got slowly to his feet. Reiger had already gone forward. He was pointing to a green light that flickered in the distance. Miller swung the wheel a little.

"That's the guy who takes our load," Reiger shouted to Fenner. "We've got through all right."

Fenner stood watching the green light come nearer. He knew now that he must start things moving. He'd played with Carlos long enough.

It was just after two o'clock in the morning when Fenner got back to the Haworth. Before he switched on his room light he knew someone was there. He didn't hear anything, but he knew he wasn't alone. He stepped inside, feeling uncomfortably exposed in the dimly lighted doorway. There was something in the air, a scent. He reached inside his coat and pulled his gun, then he groped for the wall switch and flicked the light on.

A woman's clothes on the floor at the foot of his bed caught his eye. A black dress, a handful of lace and crêpe de chine, a pair of shoes.

Glorie Laidler sat up in his bed. Two bare arms curved up over the sheet, holding the sheet firmly against her body. When she saw who it was, she lay back again, keeping her arms out and arranging her red-gold hair on Fenner's pillow.

Fenner put his gun away. The only thing he could think of was that he was tired and that he'd have to strip his bed when she had gone. He didn't fancy sleeping in the same sheets.

Glorie smiled at him sleepily.

Fenner went over to the floor lamp, put it on, and turned off the ceiling lamp. The light was softer, but it lit up the floor brightly. He saw two little red marks on his carpet which hadn't been there before. He looked at the red marks and then he looked at Glorie's shoes. He moved further into the room. There were red marks on the shoes, as if Glorie had stepped in something. Without picking the shoes up, Fenner couldn't be sure. He knew pretty well the marks were bloodstains, but he didn't want her to know he'd seen them just yet.

Fenner said, "Why have you come here?"

"It's you. You said Haworth. You said you wanted to talk. I came here and waited. I got tired of waiting, so I got into bed. I thought you wouldn't come back to-night."

"When did you come here?"

"What do you mean—when?" Her slatey eyes went a little cold.

"What time?"

"Nine o'clock. I waited until eleven and then I came to bed."

"Anyone see you come in?"

She shook her head. Fenner thought she had gone a little white. She moved restlessly in the bed. He could see the long outline of her legs under the thin sheet. A lot of the bravado had gone out of her. She said, "You sound like a big policeman askin' nasty questions."

Fenner smiled bleakly. "Just rehearsing you, baby," he said. "You haven't much of an alibi, have you?"

Glorie sat up in bed. She said, "What—what are you saying?"

Fenner shook his head. "Get under cover. You're too big a girl for this sort of thing now."

She pulled the sheet up over her, but she didn't lie down. "What do you mean—alibi?"

He reached over and picked up one of her shoes. He examined it carefully. The sole was covered with dry blood. He tossed the shoe in her lap. She gave a husky little scream and threw it from her. Then she lay back, put her hands over her face and began to cry.

Fenner went to a cupboard, took out a bottle of Scotch and gave himself a drink.

He lit a cigarette and took off his hat and coat. It was very hot and close in the room. He walked over to the open window and looked into the deserted street. "You'd better tell me," he said.

She said, "I don't know anything about it."

He wandered back to the bed and sat down. "Then the quicker you get out of this room the better pleased I'll be. I don't want to be dragged into a murder rap."

She said, between choking sobs: "I found him. He was lying on the floor. Someone had shot him."

Fenner ran his fingers through his hair. "Who?" he said gently.

"Harry—Thayler, the man I was with."

Fenner brooded. "Where is he?" he said at last.

Glorie took her hands away. Fenner experienced a little shock. She certainly wasn't crying. She was play-acting. She said, "On his boat."

"When did you find him?"

"Just before I came to you."

Fenner rubbed his eyes. He got up and put his coat and hat on again. "Wait here," he said. "I'm goin' down to have a look at him."

She said, "I'll come with you."

Fenner shook his head. "You keep out of this. Stay here. When I get back I want to talk to you."

Then he went out of the room and down to the waterfront.

He found *Nancy W* and climbed on board. He went down into the main cabin. It was dark and he couldn't find the light switch. He used his torch, but he couldn't find Thayler. He searched the whole boat, but he couldn't find anything. He turned on the light in the sleeping cabin after closing the porthole. From the clothes lying about, he thought this must be where Thayler had slept.

He went through the chest of drawers carefully.

The only thing he found which really astonished him was a small photo of Curly Robbins, taken, as far as he could judge, several years ago. He took the photo and put it in his wallet. Then he shut the drawer and snapped off the light.

He went back to the main cabin again and examined the carpet. It was only when he looked very closely that he could see that the carpet had been recently washed in one small patch. He stood up, scratching his head. He was quite certain now that Thayler was not on board.

Was Thayler dead? Could he rely on what Glorie had said? If he'd been killed, who had got rid of his body and washed up the carpet? Had Glorie killed him? The last time he'd seen those two together they weren't exactly acting friendly.

He said with exasperation, "Nuts!" and went out of the cabin. As he stepped on the jetty he noticed a big sedan drawn up without lights on the other side of the waterfront. He gave it a quick look, and then dropped flat. A choked roar came from the car as he did so and he knew someone had let off a shot-gun in his direction. He pulled his gun and kept flat. He heard the car start and the swish of tyres on the sandy road. Then the car swept out of sight round the corner.

Fenner got up and dusted himself. Things were getting complicated. He walked back to the Haworth, keeping in the shadows and using the back streets only.

Glorie lay just where he had left her. Her face was a little pinched, and the smile she gave him was only a twist of the mouth.

He pulled up the chair again and sat down. "Was he in the main cabin when you saw him?" he said abruptly.

She said, "Yes."

Fenner nodded, as if he expected that. "They've taken him away now," he said. "I don't know why they did that, because if they wanted a fall-guy you'd 've been it. Either you killed him and tossed him overboard or you didn't, and the killer came back for some reason or other and took him away. Maybe you tossed him overboard."

Glorie showed her long arms. "Do you think. I could do it? He was big."

Fenner thought of the almost perpendicular stairs leading into the cabin, and shook his head. "No," he said. "I guess that's right."

The colour came back to her face and she didn't look so drawn. She said, "If they hid him away, no one will know he's dead, will they?"

Fenner yawned. "That's right," he said.

She curled down in the bed, pulling the pillow off the bolster. "Don't you think I look snug?" she said, her eyes getting flirtatious again.

Fenner said, "Where's your sister Marian?"

She didn't jump more than an inch, but it looked like a couple of yards. Fenner leaned over her and pulled her round. Her eyes were startled. "Where's your sister?" he repeated.

She said, "What do you know about her? *How* do you know about her?"

Fenner sat down close to her. "You're as like as two peas," he said. "I've never seen anything quite like it." He put his hand inside his pocket and took out the letter he had found in Marian's bag. "Look at that," he said.

She read it through blankly, and then shook her head. "I don't know," she said. "Who's Pío? Who's Noolen?"

Fenner went over to the table, picked up a pad of note paper and a pencil and came back to the bed. "Write that letter out for me," he said.

As she struggled up, he said hastily, "Wait." He went to the cupboard and got his pyjama jacket and threw it over to her. Then he went into the bathroom and waited a few seconds. When he came out she had put the coat on and was rolling back the long sleeves.

She said, "Why do you want me to do this?"

"Do it." He spoke very curtly.

She scribbled on the pad and then gave it to him. He compared the two handwritings. There was nothing similar about them. He tossed the pad on the table again and began to walk up and down the room slowly. She watched him nervously.

"You've got a sister, haven't you?" he said at last.

She hesitated, then she said, "Yes; but we haven't seen each other for a very long time."

"How long? Why haven't you?"

"Four or five years, I forget exactly. Marian and I didn't get on so well. She'd got ideas about how I should live. We didn't quarrel, but she kept having ideas. So we split when father died."

Fenner said gently, "You're lying. If you hadn't seen each other for that length of time, why did she come to me all fussed because you were missing?"

Two little patches of red burnt in Glorie's cheeks. "I didn't know she came to you. Who are you, anyway?"

"Never mind who I am. When did you last see Marian?"

Glorie looked sulky. "I was in New York with Harry. We ran into each other. It was about a couple of weeks ago. I was up there on a trip. Marian wanted me to come to her hotel. I said I would, because she was so insistent. I had Harry with me. It was awkward. Marian wouldn't stand for Harry, so I gave her the slip and came back to Florida."

Fenner came over and sat on the bed. "Either you're telling a lot of lies, or else there's somethin' I've missed in all this," he said.

Glorie shook her head from side to side. "I'm not lying," she said. "Why should I?"

"Listen, did you say anything to your sister about twelve Chinamen?"

"Twelve Chinamen? Why should I?"

"Don't keep sayin' 'Why should I?'" Fenner said savagely. "It confuses me."

As far as he could see he was no further, now he'd met this girl, than he was before. He thought, and then said, "Why Leadler? Why not Daley?"

"Leadler's my married name," Glorie said. "I was divorced a year ago."

Fenner grunted. "Where's your husband?"

She shook her head. "I don't know," she said. "Why?"

Fenner didn't answer. Instead he said, "Your sister was murdered last week in a house in Brooklyn."

There was a long silence. Glorie said, "I don't believe it." Her eyes crawled up and down Fenner's face.

Fenner shrugged. "You don't have to," he said; "but she was murdered all right. I liked that girl. She came to me for help. I didn't like the way she met her finish, an' I'm promising myself to fix the guy who killed her."

Glorie took his coat in her hand. She twisted the coat and shook him. "Marian dead?" she said. "You sit there like that and say that to me? You haven't any pity for me! Marian—Marian—"

Fenner put his hand on her wrist and jerked her hand away. "Cut it out," he said. "You can't act. You don't give a hoot what happened to Marian."

Glorie looked at him and then giggled. She put her hand over her mouth and her eyes looked shocked. "I shouldn't 've done that," she said. "Fancy Marian getting murdered." She rolled over in the bed and buried her face in the pillows. She began to shake with laughter.

Fenner had a sudden idea. He put his hand on her head, shoved her down into the pillow, and pulled down the sheet with his other hand. Still holding her, he jerked the pyjama jacket over her shoulders and looked carefully at her back. He pulled the jacket down and pulled up the sheet, then he stepped back.

Glorie twisted round, her eyes bright. "Why—why did you do that?" she said.

"Did you know your sister had bruises all over her back?" Fenner said.

"You know everything, don't you?" and she began to cry. When Fenner saw the tears running from her eyes, he walked away to the window. He began to feel horribly tired. He said abruptly: "I'll see more of you to-morrow," and walked to the door. The sound of her sobbing followed him downstairs. He thought, "I'll go crazy if somethin' doesn't happen soon," and he went to the night clerk to arrange for another room.

The bright sunlight came through the slatted shutters and lay like prison bars across Fenner's bed.

He stirred restlessly as a clock downstairs faintly chimed ten. At the eighth chime he opened his eyes and grunted. His body still felt tired, and his head ached a little. He was dimly conscious of the sunlight, and he closed his eyes again. Then, as his mind struggled out of sleep he was aware of a weight at the foot of his bed and scent on the air. As he groaned, Glorie giggled. He looked at her through half-closed eyes, and his half-awakened senses said she looked very nice. She was curled up, with her back resting on the end of the bedstead, her long legs up to her chin, and her fingers laced round her knees. She rested her chin in the little hollow between her knees and regarded Fenner with bright eyes.

"When you're asleep you look kind and beautiful," she said. "Isn't that wonderful?"

Fenner struggled up in bed. He ran his fingers through his hair. He felt terrible.

"Would you mind goin' away?" he said patiently. "When I want to see you I'll tell you. I dislike women in my bed room on principle. I'm old-fashioned and I'm easily shocked."

Glorie giggled. "You're cute," she said simply.

Fenner groaned. Now he was sitting up his head ached sharply. "Run away," he said. "Beat it! Scram!"

Glorie threw her arms wide. Her incredibly blue eyes sparkled. "Don't you like me? Don't you think I'm mar vellous?" she said.

Fenner said unpleasantly, "Will you run away?"

Glorie slid off the bed. She looked funny in Fenner's pyjamas. They hung on her like a sack.

Fenner said, "Anyway, you look like something the cat dragged in. Why not go away and get dressed, then maybe we'll have breakfast and another talk."

Glorie giggled and began dancing round the room. Fenner thought she was the most beautiful bit of corruption he'd ever seen.

She laughed at him. "Say, you must like me!" she said.

Fenner sat up on his elbow. "Go away," he said shortly, "I don't want to be bothered just now."

She said, "Do you really mean that?" Doubt had come into her eyes, like the slow movement of a cloud across the face of the moon. She came over to the bed and sat close to him.

Fenner nodded. "Pull your freight, sister," he said. "I'll see you later."

He thought for a moment that she was going to hit him. Then she got up and wandered out of the room, leaving the door open. Fenner got out of bed and kicked the door to, and went into the bathroom. He thought: "What a hell of a note to start the morning on." After a shower he felt better and he rang for coffee. He was dressed when the waiter brought up the coffee. Two cups put him right and he went along to Glorie's room. She was dressed. Her black evening dress looked out of place in the sunlight. She was sitting by the window looking into the street.

Fenner wandered in and shut the door softly behind him. He said, "What are you going to do?"

Glorie turned and smiled at him. It was quite a shock. Her eyes were wide, candid and friendly. She said, "What can I do?"

He leaned against the wall and stared at her thoughtfully.

He said at last, "You're difficult to understand. I thought I was goin' to have a lot of trouble with you. I see I was wrong."

She swivelled round, her back to the window. "I still think you're cute," she said. Then she added, "I'm going to grow on you."

Fenner's eyes shifted past her, looked into the street. A black sedan was standing below. He'd seen that car before. Even as he started forward a man's arm came through the curtained window. The sun reflected on a gun. That was the flash picture Fenner had, a picture that paralysed him, making him

seconds late. He heard a faint phut as Glorie screamed. Not a loud scream
soft, hoarse. Then she bent at the knees. Before Fenner could do anything
about it, she slid to the floor.

The sedan went away fast. It all happened at such an incredible speed that
no one seemed conscious of it in the street. Fenner leaned out of the window,
saw the sedan swing round the corner and disappear.

He stepped away and knelt down swiftly. As he turned Glorie, his right hand
felt a wet patch on her side, just above her hip. She'd gone very white, but she
was breathing. Fenner reached out and grabbed a cushion from a near-by
chair and put it under her head. Then he ran into the bath room. He filled a
hand bowl with water, snatched up a small first-aid case he always kept with
him and went back.

She watched him come across the room, her eyes wide with fear. She said,
"I can't feel anything. Am I badly hurt?"

Fenner knelt down. "Take it easy," he said. "We'll look an' see."

He opened the case and selected a scalpel. "I guess your dress'll have to go,"
he said, cutting the silk carefully.

She said, "I'm glad I was with you," and began to cry.

Fenner cut the top of her girdle. "Keep yourself in hand," he said, working
quickly. "The shock's bound to tilt you sideways." He examined the wound,
and then grinned. "Well, I'll be damned. It's only a nick. The slug's just made
a groove in your side."

She said, "I was scared that I was going to die."

"So was I." Fenner fixed the wound with experienced fingers. "All the same,
that was nice shooting. That guy was some sniper."

Glorie said in a small voice, "It hurts now."

"Sure, it's bound to hurt." Fenner straightened and looked down at her.
"You'll have to lie up for a few days. Maybe that'll keep you out of mischief.
I'm goin' to take you home. Where do you live?"

She looked away from him, her face suddenly blank, then she gave a little
giggle that finished on a gasp of pain. "I haven't got a home," she said, putting her hand on her side.

"Where did you live before you threw in with Thayler?" She looked at him
sharply, then looked away again. "I didn't throw in with Harry—"

Fenner knelt beside her. "You're a rotten liar," he said. "You said last night
you and Thayler were doing a trip to New York together. Now you say you
didn't throw in with him. Give it to me straight."

She said jerkily, "I believe you're a detective."

Fenner snorted. "Listen, redhead, you can't lie about floors all day. I've gotta
get you somewhere. Either you tell me where you live, or else I'll send for an
ambulance."

She said, "I want to stay here."

Fenner smiled unpleasantly: "I'm not going to be your nursemaid," he said. "I gotta lot to do."

She said, "I'm safer here."

Fenner paused, thought, and then said, "I see." He went over to the bed and pulled the sheet down. Then he picked her up very gently, sitting her in a chair. She chewed her lip while he did this. He took the scalpel and cut the dress down each side.

She said, "What a mess," and went so white he thought she was going to faint.

"Hold it," he said sharply, and stood her up. "Get a grip on yourself."

She put her face against his. "You're cute," she said in a small voice.

He jerked his head away. "Cut it out!" he said, and carried her over to the bed. He was glad to get her covered

She lay with her red-gold head on the pillow and looked up at him. She looked suddenly very young and defenceless. She said, "I want to whisper."

Fenner shook his head. "Try another one. That's got whiskers on it."

She reached up her two arms. "Please!"

He bent his head and she kissed him. Her lips felt very soft against his. It was just a youthful kiss, and Fenner quite liked it. He straightened and rumpled his hair. "Take it easy," he said. "I'm going to fix things." He pulled up the sheet to her chin, cleared her clothes and the rest of the mess into the bathroom, and went downstairs.

The hotel manager looked at him with an odd expression. Fenner felt a little embarrassed. He said, "My girl friend's run into a little accident. She'll have to stay in bed. I want you to send someone out an' get her a sleeping suit an' what ever else she wants. Put it all on the bill."

The manager said quite seriously, "This is a little irre gular—"

Fenner interrupted him. "I'll say it's irregular," he said shortly, "but it ain't so irregular that it calls for a fan dance from you, so snap to it."

He went over to a telephone booth and dialled a number. A hoarse voice floated over the wire.

"Bugsey?" Fenner asked. "Listen, Bugsey. I gotta job for you. Yeah, just the job you've been wantin'. Come on over to my dump an' bring a rod."

He went into the bar and ordered two fingers of rye. He felt he wanted a drink after all the excitement. While he waited for Bugsey he remembered something. He took out his wallet. When he opened the wallet a frown came to his eyes. He said, "That's a very funny thing."

His money and his papers were all on the right-hand side of the wallet, and he knew that yesterday there had been some on the right and some on the left. He went through the papers carefully and counted his money. Nothing was

missing so far as he could remember. Then he said, "Well, well," because
Curly's photo wasn't there any more. He went through the wallet more carefully, but it wasn't there. He put the wallet back in his pocket thoughtfully and
finished the rye.

Unless someone had come in while he slept, someone other than Glorie, he
knew he hadn't far to look for the photo. He wasn't going to get away as Ross
any more. She, or whoever it was, must have seen his licence papers. He lit a
cigarette and waited for Bugsey. He knew it would be a waste of time to try
and get anything out of Glorie right now. She'd just pretend she felt bad, and
that would be the end of that.

Bugsey came into the bar with a look on his face a dog gets when he thinks
there's a bone around. He was wearing a stained suit of grey herringbone and
a greasy light felt hat. A red flower decorated his buttonhole. Fenner found
himself wondering if it had grown there.

Bugsey wiped his mouth with the back of his hand and looked at the row
of bottles with a smile of expectation. Fenner bought him a large beer and took
him to the far end of the room. When they had settled, Fenner said, "Listen,
pal, how would you like to work for me?"

Bugsey's gooseberry eyes opened. "I don't get it," he said.

"I gotta little job you might like to handle. Nothing very much, but it's worth
fifty bucks. If you an' me get along, I might put you on my pay-roll, but it'd
mean kissin' good bye to Carlos."

"Ain't you workin' for Carlos no more?"

Fenner shook his head. "Naw," he said, "I don't like his game. It stinks."

Bugsey scratched his head. "Carlos won't like it," he said uneasily.

"Never mind Carlos," Fenner said. "If I don't wantta play, I don't."

Bugsey wagged his head. "How do I earn fifty bucks?" he asked eagerly.

"This is a sweet job that means no work and not much worry. You remember the jane on the *Nancy W*?"

Bugsey passed his tongue over his lips. "Am I likely to forget her?" he said.
"What a number!"

"She's upstairs in my bed, right now."

Bugsey slopped his beer. His moonlike face showed his surprise. He said.
"In your bed?"

Fenner nodded.

"What a guy!" Bugsey was almost overwhelmed with admiration. "I bet it
cost you a heap of jack to get her in there."

Fenner shook his head again. "Fact was, Bugsey, I had to fight to keep her
out."

Bugsey put the beer down on the table with a click. "You ain't kiddin'?" he
said. "You wouldn't tell a lie about a thing like that?"

"No, she's up there all right."

Bugsey brooded, then he said in a hoarse, confidential whisper, "You might tell me how you do it. That sort of dope comes in useful."

Fenner thought it was time to get down to business.

"Never mind about the details, pal," he said. "Some guy pulled a rod on this dame and took a little meat out of her side. This guy might look in again and make a better job. I want you to sit around with a rod an' see he doesn't."

Bugsey said in a faint, strangled voice, "An' you're payin' fifty bucks for a job like that?"

Fenner looked startled. "Ain't it enough?"

"That's a laugh. I'd do it for nothin'. Maybe she'd go for me."

Fenner got up. "Okay, come on up, I'll introduce you. Only don't go gettin' ideas. You sit outside the door, get it? A dame like that hasn't any time for hoods. That's what you said, wasn't it?"

A little crestfallen, Bugsey followed him upstairs. Fenner knocked on the door and went in. Glorie was lying in a pink satin nightdress, all ribbons and frills. She gave a little giggle when Fenner paused, staring at her.

"Isn't it a dream?" she said. "Did you choose it yourself?"

Fenner shook his head. "I've got a bodyguard for you. This is Bugsey. He's goin' to hang around to keep off the nasty men."

Glorie looked Bugsey over with surprised eyes. "He looks nasty himself," she said. "Come in, Bugsey, and meet a lovely lady."

Bugsey stood in the doorway gaping.

Fenner reached forward and pulled a chair out into the passage. "This guy's goin' to sit outside and work," he said grimly. "That's what I'm payin' him for."

He pushed Bugsey out of the room again and nodded to her. "I've got a little job to do, then I'll be back for a talk. Take it easy, won't you?" Then, before she could say anything, he drew the door shut. "Get busy," he said to Bugsey, "and keep outta that room. No funny business. Get it?"

Bugsey shook his head. "I couldn't start anythin' with a dame like that. Gee! She makes my head spin."

Away from the hotel, Fenner shut himself in a telephone booth and got the Federal Building. Hosskiss came on the line after a delay. He said, "Were you the guy who slung a bomb at one of my boats?" He sounded angry.

Fenner said, "Never mind about that. Your boys asked for it. They're old-fashioned. This guy Carlos's got all sorts of modern ideas. He'll be usin' poison gas soon."

Hosskiss made growling noises, but Fenner broke in, "I want to locate a big black sedan with three C's and two sevens in the make-up of the licence plate. Can you get me that information quick?"

Hosskiss said, "You'd better come round. There's a lot I want to talk to you about."

Fenner glanced over his shoulder through the dirty glass of the booth into the street. "I'm playin' the game too close," he said. "I ain't showin' up at your place any more. Maybe we'll fix somewhere to meet later on. What about that sedan?"

Hosskiss said, "Hang on."

Fenner leant against the wall of the booth and read the various scribblings on the white paintwork. When Hosskiss came over the line again, Fenner said, "This town wants cleanin' up. The things you guys write in these booths—"

Hosskiss cut in, "Never mind about that. I think I've found your car. Would it be Harry Thayler's bus, do you think?"

Fenner screwed up his eyes. "Yeah," he said, "it could be."

"There are others in the list, of course, but Thayler seems to be the best bet."

"Never mind about the others. That'll do to go on with. Listen, Hosskiss, if I hand you Carlos an' his mob on a plate, will you get some work done for me?"

Hosskiss said he would.

"I want everything you can get on Thayler. I want to know all about a dame named Glorie Leadler, and as much as you can dig up about her sister" Marian Daley. Then there's Noolen; I want his history, too. You might see what you can find out about this guy Leadler, Glorie's husband. Then, when you've done all that, I want a line on a dame called Curly Robbins, who works at Nightingale's Funeral Parlour. I want to find out what Thayler knows about her, too."

Hosskiss got quite excited. "Hey!" he said. "That's a job of work. Diggin' up things like that will cost money."

Fenner sneered. "What the hell's the use of your organiza tion if you can't do a little thing like that? You get all that for me, an' I'll give you Carlos an' maybe I'll donate five C's to your knitting club or somethin'."

Hosskiss said, "Okay, I'll cover it. But it's goin' to take time."

"Sure it'll take time. It'll mean starting from birth cer tificates an' working up. I want all the dope, not some of it."

"Now listen, about this business of the bomb," Hosskiss began heatedly, but Fenner hung up. He stepped out of the booth, wiped his hands with his handkerchief and walked in the direction of Duval Street. While he walked, his mind was busy. So Thayler was the guy who owned the sedan. That gave him ideas. There was something very phoney about the whole business. This Glorie Leadler was playing a five-ace hand. Had she any connection with Carlos? He'd caught her in one lie, why not another? Her sister had said, "What can she want with twelve Chinamen?" Why had she said that, unless Glorie had told her about the Chinamen? If Glorie hadn't written the letter, and he didn't think she had, who was the writer? Obviously the letter must have been a plant to give him a key to the whole business. There fore it followed that the writer was anxious for him to crack it open. The handwriting was a woman's. There was only one other woman at the moment in this business and that was Curly. Had Curly written the note? Or—the idea so startled him that he stopped in the middle of the street—had Marian written it herself?

A fat man bumped into him, walked round him and went on, screwing his head to scowl at him. Fenner walked on to Nightingale's.

The buzzer sounded as he opened the door. From behind the curtain Carlos suddenly appeared. The faint cloying smell of marihuana. came from his clothes and his eyes looked like pieces of glass in his white face.

Fenner was a little startled. "Selectin' your box?" he asked pleasantly.

Carlos said, "You want anything?"

Fenner wandered round the room. "Oh, I look in an' have a chin with Nightingale," he said casually. "Good guy" when you know him. Don't see you around here much. Givin' Curly a thrill?"

Carlos leant against the counter. The atmosphere was very brittle. "Miller says you bounced him around on the boat," he said; "I don't like fightin' in my mob."

Fenner raised his eyebrows. "No? That's too bad. Every time Miller tries to make any frill when I'm around, he's goin' to be bounced, that is if the frill doesn't like him."

Carlos blinked. "Reiger didn't think much of your work, either," he said.

Fenner shook his head. "That's bad, too. But then I ain't surprised. Reiger an' I don't get on so well."

"What with one thing and another, maybe it'd be better if you didn't work for me for a while." Carlos studied his nails.

Fenner wandered over to him. "Sure," he said, "that suits me."

Carlos twisted his mouth. It was his idea of a smile. "Maybe you'd like to select a box. Nice to know that you're gettin' your wishes after you're dead."

Fenner was quite close to him now. "Meaning that things might happen? An accident or somethin'?"

Carlos shrugged. "You do know a lot now, don't you?" he said. "Not that it'd help the cops. I've changed my office an' you don't know where the boat picked up or landed the Chinks, but still, you know somethin'."

Fenner said, "I shouldn't try it. No, I guess it'd be a dopey move to try anythin' like that."

Carlos adjusted his tie. "I don't care a great deal what you think," he said, and turned away. Fenner reached out and jerked him round. "I just want to show you where we stand, hophead," and punched Carlos high up on his cheek bone. He didn't hit very hard, but he knocked Carlos off his feet.

Carlos lay on his back, supported by his elbows. A bruise showed on his soft white skin. He began to hiss through his teeth. He made Fenner think of some slug-like thing.

Fenner said, "Now you know. I never let anyone talk big about my death; it makes me nervous. If you do want to start anythin' I suppose you'll have to try, but this I promise you. If you don't pull it off, I'm comin' after you. It'll take more than your mob of hoods to stop me. I'm not goin' to bother about them, it's you I'm comin' after, an' when I catch up with you I'll bend you round a pole an' break your back for you."

Carlos got slowly to his feet. When he put his hand to his face his hand fluttered like a moth's wing.

"Dust," Fenner said. "Go home an' have a shot of liquor; you need it."

Without a word Carlos went out, closing the door behind him.

Nightingale said, "That's a hell of a thing to do."

How long he'd been standing there Fenner didn't know. The light on his glasses hid his eyes, but Fenner could see some sweat beads on his face.

Fenner said, "Why didn't you pick the punk up if he means all that to you?"

Nightingale showed his white, sharp teeth. "He means nothing to me," he said, his voice trailing off to a squeak. "All the same, it was a hell of a—"

"Skip it," Fenner broke in. "It's time someone slapped that hophead down. He thinks he's the king pin in this joint."

"He is."

"How far in are you with him?"

Nightingale made an expressive gesture. He waved his hand round the room and shrugged. "All this is his. I'm just his front."

Fenner grunted. "You keep pluggin' because you've got nothing else?"

Nightingale nodded. "Sure," he said; "I gotta live."

"Curly? Where does she come in on this?"

The weak eyes snapped behind the lenses. "You leave her outta this."

Fenner said, "She's gone soft on Carlos."

Nightingale took two little shuffling steps forward. He swung over a left that caught Fenner flush on the chin. It was meant to be a socker, but a man like Nightingale hadn't any iron in his bones. Fenner didn't even rock. He said, "You're under my weight. Forget it." Nightingale started another punch, then switched to his pocket. Fenner sunk his fist in his ribs. Nightingale went down on his knees with a sigh, rolled over on his side and got his gun out. Fenner stepped forward and stamped on his wrist. The gun clattered on the parquet, then bounced on to the pile carpet. Fenner knelt down and jerked Nightingale round by his coat collar.

"I said forget it." He shook the little man. "If you don't believe me, then you'll believe someone else some other time, but I ain't fighting with you over any dame."

Nightingale drew his lips off his teeth, started to say something, stopped, and looked beyond Fenner, over his shoulder. His anger changed to alarm. Fenner saw a man standing behind him. He saw the miniature of the man in Nightingale's glasses. He saw an arm come up, and he tried to turn. Something exploded inside his head and he fell forward. He scraped the skin off his nose on Nightingale's coat buttons.

IV

Fenner's first reaction was to the naked light hanging in a wire basket from the ceiling. Then he noticed that the room had no windows. After that, he shut his eyes again and drifted to the steady throb inside his skull. The light burned through his eyelids, and he tried to roll over away from it. When he found he couldn't move, he raised his head and looked. The movement exploded something behind his eyes, and he had to lie still again. Then, after a while, the throb went away, and he tried again.

He found he was lying on an old mattress, and his hands were tied to the ironwork of the rusty bedstead. The room was completely bare except for the bed. The floorboards were littered with cigarette butts and tobacco ash. The dust was thick. Several pages of a scattered newspaper lay about, and the fireplace contained a pile of black ashes, as if some one had recently been burning a lot of papers. It was a nasty room, full of the smell of decay, damp and stale sweat.

Fenner rested. He made no effort to free his hands. He lay quietly, his eyes screwed up a little to avoid the rays of the light, and he breathed gently. He listened with an intent ness that caught at every whispered sound. By lying like that and by listening hard, he heard sounds which at first meant nothing to him, but which he later distinguished as footsteps, the murmur of voices and the distant breaking of the rollers on the shore.

He went to sleep finally because he knew that sleep was the only thing for him at the moment. He was in no shape to try to escape. He had lost all sense of time, so when he woke he knew only that the sleep had been a good one, because he felt well again. His head ached dully, and his brain no longer rolled around inside his skull. He woke because someone was coming down the passage outside his door. He could hear the heavy footfalls on the bare boards. A key rattled in the lock and the door was kicked open. He closed his eyes. He thought it was too early to take an interest in visitors.

Someone walked over to him, and the light in his eyes went away as that someone got between him and the light. There was a long silence, then a grunt and the light began to irritate him once more. Footsteps walked to the door. Fenner opened his eyes and looked. The small squat back and short legs of the man going out of the door told him nothing, but the thick oily black hair and the coffee skin made it a good guess that he was a Cuban. He went out and locked the door again.

Fenner drew a deep breath and began to work his hands. The cords holding him were tight, but not impossibly tight. He strained and pulled, chewing on his under lip as he did so. The effort made the light go black, and he had to stop. He lay still, panting a little. The only ventilation came from the transom over the door. The room was very hot and close. Fenner could feel the sweat gumming his shirt to his back. He gently wiggled his wrists. He thought, "I've shifted them. Yes, I've done something. If I could only stop this damn headache, maybe I'd get somewhere. Now, once more." He pulled and twisted again. His right hand, made slippery with sweat, gradually slid through the circle of cord, but he couldn't do anything about his left hand. He was caught there all right.

Slowly he sat up and felt his head with his fingers very gently. The back of his skull was tender, but there was no lump or bruise. He smiled bleakly. Then he twisted round and examined the knot that was holding his left hand. It was knotted under the bed in such a way that he could only feel it, but he couldn't see it. The knot defied all the effort he made to loosen it, and he lay back on the bed, swearing softly.

He thought, "Only one up. I wonder who smacked me." Carlos? He could have gone out, watched through the door and come back quietly when Nightingale was getting tough. Or was it someone else? Where was he? More important, what was going to happen to him?

He sat up on the bed again and swung his feet to the floor. Then he stood up shakily, his left hand preventing him from standing entirely upright. His head ached a lot when he stood up, but it began to pass as he moved to the door, dragging the bed with him. He satisfied himself that the door was locked, and then, pushing the bed back to the wall, he sat down again.

He'd got to get his hand free somehow, he told himself. He lay down and began to tear at the knot feverishly. His damp fingers slid off the cord, making no impression.

The sound of footfalls made him pause, and he hastily rolled on his back and slipped his wrist through the circle of cord. He'd barely done so when the door opened and Carlos came in. Reiger and Miller stood just inside the door. Carlos came over and stood by Fenner's bed. Fenner looked up and their eyes met.

Carlos said, "Well, the punk's awake."

Reiger and Miller came farther into the room, and Reiger shut the door. They came around the bed. Fenner looked at each man slowly. He said casually, "What's the idea?"

Carlos was shivering a little. He was doped to his ears. Fenner could see the pin-point pupils. Carlos said, "We're goin' to have a little talk." He drew back his fist and hit Fenner with his small bony knuckles just below his nose. Fenner had his head moving when he saw the blow coming, but it only took a little of the steam out of the punch. He felt his teeth creak.

Carlos said, "I owe you that one, don't I?"

Fenner said nothing. He hated Carlos with his eyes, but he knew that with his left hand pinned he wouldn't stand much chance with three of them.

Carlos said, "So you're a private dick." He took from his pocket Fenner's papers and scattered them over the bed. "You certainly pulled a fast one that time."

There was a moment's silence. Carlos sat on the bed. Fenner knew that he could nail him now. If the other two cleared off he could grab Carlos by his neck and settle with him. Maybe the other two would clear off. He'd have to wait.

Carlos leaned forward and slapped Fenner across his face. He slapped him very hard, twice. Fenner blinked his eyes, but he didn't move or say anything. Carlos sat back again. His shivering made the bed rattle against the wall. He looked a little insane. He said, "Why have you come down here? What are you trying to find out?"

Fenner said with stiff lips: "I told you not to try any thing. Now, by God, I'm goin' to start after you. I ain't lettin' up until I've broken your lousy little back."

Miller exploded in a high-pitched laugh. "He's nuts," he said, "he's stark raving nuts."

Carlos had to put his hands in his pockets because they trembled so much. He said, "Listen, we're goin' to work on you. I want to know what you're doing here. Tell me quick, or I'll start on you."

Fenner sneered. He began to pull his hand out of the cord. He did it very slowly so that they didn't notice. He said, "Take my tip an' let me outta here."

Carlos stood up. He motioned to Reiger. "Work on him," he said.

Reiger got to the bed at the same time as Fenner slipped the cord. Fenner swung his leg round in a long lightning arc. He kicked Reiger just under the knee-cap. Reiger fell down, holding his knee with both hands. His eyes opened very wide with the pain and he began to curse. Fenner sat upon the bed as Miller rushed in. Miller's hands caught his hair and jerked him over, but he swung a punch into Miller rather low down. He put a lot of steam in that punch.

Miller flopped on the floor, holding his big belly in both hands. His face glistened as he began to roll, trying to get his breath.

Carlos backed away quickly. He was scared all right. Fenner got to his feet and started after him, dragging the bed with him. Reiger caught hold of the leg of the bed and hung on. Fenner pulled, striving to get at Carlos, who in his panic had circled away from the door. The bed moved a little Fenner's way, then jerked back as Reiger hauled on it.

Carlos said in a squeaky voice, "Get up an' fix him. Don't lie there, damn you!" He pulled a gun and pointed it at Fenner. "Stay where you are," he said. "I'll blast you if you move."

Fenner took another step forward, dragging the bed and Reiger with him. "Go ahead," he said. "It's the only thing that'll save you."

Miller climbed to his knees and came at Fenner with a rush. His great fat body knocked Fenner on to the bed. Fenner fell with his right arm under him, and for a second or so Miller could hit him as he liked. He smashed in a couple of punches that didn't do Fenner any good, then Fenner got one of his legs up and kicked him off the bed. Miller got to his feet again and Reiger came up behind Fenner and grabbed him round his throat. Miller stepped in then and slammed in three or four punches to Fenner's body. Miller was flabby, but he made his punches felt. Fenner knew he wasn't the one to get worried about, Reiger was the boy. Reiger was hugging his throat with an arm like an iron band and Fenner felt his head begin to swim. Getting his feet firmly on the floor, he stiffened his body and heaved backwards. He, the bed and Reiger all went over with a crash. Reiger let go and tried to wriggle clear.

Fenner was in a bad position. He was kneeling with his left hand twisted behind him and the bed resting on his back. The only way he could get out of the position was to heave the bed over again. As he straightened up, carrying the bed on his back, Reiger kicked out at him. Reiger's foot caught him behind his knee, and he went over. The muscles of his imprisoned arm seemed to catch fire, and, half crazy with the pain, Fenner slammed the bed over on top of Reiger. The iron headpiece caught Reiger under the chin and Fenner heaved on the bed with all his weight. Reiger's eyes started out of his head and he began to wave his arms violently. Fenner went on shoving.

Miller dropped on him and started beating him about the head, but Fenner didn't take off the pressure. He knew he'd got Reiger, and if he could stop him, he'd stand a chance with the other two. Reiger was going a blackish purple, his arms only waved feebly. Carlos ran round and jerked the bed away. Reiger flopped on his hands and knees, making a honking sound like a dog being sick.

Miller had opened a cut just above Fenner's eyes and the steady stream of blood bothered him. He groped round with his free hand. He dug his fingers into Miller's belly, got a grip and twisted. Miller gave a high whinny sound and tried to get away, but Fenner hung on. Still holding a fistful of Miller's flesh, he heaved again, bringing the bed crashing down on both of them.

Carlos stood peering down at them through the bed springs, but he couldn't get at them. He tried to pull the bed away, but Fenner held it with his arm. He kept the paralysing grip on Miller, who began to scream and thrash with his legs. He tried beating Fenner's face with his fists, but Fenner just twisted some more, kept his head on his chest, and hung on.

Carlos ran out, and Fenner could hear him shouting vio lently in Spanish. Miller gave a sudden heave and broke away. He went a whitish green, and flopped limply, just lay there, staring at Fenner with frightened eyes.

Fenner tried to smile, but couldn't make it. He kicked Miller away and turned the bed over slowly. He got his arm into a more natural angle. Then, working feverishly, he got the iron post out of the sockets of the bed and stood up. Even then, with his arm tied to the iron post, he was in a bad position, but not so bad as he had been. He started for the door. As he passed Reiger, who was kneeling with his back to the wall, his hand to his throat, Fenner gave him a swipe with the iron post. Reiger fell over on his side, cover ing his head with his arms.

Fenner took more steps and got outside the room. He felt as if he was walking through glue. His steps got slower as he reached the passage, and he suddenly fell on his hands and knees. He felt very light-headed and his chest began to hurt. He stayed on his hands and knees, wanting very badly to lie down, but he knew he had to go on. He put a hand on the wall and levered himself up again. He left a long smear of blood on the dirty yellow paper. He thought: "Hell, I ain't goin' to make it!" and he fell down again.

There came a lot of shouting downstairs and he tried to get back in the room again. He heard men coming up the stairs fast. He thought, "Blast this post!" and tried once more to free his hand. It seemed welded to the thing. He struggled up as two excited little Cubans came rushing at him. They all went down in a heap together. One of them grabbed him at the throat and the other tangled his legs up. These little punks were strong.

He heard Carlos's voice shout, "Not too hard!" then something crashed on his head and he fell forward. Out of the blackness his hand encountered a face and he punched feebly, then a bright light burst before his eyes and suffocating blackness blotted out everything.

Fenner thought, "I must have taken a beating. They think I can't start any more trouble." He said that because he found they hadn't bothered to tie him this time. They had taken the bed away and left him in the empty room on the floor. He gave himself a little while, but when he tried to move he found he could just twitch his body.

He thought, "What the devil's the matter with me?" He knew he wasn't tied, because he couldn't feel any cord on him, but he couldn't move. Then he became aware that the light was still on, but his eyes were so swollen that he could only see a fuzzy blur. When he shifted his head, pain like sheet lightning travelled all over him and he lay still again. Then he went to sleep.

He woke because someone was kicking him in the ribs. Not hard kicks, just heavy thumps, but the whole of his body raved at the pain.

"Wake up, punk!" Reiger said, kicking continuously. "Not feelin' so tough now, huh?"

Fenner screwed up everything he'd got in him, rolled towards the sound of the voice, and groped with his arms. He found Reiger's legs, hugged them and pulled. Reiger gave a strangled grunt, tried to save himself, and went over backwards. He landed with a crash that shook the room. Fenner crawled towards him grimly, but Reiger kicked him away and scrambled to his feet. His face was twisted with cold rage. He leant over Fenner, beat away the upraised arms, and grabbed him by his shirt front. He pulled him off the floor and slammed him down hard.

Carlos came in and paused. "You doin' that for fun?" he asked. There was a faint rasp in his voice.

Reiger turned. "Listen, Pío," he said through his teeth. "This guy's tough, see? I'm just softening him up."

Carlos went over and looked down at Fenner. He stirred him with his foot. Then he looked over at Reiger. "I don't want him to croak. I want to find out things about him. I want to know why he came all the way from New York and got in with our mob. There's somethin' phoney about this, and I don't like it."

Reiger said, "Sure. Suppose we make this guy talk?"

Carlos looked down at Fenner. "He ain't in shape to be roughed around just yet. We'll try him in a little while."

They went out.

Fenner came round again a little later. There seemed to be an iron clapper banging inside his skull. When he opened his eyes, the walls of the room converged on him. Terrified, he shut his eyes, holding on to his reason.

He stayed that way for a while, then he opened his eyes again. This time the walls moved slowly and he was no longer scared. He crawled on his hands and knees across the room and tried the door handle. The door was locked. He had only one obsession now. He wasn't going to tell them anything. They had beaten him over the head so much that he had lost much of his reason, and he was no longer aware of the pain that tortured his body.

He thought, "I've gotta get out of this. They'll go on until they kill me." Then he remembered what they had done to the Chinaman, and he went a little cold. "I couldn't take that," he thought. A cunning gleam came into his eyes and he put his hand on the buckle of his belt. He undid the belt and pulled it through the loops of his trousers. Then he climbed unsteadily to his feet. He had to put one hand against the wall to support himself.

With exaggerated care he threaded the long strip of leather through the buckle. Then he passed the loop over his head, drew the belt tight round his neck.

He said, "I gotta find a nail or a hook or something. I gotta fix the other end somewhere." He wandered round the room, searching the bare walls. He made a complete circle of the room and stopped by the door again.

He said, "What am I going to do now?"

He stood there, his head hanging on his chest, and the belt swinging from his neck. He went round the room again more carefully, but the walls were naked. There was no window, no hooks, only the electric light bulb high up out of his reach.

He wondered if by putting his foot through the loop made at the other end of the belt, he could strangle himself. He decided he couldn't. He sat on the floor again and tried to think. The clapper went on banging inside his skull, and he held his head in his hands, swaying to the beat.

Then he saw how he could do it. He said, "I guess I'm not as smart as I used to be." He crawled over to the door on his hands and knees and fastened the belt round the door handle. By lying face downwards he could hang himself all right. It'd take time, but he guessed if he stuck it he'd croak.

He spent quite a time fastening the belt securely to the handle. He made it short so that his neck was only a few inches from the brass handle, then he slid his feet away slowly until he was stretched out, his weight supported by his hands.

He had no thoughts about his finish. He could only think that he was cheating Carlos. He remained still for a few seconds, then he took his hands away, allowing his whole weight to descend on the belt. The buckle bit into his neck sharply and the leather sank into his flesh.

He thought triumphantly, "It's going to work!" The blood began to pound in his head. The agony in his lungs nearly forced him to put his hands to the ground, but he didn't. He swayed on the belt, a blackness before his eyes. Then the handle of the door snapped off and he fell to the boards with a crash.

He lay there dazed, breathing in the hot air in great gasps. Blood trickled from his neck where the buckle had bitten into him. A sick feeling of defeat was far worse than the pain that racked his tired body.

Pulling the belt from his neck, he lay on his back staring up at the dirty ceiling. The blood from his neck set him thinking. His mind was so dazed that he couldn't piece his thoughts together, but he knew that if he kept thinking he was going to find another solution.

He stayed still for a time, then he sat up again. Once more the cunning look came into his eyes. He groped for the belt and examined the buckle. It had a sharp, short spike that caught in the belt holes. Somewhere in his arms, he knew, were his main arteries. He'd only to pierce them with the spike and he'd bleed to death.

He said" "Nice way to go. I must be crazy not to have got round to that before."

Laboriously he felt for the artery. When he thought he'd found it, he took the buckle and pressed the spike into his flesh.

A tiny speck of blood appeared, and he pressed harder. The artery began to pulse and throb. Then suddenly the spike sank deep and the blood welled up. He was so exhausted that he fell back on the floor. His aching head struck the wall and he went out in a bright flash of light.

A shadowy figure materialized out of the bright mist. Fenner looked and wondered vaguely if it were an angel. It wasn't, it was Curly. She bent over him and said something he couldn't hear, and he mumbled, "Hello, baby," softly.

The room was building up into shape and the bright mist was going away. Behind Curly stood a little man with a face like a goat. Faintly, as if he were a long way off, Fenner heard him say, "He'll be all right now. Just make him lie there. If you want me, I'll come round."

Fenner said, "Give me a drink of water," and fell asleep.

When he woke again, he felt better. The clapper in his head had stopped banging and the room stayed still. Curly was sitting on a chair near him, her eyes very heavy, as if she wanted sleep.

Fenner said, "For God's sake—" but Curly got up hastily and arranged the sheet. "Don't talk yet," she said; "you're all right. Just go to sleep."

Fenner shut his eyes and tried to think. It wasn't any use. The bed felt fine and the pain had gone away from his body. He opened his eyes again.

Curly brought him some water. He said, "Don't I get anything stronger'n that?"

Curly said" "Listen, Jughead, you're sick. You're slug-nutty. So take what's given you."

After a little while, Fenner said, "Where am I, anyway?"

"You're in my room off White Street."

"Please, baby, would you mind skipping the mystery an' letting me know how I got here?"

Curly said, "It's late. You must go to sleep. I'll tell you about it to-morrow." Fenner raised himself on his elbows. He was ready to wince, but he didn't feel any pain. He was weak, but that was all. He said, "I've been sleeping too long. I want to know now."

Curly sighed. "Okay, okay. You tough guys give me a pain."

Fenner didn't say anything. He lay back and waited. Curly wrinkled her forehead. "Nightingale was mad with you. What did you do?"

Fenner looked at her, then said, "I forget."

Curly sniffed. "He told me that Pío had bounced you, and taken you to his waterfront place. I wanted to know what was happening to you. Nightingale got restless when he cooled off. He reckoned he was letting Crotti down if he didn't look after you. It didn't need much persuasion from me to get him to go and find out. He comes back with you looking as if someone had been working over you. He says for me to get a croaker and to look after you."

Fenner didn't believe it. "That little guy took me out of Carlos's place? Didn't Carlos say anythin'?"

Curly yawned. "He wasn't there. They were all over at the hotel."

Fenner said, "I see." He lay still, thinking, then he said, "What's the date?" When she told him, he said, "It's still May?" She nodded. He reckoned painfully. He'd been away from Glorie for four days. It seemed a lot longer than that. Then he said, "Carlos missed me yet?"

Curly yawned again. "Uh-huh, but he ain't linked me or Nightingale up with it. Maybe he'll get around to it. He thinks of everything."

Fenner shifted. He passed his fingers through his hair gently. His skull was very tender. "That guy won't like you too much if he finds out."

Curly shrugged. "You're right," she said, and yawned again. "There's a lot of room in your bed. Would it embarrass you if I got me some sleep?"

Fenner smiled. "You come on in."

Curly smiled and went out of the room. She came back in a little while in a pink woolly dressing-gown. Fenner said, "Well, that's homely, isn't it?"

She came round and sat on the far end of the bed. "Maybe, but it's warm," she said. She kicked off her slippers and took off the dressing-gown. "You wouldn't think it, but I'm always cold in bed," she said. She was wearing a pair of light wool pyjamas.

He watched her climb in beside him. "That sleepin' suit looks kind of unromantic, too, doesn't it?" he said.

She laid her blonde head on the pillow. "What of it?" She yawned and blinked her eyes. "I'm tired," she said. "Looking after a guy like you is hard work."

Fenner said gently. "Sure. You sleep. Maybe you'd like me to sing to you?"

Curly said "Nuts," drowsily, and fell asleep.

Fenner lay still in the darkness, listening to her deep breathing, and tried to think. He still felt dazed and his mind kept wandering. After a while he, too, went to sleep.

The morning light woke him. He opened his eyes and looked round the room, conscious that his head was clear and his body no longer ached. Although he was a little stiff as he moved in the bed, he felt quite well.

Curly sat up slowly in bed and blinked round. She said, "Hello, how you makin' out?"

Fenner grinned at her. It was a twisted grin, but it reached his eyes all right. "You've been a good pal to me," he said. "What made you do it, baby?"

She turned on her side. "Don't worry your brains about that," she said. "I told you first time I met you I thought you were nice." She closed her eyes.

Fenner said drowsily, "What are you thinking?"

She put her hand up to his face gently. She said, "I was just thinkin' how tough it is to run across a guy like you when it's too late."

Fenner moved away from her. "You mustn't look at it like that," he said seriously.

She suddenly laughed, but her eyes were serious. "I'll get you some breakfast. You'll find a razor in the bathroom."

By the time he'd shaved his beard off, breakfast was on the table. He went and sat down. "Swell," he said, looking at the food.

The dressing-gown he'd found in the cupboard must have belonged to Nightingale. It reached to his knees and pinched him across his shoulders.

Curly giggled at him. "You do look a scream."

Fenner made short work of the food, and Curly had to go outside and fry him some more eggs. She said, "guess you're mending fast."

Fenner nodded. "I'm great. Tell me, baby, does Night ingale mean anything to you?"

She poured him out some more coffee. "He's a habit. I've been with him for a couple of years. He's kind to me, and I guess he's crazy about me." She shrugged. "You know how it is. I don't know anyone I like better, so I feel I may as well make him happy."

Fenner nodded, sat back and lit a cigarette. "What's Thayler mean to you?"

Curly's face froze. The laughter went out of her eyes. "Once a dick, always a dick," she said bitterly, getting to her feet. "I ain't talking shop with you, copper."

"So you know that?"

Curly began to stack the plates. "We all know it."

"Nightingale?"

"Sure."

"But Nightingale pulled me out of that jam."

"He owes Crotti something." Curly took the plates away.

Fenner sat thinking. When she came back, he said, "Don't get that way, baby. You an' I could get places."

Curly leaned over the table. Her face was hard and suspicious. "You're not getting anywhere with me on that line," she said, "so forget it."

Fenner said, "Sure, we'll forget it all."

When she had shut herself in the bathroom, Nightingale came in. He stood looking at Fenner with a hard eye.

Fenner said, "Thanks, pal. I guess you got me out of a nasty jam."

Nightingale didn't move. He said, "Now you're okay, you better dust. This burg's too small for you and Carlos."

Fenner said, "You bet it is."

"What sort of pull you got with Crotti, policeman?" Nightingale asked. "What's the idea?"

"Crotti has no use for Carlos. I'm gunning for that guy. This is the way Crotti wants it to go."

Nightingale came further into the room. "You've gotta get out of town quick," he said. "If Carlos knows that I've helped you, what do you think he'll do to me?"

Fenner's eyes were very intent as they watched Nightingale. "I'm starting for Carlos. You better get yourself on the winning side."

"Yeah. I'm on it already. You get outta here, or I'll help to run you out." Nightingale was very serious and quiet.

Fenner knew it was no use talking to him. "Have it your own way," he said.

Nightingale hesitated, took a .38 special from his pocket, and put it on the table. "That's to see you out of town safe. Crotti did a lot for me. If you're still around by to-night, you better start shootin' when you see me—get the idea?"

He went out, closing the door gently behind him.

Fenner picked up the gun and held it loosely in his hand. "Well, well," he said.

Curly came out of the bathroom. She saw the gun. "Night ingale been in?"

Fenner nodded absently.

"Friendly?"

"About the same as you."

Curly grunted. "You ready to leave? I'm getting my car. I'll drop you anywhere."

Fenner said, "Sure." He was thinking. Then he looked at her. "Carlos is goin' to be washed up. You might like to talk now."

Curly pursed her mouth. "Nuts," she said. "Your clothes are in the cupboard. They'll do to get you to your hotel." She went to the door. "I'll get the bus."

Fenner dressed as quickly as he could. His clothes looked as though they'd been mixed up in a road smash. He didn't care. When he'd finished dressing, he went to the door and stepped into the passage. His intention was to meet Curly downstairs. He walked slowly to the head of the stairs. He found that he wasn't as tough as he thought. It was an effort to move, but he kept on. At the head of the stairs he paused. Curly was lying on the landing below.

Fenner stood very still, and stared. Then he pulled the gun from his hip pocket and went down the stairs cautiously. There was no one about. When he came nearer he could see the handle of a knife sticking out of her back. He stopped and turned her. Her head fell back, but she was still breathing.

It took a great effort for him to get her upstairs. She was heavy, and he was trembling by the time he got her on the bed. He put her down gently, then snatched up the telephone. Nightingale's number was on the address pad. He dialed, standing with his eyes on Curly.

Nightingale said primly, "This is the Funeral Parlour."

Fenner said, "Come over here quick. They've got Curly." He hung up and went over to the bed.

Curly opened her eyes. When she saw Fenner she held one of her hands out to him. "Serves me right for helping a dick," she said faintly.

Fenner didn't dare pull the knife out. He held her so that she didn't have any weight on the handle. He said, "You take it easy, baby; I'm gettin' help."

Curly twisted. "It's going to come a lot too late," she said, then her face crumpled and she began to cry.

Fenner said, "Was it Carlos?"

Curly didn't say anything. Blood stained her chin.

Fenner said, "Give me a lead. Don't be a mug and let him get away with it. He'll only think you're a sucker."

Curly said, "It was one of his Cubans. He jumped me before I could scream."

Fenner saw she was going very white. He said quickly: "Why does Thayler carry your photo around with him? What's he to you?"

Curly whispered faintly, "He's my husband." Fenner saw she was going fast. He put his hand round her back and pulled the knife out. Her eyelids fell back and she gave a little cry. Then she said, "That's a lot better."

He laid her down on the bed. "I'll even this up for you. Carlos'll pay for this," he said.

She sneered. "Okay, brave little man," she whispered. "Fix Carlos, if you like, but it won't do me any good."

Fenner remembered seeing some Scotch, and he went over to the wall cupboard and poured out two fingers. He made her swallow it.

She gasped. "That's right. Keep me alive until I've told you all you want to know"—bitterly.

Fenner took her hands. "You can put a lot straight. Is Thayler in with Carlos?"

She hesitated, then moved her head a little. "He's in it all right," she said faintly. "He's been a bad guy, and I don't owe him anything."

"What's his angle?"

"Runs the labour syndicate." She shut her eyes. Then she said, "Don't ask me anything else, will you? I'm fright ened."

Fenner felt completely helpless. Her skin now looked like waxed paper. Only a red bubble at her lips showed that she still lived.

Someone came blundering up the stairs. Fenner ran to the door. Nightingale came in. His face was glistening. He pushed past Fenner and ran across to the bed. He was too late. Curly had died just before he came in.

Fenner stepped outside the room and pulled the door to. As he walked quickly down the passage a low wail came from behind the door. It was Nightingale.

The manager of the Haworth Hotel came round the desk quickly when he saw Fenner. "What is all this?" he spluttered, his voice trembling with indignation. "What do you think this joint is?"

"Don't ask me," Fenner said, pushing past him. "If it's a joint, where are the girls?"

The manager ran to keep up with him. "Mr. Ross, I insist! I cannot have these disturbances!"

Fenner paused. "What *are* you yapping about?"

"My people are afraid to go up on floor three. There's a rough hoodlum sitting up there, not letting anyone pass. I've threatened him with the police, but he says you told him to stick around. What does it mean?"

Fenner said, "Get my check ready. I'm moving out." He went upstairs quickly, leaving the manager protesting. There was no sign of Bugsey when he reached his room, and he kicked open the door and went in.

Glorie was sitting up in bed and Bugsey was sitting close to her. They were playing cards. Bugsey wore a pair of white shorts and his hat. Sweat was running down his fat back.

Fenner stood still. "What's goin' on here?"

Glorie threw down her cards. "Where have you been?" she said. "What's happened to you?"

Fenner went in and shut the door. "Plenty," he said. Then, turning to Bugsey, "What you think you're doing—a strip tease?"

Glorie said, "He was playing for my nightie, but I beat him to it."

Bugsey grabbed his trousers, "You sure came in at the right moment," he said feverishly. "That dame's a mean card player."

Fenner wasn't in the mood for laughter. He said, "Get out quick and get a closed car. Park it at the rear of the building in a quarter of an hour."

Bugsey struggled into his clothes. "Looks like someone's been pushin' you around."

"Never mind about me," Fenner said coldly; "this is urgent."

Bugsey went out, pulling his coat on. Fenner said, "Can you get up, do you think?"

Glorie threw the sheet off and slid to the floor. "I only stayed in bed because it upset poor little Bugsey," she said. "What's been happening?"

Fenner dug himself out a new suit and changed. "Don't stand there gaping," he snapped. "Get dressed. We're moving out of this joint fast."

She began to dress. She said, "Can't you tell me where you've been?"

Fenner was busy emptying the drawers into two grips. "I was taken for a ride by a gang of toughs. Just shaken 'em off."

"Where are we going?"

Fenner said evenly, "We're goin' to stay with Noolen."

Glorie shook her head. "I'm not," she said.

Fenner finished strapping the grips and stood up. He took two quick steps across the room and put his hand on her wrist. "You're doing what I tell you," he said.

"Not Noolen's."

"That's what I said. I'm not standing for any comeback from you. You can walk, or I'll carry you."

He went to the house 'phone and rang for his check. While waiting, he paced the room restlessly. Glorie sat on the bed, watching him with uneasy eyes. She said, "What are you starting?"

Fenner looked up. "Plenty," he said. "This mob started on me, and now I'm finishing it. I'm not stopping until I've bust the mystery right outta this business and got that little punk so short he'll scream murder."

The bell-hop brought in the check and Fenner settled. Then he picked up his grips in one hand and took Glorie by her elbow with the other. "Let's go," he said, and together they went downstairs.

They found Bugsey sitting at the wheel of a big car. Bugsey was looking a little dazed, but he didn't say any thing. Fenner climbed in behind Glorie. "Noolen's. Fast," he said.

Bugsey twisted round in his seat. "Noolen's?" he said. "Why Noolen's? Listen, you don't want to go to that guy. He's the south end of a horse."

Fenner leaned forward. "Noolen's," he repeated, looking at Bugsey intently. "If you don't like it, get out an' I'll drive."

Bugsey gaped from Fenner to Glorie. She said, "Go ahead, brave heart, this fella's making his orders stick."

Bugsey said, "Oh, well," and drove off.

Glorie sat in the corner of the car, a sulky expression on her face. Fenner stared over Bugsey's broad shoulders at the road ahead. They drove all the way to Noolen's in silence. When they swept up the short circular drive Glorie said, "I don't want to go in there." She said it more in protest than in any hope of Fenner's agreeing. He swung open the door and got out.

"Come on, both of you," he said impatiently.

It was half-past eleven o'clock as they walked into the deserted lobby of the Casino. In the main hall they found a Cuban in shirt-sleeves aimlessly pushing an electric cleaner about the floor. He looked up as they crossed towards him, and his mouth went a little slack. His eyes fastened on Glorie, who scowled at him.

"Noolen around?" Fenner said.

The Cuban pressed the thumb-switch on the cleaner and laid it down almost tenderly. "I'll see," he said.

Fenner made a negative sign with his head. "You stay put," he said shortly.

He cut across the hall in the direction of Noolen's office. The Cuban said, "Hey!" feebly, but he stayed where he was.

Glorie and Bugsey lagged along in the rear. Fenner pushed open the door of the office and stood looking in. Noolen was sitting at his desk. He was counting a large pile of greenbacks. When he saw Fenner his face went blotchy and he swept the greenbacks into a drawer.

Fenner walked in. "This is no hold-up," he said shortly; "it's a council of war."

He turned his head and said to Glorie and Bugsey, who hung about outside, "Come in, you two, and shut the door."

Noolen sat very still behind his desk. When Glorie came in, he put his fingers to his collar and eased it from his neck. Glorie didn't look at him. She went over to a chair at the far end of the room and sat down. Bugsey shut the door and leaned against it. He, too, didn't look at Noolen. There was a strained tension in the room.

Noolen managed to say: "What the hell's this?"

Fenner took one of Noolen's green dapple cigars from the desk box, clamped his teeth on it and struck a match with his thumb-nail. He spent a long minute lighting the cigar evenly, then he tossed the match away and sat on the edge of the desk.

Noolen said, "You've got a lot of crust, Ross. I told you I wasn't interested in anything you've got to peddle. It still stands."

Glorie said in a flat voice: "He isn't Ross. His name is Fenner, and he's a private investigator, holding a licence."

Fenner turned his head and looked at her, but she was adjusting her skirt, a sulky, indifferent expression on her face.

Bugsey sucked in his breath. His gooseberry eyes popped. Noolen, who was reaching for a cigar when Glorie spoke, paused. His fat white hand hovered over the box like a seagull in flight, then he sat back, folding his hands on the blotter.

Fenner said, "If you were half alive, the news would have got round to you before."

Noolen fidgeted with his hands. "Get out of here," he said thickly. "Private dicks are poison to me."

"You and me've got a job to do," Fenner said, looking at the fat man with intent eyes. "The law doesn't come into this."

Noolen said viciously, "Get out!"

Without any effort, Fenner hit him on the side of his jaw. Noolen jerked back; his fat thighs, pinned under the desk, saved him from going over. Fenner slid off the desk, took four quick steps away and turned a little so that he could see the three of them.

Bugsey's hand was groping in his back pocket. His face showed the indecision that was bewildering him.

Fenner said, "Hold it. If you start somethin', I'll smack your ears for you."

Bugsey took his hand away and transferred it to his head. He scratched his square dome violently. "I guess I'll scram," he said.

"You'll stay if you're wise," Fenner said evenly. "Carlos might be interested to know what you've been doing playin' around with a dick."

Bugsey went a little green. "I didn't know you were a dick," he said sullenly.

Fenner sneered. "Tell it to Carlos. You don't have to tell it to me."

Bugsey hesitated, then he slumped against the wall.

Fenner glanced at Noolen, who sat in a heap, rubbing his jaw. All the fight had gone out of him. "Okay," he said. "Now maybe I can get down to things. You and me are goin' to run Carlos and his mob out of town. Bugsey here can either come in on our side, or go back to Carlos. I don't care a lot what he does. If he goes back he'll have a lot of explaining. If he sticks, he'll pick up five hundred bucks a week until the job's cleaned up."

Bugsey's eyes brightened. "I'll stick for that amount," he said.

Fenner felt in his wallet, took out a sheaf of notes, crumpled them into a ball, and tossed them at Bugsey. "That's some thing to go on with," he said.

Noolen watched all this in silence. Fenner came across and sat on the desk again. "How would you like to be the king-pin in this burg?" he said. "That's what you can be if you work with me."

"How?" Noolen's voice was very husky.

"We'll get your little mob and me and Bugsey and we'll make the town very hot for Carlos. We'll hi-jack his boats, we'll sabotage his organization, and we'll go gunning for him."

Noolen shook his head. "No, we won't," he said.

Fenner said evenly, "You yellow big shot! Still scared?"

"I've never worked with the cops an' I never will."

"You don't understand. Four days ago Carlos had me in his waterfront place. He made things pretty tough, but I got away. I'm making this a personal business. I'm not inviting the law to come along."

Noolen shook his head. "I ain't playin'."

Fenner laughed. "Okay, we'll make you play." He stood up. "You in this?" he said to Bugsey. Bugsey nodded. "I'll hang around," he said.

Fenner nodded to Glorie. "Come on, baby," he said. "You, me an' Bugsey'll look after this until this punk decides to fight."

Glorie got up. "I don't want to play either."

Fenner showed his teeth. "What a shame," he said, walking over to her and taking her arm. "But you're not Noolen; you'll do as you're told."

Noolen said, "Leave her alone."

Fenner took no notice. "Let's go," he said, and they went out of the room, Glorie walking stiffly beside him.

Out in the street, Fenner paused. He said to Glorie, "We'll stay at your place."

Glorie shook her head. "I told you I haven't got a place."

Fenner smiled. "We'll go where you keep your clothes. That evening dress looks sort of out of place at this time."

Glorie hesitated, then she said, "Listen, I honestly don't want to be mixed up with Carlos. Will you please excuse me?"

Fenner pushed her into the car. "It's too late, baby," he said unpleasantly. "I can't have anyone shootin' you up whenever they want to. You've got to stick by me for a while."

She heaved a sigh. "Okay. I've got a little place off Sponge Pier."

Fenner nodded to Bugsey. "Sponge Pier, fast," he said.

Bugsey climbed into the car and Fenner followed him. He sat close to Glorie, keeping his grips upright between his legs. "There's goin' to be an awful lot of fun in this joint pretty soon," he said. "Maybe I'll get somewhere or maybe I won't, but whatever happens to me, Carlos'll go first."

Glorie said, "You quite hate that guy, don't you?"

Fenner looked ahead. His eyes were very cold. "You bet," he said curtly.

About half a mile past Sponge Pier, hidden by a thick cluster of palm trees, was a small bungalow. Bugsey ran the car through the small landscape garden and parked it out side the door. A wide piazza screened by green sun-blinds encircled the house, and every window had green wooden sun-shutters.

Fenner got out of the car and Glorie followed him. She said to Bugsey, "The garage is at the back."

Fenner said, "You got a car?"

"Yes. Do you mind?"

Fenner looked at Bugsey. "Take that rented car back. We'll use this baby's. We can't afford to be extravagant."

Glorie said, "Don't mind me."

"Got a staff here?" Fenner asked, looking the house over. "I've got a woman who runs the place."

"That's fine. Bugsey can help her." Once more Fenner turned to Bugsey. "Take the car back, then come on here. Miss Leadler will tell her woman you're coming. Then you make yourself useful until I want you. Get it?"

Bugsey said "You're payin' the bill," and he drove the car away.

Fenner followed Glorie into the bungalow. It was a nice place. A small Spanish woman appeared from nowhere, and Glorie waved her hand. "This is Mr. Fenner. He'll be staying a little while. Will you fix lunch?"

The woman gave Fenner a quick look. He didn't quite like the smirk in her eyes, and she went away again.

Glorie opened a door on the left of the lobby. "Go in there and rest yourself. I want to change."

Fenner said, "Sure," and wandered into the room. It was comfortable: cushions, divans and more cushions. The open windows let out to the piazza, and the room was dim with subdued sunlight.

The Spanish woman came in and laid a table for lunch on the piazza. Fenner sat on one of the divans and smoked. He said, "When you're through, you might get me a drink." She took no notice of him, and he didn't bother to speak again. He sat quite still.

Glorie came in after a while. She wore a white silk dress, ankle length, and white doeskin sandals. Her red-gold hair was caught back off her ears by a red ribbon. Her mouth was very red and her eyes sparkled.

She said, "Like me?" and pivoted slowly.

"Yeah," he said, getting up. "You're all right."

She made a little grimace at him and went over to fix drinks.

The ice-cold cocktails had a bite. When they sat down to the meal, Fenner felt fine. They got through the meal without saying much. Fenner was conscious of Glorie's eyes. She kept looking at him and then when he glanced up, she'd look hurriedly away. They talked about the bungalow and the Spanish woman and things that didn't matter.

After the woman had cleared away, Fenner lounged on the divan. Glorie moved restlessly about the room. Fenner followed her with his eyes because she was beautiful to watch. She said suddenly, "Don't sit there doing nothing."

"What do you want me to do?"

She went over to the window and looked out. Fenner watched her with interest.

She said, "Come on, I'll show you my place."

Fenner got off the divan and followed her across the lobby and into another large room. It was very bare. Polished boards, rugs and a large divan-bed, that was all. A small dressing-room and a bathroom led off to the right. She stood aside to let Fenner pass and then shut the door behind her.

He looked into the dressing-room and then into the bath room while she waited. "Very nice," he said.

He could hear the sound of her breathing from where he stood. He didn't look at her. He kept moving about the room while she waited. Then he said suddenly, "Let's talk."

She sat limply on the bed. She put her laced fingers behind her head. Fenner looked down at her. His face was expression less.

"Thayler's the guy who runs Carlos's labour syndicate. He was married to Curly Robbins, Nightingale's assistant. Carlos has just killed her. You ran with Thayler. Did you know what his racket was?"

She said, "Sit down here, and I'll talk to you."

He sat down close to her. "Well?"

"Give me your hand."

He put his hand in hers. "Did you know?" he repeated.

She gripped it hard. "Yes, I knew," she said.

Fenner sat very still. "Did you know he was married to Curly?"

She lay with her eyes closed, her teeth biting her underlip. "No."

"You knew all about Carlos as well?"

"Yes, I knew all about him." She sat up. She wound her arms around his neck, pulling his head down to her. Before her lips could reach his mouth he shoved her away. "Cut it out," he said harshly, getting to his feet. "You don't get anywhere with me."

He went out of the room, unlocking the door and leaving it open. He passed Bugsey wandering in from outside. He didn't say anything, but went on into the garden.

V

Towards evening Fenner returned to the bungalow. He found Bugsey sitting on the porch steps, making patterns on the gravel path with a piece of wood. He said, as he went past, "Still in a pipe-dream?"

Bugsey started, but before he could say anything Fenner had passed into the bungalow. He went straight to Glorie's room.

Glorie was sitting on the window-seat, dressed in a pale green wrap. She was looking out of the window, and she turned quickly as Fenner walked in. "Beat it," she said harshly.

Fenner shut the door. "I've got a little story to tell you. The Federal Bureau have been digging up the past, and I've been looking the dope over. Some quite interesting stuff."

Glorie sat very still. "What do you mean?" she said.

Fenner sat on the bed. "I'll tell you," he said evenly. "Some of it's just guess-work, some of it's facts, but it makes a nice little story. It starts off in a hick town in Illinois. The guy who runs this town gets himself a young wife. That's all right, but the young wife has got big ideas. She begins to spend more money than her hubby can make. The name of this guy is Leadler, and he's a politician of sorts. You married him because you thought you could get out of the cheap song-and-dance show you were touring in. Well, you did. Leadler, to keep you in silk pants, helps himself to a lot of dough that belongs to the town. You both take a powder to Florida."

Glorie folded her hands in her lap. "You can't do any thing to me," she said.

Fenner shook his head. "Hell! That's not the idea," he said. "I wouldn't want to do anything to you. Let me go on. You and Leadler part. I don't know why, but as Thayler now appears on the scene, I take it you prefer a younger and richer man. Okay, you lose sight of Leadler, and you go for a cruise with Thayler. Before you turn up, he was married to Curly Robbins. Thayler absorbs the Chinks Carlos smuggles into the country. He pays Carlos so much a head, and sells the Chinks to sweat shops up the coast. Curly knew all about that, so it was dangerous to let her float around without being watched. Thayler gets her a job with Night ingale, who does odd jobs for Carlos. She gets good money, doesn't have to do much, and Nightingale can look after her. You want to divorce Leadler so you can marry Thayler. Thayler never told you he was married, and you can't find Leadler. Then one day your boat comes in to Key West and you go along for an evening's fun to the local casino. You recognize Noolen as your long-lost husband. That's a sur prise, isn't it?"

Glorie chewed her underlip. "You think you're smart, don't you?" she said, stormily.

"Noolen, or Leadler, if you like, isn't doin' so well with his casino, so he's willing to give you a divorce if you pay him for it. You want the dough to give to him, but Thayler won't part. It's stalemate for a moment. You don't care a lot for Thayler, it's his dough you want. That guy certainly rolls in dough. You want to be always sure you're going to get it, and the only way you can be sure is to marry him. The cops have turned up some dirt that proves that, while you were with Thayler, you also had a Chink running around. You two kept under cover, but not well enough. This Chink used to work for Carlos. He disappeared about a couple of months ago. Maybe Thayler found out and tipped Carlos. I don't know, but he disappeared. What happened to him, baby?"

Glorie began to cry.

Fenner went on, "Never mind. Maybe it doesn't matter. Now your mysterious sister turns up. She comes to see me. It's a funny thing, but the cops can't give me a lead on that dame. They can't dig further into your past than your song -and-dance days. This looks like your sister was a better girl than you, and she kept out of trouble. Why she came to me, and why she knew about the Chinamen, Noolen and Carlos, I can't explain yet. I'll get round to it some day, but right now it's got me beat. As far as I'm concerned, it's your sister who gets me to come down here. I find the situation lined up like this: "Noolen's frightened of Thayler and Carlos. I can under stand that now. He doesn't want anyone to know he's Leadler, and I bet you've told Thayler that, or if you haven't he thinks you have. You and Thayler are not getting on too well. You're quarrelling. Then, maybe, you learn that he's married, and you shoot him. You get scared and run to me. You like the look of me and you're looking round for someone to hook up with again, so after you've shot Thayler you come along to my hotel. Now you haven't killed Thayler. He's waitin' in his car parked by the boat. He nearly kills me and, later, he tries to shoot you. Now, why does he do that? Because he knows you've taken somethin' from the boat, after you shot him. Isn't that right?"

Glorie stopped crying. "Is that all you know?" she said.

Fenner shrugged. "It helps, doesn't it?"

Glorie didn't say anything.

"Thayler's washed up as far as you're concerned. You and I can go after him. I'm going to smash Carlos and his racket, and Thayler may as well go with him. What do you think?"

Glorie said, "I must think. Go away now. I want to get things straight."

Fenner got to his feet. "I'll be waiting in the other room. Make it snappy," he said. He went to the door and then paused. "What was your sister to you?" he said abruptly.

Glorie shifted her eyes. "Nothing," she said. "I hated her. She was mean, narrow minded and a mischief-maker."

Fenner raised his eyebrows. "I don't believe a lot you say," he said, "but maybe that's true. You're not sorrowing for her, are you?"

"Why should I?" she said fiercely. "She got what was coming to her."

Fenner stood by the door. Then he said slowly, "That gives me an idea. You and Thayler were in New York at the time of her death. You two girls were almost twins. Suppose Thayler fell for her. Suppose you came in and found them, got jealous, and killed her. Suppose Thayler got those two Cubans to carve her up and get rid of her. Were those two guys workin' for him?"

Glorie said, "Oh, run away. You'll be thinking I'm worse than I am."

Fenner was quite startled at this new idea. He came back into the room again. "Was that the way it went?" he said. "Come on, did you kill Marian Daley?"

Glorie laughed in his face. "You're nuts," she said. "Of course I didn't."

Fenner scratched his head. He said, "No, I don't think that's quite the way it went. It won't explain the guy who said she was screwy, an' it won't explain the Chink in my office. Still, it's an idea."

He stood looking at her for several moments, then walked out of the room, leaving her polishing her nails.

Outside, Fenner went into the sitting-room. A vague feeling of excitement stirred him, a feeling that he was approaching a solution of the mystery of this business. He went over to the sideboard and helped himself to a drink.

Bugsey wandered in. "Got one for me?" he said hopefully. Fenner jerked his head. "Help yourself," he said, sitting down on the divan.

Bugsey poured a long drink and stood blinking at the glass. He took a long pull and smacked his lips.

Fenner glanced at him, but said nothing.

Bugsey fidgeted with his eyes, then said cautiously, "She ain't nice, is she?"

"Who isn't?" Fenner was thinking about other things.

"Her—in there." Bugsey jerked his head. "There's somethin' the matter with her, or somethin', ain't there?"

"What is all this?" Fenner wished he'd go.

Bugsey said, "Oh, nothing," and finished his drink. He looked at Fenner furtively, then helped himself to another. "Next time you go out, you might take me with you," Bugsey said. "Somehow I don't feel too safe alone with her."

Fenner scowled at him. "Listen, pal," he said. "Would you take a little walk? I've got a lot on my mind."

Bugsey finished his drink. "Sure, sure," he said apologetically. "I guess I'll take a little nap." He shuffled off.

Fenner lay on the divan, holding the glass of Scotch, and staring out of the window. He stayed that way for a long time. Hosskiss, the Federal man, had been very helpful. He had turned all his information over to Fenner, and pro mised to try to dig up some more during the next few days. He was even hopeful of finding a line on Marian Daley, although up to now he couldn't dig up anything. Noolen, so long as he kept to Florida, was safe. He couldn't be pro secuted. Fenner wondered how smart Noolen was, and if he could be bluffed. He thought he might try and see how he got on.

He was still there when Glorie came in at sundown. She sat by his side.

Fenner said, "Well, you thought it over?"

She said, "Yes."

There was a long pause. Fenner said, "You're wondering what's goin' to happen to you, aren't you? You think if Thayler goes, you've got to start hunting around for some other man to keep you."

Glorie's eyes hardened. "You think of everything, don't you?" she said.

"Don't get high hat. I've thought about you, too. It's going to be tough, but there's no other way out. Thayler's on the skids, and the sooner you cut away from him the safer it's going to be for you. You don't need to worry. Take a look at a mirror. A dame like you won't starve."

Glorie giggled. "You're cute," she said. "I want to hate you, but you're too cute. Don't you ever make love to a girl?"

Fenner said, "Let's keep to business. Never mind what I do. I'm working now, and I never play when I work."

Glorie sighed. "I guess that's all hooey."

Fenner nodded. This was boring him. "Now what about Thayler? Did you take anything from him?"

Glorie pouted. "Why do you think I did?"

"It's a guess. Why did he want to shoot you? Revenge? Too risky. He knew you were with me. To stop you talking? Yes, that adds up."

Glorie went over to the sideboard and opened a wooden biscuit chest. She came back with a small leather wallet. She threw it into his lap. "I took that," she said defiantly.

Fenner found a number of papers in the wallet. He lit a cigarette and went through them carefully. Glorie at first sat close to him, watching; then, when she saw how absorbed he was, she got up and went out on the piazza. She fidgeted around for nearly ten minutes, then she came back again. Fenner said, without looking up from his reading, "Get a meal together, baby; I'm going to have a late night."

She went out and left him. Later, when she came back, he was sitting where she had left him, smoking. The wallet and the papers weren't any longer in sight.

"Well?" she said.

Fenner looked at her. His eyes were hard. "Any of those guys know you've got this place?"

She shook her head. "No one."

Fenner frowned. "You don't tell me that you put this joint together all on your own."

He wasn't sure whether her face had gone pale or whether it was a trick of the light. She said evenly, "I wanted some where to go when I was sick of all this. So I saved, bought the place, and no one knows about it."

Fenner grunted. "You know what's in that wallet?"

"Well, I looked at it. It didn't mean anything to me."

"No? Well, it means a hell of a lot to Thayler. There are four receipts of money paid by Carlos to him. Two I O U's from Noolen for large sums of money, and particulars of five places where they land the Chinks."

Glorie shrugged. "I can't cash that at the bank," she said indifferently.

Fenner grinned. "Well, I can," he said getting to his feet. "Give me a big envelope, will you, baby?"

She pointed to a little desk in the window recess. "Help yourself."

He went over and put the contents of the wallet in the envelope, scrawled a note, and addressed the envelope to Miss Paula Dolan, Room 1156, Roosevelt Building, New York City.

Glorie, who had been reading over his shoulder, said, "Who's the girl?"— suspiciously.

Fenner tapped the envelope with a long finger. "She's the dame who runs my office."

"Why send it to her?"

"Listen, baby, I'm playing this my way. If I liked I could turn this over to Hosskiss, the Federal man, and get him to crack down on those two guys. It would be enough for him to start an investigation. But Carlos has been tough with me, so I'm goin' to be tough with him. Maybe he'll get me before I get him, in that case the stuff gets turned over to the cops, after all. Get it?"

Glorie shrugged. "Men are either chasing women or getting themselves into a jam because of their pride," she said. "I love a guy who takes on a mob single-handed to even things up. It's like the movies."

Fenner stood up. "Yeah?" he said. "Who said single-handed?" He went out on to the piazza. "I'm going to put this in the mail. I'll be right back, and then we can feed."

On his way back from mailing the letter he passed a cable office. He paused, thought, and then went in. He wrote a cable out and took it to the desk.

The clerk checked the message and looked at Fenner hard. The message ran:

Dolan. Room 1156 Roosevelt Building, New York City. Report progress by Crossett of Daley murder. Rush. D.F.

Fenner paid, nodded, and went out again. He walked fast back to the bungalow.

Glorie was waiting for him with cocktails.

Fenner said, "I'm in a hurry. Let's eat and drink at the same time."

Glorie rang the bell. "Where are you going?" she asked.

Fenner smiled. "I'm going to see your husband," he said gently. "It's time he forgot his shyness and started to play ball."

Glorie shrugged. "A guy like that won't help you much," she said.

While they ate, Fenner kept silent. After the meal he stood up. "Listen, baby, this is serious. Until these guys have been washed up you've got to stay here. On no account must you leave this joint. You know too much and you've put Thayler in a spot. Any one of the mob would slit your throat if they saw you. So stay put."

Glorie was inclined to argue, but Fenner stopped her. "Be your age," he said patiently. "It won't take long, and it'll save you for some other poor sap."

Glorie said, "Oh, well," and went over to the divan. Fenner walked out into the kitchen.

Bugsey had just finished supper and was making eyes at the Spanish woman, who ignored him. Fenner said, "I'm going out. Maybe I'll be back to-night, maybe I won't."

Bugsey lumbered to his feet. "Shall I bring a rod?" he said.

Fenner shook his head. "You stay here," he said. "Your job is to protect Miss Leadler. You keep awake and watch out. Someone might try and rub her out."

Bugsey said, "Aw, boss, for God's sake—"

Fenner said impatiently, "You stay here."

Bugsey shuffled his feet. "That dame don't want pro tectin'. I'm the guy who wants protectin'."

"What are you yapping about? You always wanted a flock of dames. She's as good as twenty dames, isn't she?" Fenner asked him, and before he could reply he left.

Noolen said, "I thought I told you to keep outta here."

Fenner threw two pieces of paper on the desk. "Take a look at that," he said.

Noolen picked up the papers, glanced at them, then stiffened. He looked sharply at Fenner, then back to the papers again.

"You'd better burn 'em," Fenner said.

Noolen was already reaching for a match. They stood in silence until the charred ash drifted on to the floor.

Fenner said, "That's saved you a little, hasn't it, Leadler?"

Noolen went very pale. He said hoarsely, "Don't call me that, damn you!"

Fenner said, "Why did Thayler lend you ten grand?"

"How did you get those?"

"Oh, I found them. I thought maybe you'd feel more disposed to play ball if you were out of Thayler's debt."

Noolen fidgeted with his eyes. "Glorie's been talking," he said. There was a vicious, gritty quality in his voice.

Fenner shook his head. "I got it from the cops. Listen, buddy, you might just as well make up your mind. If you don't play ball with me, I'll take you back to Illinois. I guess they'd be glad to see you."

Noolen sat down. "Sure," he said. "Suppose you start from the beginning."

Fenner studied his finger-nails. "I want a little war to start," he said. "First of all I want Carlos's mob jumped. I want his boats put out of action, and I want Carlos on a plate. Then we can start on Thayler."

Noolen brooded. "That mob's tough," he said. "It ain't goin' to be easy."

Fenner grinned coldly. "Shock tactics, buddy," he said. "We'll have them running in circles. Who can you get to tackle Carlos? Got any muscle-men?"

Noolen nodded. "I know a little gang who'd do it for a consideration."

"Okay, then it's up to you to give them what they want. I've saved you ten grand, so that's something you can spend. Why did Thayler lend you that dough?"

Noolen shifted his eyes. Fenner leant forward. "Listen, you rat, if you don't come clean with me I'll throw you to the wolves. Hell! You're so yellow you'd want a pair of water-wings in your bath. Spill it, canary."

Noolen pushed back his chair. "Thayler didn't want me to divorce Glorie," he said sullenly, "so he lent me the dough. Lately he's been yellin' for it."

Fenner sneered. "You're a nice lot," he said, getting up. "Show me your hoods."

Noolen said, "I didn't say I'd do it."

"I'm goin' to smack you in a minute if you go on like this," Fenner said. "Forget I'm anything to do with the cops. This burg doesn't mean anything to me. I want Carlos and his mob kicked out of here, an' I'm having the fun of seein' it done. After that I'm clearing out. It's up to you to horn in and make yourself the King Pin when they've gone."

Noolen got up. "I think the outfit's too big, but if that's the way you put it, I'll see how it goes."

They went out together. A four-minute drive brought them to a pool room on Duval Street. Noolen walked in, followed by Fenner. The barman nodded to Noolen, who went on through the back.

In a large room with one billiard-table and two green-shaded lamps, five men stood around making the atmosphere thick with tobacco smoke. They all looked up quickly as Noolen and Fenner walked in. One of them put his cue in the rack and slouched out of the room.

Noolen said, "I wantta talk to you boys."

They came drifting up through the smoke, their faces expressionless and their cold eyes restless. Noolen jerked his thumb at Fenner. "This guy's Fenner. He's been gettin' ideas about Carlos's mob. Thinks it's time we rode them outta town."

They all looked at Fenner. Then a tall thin man, with a cut-away chin and watery, vicious eyes said, "Yeah? Well, that's a swell idea. That'll get us all a bang-up funeral, sure thing."

Fenner said quietly, "Let me know these guys."

Noolen said, "That's Schaife," indicating the man who had just spoken. "Scalfoni in the green shirt, Kemerinski holdin' the cue, and Mick Alex the guy with the squint."

Fenner thought they were a fine collection of rats. He nodded. "Let's get together," he said, wandering over to the long padded seats, raised to overlook the billiard-table. "How about some drinks?"

Schaife said to Noolen, "Who's the guy, boss?"

Noolen smiled sourly, "He's the original white-headed boy," he said. "You won't go wrong with him."

They all sat down on the bench and fidgeted until the barman brought drinks. Fenner said, "This is my party. Noolen's the guy who'll pay for it."

Scalfoni, a little dried-up Italian, said, "I gotta date with a dame in a little while. Suppose we get down to things."

The others grunted.

Fenner said, "Carlos has been the big shot in this town too long. We're going to make things so hot for him he's going to take a powder. I want you boys to get together on this. This ain't a picnic, it's war."

"What's it worth?" Schaife said.

Fenner glanced at Noolen. "That's your side of it."

Noolen thought, then he said, "Two grand each and a safe job when I'm in the saddle."

Kemerinski picked his nose thoughtfully. "You goin' to run Carlos's racket?" he said to Noolen.

Noolen shook his head. "I've got a racket that's a lot better than that. You leave all that to me."

Kemerinski looked at Schaife. "Two grand ain't an awful lot, but I'd like to smack that mob if I could get away with it."

Schaife said, "Make it three."

Noolen shook his head. "Can't do," he said briefly. "Two's ample."

There was a moment's silence, then the squint-eyed Alex said, "That's okay with me." The others hesitated, then agreed. Fenner blew out his cheeks. "So far so good," he thought.

"We shall want a boat"" he said. "Any of you guys got a motor-boat?"

Kemerenski said he had.

Fenner nodded. "There's a spot just north of Key Largo, called Black Caesar's Rock. That's where Carlos keeps his boats. That's where Thayler makes the exchange and takes the Chinks for the rest of the ride. I guess we might go out an' look that burg over."

Scalfoni swung his short legs. "I got just the thing for those guys," he said, with a cold grin. "How would you like to take a load of bombs with you?"

Fenner looked vaguely round the room. "Bombs?" he said. "Sure, bring bombs." A fixed ice-cold look crept into his eyes. "Sure," he repeated, "that's quite an idea."

Noolen said uneasily, "The cops'll make a hell of a row about bombs."

Fenner shook his head. "The cops won't worry about Carlos. They'll hang out bunting when that guy croaks."

Scalfoni got up. "When do we go?" he said. There was a tight eagerness in his voice.

"We'll go now. We'll go just as soon as the boat's ready an' you boys have collected some artillery."

Scalfoni hesitated, then shrugged. "I gotta date, but I guess she'll have to wait. This sounds like it's goin' to be quite a party."

Fenner said, "Where's your boat?"—to Kemerinski.

"It's in the harbour opposite the San Francisco Hotel."

"Okay. Suppose you boys meet me in an hour's time on the boat?"

They all said they'd do that, and Fenner went out with Noolen. He said gently, as they got into the street, "If I were you, I'd go along to the cops and get protection. If Carlos thinks you're in this he might get tough with the Casino. You keep out of sight until it's over. Tell the cops you want some officers over at your place, that you're expect ing trouble."

Noolen looked uneasy, and said he'd do that, and went off into the darkness.

Keeping to the back streets, Fenner headed for the water front. He walked fast, his hat pulled well down over his face, and his eyes searching the black shadows as he went along. He had no intention of running into any of Carlos's mob just at present. He knew Carlos must be looking for him. Fenner told himself the next twenty-four hours ought to be a lot more interesting than the last twenty-four hours.

As he approached the waterfront through Negro Beach he saw ahead of him a car drawn up under a lamp standard, with parkers on. He looked hard at the car and came on, slowing his pace and not quite knowing why he did so. Some how, in the almost deserted dark street that car looked too isolated, too obviously loitering. He suddenly ducked into a doorway because he noticed the curtain of the rear window had shifted. There was no wind, and he had an uncomfort able feeling that someone had been watching him come down the street.

The sound of an engine starting came to him in the silence, and gears grated, then the car began to move forward slowly. Fenner stood in the doorway until the red tail-light dis appeared round the bend in the road. He rubbed his chin thoughtfully, then stepped out on to the pavement again.

He didn't go forward, but stood very still, listening. Faintly he could hear the whine of a car, and a cold little smile hit his mouth. The car had gone forward only to turn. It was coming back.

He ran across the road fast and stepped into another door way in the dark shadows. Squeezing himself against the brickwork, he felt for his gun and jerked it from his shoulder holster. He thumbed back the safety-catch and held the gun, with its blunt nose to the star-filled sky.

The car swung round the bend. It was gathering speed. Its only lights were its parkers, and as it swept past a blaze of gunfire spurted from the side window.

Fenner could hear the patter of bullets thudding against the wall on the opposite side of the road, where he had been. Someone was grinding a Thompson, and Fenner couldn't help being thankful that he had crossed the road. He fired three times at the car as it went past him. He heard the crash of the glass as the windshield went, and the car lurched across the road and thudded up the kerb, then smashed into a shop window.

Running from his doorway, Fenner went a little way up the street, passing the car, and ducked down a dark alley. He went down on one knee and peered round, watching.

Three men darted out of the car. One, he thought, was Reiger. They ran for cover. Fenner got the middle man in his gun-sight and squeezed the trigger. The man staggered, tried to keep his balance, then fell on his face in the road. By that time the other two had darted into doorways. They began firing at the mouth of the alley, one with an automatic and the other with a Thompson. Fenner didn't bother about the man with the automatic, but the Thompson bothered him a lot. The bullets chipped away the brickwork of the wall, and he had to crawl away from the opening as splinters of concrete made things dangerous.

Remembering the night on the boat, Fenner crawled further away. He wasn't risking having a bomb tossed at him.

Someone called, "You better duck in here."

He saw a door on his left open and a figure standing in the doorway. "Shut that door and get under cover," he shouted. "Look lively."

It was a woman who spoke. She said unemotionally, "Shall I ring for the cops?"

Fenner slid over to her. "Beat it, sister," he said. "This is a private row. You stay indoors; you're likely to get hurt standing there." Just as he finished speaking a blinding flash and a violent explosion came in the mouth of the alley. A sudden rush of wind flung Fenner forward and he and the woman went over with a crash into the narrow passage of the house.

Fenner rolled over and kicked the front door shut. He said, "Wow! These guys 've got bombs."

The woman said with a quaver in her voice, "This joint won't stand another like that. It'll fall down."

Fenner got unsteadily to his feet. "Let me into a front room," he said quickly. He moved in the darkness where he thought a room ought to be, and stumbled over the woman, who was still sitting on the floor. She wound her arms round his legs and held him. "Forget it," she said shortly. "You start firing from my window and they'll throw another bomb at you."

Fenner said, "Then let me out of here"—savagely.

Faintly the sound of a siren coming fast reached his ears.

The woman said, "The cops!" She let go of Fenner and got to her feet. "Got a match?"

Fenner made a light and she took the spluttering flame from his fingers. She went over to a naked gas-burner and lit it with a plop. She was a short, fat, middle-aged woman with a square chin and determined eyes.

Fenner said, "I guess you did me a good turn. If I'd been outside when that pineapple went off, I should have been sticking to the wall. Now, I guess I better beat it before the cops start having a look round."

The siren came up with a scream and died away in a flurry as brakes made tyres bite into the road. She said, "You better stay here. It's too late to go out now."

Fenner hesitated, checked his watch, found he had still some forty minutes before meeting the mob, and nodded. "Somehow," he said, "you remind me of my best girl. She was always getting me out of a jam."

The woman shook her head. A little gleam of humour showed in her eyes. "Yeah?" she said. "You remind me of my old man when he was around your age. He was quick and strong and tough. He was a good man."

Fenner made noises.

She went on. "Go down the passage and sit in the kitchen. The cops'll come in a minute. I know the cops around here. I'll fix 'em."

Fenner said, "Okay," and he went into the kitchen and lit the big paraffin lamp. He shut the door and sat in a rocking-chair. The room was poor, but it was clean. The mat on the floor was thin and threadbare. There were three religious prints on the wall and two big turtle shells each side of the fireplace. He heard a lot of talking going on, but he didn't hear what was being said. To hear, he would have to open the door, and he thought they might see the light. So he just rocked himself gently and thought about Reiger. That mob was tough all right. His head still swam with the force of the explosion. Then he felt inside his coat, took out his wallet and peeled off five ten-dollar bills. He got up and put the bills under a plate on the dresser. Somehow he thought the woman wouldn't like to take money from him, and from the look of the room she needed it.

After a few minutes she came in. She nodded to him. "They've gone," she said.

Fenner got out of the chair. "That's mighty nice of you. Now I guess I'll run away."

She said, "Wait a minute, stranger. Was that Carlos's mob?"

Fenner looked at her thoughtfully. "What do you know about that mob?" he asked.

Her eyes grew hard. "Plenty. If it weren't for those punks, my Tim would be here now."

Fenner said, "Yeah, it was them all right. What happened to Tim?"

She stood still, a massive figure of granite solidness. "Tim was a good guy," she said, looking straight at Fenner. "He wasn't rich, but he got by. He had a boat and he took parties out in the gulf fishin'. Then this Carlos wanted him to take Chinks in the boat. He offered to pay, but Tim wasn't playing. He was like that. He was strong and tough, and he told Carlos no.

"Carlos couldn't get his own way, so he kills my man. Well, it ain't what happens to the one who gets killed. It's what happens to the one who gets left. Tim died quick; went out like a light. But I don't forget quick. I guess in time I'll go dead inside and I'll find things working out easier than they are now, but right now I'd like to do things to that Carlos."

Fenner got to his feet. He said gently, "Take it easy. Carlos'll pay for that, all right. It wouldn't get you anywhere if you did kill him. Leave Carlos to me. I gotta date with him."

The woman said nothing. She suddenly stuffed her apron in her mouth and her face crumpled. She waved Fenner to the door wildly, and as he went out she sank on her knees by the rocking-chair.

When Fenner got down to the harbor, Schaife was waiting for him outside the San Francisco Hotel. They went in and had two quick drinks and then Fenner followed him down to the waterfront.

Schaife said, "I've got two Thompsons and a lotta shells. Scalfoni's brought a bag of bombs. God knows if those bombs are any use. He makes 'em himself. That guy's been itchin' to throw them at someone ever since he got the idea."

Fenner said, "He'll get his chance to-night."

Kemerinski's boat was of a good size. Alex and Scalfoni were smoking, waiting. Fenner stepped aboard as Kemerinski appeared from the engine cockpit. He grinned at Fenner. "Everything okay," he said. "We can go when you say so."

Fenner said, "Sure. We've got nothing to wait for. Let her go."

The other three got on board, and Kemerinski went below and started the engine. The boat began to throb and Schaife shoved her nose off from the harbour wall.

Fenner said, "We'll land on the village side and walk over. Maybe we'll have to leave in a hurry."

Kemerinski grunted. "This old tub ain't too fast," he said, nosing the boat carefully through the lights towards the open gulf.

Scalfoni came up and climbed into the cockpit. His greasy skin shone in the dim light. "I got the bombs," he said. "Gee! I'm sure goin' to get a kick when they go bang."

Fenner took off his hat and scratched his head. "These other guys've got bombs, too," he said. "They threw one at me about an hour ago."

Scalfoni's jaw dropped. "Did it go off?" he asked.

Fenner looked at him and nodded. "Sure, it wrecked a house. I'm hoping you've made a good job with your home made bangs. We might need them."

Scalfoni said, "Jeeze!" and went away to have another look at his bag.

It didn't take much longer than fifteen minutes before Fenner spotted distant lights. He pointed them out to Kemerinski, who nodded and said, "Black Caesar."

Fenner stretched and climbed out of the cockpit. He walked over to the other three who were sitting on the fore deck, watching the lights. "Let's get this right," he said. "We've come here to put Carlos's boats out of action. We've got to do this quick and with the least trouble. Scalfoni, you carry the bombs. Schaife and me will have the Thompsons, and Alex will cover us with his rod. Kemerinski will stay with the boat. Okay?"

They grunted.

As the boat ran into the small natural harbor, Schaife unslung the two Thompsons and passed one to Fenner. Scalfoni came up from the cabin, a black bag in his hand. "Don't you guys crowd me," he said. "These pineapples are touchy things."

They all laughed.

Alex said, "Some guy'll put a slug in that bag, sure thing. It'll save you a burial, anyway."

The boat swept in a half-circle, and came up to the side of the harbour wall as Kemerinski reached forward and cut the switch. The engine died with a little flurry.

Schaife, standing in the stern, jumped on to the wall and Alex tossed him the bowline. He held the boat steady until the others landed. Kemerinski handed up the bag of bombs tenderly to Scalfoni.

Fenner said, "Watch out. Soon as you hear the bombs, get the engine started. We might have to leave in a hurry."

Kemerinski said, "Sure, that'll be okay. Watch your selves, you guys."

They moved towards the village. The road leading from the harbour was rough and narrow. Big stones lay about, and once Scalfoni tripped. The others swore at him uneasily. "Careful, you punk," Alex said; "watch how you walk."

Scalfoni said, "I'm watchin' okay. The way you're goin' on, you'd think these pills were dangerous. Maybe they won't go off at all."

Fenner said, "We'll take the back streets. Two of you go first, and Scalfoni and I'll follow you. We don't want to attract attention."

It was a hot night with a bright moon. Both Fenner and Schaife carried the Thompsons wrapped in a piece of sacking. They skirted the village and crossed the island through a series of small squares and dark alleys. The few fishermen they did meet glanced at them curiously, but could make out nothing except shadowy outlines.

After a steep climb they suddenly came to the sea again, sparkling several hundred feet below them.

Fenner said, "I guess this is it."

Down the steep incline they could see a large wooden cabin, a long concrete jetty, and six big motor-boats moored to rings set in the reinforced wall. Two lights gleamed through two windows of the cabin, and the door stood half open, sending a strip of light on the oily water.

They stood silently looking down. Fenner said, "Get the bombs out. Each of you take a couple. Scalfoni has the rest. We'll attack the cabin first. When it looks safe enough tackle the boats. They're all to be sunk."

Scalfoni opened the bag and took out two bombs. He handed them to Fenner. The bombs were made of short sections of two-inch pipe. Fenner stood waiting until Scalfoni had given each man a couple of the stuffed pipes, then he said, "Schaife and I will look after the cabin. You, Scalfoni, get down to the boats. Alex, stay here and come down if we get into trouble."

Scalfoni opened his shirt and piled bombs inside.

"You have a fall now, an' you'll certainly be in a mess," Fenner said, with a little grin.

Scalfoni nodded. "Yeah," he said, "it makes me nervous to breathe."

Fenner held the two bombs in his left hand and the Thompson in his right. "Okay," he said, "let's go."

Moving slowly, Schaife and Fenner began to slide down the incline. Fenner said, "You go to the right and I'll take the left. I don't want any shootin' unless it's necessary."

Schaife's thin face sneered. "It'll be necessary all right," he said.

Halfway down they both paused. A man had come out of the cabin and he walked along the wall.

Fenner said, "That complicates things."

The man stood on the wall, looking out to sea. Fenner began sliding down again. "Stay where you are for a bit," he said softly to Schaife. "He might hear two of us."

Down Fenner went silently. The man stood, his back turned, motionless. Fenner reached the waterfront and stood up. He put the two bombs inside his shirt. He was so conscious of the man that he didn't shrink at the coldness of the metal against his skin. Holding the Thompson at the ready, he walked soitly down the wall. When he was thirty feet from the man, his foot touched a small stone which rolled into the water, making a loud splash. Fenner froze. Stand ing quite still, his finger curled round the trigger.

The man glanced over his shoulder, saw Fenner and jerked round. Fenner said, "Hold the pose," jerking up the Thompson.

In the moonlight Fenner could see that the man was a Cuban. He could see the whites of his eyes as they bolted out of his head. The Cuban shivered a little with shock, then he dropped on his knees, his hand going inside his coat. Fenner swore at him softly and squeezed on the trigger. He gave him a very short burst from the gun. The Cuban fell back, his hands clutching at his chest; then he rolled over into the water.

Fenner moved fast. Two big drums of petrol stood close by and he ducked behind them. He got there a split second before a machine-gun opened up from the cabin. He heard the slugs rattle on the drum, and a strong smell of petrol told him the drum was pierced.

The machine-gun kept grinding and there was such a hail of bullets that Fenner had to lie flat, his face pressed into the sand, expecting any second to feel the ripping slugs tear into his body. He put his hand in his pocket and took out the two bombs. He balanced one of them in his hand, then tossed it over the drum in the direction of the cabin. He heard it strike something and then drop to the ground.

He thought, "So much for Scalfoni's home brew."

The machine-gun had stopped, and the silence that followed its vicious clatter was almost painful. He edged his way to the side of the drum and peered round cautiously. The lights of the cabin had been put out and the door had been shut. He groped for the other bomb, found it, and threw it at the door. Even as his hand came up the machine-gun spluttered into life, and he ducked back just in time.

The bomb hit the door and a sheet of flame lit up the darkness, followed by a deafening noise. Brick splinters and wood whizzed overhead, and the force of the concussion made Fenner's head reel. He revised his opinion of Scalfoni's bombs after that. The machine-gun stopped. Again looking round the drum, Fenner saw that the door had been ripped so that it hung from one hinge. The woodwork and paint was smoke-blackened and splintered. Even as he looked, two more violent explosions occurred from the back of the cabin. He guessed Schaife was doing his stuff.

Resting the Thompson on the top of the drum, he fired a long burst into the cabin and ducked down again. Some one replied from the wrecked cabin with a straggly burst from the machine-gun and then Fenner gave him half the drum. After that there was a long lull.

Glancing up, Fenner could just make out Scalfoni crawling down the slope, clutching his chest with one hand. He looked very much exposed as he moved on down, but Fenner could imagine his triumphant grin. He must have been spotted coming down, because someone started firing at him with an automatic rifle. Scalioni didn't lose his head. He put his hand inside his shirt, pulled out a bomb, and heaved it at the cabin. Fenner followed the bomb in flight, then flattened himself in the sand. He had a horrible feeling that the bomb would fall on his head.

The bomb struck the cabin and exploded with a tearing, ripping noise. A long flash lit up the sky and then the roof of the cabin caught on fire. Scalfoni came down fast without drawing any more shooting. Bent double, he ran past the cabin and joined Fenner behind the drum.

"Jeeze!" he said excitedly. "They work! What a night! I wouldn't 've missed this for all the janes in the world."

Fenner said, "Watch out! They'll be coming out."

Scalfoni said, "Lemme give 'em just one more. Just one more to make up their mind for them."

Fenner said, "Sure, enjoy yourself."

Scalfoni slung the bomb into the open doorway. The explosion that followed was so violent that although they were crouching down behind the drum they both suffered a little from the concussion.

A moment later someone screamed, "I'm done. I'm comin' out. Don't do any more—don't do any more."

Fenner didn't move. "Come on out, with your mitts high."

A man came staggering out of the blazing cabin. His face and hands were cut with flying glass, and his clothes were almost all torn off. He stood swaying in the flickering light of the flames, and Fenner saw that it was Miller. He came out from behind the drum, his lips just off his teeth.

Schaife came running up, his thin face alight with excite ment. "Any more of them?" he asked.

Miller said, "The others are dead—don't touch me, mister."

Fenner reached out and grabbed him by his tattered shirt. "I thought I settled your little hash a while back," he said unpleasantly.

Miller gave at the knees when he recognized Fenner. "Don't start on me!" he blubbered.

Fenner cuffed him with his free hand. "Who else is in there?" he said. "Come on, canary" sing!"

Miller stood trembling and shuddering. "There ain't any more," he whined. "They're all dead."

Alex came running up. Fenner said to him, "Take care of this guy. Treat him nicely. He's had a nasty shock."

Alex said, "Yeah?" swung his fist and knocked Miller down, then he booted him hard.

Fenner said, "Hey! Don't get too tough. I want to talk with that punk."

Alex said, "That's all right. I'll have him in the right frame of mind." He went on booting Miller.

Fenner left them and went down the wall towards the boats. Scalfoni was waiting for orders.

Fenner said, "Scuttle 'em. Keep one. We'll go round the island an' pick Kemerinski up. It'll save walkin'."

He went back to Miller, who had dragged himself off the ground and was imploring Alex to let him alone. Fenner told Alex to go and help Scalfoni. Fenner said to Miller, "I told your little louse what would happen. This is only the start of it. Where's Thayler?"

Miller didn't say anything. His head was sunk on his great chest and he made a strangled sobbing noise. Fenner rammed the Thompson into his ribs. "Where's Thayler?" he repeated. "Talk, you punk, or I'll spread your insides."

Miller said, "He don't come here. Honest, I don't know where he is."

Fenner showed his teeth. "We'll see about that," he said.

Scalfoni came running up. "They're fillin'," he said. "Suppose I toss in a few bombs to make sure."

Fenner said, "Why not?"

A few minutes later the shattering roar of the bombs exploding filled the silent harbor, and clouds of dense black smoke drifted from the boats.

Fenner said to Miller, "Come on, punk, you're going for a ride." He had to shove Miller in front of him at the end of the Thompson. Miller was so terrified that he could hardly walk. He kept on mumbling, "Don't give it to me. I want to live, mister, I want to live."

The others were already in the boat waiting for them.

When they got on board, Schaife started the engine. "Gee!" he said. "This is the grandest night's work I've ever done. I never thought we'd get away with it."

Fenner groped for a cigarette and lit it. "The fun'll start as soon as Carlos hears about it," he remarked. "I said shock tactics would succeed, and they have. Now Carlos knows what he's up against, the rest isn't going to be so easy."

They ran the boat round the island and signalled to Kemerinski, who started up his boat and joined them outside the harbour. They all got into Kemerinski's boat, Alex dragging Miller along with him. Scalfoni was the last to leave and, before he did so, he opened the cocks and scuttled the boat.

As he climbed on board Kemerinski's boat he said, "I guess it's tough sinkin' these boats. I could have done with one of them myself."

Fenner said, "I thought of that, but Carlos still has a fair-size gang, an' he'd have got them back. This is the only way."

As Kemerinski headed the boat out to sea he wanted to know what had happened. "I heard the uproar," he said excitedly. "It certainly got the village steamed up. They guessed what was goin' on, and no one had the guts to go an' watch the fun."

Fenner said to Alex, "Bring the punk into the cabin. I want to talk to him."

Alex said, "Sure," and brought Miller down into the small brightly lit cabin.

Miller stood shivering, staring at Fenner with bloodshot eyes.

Fenner said, "Here's your chance, canary. You talk and you'll survive. Where can I find Thayler?"

Miller shook his head. "I don't know," he mumbled. "I swear I don't know."

Fenner looked at Alex. "He don't know," he said.

Alex swung his fist hard into Miller's face. There was the faint sound of his arm in flight, then a thud as his fist crushed Miller's face.

Fenner repeated coldly, "Where's Thayler?"

Miller sobbed, and mumbled something. Fenner said, "Okay, leave him to me." He reached inside his coat and pulled out his gun. He walked over to Miller and bent over him. "Get up," he said harshly. "I'm not making a mess inside here. Come on up on deck."

Miller looked into the gun barrel, his eyes bulging, then he said in a low, even voice, exhausted with terror, "He's over at the Leadler dame's joint."

Fenner remained squatting. He was very still. "How did he know about it?" he said at last.

Miller leaned his head against the wall. Blood continued to drip from his nose and his eyes never left the gun. "Bugsey 'phoned him," he whispered.

"Bugsey?"

"Yeah."

Fenner drew a deep breath. "How do you know this?"

With Miller, fear had worn itself out, leaving him with the calmness of death. He said as if he was very tired, "I was just goin' over when you arrived. Thayler 'phoned me. He said Bugsey had got him on the 'phone and told him where the Leadler dame was hiding. Thayler said for me to come, and he was gettin' Nightingale, too."

Fenner straightened and ran to the cabin door. He shouted to Kemerinski, "Push your tub. We've got to get back fast."

Kemerinski said, "She can't do any more. She'll bust."

"Then bust her," Fenner said. "I want more speed."

When the boat slid into Key West harbour Fenner said, "Alex, you take this Miller to Noolen. Tell him to hide him until I give the word, then I'll hand him over to the cops."

Alex said, "Hell! Suppose we bump him an' shove him into the drink?"

Fenner's eyes snapped. "Do what I say."

Schaife was already making the boat fast. They all crowded off the boat. Then Fenner saw the sedan parked in the shadow. He yelled, "Get down— look out!" and flung himself flat.

Out of the wide window of the car came gunfire. Fenner had his gun out and fired three times. The others had fallen flat except Miller, who was apparently too dazed to do any thing. A stream of bullets from the sedan cut across his chest and he crumpled up soundlessly.

Scalfoni suddenly got to his feet, ran a little way towards the car and tossed his last bomb. Even as the bomb left his hand he clawed at his throat and went over solidly. The bomb, falling short, exploded violently and rocked the car over on its side.

Fenner scrambled to his feet, yelling like a madman and rushed across the street, firing from his hip. Three men crawled out of the car. One of them fumbled with a Thomp son. They all seemed dazed with the concussion. Fenner fired at the man with the Thompson, who pitched forward on his face.

Schaife came blundering up, charged one of the remaining men, and went over with him, hammering at his head with his gun butt.

The remaining man twisted aside and fired point blank at Fenner, who hardly noticed the streak of blood that appeared suddenly in the middle of his right cheek. He kicked the man's legs from under him, stamped on his wrist so that his gun fell from his hand, and then leaned over him, clubbing him senseless with his gun butt. As he straightened up another car came round the corner and charged down. Out of it, gunfire.

Fenner thought, "This is the bunk." He zigzagged behind the overturned sedan. Bullets chipped the street at his feet. Schaife, trying to get under cover, gave a croaking yell and began to walk in circles. More gunfire from the car, and down he went.

From behind the sedan Fenner fired four shots at the other car, then he glanced round to see who was left. Alex and Kemerinski had got back to the boat. Even as he looked, Kemerinski opened up with the Thompson. The night was suddenly alive with gunflashes and noise.

Fenner thought that it was time he got moving. Alex and Kemerinski in their position could take care of any number of hoods. He wanted to get to the bungalow. He waited his opportunity, then, keeping the overturned car between him and the line of fire, he backed away quickly and ducked down the nearest alley.

In the distance he could hear the sound of police whistles, and he dodged down another alley away from the approaching sound. He was too busy to risk getting hauled in by the cops.

A taxi crawled past the alleyway as he emerged into the main street. Running forward, Fenner signalled the driver, who crowded on brakes. Fenner jerked open the door, giving the driver the bungalow address. "Make it fast, buddy," he said. "I mean fast."

The driver engaged his gears and the taxi shot away. "What's breaking around here?" he asked, keeping his eyes, on the road. "Sounds like a battle going on."

"Sure," Fenner said, leaning back, "battle's the right word."

The driver leaned his head out of the cab and spat. "I'm glad I'm going the other way. It sounds kind of dangerous around here."

Fenner didn't let the driver take him right to the bungalow. He got him to stop at the corner of the road, then he ran fast down towards the bungalow. Lights were showing in the front rooms, and as he walked up the short circular drive he saw someone come away from the front door. He put his hand inside his coat and loosened his gun from its shoulder holster.

A boy with a peaked cap paused at the sound of Fenner's approach, and then came towards him. He was a messenger. He said, "You ain't Mr. D. Fenner?"

Fenner said, "Sure. Got a telegram for me?"

The boy gave him an envelope and his book. While Fenner scratched his initials, the boy said, "Been ringin' for quite a while. The lights are on, but no one's at home."

Fenner gave him a quarter. "That's how we fool burglars, son," he said, and went on up to the house. He shoved the cable into his pocket and tried the front door, opened it, and stepped inside.

In the front sitting-room Bugsey lay on the carpet, a small pool of blackish blood making a circle round his head. His gooseberry eyes were half shut and stared sightlessly at Fenner. His mouth puckered, showing his yellow teeth in a frightened, whimpering snarl.

Fenner stood looking. He could do nothing. Bugsey was dead all right. Fenner pulled his gun out and walked slowly into the hall. He stood listening, then he went into the bedroom. Thayler sat in the small tub chair, a look of startled surprise on his face. A little congealed blood traced its way from his mouth to his shirt-front. His eyes were blank and fixed.

Fenner said aloud, "Well, well," and then he looked round the room. It was easy to see what had happened. Thayler had been sitting facing the door. Possibly he'd been talking to Glorie. Then someone Thayler knew walked in. Thayler must have looked up, seen who it was, not taken fright, and then that someone had shot him through his chest.

Fenner went over to him and touched his hand. It was growing cold, but there was still a little warmth in it.

A chair grated as if someone had eased it back. The sound came from the kitchen. Fenner stood very still, listening. The chair grated again. Fenner stepped to the door and peered out. Then, moving very silently, he entered the kitchen, holding his gun forward.

Nightingale stood holding on to the back of a kitchen chair. He held a blunt-nose automatic in his hand, but when he recognized Fenner his hand dropped limply to his side.

Fenner said, "Hurt?" There was something about the way Nightingale was holding himself that made him ask the question.

"I got 'em all in my belly," Nightingale said slowly. He began to work his way round the chair, and when Fenner came over to help him he said a little feverishly, "Don't touch me." Fenner stood back and watched him manoeuvre himself down into the chair. When he finally sat, sweat ran down his face.

Fenner said, "Take it easy. I'll get a croaker."

Nightingale shook his head. "I got to talk," he said hurriedly. "No croaker can give me a new belly." He bent forward slowly, pressing his forearms against his lower body.

"What happened?"

"I shot Thayler, and that rat Bugsey got me. I thought I could trust him. He put five slugs into me before I could shoot him. Then I fixed him all right."

Fenner said, "Why kill Thayler?"

Nightingale stared dully at the floor. When he spoke again his voice was very thick. "They killed Curly. That settled it. I wanted to get Carlos, too, but I guess I shan't now."

"They killed her because you and she got me out of the fix."

"Yeah, but Thayler always wanted her out of the way. She knew too much. She and me, we knew too much. We knew about you. Glorie was at the bottom of everything. She and her Chinaman."

"What Chinaman?" Fenner asked softly.

"Chang. The guy they planted in your office."

"You knew about that?"

Nightingale shut his eyes. He pressed his arms against his belly much harder. It was only by doing that, and by bending well forward, that he kept himself from falling apart. He said at last, in a faint, strangled voice, "Yeah, I knew about it. Carlos found out about the Chink. Glorie was cheating with him. When Thayler took her to New York for a trip, Chang went along, too. That Chink did jobs for Carlos. Carlos thought he was fooling around with Glorie, so he sent a couple of guys to watch. They found out and they killed him. It was Thayler who had him moved to your office."

Fenner stood very still, thinking, "Why? Why to me, for God's sake?"

Nightingale shook his head. "I don't know. He'd got some deep game." He spoke slower, taking more pains to utter each word clearly. "Something phoney happened on that New York trip. Something that started all this."

"Chang? Was Glorie fond of him?" Fenner thought he was seeing an end to this business.

Nightingale shivered a little, but he wouldn't give up. Pain was eating into him and he was dying fast, but he pretended that he wasn't suffering. He wanted to show Fenner that he could take anything that was handed out without a squawk.

Nightingale said, "She was crazy about him." He began to sway a little in the chair.

"Where is she now?"

"She took it on the lam when the shooting started. Any way, Thayler would have given her the heat if I hadn't broken in. I wish now ... that ... I'd 've waited ... before I shot him."

Fenner was too late to catch him. He rolled off the chair on to the floor. Fenner knelt down and lifted his head. "Crotti's a good guy," Nightingale said faintly. "You tell him I stood by you. That'll make things ... even." He peered up at Fenner through his thick lenses, tried to say something and couldn't quite make it.

Fenner said, "I'll tell him. You've been a good guy to me."

Nightingale whispered, "Get after ... Carlos. He's got a dive ... back of Whiskey Joe's...."

He grinned at Fenner, then his face tightened and he died.

Fenner laid his head gently on the floor and stood up. He wiped his hands with his handkerchief, staring blankly at the opposite wall. Just Carlos now, he told himself, then maybe he'd get through with this business. As he put his handkerchief away he found the telegram. He pulled it out of his pocket and ripped the envelope. It ran:

Dead woman you thought Marion proved by finger prints to be kidnapped daughter of Andrew Lindsay. Suggest Marian not all she seems. Paula.

Fenner crumpled the cable slowly in his hand. "So that's that," he said. "Now I guess I can finish this."

He took one more look at Nightingale, then walked softly out of the bungalow.

Where was Glorie? Now Thayler was dead she was foot loose again. Fenner thought he might find her with Noolen. She might, of course, have gone anywhere, but Noolen was worth trying. When a dame sees three men shot to death, and misses the same death by such a close margin, she's not likely to make smart plans. She had the skids under her, and she'd go to the one person left whom she knew well. She ought to know Noolen all right, Fenner argued. He was her husband, wasn't he?

He got back on the main street, hired himself a taxi, and went over to the Casino. Two patrolmen stood near the entrance, and they both gave him a hard look as he ran up the steps. Fenner grinned as he saw this evidence of Noolen's caution. He went through the big hall that was just closing down. Only one light burned, and apart from two Cubans in shirt-sleeves, covering the tables with dust-sheets, the hall was empty. They glanced up when Fenner came in.

"Noolen in still?" Fenner asked, heading for the office.

"He's busy right now," one of the Cubans said, trying to intercept him. Fenner beat him to the door, pushed it open and went in.

Noolen, Kemerinski and Alex sat around the desk. A black unlabelled bottle and glasses stood before them, and they all were smoking. They all looked up, their faces startled, then, seeing Fenner, they relaxed. Noolen scowled at him. "What do you call this?" he said bitterly. "Schaife and Scalfoni dead, and these two guys nearly shot to hell. This your idea of smashing Carlos?"

Fenner wasn't in the mood to play around with Noolen. He put his hands flat on the desk and looked Noolen in the face. "Pipe down, you jerk. What've you got to bellyache about? Schaife and Scalfoni dead? So what? Think you can fight a war without any casualties. What about the other side? We've wiped out all their boats. We've burnt their base. Thayler's dead, Nightingale's dead, Miller's dead, Bugsey's dead, and six or seven others of the mob. Ain't that giving value for money?"

Noolen sat staring at him. "Thayler?" His voice hardly reached above a whisper.

Fenner nodded. "That leaves Carlos and Reiger. I par ticularly want those two guys myself. Then the gang's washed up."

Kemerinski said, "This guy knows what he's talkin' about. I'll play along with him still."

Alex nodded and grunted.

Fenner said, "Okay. What are we waitin' for? Where's Whiskey Joe's?"

"It's a joint near Nigger Beach."

Fenner turned to Noolen. "I'm goin' after Carlos. When I get back I've got something to say to you. Stick around. This is the finish of this business."

He turned to the other two: "Get a couple of Thompsons. We're goin' to Whiskey Joe's. Carlos 's over there."

Alex went away. Kemerinski said, "Just we three?" He sounded a little uneasy.

Fenner shook his head. "I'm going. You two come in later and clear up the mess."

Fenner went out with Kemerinski. Alex was waiting in the car, nursing two Thompsons. As Kemerinski drove off, Fenner said, "You two take the guns. You wait outside until you hear shooting, then come in and blast everything you see. Don't stop shooting until there's nothin' to shoot at—get it?"

Alex said, "This has been a swell night."

The big car went down Duval Street fast. Duval Street stretched right across the whole length of the island. It was late, and they met no cars. Kemerinski drove very fast. He cut speed as he reached South Street and swung the car to the right. At the bottom of South Street he drew to the kerb and killed the engine. "Whiskey 's over on the corner at Nigger Beach."

Fenner got out of the car and began walking down the street. The other two followed him, holding the Thompsons under their coats.

Fenner said, "He's got a place at the back. Would you know it?"

Alex said, "There's a warehouse round the back, maybe that's it."

"We'll go and look at it."

Whiskey Joe's bar had closed for the night. It was just a small pile of black woodwork in the darkness. Alex said, "Down this alley"" softly.

Fenner said, "Stick around while I have a look. I'll be back."

He went down the alley, which was very dark and smelt of decay and dark-alley smells. He walked carefully, not sneaking, but making no noise. At the end of the alley was a small square. Turning right and coming up behind Whiskey Joe's, he could make out a big square building with a flat roof. That, too, was a black silhouette against the star-filled sky. He got closer, found a door, tried it cautiously. It was locked. He moved along, looking for a window, turned the corner and worked his way along the south side. Still no windows. Round the next corner an iron ladder set close to the wall led upwards into the darkness. Fenner guessed it would take him on to the roof.

He went back fast and noiselessly to the other two waiting at the mouth of the alley. "I think I've found the dump," he said. "There's only one door. All you two've got to do is to lie out there and start with the meat-grinder soon as they come out. Don't show yourselves, just lie flat and grind away."

He could see Kemerinski's teeth as he grinned. "I'll go up on the roof and send 'em out to you. Don't make mistakes, an' when you've done the job, beat it. I'll look after myself."

The two grunted to show they understood, and then Fenner retraced his steps to the building. He climbed up the iron ladder, testing each rung before he put his weight on it. He counted forty rungs before he reached the top. As his head came over the balustrade he saw in the centre of the roof a square sky-light, through which a light was shining.

Fenner knew that he'd have to be mighty careful how he crossed over. The slightest sound he made would be heard by anyone underneath. Before getting on to the roof he walked along the balustrade and looked over. He spotted Alex and Kemerinski hiding in a long ditch that was exactly opposite the door of the warehouse. They saw him and waved. He raised his hand, and then lowered himself from the balustrade to the roof.

Holding his gun in his right hand, he inched his way across the space that divided him from the skylight. It took him quite a time, but he did it without a sound. Pushing his hat to the back of his head he looked down into the room. Carlos was there. Reiger was there, and another man he didn't know. They were within six feet of Fenner. The room was very low, like a loft, and Fenner was so startled that he hurriedly jerked back.

Carlos was smoking on the bed. Reiger lolled, his head against the wall, in a chair; he was asleep. The other man dozed on the floor.

Fenner looked at the cross-pieces between the panes of the skylight; he felt their thickness gently with his thumb. There was no substance in them. Then he straightened and, reaching out with his right foot, he placed it gently in the exact centre of the cross-pieces. He took a deep breath and pushed down with all his weight.

The cross-pieces gave with a splintering noise and he and the glass crashed down into the room. He landed on his feet, staggered, and jerked up his gun.

Carlos lay very still on the bed, his cigarette jerking up and down in his mouth. The man on the floor went for his gun unconsciously. He was so dazed that his instinct took him to death. If he hadn't been dozing nothing on this earth would have made him go for the gun. Fenner shot him between the eyes.

Reiger and Carlos were like frozen statues. They just stared at Fenner with fixed glassy eyes.

Fenner said, "I want you," to Carlos.

The ash from Carlos's cigarette fell on his chest. He looked wildly at Reiger and then back to Fenner. "Gimme a break," he said hoarsely.

Fenner said, "Shut up. I've been layin' for you two. Now you're going to get what's coming to you. I'm not going to do it. You two guys can do it to yourselves. You can fight it out. The one who wins goes out of this joint. I won't touch him. Maybe you've heard I keep my word. Either that, or I'll knock the two of you off."

Reiger relaxed suddenly. He said, "I kill him and you don't touch me?" He sounded incredulous.

Carlos crouched further against the wall. "Reiger!" he screamed. "Don't do it! I'm your boss, do you hear? You're not to do it."

Reiger got slowly out of his chair; he had a fixed grin on his face.

Fenner said, "Wait. Put your mitts up and face the wall."

Reiger scowled at him, but Fenner rammed his gun hard into his side. He put his hands up and turned round. Fenner took a gun out of his hip pocket and stepped back. "Stay there an' don't move." He went over to Carlos, grabbed him by his shirt-front, and dragged him off the bed. A quick frisk told him Carlos hadn't a gun.

Fenner walked to the corner of the room near the door and leaned against the wall. "What you waiting for? Don't one of you want to go home?"

Carlos began to scream at Reiger, but the look on Reiger's face told him he'd have to fight. Reiger, his hands held low, a set animal expression on his face, began to stalk after Carlos, who circled the room swearing in a soft continuous flow. The room was too small to keep that up long. Reiger suddenly rushed in blindly, grabbing Carlos round the waist. Carlos screamed with terror, beat Reiger about his head with his clenched fists, and tried to get away. Reiger began to hit Carlos in the ribs, driving in punches that sounded hollow. They swayed round the room, punching and mauling each other, then Carlos's heel caught in the mat and he went over with Reiger on top of him. Reiger hammered his head on the boards. He turned his head and grinned at

Fenner. "I've got the louse now," he panted. "I've got him now!"

Carlos reached up with his hands and drove two hooked fingers into Reiger's eyes. A horrible sound issued from Reiger's chest and burst from his mouth in a sobbing croak. He fell away from Carlos. Holding one hand to his eyes and beating the air with the other, he began to blunder round the room. Carlos crawled to his feet, shook his head, and waited for Reiger to go past him again. As he did so, he shot out a foot and brought Reiger down. Reiger fell on his face and lay there, moaning and kicking with his feet.

Carlos had forgotten that Fenner was in the room. He saw only Reiger. Dropping on Reiger's back, he pinned him with his knees and fastened his red fingers round Reiger's throat. Reiger gurgled, groped feebly for Carlos's hands and then went limp. Carlos threw him away and stood up trembling.

Fenner leaned against the wall, covering Carlos with his gun. "You're lucky," he said. "Beat it before I change my mind. Go on—dust, you—"

Carlos took two staggering steps to the door and flung it open. Fenner heard him blundering downstairs and he heard him fumbling at the lock. He stood, his head on one side, listening. Then out of the night came a sound of two Thompsons firing. Both gave a long burst, then there was silence.

Fenner put his gun away slowly and groped for a cigarette. "I guess I've had about enough of this burg. I'll go home and take Paula out for a change," he said to himself. He climbed out of the skylight and let himself down the iron ladder. As he did so he heard the sound of a car starting. It was Alex and Kemerinski calling it a day.

He went round and looked at Carlos. He had a tidy mind. He had had no doubt that those two would do a good job, but he liked to be sure. He need not have bothered. They'd done a good job.

He brushed down his clothes with his hand, thinking busily, then he turned and walked back towards Noolen's place.

Noolen started out of his chair when Fenner came in. He said, "What happened?"

Fenner looked at him. "What do you think? They're horseflesh—both of them. Where's Glorie?"

Noolen wiped his face with his handkerchief. "Dead? Both of them?" He couldn't believe it.

Fenner repeated impatiently, "Where's Glorie?"

Noolen put two trembling hands on the desk. "Why?"

"Where is she, damn you!" Fenner's eyes were intent and ice-cold.

Noolen pointed. "She's upstairs. You can leave her out of this, Fenner. I'm goin' to look after her now."

Fenner sneered. "What's the idea? You're not falling for any line of repentance she's likely to hand out, are you?"

Noolen's face went a faint red. "I don't want any cheap cracks from you," he said. "After all, she's my wife."

Fenner pushed back his chair. "For God's sake," he said, getting to his feet, "there's no fool like an old fool! Okay, if that's the way it stands." He shrugged. "Quite a dame, this Glorie. Off with the dead money-bags and on with the new."

Noolen sat there, his hooded eyes fixed, and his mouth a little twisted. He said, "Cut out your cracks, Fenner; I don't like them."

Fenner turned to the door. "I'm going to see that dame," he said. "Where shall I find her?"

Noolen shook his head. "You ain't," he said. "Start somethin' here and you'll get a heap of grief."

"So? Okay, then I don't see her; but I'll tell you what I'll do. I'll be back in an hour's time with the cops and a warrant for her arrest."

Noolen sneered. "You got nothing on that dame," he said.

"Sure, I haven't. Only a murder rap. Still, what's a murder rap? Small change in your circle."

Noolen's fat hands twitched, and his puffy face took on a greenish tinge. "What are you talkin about?" he said, with stiff lips.

Fenner moved to the door. "You'll know. I haven't time to play around with you. I either see her now, or see her in jail. I don't give a damn which way it is."

Noolen's face glistened in the light of the desk lamp. He said, "Top door on the right upstairs."

Fenner said, "I won't be long, and you stay right where you are." He went out and shut the door behind him.

When he got to the door on the right at the head of the stairs, he turned the handle and walked in. Glorie started up from a chair, her face white, and her mouth making a big O in her face.

Fenner shut the door and leaned against it. "Keep your stockings up," he said slowly. "You and me are just going to have a little talk, that's all."

She dropped back in the chair. "Not now," she said, her voice tight. "It's late—I want to go to sleep ... I'm tired ... I told him downstairs not to let anyone up."

Fenner selected a chair opposite her and sat down. He pushed his hat to the back of his head and dug in his vest-pocket for a packet of cigarettes. He shook two loose and offered them.

She said, "Get out of here! Get out of here! I don't want—"

Fenner took one of the cigarettes and put the packet back in his pocket. He said, "Shut up!" Then he lit the cigarette and blew a thin cloud of smoke up to the ceiling. "You an' me are going to have a little talk. I'm talking first, then you are."

She got out of the chair and started for the door, but Fenner reached out, caught her wrist, and pulled her round. She swung blindly for his face with hooked finger-nails. He caught her hand, imprisoned her two wrists in one hand and smacked her face with his other hand. Four red bars appeared on the side of her face, and she said, "Oh!"

He let go of her hands and pushed her away roughly. "Sit down and shut up!"

She sat down, her hand touching her cheek gently. She said, "You're going to be sorry for that."

Fenner eased himself in the chair so that it creaked. "That's what you think," he said, yawning. "Let me tell you another little story. It'll slaughter you."

She clenched her fists and pounded them on her knees. "Stop! I know what you're going to say. I don't want to hear!"

Fenner said, "For you there has never been anyone but Chang. When Carlos killed him, your life stopped. Nothing mattered to you. All you had to live for was to get even with Carlos for taking away the one thing that made your horrible life worth while. That's right, isn't it?"

She put her hands over her face and shivered, then she said, "Yes."

"Thayler and you went to New York for a short trip. You couldn't even be parted from Chang for a few days, so he came up and you saw him, when Thayler was busy else where. Carlos sent two of his Cubans and they found Chang and killed him. That's right, too, isn't it?"

"They came in the night when I was with him," she said. Her voice was expressionless. "One of them held me while the other cut his throat. I was there when they did it. They said they'd kill me if he resisted, so he just lay on the bed and let that awful Cuban cut his throat. Somehow, he man aged to smile at me when he was doing it. Oh, if you could have been there! If you could have seen him lying there with the Cuban bending over him. The sudden look of terror and pain in his eyes as he died! I could do nothing, but I swore that I'd get Carlos, I would smash everything he had built up."

Fenner yawned again. He was feeling tired. "You're not very nice," he said. "I can't feel any pity for you, because you always thought of yourself first. If you were really fine you would have had your revenge, even if it brought you down, too, but you hadn't the guts to lose what you already had, so you had to plot and plan to keep Thayler and get Carlos thrown to the wolves."

Glorie began to cry.

Fenner went on, "While this was going on, Thayler had found himself a new toy. Thayler was a nasty bit of work, too. There was a girl called Lindsay. Maybe he met her at a party. He liked her and somehow he got her to go to his house. He knew you weren't about and he persuaded her to drop in. I can guess what happened. He tried to make her, but she fought him. That's how she got bruised, huh?"

Glorie went on crying.

"Well, he overdid it, didn't he? She died. When you got home, after Chang had been killed, you found Thayler run ning in circles with a corpse on his hands. That's the way it went, isn't it?"

"Yes." She put her handkerchief to her eyes and began to rock herself backwards and forwards.

"You found the Lindsay dame dead, and her body badly bruised. Now, baby, it's your turn. Shoot! What did you do?"

Glorie said, "You know all about it. Why ask me?"

"But why did you come to me?"

"I heard about you. I thought I saw my chance of saving Harry and starting trouble for Carlos. I heard you were tough and wouldn't stop at anything. I got a black wig, and wore simple clothes and came to you. I thought if—"

"You came to me as Marian Daley. You said your sister was missing. You thought if I took up the case I'd start eventually on Carlos. You gave me the hint. You said twelve Chinamen, because they always ship Chinamen over in dozens from Cuba, and I'd be smart enough to see that that was Carlos's racket. You planned with Thayler to have the Lindsay dame's body, without arms or legs or head, planted somewhere where I could find it, and I'd think that it was the body of Marian Daley. Since Marian never existed, Thayler couldn't be tried for killing a non-existent person. So you tried to establish an identity between Marian and the body. To do this you got Thayler to fake up marks on your back, and when you came to see me he telephoned to give you an excuse for undressing. I saw the marks, and naturally enough they impressed me. It was a rotten plan, and it could never have held water in a court of law, but you might have confused the issue if you'd have played your cards right. But Thayler made mistakes.

"He wanted to get the body cut up and taken away from his house. He wanted to get your identity established with me as quickly as possible, otherwise the fact that the body, when found, could have proved that it couldn't have been yours from a doctor's evidence of time of death. First, you had to see me, then I was to be held up for a day or so, to give him time to set the stage the way he wanted. To hold me up, he planted Chang on me. You didn't know this. He got his Cubans to take Chang along and put him in my office, hoping that the cops would come up and hold me for question ing. I beat him to it, found out where the Cubans came from, got there, killed them before they could get rid of one of the hands and arms of the Lindsay dame. By slipping up like that, he made a complete mess of things. That's the way it went, isn't it?"

Glorie sat limply in the chair. She said, "Yes, that's right. It was a mad idea, but Harry was so scared he'd have done anything I told him to. I hadn't much time to make plans, but I thought it was an opportunity to get Carlos. I shook Harry down for ten grand. I gave you six, because I knew then that you'd follow up the case. I forged the letter giving you the necessary clues and then, when your secretary took me to the hotel, I waited my opportunity and ran away. That was the end of Marian Daley. I went back to Key West with Harry and waited for you to come. Thayler had told the Cubans to leave the body and the clothes at the Grand Central in a trunk. We were going to give you a tip so that you could have found them. I left that to Harry, but he messed it."

Fenner lay back in his chair and stared at the ceiling. "It was cock-eyed," he said. "If you'd 've come to see me and told me about Carlos, I'd have gone for him just the same. A guy who handles people the way he did deserves all he gets."

Glorie sat up very straight. "You talk as if he's dead," she said.

Fenner looked at her. "He's dead all right. You're lucky. Seems like you've always managed to find a sucker to do your dirty work. Anyway, it was nice to see him go."

Glorie drew in a long shuddering breath. She started to say something, but Fenner interrupted. "The guy who killed Lindsay's daughter is dead. You're still my client. The Lindsay business is for the cops to work out. Maybe they'll find out about Thayler. Maybe they'll even get a line on you, but I'm not helping them. As far as I'm concerned, I'm through. You can link up with Noolen and go with him as fast as you like. I don't like you, baby, an' I don't like Noolen. I'll be glad to get back home. Whatever happens to you means nothing to me. You can be sure something will happen to you. A jane with your outlook can't last long. I'll leave it like that."

He got up and wandered to the door, then, without looking back, he went out of the room.

Noolen was standing in the hall, staring up, as he walked down the stairs. He didn't even bother to look at him. Out in the street he took a deep breath, pulled at his nose thought fully, then set off at a fast pace in the direction of the Pan-American Airport.

The End

Some Orchids for James Hadley Chase
By John Fraser

Once or twice in a generation someone writes a book that establishes a new standard in literature; a book that starts a new trend of fashion; a book that everyone knows and talks about and which several million people read. And one which must certainly be included in that class is the world-famous *No Orchids for Miss Blandish*.

> *Sunday Dispatch*, quoted on back of 1961 Panther edition.

Now for a header into the cesspool.

> George Orwell (1944)

James Hadley Chase's *No Orchids for Miss Blandish* (1939) did for the gangster novel what Raymond Chandler's *The Big Sleep* did in the same year for the private-eye novel.

Both works were clarifiers, intensifiers, transformers.

A millionaire's beautiful red-headed daughter (no first name, always Miss Blandish) falls into the clutches of a family-type Depression-era gang run by heavy-set, sinister Ma Grisson (with an "n"). Through a combination of beatings and dope, principally the latter, Ma turns her into a sex slave for her sadistic son Slim, an extrapolation from two of real-life Ma Barker's four sons and "Popeye" Vitelli in William Faulkner's *Sanctuary* (1931).

When the authorities fail to find her, Miss Blandish's father hires a tough private-eye, Dave Fenner, who cracks the case and helps the cops to wipe out the gang and rescue Miss Blandish.

Chandler eroticized the private-eye genre by amplifying the chivalrous aspects. Chase eliminates them almost entirely and puts rape and the possibility of rape at the centre of a narrative in which women can't count on conventional protections of any kind.

Nor can men. This is a novel in which fear, as well as greed and lust, is a powerful motivator.

There are no magic shields, no moral entitlements. Dumb-but-nice hatcheck-girl Maisey, well-intentioned minor racketeer Rocco, neutral hideout-operator Johnny, would-be-protective playboy McGowan, are all wiped away. But it isn't a downer. It isn't noir-depressive.

In "Raffles and Miss Blandish" (1944), George Orwell called the book "a brilliant piece of writing, with hardly a word wasted or a false note anywhere." The chapters are too long, and I wouldn't have expected customers to be able to take bottles of Scotch to their tables in a Kansas hash-house, and so on. But the flaws are minor.

The book reads as though everything has unscrolled with perfect clarity in front of Chase's mind's eye.

The text that I shall be referring to, and which Orwell himself was evidently using, is that of the first Jarrolds edition, which is also available in the 1961 Corgi paperback. For more about the various editions, see Footnote 1 and Footnote 5.

This is the Depression-era Midwest of John Dillinger, Bonnie and Clyde, the Karpis-Barker gang, and others, rather than Al Capone's Chicago. The characters don't have to master the complicated rules of big-city political machines and large-scale bootlegging operations.

There are no coincidences and no hints of Fate at work, either pro or con. Basically, people are defeated and/or killed because others with whom they are in conflict, on either side of the law, are stronger, smarter, and more ruthless than they are.

Orwell considered this Fascism. But since there are no intimations that the strong ought to prevail simply by virtue of being stronger, I don't think it is, and it seems to me a healthier attitude than the programmatic noir pessimism of the James M. Cain variety.

Nor, Orwell to the contrary, are the characters simply seeking power over others. What they're mainly after is money—money and the security that it can bring.

The ultra-violences pilloried by Orwell are indeed unforgettable, especially Slim's killing of the minor hoodlum Riley ("The knife went in slowly as if it were going into butter."), the third-degreeing of Eddie Schultz, and, at the outset, the killing by Bailey of Miss Blandish's playboy date for the evening, who has drunkenly knocked him down during the snatch.

> "He drove his left into MacGowan's body and, as the boy came forward, he socked him across the eyes and nose with the life-preserver. Miss Blandish heard the bone go, quite distinctly, like the sharp note of breaking wood. Jerry folded up. He lay on his back in the road, lit by the headlights, his long legs threshing in agony, as he held his hands to his face."

Bailey proceeds to kick him to death.

When Ma Grisson, after slapping Miss Blandish silly, tells her that if her father gets tricky about the ransom money, "I'm goin' to take you apart in bits, an' those bits will be sent to your pa every goddam day until he learns to play ball," we believe her.

Miss Blandish "was blind with shock. Her world had caved in, leaving her terrified and broken."

But despite their intensity, and their contributions to the atmosphere of anxiety, such incidents take up very little space. For the most part the killings are practical and non-sadistic—eliminating inconvenient witnesses, escaping from cops.

The third-degreeing of Eddie Schultz is practical—the classic scenario of the one man who can lead them to Miss Blandish being a tough egg who won't squeal otherwise.

Orwell's statement that "the police kill off the criminals as cruelly as the angler kills the pike" is a curious way of describing the storming of the town fortress in which the gang blaze away with tommy guns until the end. The police and the F.B.I. have evidently not been strong-arming their way to a solution before Blandish brings in Fenner, who cooperates with them.

Making others suffer, psychologically as well as physically, can still be enjoyable, and a woman can be as cruel to a woman as a man can. Slim has evidently been a sadist since childhood, though Ma's cruelty seems practical rather than sexual.

Orwell is misleading, though, when he says that "such things as affection, friendship, good nature or even ordinary politeness simply do not enter."

The relationship between Fenner and his perky, playful secretary Paula is charming. Fenner's reassurance to Blandish ("'I'll get those thugs,' he said softly, 'if it's the last thing I do.'") is not that of someone simply in it for the money. And at the end he displays considerable sensitivity in his handling of the rescued Miss Blandish, who after three months in the Grissons' hands will now have to live with unbearable memories.

Orwell is also, it seems to me, needlessly sniffy about the phenomenon of *No Orchids* being especially popular during the Blitz and ordinary soldiers relaxing with "Action Mags" in combat situations.

What ought they to have been reading? Something by Orwell's favourites like Fielding or George Meredith? One of those "old-style" English novels in which "you knocked your man down and chivalrously waited for him to get up before knocking him down again"? (untitled review, April 23, 1936)

When you're unbearably stressed and mind-weary, you can seek the comfort of the innocently familiar, such as your favourite childhood books; or else surrender to a high-energy buzz that, in its coarser way, also eliminates moral complexities and the need for thought.

In *Now It Can Be Told* (1920), the war correspondent Philip Gibbs reported of the Western Front that in fact, "Even with hours of leisure, men who had been 'bookish' could not read... The most 'exciting' novel was dull stuff up against that world convulsion." (p.139).

But, as so often happens, Orwell raises the important questions, and it is his essay that has kept *No Orchids for Miss Blandish* alive for serious consideration.

In *British Gangster and Exploitation Paperbacks of the Postwar Years* (1997), Maurice Flanagan reprints the blurb for the revised Panther edition of 1961. It includes the statement that *"No Orchids for Miss Blandish* was written in six week-ends during the late summer of 1938" (p.9). Steve Holland, in his introduction to Flanagan's book, says,

> *"No Orchids for Miss Blandish* was written over six weekends during the summer of 1938. At the time its author, James Hadley Chase (the pseudonym of René Lodge Brabazon Raymond (1906-1985) was working as a bookseller for the wholesalers Simpson Marshall, handling distribution to retail outlets and the tuppeny lending libraries. Writing a hard-boiled novel was purely marketing on behalf of its author, who had seen how quickly copies of *The Postman Always Rings Twice* by James M. Cain were sold."

To me, as to others, this sounds a bit like myth-making, presumably by Chase himself.

In *The Mushroom Jungle*, Holland describes some remarkable feats of speed-writing, and Chase could obviously work fast, since his solid *He Won't Need It Now* also appeared in 1939. I can see doing *No Orchids* in twelve consecutive days, wired on very strong sweet tea, the English non-alcoholic stimulant of preference back then. But in six separate spurts? At a time when the working week lapped over into Saturday mornings?

Still, Chase provides an interesting account of his creative processes in a 1965 interview in the *Nouvelle Observateur,*

> "I always work in the same way. I sit in an armchair and wait. One day an idea grabs me, but most often it doesn't go anywhere. I go on waiting, I work at it, this can go on for a couple of months. I don't do anything but think about it. It becomes more complicated, evolves, transforms itself. I don't make any notes. When I sense it's reached the right point, I begin writing directly onto the typewriter. Working very early in the morning. Everything, absolutely everything, comes from here (he taps his brow with his finger)." (Translation mine)

So if when he sat down to write *No Orchids* he was simply transcribing what was there in his head ...?

The only English edition of *Postman* up to that point appears to have been in 1934, and the only English edition of Faulkner's *Sanctuary* in 1931. American pulp 'zines were coming into England in the Thirties. But I don't think that copies of books published in the States would have been imported for sale.

Obviously the central situation of *Sanctuary* is lodged in Chase's consciousness—a girl from a good family falls into the hands of low-lifes and is memorably raped (after a fashion) by a degenerate gunman.

And a blurb on a 1941 paperback impression of the first edition of *No Orchids* announces, "For the vast audience who hailed 'The Postman Always Rings Twice' and [Horace McCoy's] 'They Shoot Horses, Don't They?' may I offer the deadliest of all those tales."

But *No Orchids* has nothing in common stylistically with either *Sanctuary* or *Postman*.

On the other hand, Paul Cain's *Fast One*, which it does resemble, came out in England in March 1936, a cheap edition of Graham Greene's *A Gun for Sale* (aka *This Gun for Hire*) appeared in January of 1938, and Greene's *Brighton Rock* was published in July of the same year.

My own guess, though, is that none of these, whatever they may have suggested about sales possibilities, was the grain of sand in the oyster.

One such grain was most likely provided by Jonathan Latimer's *The Dead Don't Care*, published in London in January 1938. Chase's titling his second novel *The Dead Stay Dumb* may have been a tip of the hat to that effect.

The greater part of this, Latimer's fourth Bill Crane novel, is as good as a vacation among the drinking rich in the still unspoiled Florida of the Thirties.

But in the last two chapters we find that rich, small, drunky, likable Camelia Essex, who has been snatched outside a nightclub earlier, is being held in a cabin-cruiser off the Florida keys by pock-marked, stocky Frankie, plump soprano-voiced, clammy-handed Toad, skeletal Dopey (not named after the Disney character), and granite-faced George, owner of the boat.

Frankie and George, with investigator Bill Crane and Cam's fiancé Tony Lamphier bound and helpless in the same cabin, are all set to start raping her ("'Want me to hold her?' George called") when . . . . well, read the book.

The following passage from earlier in the novel seems to me granular:

> [Crane] wondered what it was like to be a woman and held by kidnapers. He often wondered what it was like to be a woman, but never before in connection with kidnapping. He supposed it was pretty bad. In the first place, when you were kidnapped, man or woman, you were always in doubt whether your captors would ultimately kill you or release you. But with a woman there was another consideration. With a pretty girl like Camelia Essex, especially, there was another consideration.

It was funny people never spoke about this. It was like solo transoceanic flyers. You never heard how they went to the bathroom. It was just something you never spoke about. And so was being raped by kidnapers. What was standard practice? He was a detective, but he didn't know. How the hell could you know? A girl wouldn't say: Why, yes, thank you, I was raped. He didn't think the average kidnaper was above a little rape. (Ch. 6)

Something else in all likelihood was also going on in Chase's creative processes.

This was the summer of 1938, when master political Capone-figure Adolf Hitler and his perfectly cast gangster crew—fat, pseudo-jovial Herman Goering, twisted crippled Josef Goebbels, chinless bespectacled slug-like Heinrich Himmler, arrogant faux-aristocrati Joachim von Ribbentrop, and others—were in full career.

The 1919 Treaty of Versailles was in tatters, Germany had reintroduced conscription and been re-arming, the Rhineland area was snatched back from France in 1936, German planes had been assisting General Franco's forces in Spain, and in March 1938, after nibbling at the edges, Germany annexed the whole of Austria, all this without any opposition from Britain and France.

War with Nazi Germany was now a possibility for any seriously thinking person (my own father bought a 1928 Overland Whippet for ten pounds in which to evacuate us from London if needs be), and it promised to be cataclysmic.

H.G. Wells, that nearest thing to a modern seer, had been predicting the devastations of aerial bombardment since *The War in the Air* (1908) and *The World Set Free* (1914), with London lying in ruins in the opening part of the very depressing 1936 movie *Things to Come,* the filming of his *The Shape of Things to Come* (1933).

Through the narrator at the end of his novel *Coming Up for Air* the following year, George Orwell was predicting that war would be the end of the old muddling-along-somehow England, and that rubber truncheons, barbed wire, and "all the things you've got at the back of your mind, the things you're terrified of, the things that you tell yourself are just a nightmare or only happen in foreign countries," were on their way.

In "Raffles and Miss Blandish," as I have said, Orwell characterizes *No Orchids* (so vastly better a seller than his own novel) as being essentially about the pursuit of power.

I think that that gets it a bit wrong, over and above the fact that what the gangsters, small and larger, are after is money.

No Orchids is surely about how to cope with groups who are ruthless in their own exercise of power. As Lee Horsley says of Slim Grisson in *The Noir*

Thriller, we have tests here of "a society's resolve."

Miss Blandish's drunken upper-class squire for the night, taking the kind of gentlemanly swing at Bailey that Orwell seemingly favoured in the comments I quoted earlier, is shattered by Bailey's cosh and kicked to death.

The police and the FBI get nowhere in the case for three months, during which Miss Blandish, her world collapsed, her over-class self treated with a total lack of respect, is in hell among the effectively organized plebs.

Finally her father, the Meat King, buys the services of a private operator who, while not driven simply by greed, is not afraid to cut some corners, roughing up Mexican night-club owner Pete (at some risk to himself from the staff), getting hard-as-nails gun-moll Anna Borg to release crucial facts by threatening to grill her boyfriend Eddie Schultz's face with her portable electric stove, and getting to Johnny's place a short jump ahead of the mob, where he just misses being machine-gunned and hand-grenaded.

After which he picks up Eddie and watches while the wrecking-crew work on him in the notorious third-degree episode.

> "Eddie . . . didn't say anything. Fenner turned sour. 'Quit playin'
> with him, can't you?' he said to the cops. 'This guy's tough, ain't
> he? Well, get tough too.'"

Which sounds like good advice, and it works.

Fenner's approach isn't cost-free.

He sends poor, nice, scared hat-check girl Maysie to scout for Miss Blandish in the Grissons' lair and gets her killed.

But it would have made good sense to members of the European Resistance, I imagine. And one shouldn't put too much store by the wartime movie images of chivalrous British youth.

Behaving decently when not actually fighting was one thing, and very important, as witness the horrors of the totally unchivalrous Battle of Stalingrad. In *Now It Can Be Told,* Philip Gibbs had convincingly reported seeing "Our men treat[ing] their prisoners, nearly always, after the blood of battle was out of their eyes, with a good-natured kindness that astonished the German themselves."(p. 406). Some traditions don't wither away. There were astonishing episodes at the end of WW2 when liberated prisoners of war in the infamous Japanese camps did not turn on their bewildered guards and rend them.

But when it came to killing, the pertinent ethos soon became that of the great teacher of hand-to-hand combat, W.E. ("Dan") Fairbairn, of whom one admirer, as quoted on Google, recalls, "All of us who were taught by Major Fairbairn soon realized that he had an honest dislike for anything that smacked of decency in fighting."

According to a blurb, Chase's "book was the most read by the men and women of the [British] Armed Forces."

At age thirty-two and with nothing special to show from his life to date, but within his head the consciousness of a book that he might be able to write, Chase may well have felt that he had nothing to lose by giving up on a programmatic "decency," and that he would let his imagination take him wherever the demands of his story required.

He had obviously been thinking and reading about gangsters, and about the very different crime culture of the States, for some time, and he was indeed presenting, as Orwell suggests, "a distilled version of the modern political scene."

As someone who, like Orwell, hadn't been able to go to university, he was probably exasperated by charming, chattering, upper-classish types like Robert Donat's Richard Hannay in Hitchcock's espionage thriller *The Thirty-Nine Steps* (1935) and Michael Redgrave in *The Lady Vanishes* (1938), that exhibition of too-too-terribly-English fumblings in the attempt to cope with, or even acknowledge the reality of, Fascist Europe.

An obvious grain of sand came from Horace McCoy's *No Pockets in a Shroud*, published first in Britain in 1937, in which, as it happens, one of the characters is named Grisson.

The protagonist, feckless, womanizing journalist Michael Dolan, conscious of Hitler's and Mussolini's predations over in Europe, and naively setting out to tell the truth about local corruption in his new little newspaper, is pretty irritating. When he runs up against his home-town equivalent of the Klan, to which apparently all the right-thinking establishment citizens belong, and is bumped off, it is really only to be expected.

Which leaves future prospects pretty bleak, except maybe for the two undercover Communists who have been involved with him.

However, in a curious episode, he steps entirely out of character when he tells a rich local Senator whose carefree daughter he has impulsively married and whom he's trying to extract money from for his paper, how during an earlier sexcapade he'd got some cop friends of his to deal with a private-eye who'd been tailing him.

> "Well, the coppers don't particularly care for private dicks at best, so we took this fellow to a little room down in the basement. A sound-proofed room, Senator, with only one chair—a replica of an electric chair—in the middle, with a big spotlight shining in the face of whoever sits in it. We strapped this fellow in and bruised him up a little, but still he wouldn't talk. So we went to work on him with the rubber hose—and a couple of hours later he admitted that Fred Coughlin had hired him." (p. 96)

After which he puts the crooked Coughlin out of action with a photo of him in a hotel with an under-age schoolgirl.

I am not, heaven forbid, suggesting that Chase was consciously writing an allegory. The term "allegory" too easily invites emotional distancing and the replacement of mixed bundles of banknotes with gambling chips—or Monopoly money.

But we do have an obvious overlapping of the *Sanctuary* image of rape at the hands of low-lifes as an ultimate powerlessness, the power-charged and power-seeking activities of American gangsters, and what Hitler and his gang had been up to in their dealings with other countries.

And, yes, Slim Grisson's weapon of choice is the knife.

And if we recall only one thing about gang-leader Mackie Messer in Brecht and Weill's *The Threepenny Opera* (1928; brilliantly filmed by G.W. Pabst in 1931), it is that he is Mack the Knife.

And the massacre of Hitler's principal rival Ernst Röhm and other Brownshirt leaders in the summer of 1934 was "The Night of the Long Knives."

And the most unforgettable episode in *No Orchids* is when Slim slowly pushes his switchblade into the bared belly of lesser gangster Frankie Riley, tied to a tree.

And, yes, a length of rubber hose and a rubber truncheon are both rubber, and there is something disquieting about an innocent gardening aid containing pain and a truncheon being flexible, perverting a substance that in rubber bands and bouncing balls is a bit playful.

The rubber truncheon, the ominously named Totschläger (beater-to-death), was a basic tool of social control in Fascist Europe, and had already figured prominently in interrogations in Eric Ambler's *Cause for Alarm* (1936) and *Background to Danger* (1937).

Footnote 1

The text of the first edition of *No Orchids* (Jarrolds, 1939) is the best one. It reappears in the 1961 Robert Hale edition and the 1977 Corgi edition. It might be thought of as the "H'yah" edition.

On the second or third page, small-time gangster Bailey, sitting in Minnie's hash-house on a hot dry July morning in small-town Kansas, calls out to blonde, busty Minnie, "H'yah, Gorgeous" when he wants some service.

In the revised 1942 text, "H'yah" is dropped, presumably because that's simply what one would say by way of a first greeting. Nor does it appear in subsequent editions.

"Hey, juicy fruit" is an improvement over "H'yah." But the 1942 revisions, which are mainly in the first half of the novel, are cumulatively regrettable.

The in-places-tightened phrasing breaks the rhythm of the prose. Normal lecherous feelings on the part of minor characters are eliminated. Miss Blandish is given some un-speakable lines of dialogue of the "You can't do this to me!" variety that make her seem snobbish, spoiled, and wimpy.

At the same time, we lose a fifty-line passage in which she movingly describes to gang-member Eddie Schultz, who has some sympathy for her, her nightmarish perception of Slim through a drugged haze.

And Slim, who in the original version is a homicidal but sexually immature gangster who from the outset wants her fabulous pearl necklace for the gang and her body for himself, is turned in places into a drooling retard romantically in awe of her (he gives her back the pearls) and saving her from being bumped off by "the old wolf."

In other parts, such as the episode in which he and Eddie tangle with the cops while looking for mystery-woman Anna Borg, he behaves perfectly normally. The result is incoherence.

The whole description of his first rape of Miss Blandish is cut. So is an earlier reference to his having seriously molested a little girl when he was a schoolkid.

There is also less sex on the part of minor characters and bit-players, like the drunks at the dance-party where we first see Miss Blandish, and Riley fondling her silk-covered thighs in the car. It makes the novel feel colder.

But the rewriting, as I said, is largely in the first half, before Fenner enters the scene. The endgame in which Slim is on the run with the dazed Miss Blandish in tow is one of the best parts of the book.

Until late in the game, I myself, after a quick skim, hadn't bothered with the first-edition text (Corgi), having assumed that the other, being more staccato, was the right one.

The 1942 Howell, Soskin American edition has some of the same cuts and additions.

Footnote 2

The novel has been filmed at least twice, as *No Orchids for Miss Blandish* (1948), with Jack LaRue as Slim, and by Robert Aldrich as *The Grissom Gang* (1971).

The Aldrich movie, scripted by Leon Griffiths, who earlier did one of the most unsparing and atmospheric Hammer horrors, *The Flesh and the Fiends* (1960), brilliantly incarnates the narrative in a sweaty, three-dimensional, expressionistically coloured early Thirties America, with perfect casting.

Its basic derivation from the 1961 text works just fine.

Scott Wilsan is poignant as Slim, hopelessly, ridiculously, undeflectably in love *(l'Amour fou)*. Miss (Barbara) Blandish, as played impeccably by Kim Darby, isn't a gorgeous redhead without much identity, but a spoiled, snotty, explicitly snobbish little girl who is now learning something about the Depression-era underclass and mounting her own kind of unlovable resistance.

The movie is an impressive testimony to the continuing power of the fable, mutating from Faulkner's Twenties South, via Thirties England, back to the States again.

Aldrich handles it as a labour of cinematic love, allowing things to proceed at the right emotional pace without a stop-watch-holding producer in mind, and achieves real pathos towards the end as Barbara reflects that she will now be restored to a father who will hate and reject her as damaged goods (he does) and that Slim has indeed been her one true love.

It is Aldrich's most deeply serious movie. The account of it by Geoff Andrew in the 2002 *Time Out* movie annual is perfect.

Has the book been filmed under some other title elsewhere, I wonder? It feels like a natural for Japanese or Hong-Kong cinema.

It has also been made into two plays, the first by Chase himself and enjoying a long run in Britain, the second by Robert David MacDonald.

Footnote 3

The 1948 sequel to *No Orchids*, *The Flesh of the Orchid*, is a cluttery pursuit-and-hide narrative in which Chase seems to have given up the attempt to make his characters' speech sound American.

It largely lacks nail-biting suspense because (a) you are pretty sure that Carol Blandish, nineteen-year-old daughter of Slim Grisson and Miss Blandish (who presumably survives or never makes her suicide leap at the end of *No Orchids*), will finally be free of the more or less unlikable types who want a piece of her action as a prospective millionairess and (b) you don't much care what happens to the characters who help her.

But the narrative achieves remarkable intensity in the finale, when professional hitman Max Sullivan, in hospital after being paralyzed on one side by a stroke, learns that Carol is in the room opposite his own after he's undergone cranial surgery.

In his implacable determination to drag himself along the floor and kill her, with Chase writing at what is obviously full creative stretch, we see something essentially different—woman as mysterious object.

> "She lay on her back, the sheet drawn up to her chin, her face the colour of snow in the bluish light. She looked as if she were dead— very lovely and calm—but he could see the slight rise and fall of her breasts as she breathed. Her head was swathed in bandages, and only a wisp of her beautiful red hair showed beneath the bandages.
>
> Max saw nothing of this: all he saw was someone to kill, just out

of his reach, and, trembling with fury, he caught hold of the bed-rail and tried to lever himself up, but the dead side of his body proved too heavy.

He thought for a moment that he was going to have another stroke. To be so close to her, to have had to suffer so much to get to her, and for her still to be safe and beyond his reach was more than he could endure."

I suspect that writing like that is rare in Chase.

Footnote 4

Since writing these comments, I have googled for "No Orchids for George Orwell" (it seemed a natural title) and come up with Susan Harris Smith's article of that name in *Armchair Detective*, vol. 9, pp. 114-115. She is unintimidated by the prestigious "Raffles and Miss Blandish," points to inaccuracies in Orwell's account of *No Orchids*, and speaks up for aspects of the value system in *No Orchids* as opposed to that in the Raffles books that Orwell prefers.

However, the text of *No Orchids* that she refers to is different from both the 1939 one and the revised 1942 one.

Neither of them contains the passage that she quotes from near the end of the novel in which Miss Blandish laments the emptiness of her life before the kidnapping and deplores her general value system.

Nor does Bailey express in them a desire to become a chicken farmer—Bailey, who has furiously kicked Miss Blandish's date in the head until he dies.

Her Panther edition (1961), which is the same as the 1980 Penguin one, is heavily revised. The prose is conventionally better at the outset, where Chase provides physical descriptions of the characters, and the book as a whole is a smoother read. But it has been "improved" the way 42nd Street has been improved. Eddie Schultz, for example, cracks after being merely slapped hard by one of the cops.

The passage of self- and class-criticism from which Smith quotes feels tacked on and, in its lucidity, inconsistent with the suicide leap that almost immediately ensues on it.

The physical description of Bailey also feels tacked on, having no expressive relationship to his character.

And yes, the Bailey of this book speaks of wanting to become a chicken-farmer. And no, of course this Bailey doesn't kick McGowan to death. He simply shoots him.

The 1948 Novel Library *The Villain and the Virgin* and the 1951 Avon *No Orchids* are the same text with different covers and title pages. Both covers describe it as "revised and edited." So far as I can see, this is the original text with some cuts but no additions.

Ma Grisson no longer slaps Miss Blandish silly, and may simply be threatening her with the rubber hose, rather than using it. Rico doesn't have an orgasm before being knifed. Eddie Schultz caves in before the police beating starts. Miss Blandish doesn't go to her death through the hotel window. The last words of the novel are now, "I want to be alone now. I've got to think," a change which admittedly makes sense of her subsequently bearing the daughter who figures in *Flesh of the Orchid*.

###

Some readers may prefer one of the revised editions. Presumably Chase himself wanted to make the novel more likable. But Orwell was talking about the first edition, and the revised editions are different not only in details, which are numerous, but in the central emphasis where Slim Grisson is concerned.

The first version is the fullest, the most self-consistent, and the best. Despite minor flaws like "H'yah."

According to Steve Holland, Jarrolds reprinted the hardcover in 1940, 1942, and 1947, "to keep up with the library demand." (SH/BGE), the libraries being the tuppenny lending libraries.

In any event, *No Orchids* exists in at least five different versions.

1. Jarrolds, 1939 hardcover and 1941 (?) paperback; Corgi, 1961, paperback.

Miss Blandish is wearing pearls.

2. Jarrolds, 1942, revised. Hardcover and paperback; Harlequin paperback, 1951.

Miss B. is wearing diamonds. Substantial changes.

3. Howell, Soskin (U.S.), 1942.

The 1939 text with some of the same changes as in the 1942 Jarrolds edition. Miss B. still wearing pearls.

4. Avon, 1951; Diversey (Avon), 1948, 1949, as *The Villain and the Virgin.*

Pearls. No self-critical speech by Miss B. No suicide at the end. Eddie is socked on the head but not on knees and arm. Rocco doesn't have an orgasm before being knifed. Other changes.

5. Panther, 1961; Penguin, 1980; heavily revised.

Diamonds. Self-critical speech, and suicide at the end, but the rich lady's reaction to it omitted. Eddie gives in before being socked at all. Flynn and not Slim accompanies Eddy to the apartment building in search of Anna. Rocco, lying down, is knifed several times. There are other changes.

If all this sounds confusing, it is.

Footnote 5

In Donald Thomas's *An Underworld at War* (2003), Chase—but better call him Raymond now—is described as "an English writer and serving RAF pilot" (p.314). In the article on him in the multivolume *Dictionary of Literary Biography*, we find him "becoming a squadron leader." When myths get established, they're hard to shake.

René (pronounced "Rennie"?) Raymond was born in 1906. There is no way in which a thirty-three-year old with no previous flying experience would be taken on for training as a pilot—especially not a fighter pilot—in what the demands of the new technologies made very much a young man's service.

Moreover, Raymond himself is quoted in Robert Deleuse's "A la poursuite de James Hadley Chase" as telling an interviewer that at the start of the war "I was attached to the Air Ministry, where I had to turn up every morning at 8:30. So, in order to continue writing, I got up every day at 5:30." (Translation mine.).

Later on, he and the cartoonist David Langdon took over the editorship of the *Royal Air Force Journal* and turned it into what appears to have been a very professional publication. In the 1946 book of selections from it, *Slipstream*, both are Squadron Leaders.

"Squadron Leader" isn't a term like "Platoon-Commander." It's simply a rank, the equivalent of Major in the Army.

But myths die hard, and Chase in his photos does look very R.A.F.

Footnote 6

When Chase died in 1985, an obituary writer for the London *Times* observed at the end, with oh such knowing condescension,

> In an age hardened to James Bond and Mickey Spillane, it becomes difficult to understand why these harmless, professional thrillers, more competent than most of their genre, but otherwise unremarkable, were ever thought shocking. *No Orchids for Miss Blandish* was remembered as a symbol long after it was forgotten as a book. (Clipping dated 7/2/85).

The novel has had better legs than that.

—excerpted from *Found Pages*

John Fraser was born in North London in 1928. He married Midwestern artist Carol Hoorn in 1961 and together they moved to Halifax, Nova Scotia, in 1961, where Fraser taught at Dalhousie University until his retirement. He is the author of three books, *Violence in the Arts* (1974), *America and the Patterns of Chivalry* (1982), and *The Name of Action: Critical Essays* (1985). "Found Pages" is a very long accumulation of information, speculation, and literary-critical opinion about mid-century English gangster fiction.

JAMES HADLEY CHASE BIBLIOGRAPHY

No Orchids for Miss Blandish (1939; reprinted as The Villain and the Virgin, 1948)

The Dead Stay Dumb (1940; reprinted as Kiss My Fist!, 1952)

Twelve Chinks and a Woman (1940; reprinted as 12 Chinamen and a Woman, 1950, and as The Doll's Bad News, 1974)

Miss Callaghan Comes to Grief (1941)

Get a Load of This (1941; stories)

Miss Shumway Waves a Wand (1944)

Eve (1945)

I'll Get You for This (1947)

Last Page (1947; play, filmed as Man Bait)

The Flesh of the Orchid (1948)

You Never Know With Women (1948)

You're Lonely When You're Dead (1949)

Lay Her Among the Lilies (1950; reprinted as Too Dangerous to be Free, 1951)

Figure It Out for Yourself (1950; reprinted as The Marijuana Mob, 1952)

Strictly for Cash (1951)

The Double Shuffle (1952)

The Fast Buck (1952)

I'll Bury My Dead (1953)

This Way for a Shroud (1953)

Tiger by the Tail (1954)

Safer Dead (1954; reprinted as Dead Ringer, 1955)

You've Got it Coming (1955)

There's Always a Price Tag (1956)

The Guilty are Afraid (1957)

Not Safe to be Free (1958; reprinted as The Case of the Strangled Starlet, 1958)

Shock Treatment (1959)

The World in My Pocket (1959)

What's Better Than Money (1960)

Come Easy Go Easy (1960)

A Lotus for Miss Quon (1961)

Just Another Sucker (1961)

I Would Rather Stay Poor (1962)

A Coffin from Hong Kong (1952)

Tell it to the Birds (1963)

One Bright Summer Morning (1963)

The Soft Centre (1964)

This is for Real (1965)

The Way the Cookie Crumbles (1965)

You Have Yourself a Deal (1966)

Cade (1966)

Have This One on Me (1967)

Well Now, My Pretty (1967)

An Ear to the Ground (1968)

Believed Violent (1968)

The Whiff of Money (1969)

The Vulture is a Patient Bird (1969)

There's a Hippie on the Highway (1970)

Like a Hole in the Head (1970)

An Ace Up My Sleeve (1971)

Want to Say Alive? (1971)

You're Dead Without Money (1972)

Just a Matter of Time (1972)

Knock, Knock! Who's There? (1973)

Have a Change of Scene (1973)

So What Happens to Me? (1974)

Goldfish Have No Hiding Place (1974)

Believe This, You'll Believe
   Anything (1975)
The Joker in the Pack (1975)
Do Me a Favour Drop Dead (1976)
My Laugh Comes Last (1977)
I Hold the Four Aces (1977)
Consider Yourself Dead (1978)
Can of Worms (1979)
You Must be Kidding (1979)
Try This One for Size (1980)
You Can Say That Again (1980)
Hand Me a Fig Leaf (1981)
Have a Nice Night (1982)
We'll Share a Double Funeral
   (1982)
Not My Thing (1983)
Hit Them Where it Hurts (1984)

Omnibus Editions

Three of Spades (1974; includes
   The Double Shuffle, Shock
   Treatment and Tell It to the Birds)
Meet Mark Girland (1977; includes
   This is for Real, You Have Yourself
   a Deal and Have This One on Me)
Meet Helga Rolfe (1984; includes
   An Ace Up My Sleeve, A Joker in
   the Pack and I Hold Four Aces)

As Raymond Marshall
(reprinted as by Chase except *)

Lady Here's Your Wreath (1940)
Just the Way It Is (1944)
Blonde's Requiem (1945)*
Make the Corpse Walk (1946)
No Business of Mine (1947)*
Trusted Like a Fox (1948; reprinted
   as Ruthless, 1955)

The Paw in the Bottle (1949)
Mallory (1950)
In a Vain Shadow (1951; reprinted
   as by Marshall as Never Trust a
   Woman, 1957)
But a Short Time to Live (1951;
   reprinted as The Pick-Up, 1955)
Why Pick on Me? (1951)
The Wary Transgressor (1952)
The Things Men Do (1953)
The Sucker Punch (1954)
Mission to Venice (1954)
Mission to Siena (1955)
You Find Him—I'll Fix Him (1956)
Hit and Run (1958)

As James L. Docherty
(reprinted as by Chase)

He Won't Need it Now (1939)

As Ambrose Grant
(reprinted as by Chase)

More Deadly Than the Male (1946)

As René Raymond
(reprinted as by Chase)

The Mirror in Room 22 (1946;
   story, appeared in Slipstream: A
   Royal Airforce Anthology edited
   by René Raymond and David
   Langdon)

For further info on the works of
James Hadley Chase, visit
www.hadleychase.co.nr, compiled
by Dr. P. C. Sarkar. This is the
definitive Chase website.

Made in the USA
Charleston, SC
06 April 2016